William Black

Green Pastures and Piccadilly

William Black

Green Pastures and Piccadilly

ISBN/EAN: 9783337049645

Printed in Europe, USA, Canada, Australia, Japan

Cover: Foto ©Andreas Hilbeck / pixelio.de

More available books at **www.hansebooks.com**

GREEN PASTURES AND PICCADILLY

A Novel.

By WILLIAM BLACK,

AUTHOR OF

"A PRINCESS OF THULE," "MADCAP VIOLET," "A DAUGHTER OF HETH,"
"THE STRANGE ADVENTURES OF A PHAETON," &c.,

IN CONJUNCTION WITH AN AMERICAN WRITER.

NEW YORK:
HARPER & BROTHERS, PUBLISHERS,
FRANKLIN SQUARE.
1878.

WILLIAM BLACK'S NOVELS.

GREEN PASTURES AND PICCADILLY. 8vo, Paper, 50 cents; 12mo, Cloth, $1 50.

MADCAP VIOLET. 8vo, Paper, 50 cents; 12mo, Cloth, $1 50.

THREE FEATHERS. Illustrated. 8vo, Paper, 50 cents; 12mo, Cloth, $1 50.

A DAUGHTER OF HETH. 8vo, Paper, 35 cents.; 12mo, Cloth, $1 50.

A PRINCESS OF THULE. 8vo, Paper, 50 cents; 12mo, Cloth, $1 50.

IN SILK ATTIRE. 8vo, Paper, 35 cents; 12mo, Cloth, $1 50.

KILMENY. 8vo, Paper, 35 cents; 12mo, Cloth, $1 50.

LOVE OR MARRIAGE? 8vo, Paper, 30 cents.

THE MAID OF KILLEENA, THE MARRIAGE OF MOIRA FERGUS, and Other Stories. 8vo, Paper, 40 cents.

THE MONARCH OF MINCING-LANE. 8vo, Paper, 50 cents; 12mo, Cloth, $1 50.

THE STRANGE ADVENTURES OF A PHAETON. 8vo, Paper, 50 cents; 12mo, Cloth, $1 50.

PUBLISHED BY HARPER & BROTHERS, NEW YORK.

Either of the above volumes will be sent by mail, postage prepaid, to any part of the United States, on receipt of the price.

CONTENTS.

GREEN PASTURES AND PICCADILLY.

CHAPTER I.

You may be sure there was a stir among our women-folk when they heard that a young man had come courting the earl's daughter. We have among us—or over us, rather—a miniature major-domo of a woman, a mere wisp of a thing, who has nevertheless an awful majesty of demeanor, and the large and innocent eyes of a child, and a wit as nimble and elusive as a minnow; and no sooner is this matter mentioned than she says,

"Oh, the poor child! And she has no mother."

"That," it is observed by a person who has learned wisdom, and does not talk above his breath in his own house—"that is a defect in her character which her future husband will no doubt condone."

She takes no heed. The large and tender eyes are distant and troubled. She has become a seer, a prophetess of evil things in the days to come.

"Think of the child!" she says to our gentle visitor—who was once being courted herself, but is now a brisk young matron blushing with the honors of a couple of bairns—"think of her being all alone there, with scarcely a woman friend in the world. She has no one to warn her, no one to guide her—"

"But why," says our young matron, with mild wonder—"why should she want warning? Is it such a terrible thing to get married?"

Common-sense does not touch the inspired.

"The getting married? No. It is the awakening after. How can she tell—how can she know—that this young man, if he really means to marry her, is at the present moment courting her

deadliest rival? Whom has she to fear in the future as much as
her old idealized self? He is building up a vision, a phantom,
no more like that poor girl than I am like her; and then, when
he finds out the real woman after marriage, his heart will go back
to the old creation of his own fancy, and he will wonder how she
could have changed so much, and grieve over his disappointment.
Yes, you may laugh"—this is a sudden onslaught on another
meek listener—"but every woman knows what I say is true.
And is it our fault that men won't see us as we are until it is too
late? We have to bear the blame, at all events. It is always
the woman. Once upon a time—and it only happens once—she
was a beautiful, angelic creature; she was filled with noble aspirations; wisdom shone in her face; I suppose the earth was
scarcely good enough for her to walk on. Then she marries;
and her husband discovers, slowly and surely, not his own blunder, but that his imaginary heroine has changed into an ordinary
woman, who has an occasional headache like other people, and
must spend a good deal of her life in thinking about shops and
dinners. He tries to hide his dismay; he is very polite to her;
but how can she fail to see that he is in love, not with herself at
all, but with that old ideal of his own creation, and that he bitterly regrets in secret the destruction of his hopes? That is no
laughing matter. People talk about great tragedies. The fierce
passions are splendid because there is noise and stamping about
them. But if a man stabs a woman and puts her out of the
world, is she not at peace? And if a man puts a bullet through
his head, there is an end of his trouble. But I will tell you my
belief, that all the battles and wars that ever were in the world
have not caused the fifteenth part of the misery and tragic suffering that have been caused by this very thing you are laughing at
—those false ideals formed before marriage. You may laugh if
you like."

Indeed, we were not disposed to laugh. She was really in earnest. She had spoken rapidly, with something of an indignant
thrill in her voice, and a proud and pathetic look in her dark
eyes. We had, after all, a certain fondness for this gentle orator; and it was difficult to resist the eager pleading of her impas-
sioned words when, as now, her heart was full of what she was
saying.

Or was it the beautiful May morning, and the sunlight shining on the white hawthorn and the lilacs, and the sleepy shadow of the cedar on the lawn, and the clear singing of the larks far away in the blue, that led us to listen so placidly to the voice of the charmer? A new-comer broke the spell. A heavy-footed cob came trotting up to the veranda; his rider, a tall young man with a brown beard, leaped down on the gravel, and called aloud in his stormy way,

"Donnerwetter! It is as warm to-day—it is as warm as July. Why do you all sit here? Come! Shall we make it a holiday? Shall we drive to Guildford?—Weybridge?—Chertsey?—Esher?"

The two women were sneaking off by themselves, perhaps because they wished to have a further talk about poor Lady Sylvia and her awful fate; perhaps because they were anxious, like all women, to leave holiday arrangements in other hands, in order to have the right of subsequently grumbling over them.

"Stay!" cries one of us, who has been released from the spell. "There is another word to be said on that subject. You are not going to ride rough-shod over us, and then sneak out at the back-door before we have recovered from the fright. This, then, is your contention—that a vast number of women are enduring misery because their husbands have become disillusionized, and cannot conceal the fact? And that is the fault of the husbands. They construct an ideal woman, marry a real one, and live miser-able ever after, because they can't have that imaginative toy of their brain. Now don't you think, if this were true—if this wretchedness were so wide-spread—it would cure itself? Have mankind gone on blundering for ages, because of the non-arri-val of a certain awful and mysterious Surrey prophetess? Why haven't women formed a universal association for the destruction of lovers' dreams?"

"I tell you, you may laugh as you like," is the calm reply, "but what I say is true; and every married woman will tell you it is true. Why don't women cure it? If it comes to that, wom-en are as foolish as men. The girl makes her lover a hero; she wakes up after marriage to find him as he really is, and the high-est hope of her life falls dead."

"Then we are all disappointed, and all miserable. That is your conclusion?"

"Not all," is the answer; and there is a slight change of tone audible here, a slight smile visible on her lips. "There are many whose imagination never went the length of constructing any ideal, except that of a moor covered with grouse. There are others who have educated themselves into a useful indifferentism or cynicism. Unfortunately it is the nobler natures that suffer most."

"Well, this is a tolerably lively prospect for every girl who thinks of getting married. Pray, Frau Philosophin, have you been constructing all these fiddle-stick theories out of your own head, or have you been making a special study of Sylvia Blythe?"

"I know Lady Sylvia better than most people. She is a very earnest girl. She has ideals, convictions, aspirations—a whole stock in trade of things that a good many girls seem to get on very well without. If that poor girl is disappointed in her marriage, it will kill her."

"Disappointed in her marriage!" calls out the young man, who has been standing patiently with the bridle of his cob in his hand. "Why do you think that already? No, no. It is the girl herself—she lives in that solitary place, and imagines mere foolish things—it is she herself has put that into your mind. Disappointed! No, no. There is not any good reason—there is not any good sense in that. This young fellow Balfour, every one speaks well of him; he will have a great name some day; he is busy, a very active man. I hear of him in many places."

"I wish he was dead!" says my lady; and, curiously enough, at this moment her eyes fill with tears, and she turns and walks proudly away, accompanied by her faithful friend.

The young man turns in amazement.

"What have I done? Am I not right? There is nothing bad that Balfour has done?"

"There is plenty bad in what he means to do, if it is true he is going to carry off Lady Sylvia Blythe. But when you, Herr Lieutenant, gave him that fine certificate of character, I suppose you didn't know that people don't quite agree about Mr. Hugh Balfour? I suppose you don't know that a good many folks regard him as a bullying, overbearing, and portentously serious Scotchman, a little too eager to tread on one's corns, and not very particular as to the means he uses for his own advancement? Is it very creditable, for example, that he should be merely a warming-pan for young Glynne in that wretched little Irish borough? Is it decent that he should apparently take a pride in insulting the deputations that come to him? A member of Parliament is supposed to pay some respect to the people who elected him."

Here the brown-visaged young man burst into a roar of laughter.

"It is splendid—it is the best joke I have known. They insult him; why should he not turn round and say to them, 'Do you go to the devil!' He is quite right. I admire him. Sackerment!—I would do that too."

So much for a morning gossip over the affairs of two people who were not much more than strangers to us. We had but little notion then that we were all to become more intimately related, our lives being for a space intertwisted by the cunning hands of circumstance. The subject, however, did not at all depart from the mind of our sovereign lady and ruler. We could see that her eyes were troubled. When it was proposed to her that she should make a party to drive somewhere or other, she begged that it might be made up without her. We half suspected whither she meant to drive.

Some hour or two after that you might have seen a pair of ponies, not much bigger than mice, being slowly driven along a dusty lane that skirted a great park. The driver was a lady, and she was alone. She did not seem to pay much heed to the beautiful spring foliage of the limes and elms, to the blossoms of the chestnuts, nor yet to the bluebells and primroses visible on the other side of the gray paling, where the young rabbits were scurrying into the holes in the banks.

There was a smart pattering of hoofs behind her; and presently she was overtaken by a young gentleman of some fourteen years or so, who took off his tall hat with much ceremony, and politely bade her good-morning.

"Good-morning, Mr. John," said she, in return. "Do you know if Lady Sylvia is at home?"

"I should think she was," said the boy, as he got down from his horse, and led it by the side of the pony-chaise, that he might the better continue the conversation. "I should think she was. My uncle's gone to town. Look here; I've been over to the 'Fox and Hounds' for a bottle of champagne. Sha'n't we have some fun? You'll stay to lunch, of course?"

In fact, there was a bottle wrapped round with brown paper under his arm.

"Oh, Mr. John, how could you do that? You know your cousin will be very angry."

"Not a bit," said he, confidently. "Old Syllabus is a rattling good sort of girl. She'll declare I might have had champagne at the hall—which isn't true, for my noble uncle is an uncommonly sharp sort of chap, and I believe he takes the key of the wine-cellar with him—and then she'll settle down to it. She's rather serious, you know, and would like to come the maternal over you; but she has got just as good a notion of fun as most girls. You needn't be afraid about *that*. Old Syllabus and I are first-rate friends; we get on capitally together. You see, I don't try to spoon her, as many a fellow would do in my place."

"That is very sensible of you—very considerate."

The innocence of those eyes of hers! If that brat of a schoolboy, who was assuming the airs of a man, could have analyzed the tender, ingenuous, lamb-like look which was directed toward him —if he could have seen through those perfectly sweet and approving eyes, and discovered the fiendish laughter and sarcasm behind—he would have learned more of the nature of women than he was likely to learn in any half-dozen years of his idiotic existence. But how was he to know? He chattered on more freely than ever. He had a firm conviction that he was impressing this simple country person with his knowledge of the world and of human nature. She had been but once to Oxford. He had never even seen the place; but then, as he was going there some day, he was justified in speaking of the colleges as if they were all on their knees before him, imploring him to accept a fellowship. And then he came back to his cousin Sylvia.

"It's an awful shame," said he, "to shut up the poor girl in that place. She'll never know anything of the world: she thinks there's nothing more important than cowslips and daisies. I don't suppose my uncle is overburdened with money—in fact, I believe he must be rather hard up—but I never heard of an earl yet who couldn't get a town-house somehow, if he wanted to. Why doesn't he get another mortgage on this tumble-down old estate of his, and go and live comfortably in Bruton Street, and show poor old Syllabus something of what's really going on in the world? Why, she hasn't even been presented. She has got no more notion of a London season than a dairy-maid. And yet

I think if you took her into the Park she would hold her own there: what do you think?"

"I think you would not get many girls in the Park more beautiful than Lady Sylvia," is the innocent answer.

"And this old place! What's the good of it? The whole estate is going to wreck and ruin because my uncle won't have the rabbits killed down, and he won't spend any money on the farm buildings. And that old bailiff, Moggs, is the biggest fool I ever saw: the whole place is overrun with couch-grass. I am glad my uncle gave him one for himself the other day. Moggs was grumbling about the rabbits. 'Moggs,' said my uncle, 'you let my rabbits alone, and I shall say nothing about your couch.' But it's an awful shame. And he'll never get her married if he keeps her buried down here."

"But is there any necessity that your cousin should marry?"

"I can tell you it is becoming more and more difficult every year," said this experienced and thoughtful observer, "to get girls married. The men don't seem to see it, somehow, unless the girl has a lot of money and good looks as well. Last year I believe it was something awful; you could see at the end of the season how the mothers were beginning to pull long faces when they thought of having to start off for Baden-Baden with a whole lot of unsalable articles on hand."

"Yes, that is a serious responsibility," is the grave answer. "But then, you know, there need be no hurry about getting your cousin married. She is young. I think if you wait you will find at the right moment the beautiful prince come riding out of the wood to carry her off, just as happens in the story-books."

"Well, you know," said this chattering boy, with a smile, "people have begun to talk already. There is that big boor of a Scotch fellow—what's his name?—Balfour—has been down here a good many times lately; and, of course, gossips jump at conclusions. But that is a little too ridiculous. I don't think you will catch old Syllabus, with all her crotchets, marrying a man in the rum-and-sugar line. Or is it calico and opium?"

"But I thought he had never had anything to do with the firm? And I thought it was one of the most famous merchant houses in the world?"

"Well, I don't suppose he smears his hands with treacle and wears an apron; but—but it is too ridiculous. I have no doubt when my uncle has got all he wants out of him, he won't trouble Willowby again. Of course I haven't mentioned the matter to old Syllabus. That would be no use. If it were true, she would not confess it: girls always tell lies about such things."

"There you have acted wisely; I would not mention such idle rumors to her, if I were you. Shall I take the bottle from you?"

"If you would," said he. "And I shall ride now; for we have little time to spare; and I want you to see old Syllabus's face when I produce the champagne at lunch."

So the lad got on his horse again, and the cavalcade moved forward at a brisk trot. It was a beautiful country through which they were passing, densely wooded here and there, and here and there showing long stretches of heathy common with patches of black firs standing clear against the sky. And the bright May sunlight was shining through the young green foliage of the beeches and elms; the air was sweet with the scent of hawthorn and lilac; now and again they heard the deep "joug, joug" of a nightingale from out of a grove of young larches and spruce.

By-and-by they came to a plain little lodge, and passed through the gates, and drove along an avenue of tall elms and branching chestnuts. There was a glimmer of a gray house through the trees. Then they swept round by a spacious lawn, and drew up in front of the wide-open door, while Mr. John, leaping down from his horse, rung loudly at the hall. Yet there seemed to be nobody about this deserted house.

It was a long, low, rambling building of gray stone, with no architectural pretensions whatsoever. It had some pillars here and there, and a lion or two, to distinguish it from a county jail or an asylum: otherwise there was nothing about it to catch the eye.

But the beauty of Lady Sylvia's home lay not in the plain gray building, but in the far-reaching park, now yellowed all over with buttercups, and studded here and there with noble elms. And on the northern side this high-lying park sloped suddenly down to a long lake, where there was a boat-house and a punt or two for pushing through the reeds and water-lilies along the shore, while beyond that again was a great stretch of cultivated country, lying warm and silent in the summer light. The house was strangely still; there was no sign of life about it. There was no animal of any kind in the park. There was no sound but the singing of birds in the trees, and the call of the cuckoo, soft and muffled and remote. The very winds seemed to die down as they neared the place; there was scarcely a rustle in the trees. It was here, then, that the Lady Sylvia had grown up; it was here that she now lived and walked and dreamed in the secrecy and silence of the still woodland ways.

———

CHAPTER II.

THE MISTRESS OF WILLOWBY.

THE Lady Sylvia arose with the early dawn, and dressed and stole noiselessly down the stairs and through the great stone hall. Clad all in a pale blue, with a thin white garment thrown round her head and shoulders, she looked like a ghost as she passed through the sleeping house; but she was no longer like a ghost when she went out on to the high terrace, and stood there in the blaze of a May morning. Rather she might have been taken for the very type of English girlhood in its sweetest spring-time, and the world can show nothing more fair and noble and gracious than that. Perhaps, as her boy cousin had said, she was a trifle serious in expression, for she had lived much alone, and she had pondered, in her own way, over many things. But surely there was no excess of gloom about the sweet young face—its delicate oval just catching the warm sunlight—or about the pretty, half-parted, and perhaps somewhat too sensitive lips; nor yet resting on the calm and thoughtful forehead that had as yet no wrinkle of age or care. However, it was always difficult to scan the separate features of this girl; you were drawn away from that by the irresistible fascination of her eyes, and there shone her life and soul. What were they—gray, blue, or black? No one could exactly tell; but they were large, and they had dark pupils, and they were under long eyelashes. Probably, seeing that her face was fair—and even paler than one might have expected—and her hair of a light, wavy, and beautiful brown, those eyes were blue or gray; but that was of little consequence. It was the story they told that was of interest. And here, indeed, there was a certain seriousness about her face, but it was the seriousness of sincerity. There was no coquetry in those tender and earnest eyes. Familiar words acquired a new import when Lady Sylvia spoke them; for her eyes told you that she meant what she said, and more than that.

It was as yet the early morning, and the level sunshine spread a golden glory over the eastward-looking branches of the great elms, and threw long shadows on the greensward of the park. Far away the world lay all asleep, though the kindling light of the new day was shining on the green plains, and on the white hawthorns, and on this or that gray house remotely visible among the trees. What could be a fitter surrounding for this young English girl than this English-looking landscape? They were both of them in the freshness and beauty of their spring-time, that comes but once in a year and once in a life.

She passed along the terrace. Down below her the lake lay still; there was not a breath of wind to break the reflections of the trees on the glassy surface. But she was not quite alone in this silent and sleeping world. Her friends and companions, the birds, had been up before her. She could hear the twittering of the young starlings in their nests as their parents came and went carrying food, and the loud ahd joyful "tirr-a-wee, tirr-a-wee, prooit, tweet!" of the thrushes, and the low currooing of the wood-pigeon, and the soft call of the cuckoo, that seemed to come in whenever an interval of silence fitted. The swallows dipped and flashed and circled over the bosom of the lake. There were blackbirds eagerly but cautiously at work, with their short spasmodic trippings, on the lawn. A robin, perched on the iron railing, eyed her curiously, and seemed more disposed to approach than to retreat.

For, indeed, she carried a small basket, with which the robin was doubtless familiar; and now she opened it and began to scatter handfuls of crumbs on the gravel. A multitude of sparrows, hitherto invisible, seemed to spring into life. The robin descended from his perch. But she did not wait to see how her bounties were shared: she had work farther on.

Now the high-lying park and ground of Willowby Hall formed a dividing territory between two very different sorts of country. On the north, away beyond the lake, lay a broad plain of cultivated ground, green and soft and fair, dotted with clusters of farm buildings and scored by tall hedge-rows. On the south, on the other hand, there was a wilderness of sandy heath and dark-green common, now all ablaze with gorse and broom; black pine woods high up at the horizon; and one long, yellow, and dusty road, apparently leading nowhere, for there was no trace of town or village as far as the eye could see.

It was in this latter direction that Sylvia Blythe now turned her steps; and you will never know anything about her unless you know something of these her secret haunts and silent ways. These were her world. Beyond that distant line of fir wood on the horizon her imagination seldom cared to stray. She had been up to London, of course; had stayed with her father at a hotel in Arlington Street; had been to the opera once or twice; and dined at some friends' houses. But of the great, actual, struggling, and suffering world—of the ships carrying emigrants to unknown lands beyond the cruel seas, of the hordes driven down to death by disease and crime in the squalid dens of great cities, of the eager battle and flushed hopes and bitter disappointments of life —what could she know? Most girls become acquainted at some time or other with a little picturesque misery. It excites feelings of pity and tenderness, and calls forth port-wine and tracts. It comes to them with the recommendation of the curate. But even this small knowledge of a bit of the suffering in the world had been denied to Lady Sylvia; for her father, hearing that she contemplated some charitable visitation of the kind, had strictly forbidden it.

"Look here, Sylvia," said he, "I won't have you go trying to catch scarlet fever or something of that sort. We have no people of our own that want looking after in that way; if there are, let them come to Mrs. Thomas. As for sick children and infirm grandfathers elsewhere, you can do them no good; there are plenty who can—leave it to them. Now don't forget that. And if I catch either Mr. Shuttleworth or Dr. Grey allowing you to go near any of these hovels, I can tell you they will hear of it."

And so it came to be that her friends and dependents were the birds and rabbits and squirrels of the woods and the heath; and of these she knew all the haunts and habits, and they were her companions in her lonely wanderings. Look, for example, at this morning walk of hers. She passed through some dense shrubberies—the blackbirds shooting away through the laurel-bushes —until she came to an open space at the edge of a wood where

there was a spacious dell.   Here the sunlight fell in broad patches on a tangled wilderness of wild flowers—great masses of blue
hyacinths, and white starwort, and crimson campion, and purple
ground-ivy.   She stayed a minute to gather a small bouquet,
which she placed in her dress; but she did not pluck two snow-
white and waxen hyacinths, for she had watched these strangers
ever since she had noticed that the flowers promised to be white.

> "Should he upbraid,
> I'll own that he'll prevail,"

she hummed carelessly to herself as she went on again; and now
she was in a sloping glade, among young larches and beeches,
with withered brackens burning red in the scattered sunlight,
with the new brackens coming up in solitary stalks of green,
their summits not the fiddle-head of the ordinary fern, but resembling rather the incurved three claws of a large bird.   She
paused for a moment; far along the path in front of her, and
quite unconscious of her presence, was a splendid cock pheasant,
the bronze plumage of his breast just catching a beam of the
morning light.   Then he stalked across the path, followed by his
sober-colored hen, and disappeared into the ferns.   She went on
again.   A squirrel ran up a great beech-tree, and looked round at
her from one of the branches.   A jay fled screaming through the
wood — just one brief glimpse of brilliant blue being visible.
Then she came to a belt of oak paling, in which was a very dilapidated door; and by the door stood a basket much larger than
that she had carried from the Hall.   She took up the basket, let
herself out by the small gate, and then found herself in the open
sunshine before a wide waste of heath.

This was Willowby Heath — a vast stretch of sandy ground
covered by dark heather mostly, but showing here and there brilliant masses of gorse and broom, and here and there a small larch-
tree not over four feet in height, but gleaming with a glimmer
of green over the dark common.   A couple of miles away, on a
knoll, stood a windmill, its great arms motionless.   Beyond that
again the heath darkened as it rose to the horizon, and ended in
a black line of firs.

She hummed, as she went, this idle song; and sometimes she
laughed, for the place seemed to be alive with very young rabbits, and those inexperienced babes showed an agony of fear as

they fled almost from under her feet, and scurried through the dry heather to the sandy breaks. It was at one of the largest of these breaks — a sort of ragged pit some six feet deep and fifty feet long—that she finally paused, and put down her heavy load. Her approach had been the signal for the magical disappearance of about fifty or sixty rabbits, the large majority being the merest mites of things.

Now began a strange incantation scene. She sat down in the perfect stillness; there was not even a rustle of her dress. There was no wind stirring; the white clouds in the pale blue overhead hung motionless; the only sound audible was the calling of a peewit far away over the heath.

She waited patiently in this deep silence. All round and underneath this broken bank, in a transparent shadow, were a number of dark holes of various sizes. These were the apertures for the gnomes to appear from the bowels of the earth. And as she waited, behold! one of those small caverns became tenanted. A tiny head suddenly appeared, and two black eyes regarded her with a sort of blank, dumb curiosity, without fear. She did not move. The brown small creature came out farther; he sat down like a little ball on the edge of the sandy slope; he was just far enough out for the sunlight to catch the tips of his long ears, which thereupon shone transparent, a pinky gray. Her eyes were caught by another sudden awakening of life. At the opposite side of the dell a head appeared, and bobbed in again— that was an old and experienced rabbit; but immediately afterward, one, two, three small bodies came out to the edge and sat there — a mute, watchful family, staring and being stared at. Then here, there, everywhere, head after head became visible; a careful look round, a noiseless trot out to the edge of the hole, a motionless seat there, not an ear or a tail stirring. In the mysterious silence every eye was fixed on hers; she scarcely dared breathe, or these phantasmal inhabitants of the lower world would suddenly vanish. But what was this strange creature, unlike his fellows in all but their stealthy watchfulness and silent ways? He was black as midnight; he was large and fat and sleek; he was the only one of the parents that dared to come out and make part of this mystic picture.

"Satan!" she called; and she sprung to her feet and gave one loud clap of her hands.

There was nothing but the dry sand-bank, staring with those empty holes. She laughed lightly to herself at that instantaneous scurry; and, having opened the basket, she scattered its contents—chopped turnips—all around the place, and then set off homeward. She arrived at the Hall in time to have breakfast with her cousin, though that young gentleman was discontentedly grumbling over the early hours they kept in his uncle's house.

"Syllabus," said he, "are you going to stand champagne for lunch?"

"Champagne?—you foolish boy!" said she; "what do you want champagne for?"

"To celebrate my departure," said he. "You know you'll be awfully glad to get rid of me. I have worried your life out in these three days. Let's have some champagne at lunch, to show you don't bear malice. Won't you, old Syllabus?"

"Champagne?" said she. "Wine is not good for school-boys. Is it sixpence you want to buy toffy with on the way to the station?"

After breakfast she had her rounds of the garden and greenhouses to make: she visited the kennels, and saw that the dogs had plenty of water; she went to the lake to see that the swans had their food; she had a dumb conversation with her pony that was grazing in the meadow. How could the sweet day pass more pleasantly? The air was fresh and mild, the skies blue, the sun warm on the buttercups of the park—in fact, when she returned to the Hall she found that her small bronze shoes and the foot of her dress were all dusted over with a gold powder.

But this was not to be an ordinary day. First of all, she was greatly troubled by the mysterious disappearance of Johnny Blythe, who, she was afraid, would miss his train in the afternoon; then she was delighted by his appearance in company with a visitor, who was easily persuaded to stay to lunch; then there was a pretty quarrel over the production of that bottle of public-house champagne—at which the girl turned, with a little flush in her cheek, to her visitor, whom she begged to forgive this piece of school-boyish folly. Then Mr. John was bundled off in the wagonette to the station; and she and her visitor were left alone.

What had Madame Mephistopheles to do with this innocent girl?

"Oh, Lady Sylvia," she said, "how delightfully quiet you are here! Each time I come, the stillness of the Hall and the park strikes me more and more. It is a place to dream one's life away in—among the trees on the fine days, in the library on the bad ones. I suppose you don't wish ever to leave Willowby ?"

"N-no," said the girl, with a faint touch of color in her face. And then she added, "But don't you think that one ought to try to understand what is going on outside one's immediate circle ? One must become so ignorant, you know. I have been reading the leading articles in the *Times* lately."

"Oh, indeed !"

"Yes; but they only show me how very ignorant I must be, for I can scarcely find one that I can understand. And I have been greatly disappointed, too, with another thing. Have you seen this book ?"

She went and fetched from an adjoining table a volume, which she placed in her visitor's hands. It was entitled "The Ideas of the Day on Policy."

"There was a friend of papa's here one evening," said Lady Sylvia, demurely, " and we were talking about the greatly different opinions in politics that people held, and I asked him how an ignorant person like myself was to decide which to believe. Then he said, 'Oh, if you want to see all the *pros* and *cons* of the great political questions ranged opposite each other, take some such book as Buxton's "Ideas of the Day ;" then you can compare them, and take which one strikes you as being most reasonable.' Well, I sent for the book; but look at it ! It is all general principles. It does not tell me anything. I am sure no one could have read more carefully than I did the articles in the *Times* on the Irish Universities Bill. I have followed everything that has been said, and I am quite convinced by the argument; but I can't make out what the real thing is behind. And then I go to the book that was recommended to me. Look at it, my dear Mrs. ——. All you can get is a series of propositions about national education. How does that help you to understand the Irish Universities?"

Her visitor laughed and put down the book. Then she placed her hand within the girl's arm, and they went out for a stroll in the park, through the long warm grass and golden buttercups and blue speedwells.

"Why should you take ·such a new interest in politics, Lady Sylvia?" said Madame Mephistopheles, lightly.

"I want to take an interest in what concerns so many of my fellow‑creatures," said the girl, simply. "Is not that natural? And if I were a man," she added, with some heightened color, "I should care for nothing but politics. Think of the good one might do—think of the power one might have! That would be worth living for, that would be worth giving one's life for—to be able to cure some of the misery of the world, and make wise laws, and make one's country respected among other nations. Do you know, I cannot understand how men can pass their lives in painting pretty pictures and writing pretty verses, when there is all that real work to be done—millions of their fellow‑creatures growing up in ignorance and misery—the poor becoming poorer every day, until no one knows where the wretchedness is to cease."

These were fine notions to have got into the head of an ingenuous country maiden; and perhaps that reflection occurred to herself too, for she suddenly stopped, and her face was red. But her kind friend took no notice of this retiring modesty. On the contrary, she warmly approved of her companion's ways of thinking. England was proud of her statesmen. The gratitude of millions was the reward of him who devised wise statutes. What nobler vocation in life could there be for a man than philanthropy exalted to the rank of a science? But at the same time—

Ah! yes, at the same time a young girl must not fancy that all politicians were patriots. Sometimes it was the meaner ambitions connected with self that were the occasion of great public service. We ought not to be disappointed on discovering that our hero had some earthly alloy in his composition.

Indeed, continued this Mephistopheles, there was always a danger of allowing our imaginative conceptions of people to run too far. Young persons, more especially, who had but little practical experience of life, were often disappointed because they expected too much. Human nature was only human nature. Lady Sylvia now, for example, had doubtless never thought about marriage; but did she not know how many persons were grievously disappointed merely because they had been too generously imaginative before marriage?

"But how can any one marry without absolute admiration and

absolute confidence ?" demanded the girl, with some pride, but with her eyes cast down.

And there was no one there to interpose and cry, "Oh, woman, woman, come away, and let the child dream her dream ! If it is all a mistake—if it has to be repented for in hot tears and with an aching heart—if it lasts for but a year, a month, a day—leave her with this beautiful faith in love and life and heroism which may soon enough be taken away from her.

CHAPTER III.

THE MEMBER FOR BALLINASCROON.

IN the first-floor room of a small house in Piccadilly a young man of six-and-twenty or so was busily writing letters. By rights the room should have been a drawing-room—and a woman might have made of it a very pretty drawing-room indeed—but there were no flowers or trailing creepers in the small balcony; there were no lace curtains to prevent the sunlight streaming through the open French windows full on the worn and faded carpet; while this half study, half parlor, had scattered about in it all the signs of a bachelor's existence in the shape of wooden pipes, time-tables, slippers, and the like. When the letters were finished the writer struck a bell before him on the table. His servant appeared.

"You will post those letters, Jackson," said he, "and have a hansom ready for me at 3.15."

"Yes, sir," said the man ; and then he hesitated. "Beg your pardon, sir, but the gentlemen below are rather impatient, sir—they are a little excited, sir."

"Very well," said the young man, carelessly. "Take my bag down. Stay ; here are some papers you had better put in."

He rose and went to get the papers—one or two thin blue-books and some drafted bills—and now one may get a better look at the Member for Ballinascroon. He was not over five feet eight ; but he was a bony, firm-framed young man, who had much more character than prettiness in his face. The closely cropped beard and whiskers did not at all conceal the lines of strength about his cheek and chin; and the shaggy dark-brown eyebrows gave shadow and intensity to the shrewd and piercing gray eyes. It was a face that gave evidence of keen resolve, of ready action, of persistence. And although young Balfour had the patient and steady determination of the Scotch — or, let us say, of the Saxon—as part of his birthright, and although even that had been overlaid by the reticence of manner and the gentleness—the almost hesitating gentleness—of speech of an Oxford don, any one could see that there was something Celtic-looking about the gray eyes and the heavy eyebrows, and every one who knew Balfour knew that sometimes a flash of vehement enthusiasm, or anger, or scorn, would break through that suavity of manner which some considered to be just a trifle too supercilious.

On this occasion Hugh Balfour, having made all the preparations for his departure which he considered to be necessary, went down-stairs to the large room on the ground-floor. There was a noise of voices in that apartment. As he entered, these angry sounds ceased; he bowed slightly, went up to the head of the room, and said, "Gentlemen, will you be seated?"

"Sorr," said a small man, with a large chest, a white waistcoat, and a face pink with anger or whiskey, or both—" sorr, 'tis twenty-three minutes by my watch ye have kept us waiting—"

"I know," said the young man, calmly; "I am very sorry. Will you be good enough to proceed to business, gentlemen?"

Thus admonished, the spokesman of the eight or ten persons in the room addressed himself to the speech which he had obviously prepared. But how could he, in the idyllic seclusion of the back parlor of a Ballinascroon public-house, have anticipated and prepared for the interruptions falling from a young man who, whether at the Oxford Union or at St. Stephen's, had acquired a pretty fair reputation for saying about the most irritating and contemptuous things that could vex the soul of an opponent?

"Sorr," said the orator, swelling out his white waistcoat, "the gentlemen" (he said gintlemen, but never mind) —"the gentlemen who are with me this day are a deputation, a deputation, sorr, of the electors of the borough of Ballinascroon, which you have the honor, sorr, to represent in Parliament. We held a meeting, sorr, as you know. You were invited to attend that meeting. You refused to attend that meeting—although it was called to consider your conduct as the representative of the borough of Ballinascroon."

Mr. Balfour nodded: this young man did not seem to be much impressed by the desperate nature of the situation.

"And now, sorr," continued the orator, grouping his companions together with a wave of his hand, "we have come as a deputation to lay before you certain facts which your constituents, sorr, hope will induce you to take that course—the only course, I may say—that an honorable man could follow."

"Very well."

"Sorr, you are aware that you succeeded the Honorable Oliver Glynne in the representation of the borough of Ballinascroon. You are aware, sorr, that when Mr. Glynne contested the borough, he spent no less than £10,800 in the election—"

"I am quite aware of these facts," interrupted Balfour, speaking slowly and clearly. "I am quite aware that Mr. Glynne kept the whole constituency drunk for three months. I am quite aware that he spent all that money, for I don't believe there was a man of you came out of the election with clean hands. Well?"

The orator was rather disconcerted, and gasped a little; but a murmur of indignant repudiation from his companions nerved him to a further effort.

"Sorr, it ill becomes you to bring such charges against the borough that has placed you in Parliament, and against the man who gave you his seat. Mr. Glynne was a gentleman, sorr; he spent his money like a gentleman; and when he was unseated" (he said onsated, but no matter), "it was from no regard for you, sorr, but from our regard for him that we returned you to Parliament, and have allowed you to sit there, sorr, until such times as a General Election will enable us to send the man of our true choice to represent us at St. Stephen's."

There was a loud murmur of approval.

"I beg your pardon," said Balfour. "I must correct you on one point. You don't allow me to sit in Parliament. I sit there of my own choice. You would turn me out if you could to-morrow; but you see you can't."

"I consider, sorr, that in that shameless avowal—"

Here there was a flash of light in those gray eyes; but the indiscreet orator did not observe it.

"—You have justified the action we have taken in calling on a public meeting to denounce your conduct as the representative of Ballinascroon. Sorr, you are not the representative of Ballinascroon. I will make bold to say that you are sitting in the honorable House of Commons under false pretences. You neglect our interests. You treat our communications, our remonstrances, with an insulting indifference. The cry of our fellow-countrymen in prison—political prisoners in a free country, sorr —is nothing to you. You allow our fisheries to dwindle and disappear for want of that help which you give freely enough to your own country, sorr. And on the great question that is making the pulse of Ireland beat as it has never beaten before, that is making her sons and her daughters curse the slavery that binds them in chains of iron, sorr, you have treated us with ridicule and scorn. When Mr. O'Byrne called upon you at the Reform Club, sorr, you walked past him, and told the menial in livery to inform him that you were not in the club. Is that the conduct of a member of the honorable House of Commons, sorr? Is it the conduct of a gentleman?"

Here arose another murmur of approval. Balfour looked at his watch.

"Gentlemen," said he, "I am sorry I must leave you at 3.15; my train goes at 3.30 from Paddington. Do I understand you that that is all you have to say?"

Here there were loud cries of "No! no! Resign! resign!"

"—Because I don't think it was worth your while to come all the way to London to say it. I read it every week in the columns of that delightful print, the *Ballinascroon Sentinel*. However, you have been very outspoken, and I shall be equally frank. You can't have all the frankness on your side, you know. Let me say, then, that I don't care a brass farthing what any meeting in Ballinascroon thinks, or what the whole of the three hundred and eighty electors think about me. I consider it a disgrace to the British constitution that such a rotten and corrupt constituency should exist. Three hundred and eighty electors—a population of less than five thousand—and a man spends close on £11,000 in contesting the place! Disfranchisement is too good for such a hole: it should be burned out of the political map. And so you took me as a stop-gap. That was how you showed your gratitude to Mr. Glynne, who was a young man, and a foolish young man, and allowed himself to be led by your precious electoral agents. Of course I was to give up the seat to him at the next General Election. Very well; I have no objection to that: that is a matter between him and me; though I fancy you'll find him just as resolved as myself not to swallow your Home Rule bolus. But, as between you and me, the case is different. You wished to make use of me: I have made use of you. I have got into the House; I have learned something of its ways; I have served, so far, a short apprenticeship. But do you think that I am going to give up my time and my convictions to your wretched projects? Do you think I would bolster up your industries, that are dwindling only through laziness? Do you think I am going to try to get every man of you a post or a pension? Gracious heavens! I don't believe there is a man-child born in the town but you begin to wonder what the Government will do for him. The very stones of Westminster Hall are saturated with Irish brogue; the air is thick with your clamor for place. No, no, thank you; don't imagine I am going to dip my hands into that dirty water. You can turn me out at the end of this Parliament—I should have resigned my seat in any case— but until that time I am Hugh Balfour, and not at all your very obedient servant."

For the moment his Celtic pulse had got the better of his Saxon brain. The deputation had not at all been prepared for this scornful outburst; they had expected to enjoy a monopoly of scolding. Ordinarily, indeed, Hugh Balfour was an extremely reticent man; some said he was too proud to bother himself into a passion about anything or anybody.

"Sorr," said the pink-faced orator, with a despairing hesitation in his voice, "after the language—after the language, sorr, which we have just heard, my friends and myself have but one course to pursue. I am astonished—I am astounded, sorr—that, holding such opinions of the borough of Ballinascroon as those you have now expressed, you should continue to represent that borough in Parliament—"

"I beg your pardon," said Balfour, with his ordinary coolness, and taking out his watch, "if I must interrupt you again. I have but three minutes left. Is there anything definite that you wish to say to me?"

Once more there was a murmuring chorus of "Resign! resign!"

"I don't at all mean to resign," said Balfour, calmly.

"Sorr, it is inconceivable," began the spokesman of the party, "that a gentleman should sit in Parliament to represent a constituency of which he has such opinions as those that have fallen from you this day."

"I beg your pardon; it is not at all inconceivable; it is the fact. What is more, I mean to represent your precious borough until the end of the present Parliament. You will be glad to hear that that end may be somewhat nearer than many people imagine; and again the bother comes from your side of the water. Since the Government were beaten on their Irish Universities Bill they have been in a bad way; there is no doubt of it. Some folks say there will be a dissolution in the autumn. So, you see, there is no saying how soon you may get rid of me. In that case, will you return Mr. Glynne?"

Again there was a murmur, but scarcely an intelligible one.

"I thought not. I fancied your gratitude for the £11,000 would not last as long. Well, you must try to find a Home Rule candidate who will keep the town drunk for three months at a stretch. Meantime, gentlemen, I am afraid I must bid you good-morning."

He rung the bell.

"Cab there, Jackson?"

"Yes, sir."

"Good-morning, gentlemen."

With that the deputation from Ballinascroon were left to take their departure at their own convenience, their representative in Parliament driving off in a hansom to Paddington Station.

He had scarcely driven away from the door when his thoughts were occupied by much more important affairs. He was a busy man. The deputation could lie by as a joke.

Arrived at the station, Balfour jumped out, bag in hand, and gave the cabman eighteen-pence.

"What's this, sir?" the man called out, affecting to stare at the two coins.

Balfour turned.

"Oh," said he, innocently, "have I made a mistake? Let me see. You had better give me back the sixpence."

Still more innocently the cabman—never doubting but that a gentleman who lived in Piccadilly would act as such—handed him the sixpence, which Balfour put in his pocket.

"Don't be such a fool next time," said he, as he walked off to get his ticket.

He had a couple of minutes to spare, and after having taken his seat, he walked across the platform to get an evening paper. He was met by an old college companion of his.

"Balfour," said he, "I wanted to see you. You remember that tall waiter at the Oxford and Cambridge, the one who got ill, had to give up—"

"And you got him into some green-grocery business or other. Yes."

"Well, he is desperately ill now, and his affairs are at the worst. His wife doesn't know what to do. I am getting up a little subscription for her. I want a couple of guineas from you."

"Oh," said Balfour, somewhat coldly, "I rather dislike the notion of giving money to these subscriptions without knowing something of the case. I have known so many dying people get rapidly better after they got a pension from the Civil List, or a donation from the Literary Fund, or a purse from their friends. Where does the woman live?"

"Three, Marquis Street, Lambeth."

"Take your seats, please."

So these two parted, and Balfour's acquaintance went back to the carriage, in which he had left his wife and her sisters, and to these he said,

"Did you ever know anything like the meanness of these Scotch? I have just met that fellow Balfour—he has thirty thousand a year if he has a penny—and I couldn't screw a couple of guineas out of him for a poor woman whose husband is dying. Fancy! Now I can believe all the stories I have heard of him within the last year or two. He asks men to dinner; has champagne on the sideboard; pretends he is so busy talking politics that he forgets all about it; his guests have to content themselves with a glass of sherry, while he has a little claret and water. He hasn't a cigar in the house. He keeps one horse, I believe—an old cob—for pounding up and down in Hyde Park of a morning; but on his thirty thousand a year he can't afford himself a brougham. No wonder those Scotch fellows become rich men. I have no doubt his father began with picking up pins in the street."

Quite unconscious of having provoked all this wrathful animadversion, Balfour was already deeply immersed in certain Local Taxation Bills he had taken out of his bag. Very little did he see of the beautiful landscapes through which the train whirled on that bright and glowing afternoon; although, of course, he had a glance at Pangbourne; that was something not to be missed even by a young and enthusiastic politician. At the Oxford Station he was met by a thin, little, middle-aged man, with a big head and blue spectacles. This was the Rev. Henry Jewsbury, M.A., and Fellow of Exeter.

"Well, Balfour, my boy," called out this clergyman, in a rich and jovial voice, which startled one as it came from that shrunken body, "I am glad to see you. How late you are! You'll just be in time to dine in hall: I will lend you a gown."

"All right. But I must send off a telegram first."

He went to the office. This was the telegram: "H. Balfour, Exeter College, Oxford, to E. Jackson, —— Piccadilly, London: Go to three Marquis Street, Lambeth; make inquiries if woman in great distress. Give ten pounds. Make strict inquiries."

"Now, Jewsbury, I am with you. I hope there are no men coming to your rooms to-night; I want to have a long talk with you about this Judicature business. Yes, and about something more important even than that."

The Rev. Mr. Jewsbury looked up.

"The fact is," said the young man, with a smile, "I have been thinking of getting married."

———

CHAPTER IV.

ALMA MATER.

IT was a singular change for this busy, hard-headed man to leave the whirl of London life—with its late nights at the House, its conversational breakfasts, its Wednesday and Saturday dinner parties and official receptions, and so forth—to spend a quiet Sunday with his old friends of Exeter. The very room in which he now sat, waiting for Mr. Jewsbury to hunt him out a gown, had once been his own. It overlooked the Fellows' Garden—that sacred haunt of peace and twilight and green leaves. Once upon a time, and that not very long ago, it was pretty well known that Balfour of Exeter might have had a fellowship presented to him had he not happened to be too rich a man. No one, of course, could have imagined for a moment this ambitious, eager, active young fellow suddenly giving up his wealth, and his chances of marrying, and his political prospects, in order that he might lead a quiet student life within the shadow of these gray walls. Nevertheless, that dream had crossed his mind more than once: most commonly when he had got home from the House about two in the morning, tired out, vexed with the failure of some pet project, unnerved by the apathy of the time, the government he supported being merely a government of sufferance, holding office only because the rival party was too weak to relieve it from the burden.

And indeed there was something of the home-returning feeling in his mind as he now slipped on the academical gown and hurried across to the great yellow-white hall, in which the undergraduates were already busy with their modest beef and ale. There were unknown faces, it is true, ranged by the long tables; but up here on the cross-table, on the platform, he was among old friends; and there were old friends, too, looking over at him from the dusty frames on the walls. He was something of a lion now. He had been a marked man at Oxford; for although he had never made the gallery of the Union tremble with resonant eloquence (he was, in fact, anything but a fluent speaker), he had abundant self-possession, and a tolerably keen instinct of detecting the weak points in his opponent's line of argument. Besides —and this goes for something—there was an impress of power in the mere appearance of the man, in his square forehead, his firm lips, and deep-set, keen gray eyes. He had an iron frame, too— lean, bony, capable of enduring any fatigue. Of course the destination of such a man was politics. Could any one imagine him letting his life slip away from him in these quiet halls, mumbling out a lecture to a dozen ignorant young men in the morning, pacing up and down Addison's Walk in the afternoon, and glad to see the twilight come over as he sat in the common-room of an evening, with claret and cherries, and a cool wind blowing in from the Fellows' Garden?

It was to this quiet, little, low-roofed common-room they now adjourned when dinner in hall was over, and the undergraduates had gone noiselessly off, like so many rabbits to their respective burrows. There were not more than a dozen round the polished mahogany table. The candles were not lit; there was still a pale light shining over the still garden outside, its beautiful green foliage inclosed on one side by the ivied wall of the Bodleian, and just giving one a glimpse of the Radcliffe dome beyond. It was fresh and cool and sweet in here; it was a time for wine and fruit; there were no raised voices in the talk, for there was scarcely a whisper among the leaves of the laburnums outside, and the great acacia spread its feathery branches into a cloudless and lambent sky.

"Well, Mr. Balfour," said an amiable old gentleman, "and what do the government mean to do with us now?"

"I should think, sir," said Mr. Balfour, modestly, "that if the government had their wish, they would like to be drinking wine with you at this moment. It would be charitable to ask them to spend an evening like this with you. They have had sore times of it of late; and their unpopularity is growing greater every day—why, I don't know. I suppose they have been too much in earnest. The English public likes a joke now and again in the conduct of its affairs. No English cabinet should be made up without its buffoon — unless, indeed, the Prime Minister can assume the part occasionally. Insincerity, impertinence, maladministration—anything will be forgiven you if you can make the House laugh. On the other hand, if you happen to be a very earnest person, if you are foolish enough to believe that there are great wrongs to be righted, and if you worry and bother the country with your sincerity, the country will take the first chance —no matter what services you have rendered it—of kicking you out of office. It is natural enough. No one likes to be bothered by serious people. As we are all quite content, why should we be badgered with new projects? May I ask you to hand me those strawberries?"

The old gentleman was rather mystified; but Mr. Jewsbury was not—he was listening with a demure smile.

"They tell me, Mr. Balfour," said the old gentleman, "that if there should be a General Election, your seat may be in danger."

"Oh, I shall be turned out, I know," said Balfour, with much complacency. "My constituents don't lose many opportunities of letting me know that. They burned me in effigy the other night. I have had letters warning me that I had better give Ballinascroon a wide berth if I happened to be in that part of Ireland. But I dare say I shall get in for some other place; I might say that, according to modern notions, the money left me by my father entitles me to a seat. You know how things go together. If you open a system of drainage works, you become a knight. If you give a big dinner to a foreign prince, you become a baronet. If you could only buy Arundel Castle, you would be an earl. And as I see all round me in Parliament men who have no possible claim to be there except the possession of a big fortune—men who go into Parliament, not to help in governing the country at all, but merely to acquire a social distinction to which their money entitles them—I suppose I have that right too. Unfortunately I have not a local habitation and a name anywhere. I must begin and cultivate some place—buy a brewery, or something like that. Regattas are good things: you can spend a good deal of money safely on regattas—"

"Balfour," cried Jewsbury, with a laugh, "don't go on talking like that."

"I tell you," said the young man, seriously, "there was not half as much mischief done by the old pocket-borough system as there is by this money qualification. For my part, I am Tory enough to prefer the old pocket-borough system, with all its abuses. The patrons were men of good birth, who had therefore leisure to attend to public affairs—in fact, they had the tradition that they were responsible for the proper government of the country. They had some measure of education, experience of other countries, an acquaintance with the political experiments of former times, and so forth. So long as they could present to a living —to a seat in the House, I mean—a young fellow of ability had a chance, though he had not a penny in his pocket. What chance has he now? Is it for the benefit of the country that men like —— and —— should be running about from one constituency to another, getting beaten every time, while such brainless and voiceless nonentities as —— and —— are carried triumphantly into Parliament on the shoulders of a crowd of publicans? What is the result? You are degrading Parliament in public estimation. The average member has become a by-word. The men who by education and experience are best fitted to look after the government of a nation are becoming less and less anxious to demean themselves by courting the suffrages of a mob, while the h-less men who are getting into Parliament on the strength of their having grown rich are bringing the House of Commons down to the level of a vestry. Might I trouble you for those strawberries?"

The old gentleman had quite forgotten about the strawberries. He had been listening intently to this scornful protest. When Balfour spoke earnestly—whether advancing a mere paradox or not—there was a certain glow in the deep-set eyes that exercised a singular fascination over some people. It held them. They had to listen, whether they went away convinced or no.

"What an extraordinary fellow you are, Balfour!" said his friend to him, as they were on their way from the common-room to Mr. Jewsbury's easy-chairs and tobacco. "Here you have been inveighing against the money qualification of Members of Parliament, and you yourself propose to get into the House simply on the strength of your money."

"Why not?" said the young man. "If my constituents are satisfied, so am I. If that is their theory, I accept it. You called me no end of names because I took the seat those people at Ballinascroon offered me. I was reaping the harvest sown by bribery and I don't know what. But that was their business, not mine. I merely made use of them, as I told a deputation from them this very forenoon. I have not given them a penny. What I might have given, if there was a chance of my getting in again, and I could do it safely, I don't know."

"Always the same!" exclaimed his friend, as they were going up the narrow wooden stairs. "When you are a little older, Balfour, you will learn the imprudence of always attributing to yourself the meanest motives for your conduct. The world takes men at their own valuation of themselves. How would you like other people to say of you what you say yourself?"

There was no answer to this remark, for now the two friends had entered the larger of Mr. Jewsbury's two rooms—a sufficiently spacious apartment, decorated in the severe modern style, but still offering some compromise to human weakness in the presence of several low, long, and lounging easy-chairs. Moreover, there were pipes and a stone canister of tobacco on a small table. Mr. Jewsbury lit a couple of candles.

"Now," said he, dropping into one of the easy-chairs and taking up a pipe, " I won't listen for a moment to your Judicature Bill, or any other bill; and I won't bore you for a moment with any gigantic scheme for reforming the college revenues and endowing scientific research. I want to know more about what you said at the station. Who is it?"

The young man almost started up in his chair—he leaned forward—there was an eager, bright light in his face.

" Jewsbury, if you only knew this girl—not to look at her merely, but to know her nature; if you could only imagine—" Then he sunk back again in his chair, and put his hands in his pockets. " What is the use of my talking about her? You see, it will be a very advantageous thing for me if I can persuade this girl to marry me — very advantageous. Her father is a poor man; but then he is an earl—I may as well tell you his name; it is Lord Willowby—and he has got valuable connections. Willowby is not much in the Lords. To tell you the truth, I dislike him. He is tricky, and meddles with companies—perhaps that is to be forgiven him, for he hasn't a penny. But he could be of use to me. And his daughter could be of greater use, if she were my wife. Lady Sylvia Balfour could get a better grip of certain people than plain Mr. Hugh—"

His companion had risen from his chair, and was impatiently pacing up and down the floor.

" Balfour," he cried out, " I am getting tired of this. You know you are only shamming. You are the last man in the world to marry for those miserable motives you are now talking about."

" I am not shamming at all," said Balfour, calmly. " I am only looking at the business side of this question. What other would you like to hear about? I don't choose to talk about the girl herself—until you have known her; and then I may tell you what I think about her. Sit down, like a good fellow. Is it my fault that I am ambitious?—that I want to do something in politics?"

His friend sat down resignedly.

" She has accepted you?" he said.

" Not openly — not confessedly," said the young man; and then his breath began to come and go a little more rapidly. " But—but she could not mistake what I have said to her — if she had been angry, she would have sent me off : on the contrary, it is only because I don't wish to annoy her by undue precipitancy; but I think we both understand."

"And her father?"

"Oh, I suppose her father understands too," said Balfour, carelessly. "I suppose I shall have to ask him formally. I wish to Heaven he would not have his name mixed up with those companies."

"The Lady Sylvia—it is a pretty name," said his friend, absently.

"And she is as sweet and pure and noble as her name is beautiful," said Balfour, with a sudden proud light in his eyes—forgetting, indeed, in this one outburst all his schooled reticence. "You have no idea, Jewsbury, what a woman can be until you have known this one. I can tell you it will be something for a man that has to muddle about in the hypocrisies of politics, and to mix among the cynicisms and affectations and mean estimates of society, to find at home, always by him, one clear burning lamp of faith—faith in human nature, and a future worth striving for. You don't suppose that this girl is any of the painted fripperies you meet at every woman's house in London? Good God! before I would marry one of those bedizened and microcephalous playthings—"

He sunk back in his easy-chair again, with a shrug and a laugh. The laugh was against himself; he had been betrayed into a useless vehemence.

"The fact is," said he, "Jewsbury, I am not fair to London women—or rather, I mean, to those London girls who have been out a few seasons and know a good deal more than their mothers ever knew before them. Fortunately the young men they are likely to marry are fit matches for them. They are animated by the same desire—the chief desire of their lives—and that is, to escape the curse imposed on the human race at the gates of Paradise."

"The curse was double," said his clerical friend, with a laugh.

"I know," said Balfour, coolly, "and I maintain what I say. There is no use beating about the bush."

Indeed, he had never been in the habit of beating about the bush. For him, what was, was; and he had never tried to escape the recognition of it in a haze of words. Hence the reputation he enjoyed of being something more than blunt-spoken—

of being, in fact, a pretty good specimen of the perfervid Scotchman, arrogant, opinionated, supercilious, and a trifle too anxious
to tread on people's corns.

"Do you see," he said, suddenly, after a second or two of
quiet, "what Lady —— has done for her husband? She fairly
carried him into office on the strength of her dinners and parties; and now she has *badinaged* him into a peerage. She is a
wonderfully clever woman. She can make a newspaper editor
fancy himself a duke. By-the-way, I see the prince has taken
to the newspapers lately; they are all represented at his garden
parties. If you have a clever wife, it is wonderful what she can
do for you."

"And if you have a stupid wife, can you do anything for
her?" inquired Mr. Jewsbury, to whom all this business — this
theatrical " business " of public life—was rather unintelligible.

Balfour burst out langhing.

"What would you think of a cabinet minister being led by
the nose—what would you think of his resigning the whole of
his authority into the hands of the permanent secretary under
him—simply because that secretary undertakes the duty of getting the minister's wife, who is not very presentable, included in
invitations, and passed into houses where she would never otherwise be seen? She is a wonderful woman, that woman. They
call her Mrs. Malaprop. But Tommy Bingham gets her taken
about somehow."

The two friends smoked in silence for some time; the Irish
Universities, the High Court of Judicature, the Endowment of
Research, may perhaps have been occupying their attention. But
when Balfour spoke next, he said, slowly,

"It must be a good thing for a man to have a woman beside
him whose very presence will make the world sweet and wholesome to him. If it were not for a woman here or there—and it
is only by accident they reveal themselves to you — what *could*
one think of human nature?"

"And when are you to see this wonderful rose that is able to
sweeten all the winds of the world?" his friend asked, with a
smile.

"I am going down with Lord Willowby on Monday for a few
days. I should not wonder if something happened during that
time."

CHAPTER V.

POLITICS AND NIGHTINGALES.

THE Lady Sylvia was seated before a mirror, and her maid was dressing her hair. The maid was a shrewd, kindly, elderly person, who exercised a good deal of control over her young mistress, and at this moment she was gently remonstrating with her for her impatience.

"I am sure, my lady, they cannot be here for half an hour yet," said she.

"And if I am too soon?" said the young lady, with just a trifle of petulance. "I wish to be too soon."

The maid received this admonition with much composure, and was not driven by it into scamping her work. The fact was, it was not she who was responsible for the hurry, if hurry there had to be. There was a book lying on the table. It was a description of the three Khanates of Turkistan when as yet these were existing and independent states. That was not the sort of book that ordinarily keeps a young lady late for dressing; but then there was a good deal of talk, about this time, over the advance of General Kaufmann on Khiva; and as there was a member of the House of Commons coming to dine with a member of the House of Lords, they might very probably refer to this matter; and in that case, ought not a certain young lady to be able to follow the conversation with something of intelligent interest, when even that school-boy cousin of hers, Johnny Blythe, could prattle away about foreign politics for half an hour at a stretch?

"Thank you, Anne," said she, meekly, when the finishing touch was put to her dress; and a couple of minutes afterward she was standing out-of-doors, on the gray stone steps, in the warm sunset glow.

She made a pretty picture as she stood there, listening and expectant. She was dressed in a tight-fitting, tight-sleeved dress of cream-white silk, and there was not a scrap of color, or ribbon, or ornament about it. She wore no jewellery; there was not even a soft thin line of gold round her neck. But there was a white rose in her brown hair.

Suddenly she heard a sound of wheels in the distance; her heart began to throb a bit, and there was a faint flush of color in the pale and calm and serious face. But the next minute that flush had died away, and only one who knew her well could have told that the girl was somewhat excited by the fact that the dark pupils of the gray eyes seemed a trifle larger than usual, and full of a warm, anxious, glad light.

She caught sight of the wagonette as it came rolling along the avenue between the elms. A quick look of pleasure flashed across her face. Then the small, white, trembling fingers were nervously closed, and a great fear possessed her that she might too openly betray the gladness that wholly filled her heart.

"How do you do, Lady Sylvia?" cried Hugh Balfour, with more gayety than was usual with him, as he came up the stone steps and shook hands with her.

He was surprised and chagrined by the coldness of her manner. She caught his eyes but for a moment, and then averted hers, and she seemed to withdraw her hand quickly from his hearty and friendly grasp. Then why should she so quickly turn to her father, and hope he was not tired by his stay in London? That was but scant courtesy to a guest; she had scarcely said a word to him, and her manner seemed either extremely nervous or studiously distant.

Lord Willowby — a tall, thin, sallow-faced man, who stooped a little—kissed her, and bestowed upon her a ferocious smile. That smile of his lordship's, once seen, was not to be forgotten. If Johnny Blythe had had any eye for the similitudes in things; if he had himself poured out a glass of that mysterious and frothy fluid he had bought at the "Fox and Hounds;" if he had observed how the froth hissed up suddenly in the glass, and how it instantly disappeared again, leaving only a blank dulness of liquid — then he might have been able to say what his uncle's smile was like. It was a prodigious grin rather than a smile. It flamed and shot all over his contorted visage, wrinkling up his eyes and revealing his teeth; then it instantaneously disappeared, leaving behind it the normal gloom and depression of distinctly melancholy features.

"I hope you enjoyed the drive over from the station?" said

Lady Sylvia, in a timid voice, to Mr. Balfour; but her eyes were still cast down.

He dared not tell her that he had not consciously seen a single natural object all the way over, so full was his heart of the end and aim of the journey. "Oh, beautiful! beautiful!" said he. "It is a charming country. I am more and more delighted with it each time I see it. Is not that—surely that is Windsor?"

All over the western sky there was a dusky blaze of red; and at the far horizon-line, above the dark-blue woods, there was a tiny line of transparent brown—apparently about an inch in length—with a small projection just visible at each end. It was Windsor Castle; but he did not look long at Windsor Castle. The girl had now turned her eyes in that direction too; he had a glimpse of those wonderful clear depths under the soft, dark eyelashes; the pale, serious, beautiful face caught a touch of color from the glow in the west. But why should she be so cold, so distant, so afraid? When they went into the hall, he followed mechanically the man who had been told off to wait on him. He said nothing in reply when he heard that dinner was at seven. He could not understand in what way he had offended her.

Mechanically, too, he dressed. Surely it was nothing he had said in the House? That was too absurd: how could this girl, brought up as she had been, care about what was said or done in Parliament? And then he grew to wonder at himself. He was more disturbed by a slight change of manner in this girl than by anything that had happened to him for years. He was a man of good nerve and fair self-confidence. He was not much depressed by the hard things his constituents said of him. If a minister snubbed him in answer to a question, he took the snub with much composure; and his knowledge that it would appear in all the papers next morning did not at all interfere with his dinner of that evening. But now, had it come to this already, that he should become anxious, disturbed, restless, merely because a girl had turned away her eyes when she spoke to him?

The dinner gong was sounding as he went down-stairs. He found Lord Willowby and his daughter in the drawing-room—a spacious, poorly furnished chamber that was kept pretty much in shadow by a large chestnut-tree just outside the windows. Then a servant threw open the great doors, and they went into the dining-room. This, too, was a large, airy, poorly furnished room;

but what did that matter when the red light from the west was painting great squares of beautiful color on the walls, and when one could look from the windows away over the level country that was now becoming blue and misty under the deepening glow of the sunset? They had not lit the candles as yet; the fading sunlight was enough.

"My dear fellow," remonstrated Lord Willowby, when the servant had offered Balfour two or three sorts of wine, he refusing them all, "what can I get for you?"

"Nothing, thank you. I rarely drink wine," he said, carelessly. "I think, Lady Sylvia, you said the archery meeting was on Wednesday?"

Now here occurred a strange thing, which was continued all through dinner. Lady Sylvia had apparently surrendered her reserve. She was talking freely, sometimes eagerly, and doing what she could to entertain her guest. But why was it that she resolutely refused to hear Balfour's praises of the quiet and beautiful influences of a country life, and would have nothing to do with archery meetings and croquet parties, and such trivialities; but, on the contrary, was anxious to know all about the chances of the government—whether it was really unpopular—why the Conservatives had refused to take office—when the dissolution was expected—what the appeal to the country on the part of ministers would probably be?

So much for her. Her desire to be instructed in these matters was almost pathetic. If her heart could not be said to beat with the great heart of the people, that was not her fault; for to her the mass of her fellow-countrymen was but an abstract expression that she saw in the newspapers. But surely she could feel and give utterance to a warm interest in public affairs, and a warm sympathy with those who were giving up day and night to the thankless duties of legislation?

Now as for him. He was all for the country and green fields, for peace and grateful silence, for quiet days, and books, and the singing of birds. What was the good of that turmoil they called public life? What effect could be produced on the character by regarding constantly that clamorous whirl of eager self-interest, of mean ambitions, of hypocrisy and brazen impudence and ingratitude? Far better, surely, the independence and self-respect of a private life, the purer social and physical atmosphere of the still country ways, the simple pleasures, the freedom from care, the content and rest.

It was not a discussion ; it was a series of suggestions, of half-declared preferences. Lord Willowby did not speak much. He was a melancholy faced man, and apathetic until there occurred the chance of his getting a few pounds out of you. Lady Sylvia and Mr. Balfour had most of the conversation to themselves, and the manner of it has just been indicated.

Mr. Balfour would know all about the church to which this young lady went. Was it High or Low, ancient or modern ? Had she tried her hand at altar screens ? Did she help in the Christmas decorations ? Lady Sylvia replied to these questions briefly. She appeared far more interested in the free fight then going on between Cardinal Cullen and Mr. O'Keeffe. What was Mr. Balfour's opinion as to the jurisdiction of the Pope in Ireland?

Mr. Balfour was greatly charmed by the look of the old-fash-ioned inn they had passed. Was it the " Fox and Hounds ?" It was so picturesquely situated on the high bank at the top of the hill. Of course Lady Sylvia had noticed the curious painting on the sign - board. Lady Sylvia, looking very wise and profound and serious, seemed rather anxious to know what were the chances of the Permissive Bill ever being passed, and what effect did Mr. Balfour think that would have on the country. She was quite convinced—this person of large experience of jails, reform-atories, police stations, and the like—that by far the greater pro-portion of the crimes committed in this country were the result of drinking. On the other hand, she complained that so many conflicting statements were made. How was one to get to know how the Permissive Bill principle had worked in Maine ?

Lord Willowby only stared at first ; then he began to be amused. Where the devil (this was what he thought) had his daughter picked up these notions ? They were not, so far as he knew, contained in any school-room " Treasury of Knowledge."

As the red light faded out in the west, and a clear twilight filled the sky, it seemed to Balfour that there was something strange and mystical in the face of the girl sitting opposite to him. With those earnest and beautiful eyes, and those proud and sensitive lips, she might have been an inspired poetess or prophetess, he imagined, leading her disciples and worshippers by the earnestness of her look and the grave sweet melody of her voice. As the twilight grew grayer within the room, this magnetic influence seemed to grow stronger and stronger. He could have believed there was a subtle light shining in that pale face. He was, indeed, in something like a trance when the servants brought in the candles ; and then, when he saw the warmer light touch this magical and mystic face, and when he discovered that Lady Sylvia was now less inclined to let her eyes meet his, it was with a great regret he bade good-bye to the lingering and solemn twilight and the vision it had contained.

Lady Sylvia rose to withdraw from the table.

"Do you know," said she to Mr. Balfour, "this is the most beautiful time of the day with us. Papa and I always have a walk through the trees after dinner in the evening. Don't let him sit long."

"As for myself," said Balfour, promptly—he was standing at the time—"I never drink wine after dinner—"

"And you never drink wine during dinner," said his host, with a sudden and fierce smile, that instantly vanished. "Sit down, Balfour. You must at least try a glass of that Madeira."

"Thank you, I am not thirsty," said the younger man, with great simplicity. "Really I would just as soon go out now—"

"Oh, by all means," said his host. "But don't hurry any man's cattle. Sylvia will take you for a stroll to the lake and back—perhaps you may hear a nightingale. I shall join you presently."

Of course it was with the deepest chagrin that the young man found himself compelled to accept of this fair escort; and of course it was with the greatest reluctance that the Lady Sylvia threw a light scarf over her head and led the way out into the cool, clear evening. The birds were silent now. There was a pale glow in the north-western skies; and that again was reflected on the still bosom of the lake. As they walked along the high stone terrace, they caught sight of the first trembling star, far over the great dark masses of the elms.

But in her innocent and eager desire to prove herself a woman of the world, she would not have it that there was any special beauty about this still night. The silence must be oppressive to him ; he would weary of this loneliness in a week. Was there any sight in the world to be compared to Piccadilly in the evening, with its twin rows of gas lamps falling and rising with the hollow and hill—and the whirl of carriages—the lighted windows —with the consciousness that you were in the very heart of the life and thinking and excitement of a great nation?

"We are going up, the week after next," said the Lady Sylvia, "to see the Academy. That is Wednesday, the 21st; and we dine with my uncle in the evening." Then she added, timidly, "Johnny told me they had sent you a card."

He did not answer the implied question for a second or two. His heart was filled with rage and indignation. Was it fair— was it honorable—to let this innocent girl, who knew no more of London life or reputations than a child, go to dine at that house? Must not her father know very well that the conduct of Major the Honorable Stephen Blythe, in regard to a betting transaction, was at that very time under the consideration of the committee of the County Club?

There was a good deal of fierce virtue about this young man; but it may be doubted if he would have been so indignant had any other girl told him merely that she was going to dine with her uncle — that uncle, moreover, being heir-presumptive to an earldom, and not as yet convicted of having done anything un- usually disreputable. But somehow the notion got into Balfour's head that this poor girl was not half well enough looked after. She was left here all by herself, when her father was enjoying himself in London. She needed more careful and· tender and loving guidance. And so forth, and so forth. The anxiety young men show to undertake the protection of innocent maidens is touching in the extreme.

"Yes," said he, suddenly. "I shall dine with Major Blythe on the 21st."

He had that very day written to say he would not. But a shilling telegram would put that right, and would also enable Major Blythe to borrow a five-pound note from him on the first possible occasion.

And so these two walked together on the high stone terrace, in the fading twilight and under the gathering stars. And as they came near to one dark patch of shrubbery, lo! the strange silence was burst asunder by the rich, full song of a nightingale, and they stood still to hear. It was a song of love he sung—of love and youth and the delight of summer nights: how could they but stand still to hear?

CHAPTER VI.

A LIFE-PLEDGE.

LORD WILLOWBY had fallen asleep. Through the white curtains of the window they could see him lying back in an easychair, a newspaper dropped on his knee. Why should they go in to wake him?

The wan light was dying away from the bosom of the lake down there, and there was less of a glow in the northern skies; but the stars were burning more clearly now—white and throbbing over the black foliage of the elms. The nightingale sung from time to time, and the woods were silent to hear. Now and again a cool breeze came through the bushes, bringing with it a scent of lilacs and sweetbrier. They were in no hurry to re-enter the house.

Balfour was talking a little more honestly and earnestly now; for he had begun to speak of his work, his aims, his hopes, his difficulties. It was not a romantic tale he had to tell on this beautiful night, but his companion conferred romance upon it. He was talking as an eager, busy, practical politician; she believed she was listening to a great statesman, to a leader of the future, to her country's one and only savior. It was of no use that he insisted on the prosaic and commonplace nature of the actual work he had to do.

"You see, Lady Sylvia," he said, "I am only an apprentice as yet. I am only learning how to use my tools. And the fact is, there is not one man in fifty in the House who fancies that any tools are necessary. Look how on the most familiar subjects—those nearest to their own doors—they are content to take all their information from the newspapers. They never think of inquiring, of seeing, for themselves. They work out legislation as a mere theorem; they have no idea how it is practically applied. They pass Adulteration Acts, Sanitary Acts, Lodging-house Acts; they consider Gas Bills, Water Bills, and what not; but it is all done in the air. They don't know. Now I have been trying to

cram on some of these things, but I have avoided official reports.
I know the pull it will give me to have actual and personal experience—this is in one direction only, you see—of the way the
poorer people in a great town live: how taxation affects them,
how the hospitals treat them, their relations with the police,
and a hundred other things. Shall I tell you a secret, Lady
Sylvia?"

These were pretty secrets to be told on this beautiful evening!
secrets not of lovers' dreams and hopes, but secrets about Gas
Bills and Water Bills.

"I lived for a week in a court in Seven Dials, as a French pol-
isher. Next week I am going to spend in a worse den—a haunt
of thieves, tramps, and hawkers; a very pretty den, indeed, to be
the property of the Ecclesiastical Commissioners, and almost under the shadow of Westminster Abbey!"

She uttered a slight exclamation—of deprecation and anxious
fear. But he did not quite understand.

"This time, however," he continued, "I shall be not so badly
off; for I am going to live at a common lodging-house, and there
the beds are pretty clean. I have been down and through the
whole neighborhood, and have laid my plans. I find that by paying eightpence a night—instead of fourpence—I shall have one
of the married people's rooms to myself, instead of having to
sleep in the common-room. There will be little trouble about it.
I shall be a hawker, my stock in trade a basket; and if I disappear at three in the morning—going off to Covent Garden, you
know—they won't expect to see me again till nine or ten in the
evening, when they meet in the kitchen to smoke and drink beer.
It is then I hope to get all the information I want. You see
there will be no great hardship. I shall be able to slip home in
the morning, get washed, and a sleep. The rooms in these common lodging-houses are very fairly clean; the police supervision
is very strict."

"It is not the hardship," said Lady Sylvia to her companion,
and her breath came and went somewhat more quickly, "it is the
danger—you will be quite alone—among such people."

"Oh," said he, lightly, "there is no danger at all. Besides, I
have an ally—the great and powerful Mrs. Grace. Shall I tell
you about Mrs. Grace, the owner of pretty nearly half of Happiness Alley?"

The Lady Sylvia would hear something of this person with the pretty name, who lived in that favored alley.

"I was wandering through the courts and lanes down there one day," said Balfour, "and I was having a bad time of it; for I had a tall hat on, which the people regarded as ludicrous, and they poured scorn and contempt on me, and one or two of the women at the windows above threw things at my hat. However, as I was passing one door, I saw a very strong-built woman suddenly come out, and she threw a basket into the middle of the lane. Then she went back, and presently she appeared again, simply shoving before her—her hand on his collar—a man who was certainly as big as herself. 'You clear out!' she said; and then with one arm—it was bare and pretty muscular—she shot him straight after the basket. Well, the man was a meek man, and did not say a word. I said to her, 'Is that your husband you are treating so badly?' Of course I kept out of the reach of her arm, for women who are quarrelling with their husbands are pretty free with their hands. But this woman, although she had a firm, resolute face and a gray mustache, was as cool and collected as a judge. 'Oh dear no,' she said; 'that is one of my tenants. He can't pay, so he's got to get out.' On the strength of this introduction I made the acquaintance of Mrs. Grace, who is really a most remarkable woman. I suppose she is a widow, for she hasn't a single relative in the world. She has gone on renting house after house, letting the rooms, collecting her rents and her nightly fees for lodgers, and looking after her property generally with a decision and ability quite out of the ordinary. I don't suppose she loses a shilling in the month by bad debts. 'Pay, or out you go,' is her motto with her tenants; 'Pay first, or you can't come in,' she says to her lodgers. She has been an invaluable ally to me, that woman. I have gone through the most frightful dens with her, and there was scarcely a word said; she is not a woman to stand any nonsense. And then, of course, her having amassed this property, sixpence by sixpence, has made her anxious to know the conditions on which all the property around her is held, and she has a remarkably quick and shrewd eye for things. Once, I remember, we had been exploring a number of houses that were in an infamous condition. 'Well,' I said to her, 'how do the sanitary inspectors pass this over?' She answered that the sanitary inspectors were only the servants of the

Medical Officer of Health. 'Very well, then,' I said, 'why doesn't the Medical Officer of Health act?' You should have seen the cool frankness with which she looked at me. 'You see, sir,' she said, 'the Medical Officer of Health is appointed by the vestry; and these houses are the property of Mr. ——, who is a vestry-man; and if he was made to put them to rights, he might as well pull them down altogether. So I suppose, sir, the inspectors don't say much, and the Medical Officer he doesn't say anything, and Mr. —— is not put to any trouble.' There is nothing of that sort about Mrs. Grace's property. It is the cleanest bit of whitewash in Westminster. And the way she looks after the water-supply— But really, Lady Sylvia, I must apologize to you for talking to you about such uninteresting things."

"Oh, I assure you," said the girl, earnestly and honestly, "that I am deeply interested — intensely interested; but it is all so strange and terrible. If—if I knew Mrs. Grace, I would like to —to send her a present."

It never occurred to Balfour to ask himself why Lady Sylvia Blythe should like to send a present to a woman living in one of the slums of Westminster. Had the girl a wild notion that by a gift she could bribe the virago of Happiness Alley to keep watch and ward over a certain Quixotic young man who wanted to be-come a Parliamentary Haroun-al-Raschid?

"Mr. Balfour," said Lady Sylvia, suddenly, "have you asked this Mrs. Grace about the prudence of your going into that lodg-ing-house?"

"Oh yes, I have got a lot of slang terms from her—hawkers' slang, you know. And she is to get me my suit of clothes and the basket."

"But surely they will recognize you as having been down there before."

"Not a bit. I shall have my face plentifully begrimed; and there is no better disguise for a man than his taking off his col-lar and tying a wisp of black ribbon round his neck instead. Then I can smoke pretty steadily; and I need not talk much in the kitchen of an evening. But why should I bother you with these things, Lady Sylvia? I only wanted to show you a bit of the training that I think a man should go through before he gets up in Parliament with some delightfully accurate scheme in his hand for the amelioration of millions of human beings—of whose condition he does not really know the smallest particular. It is not the picturesque side of legislation. It is not heroic. But then if you want a fine, bold, ambitious flight of statesmanship, you have only got to go to Oxford or Cambridge; in every college you will find twenty young men ready to remodel the British Constitution in five minutes."

They walked once more up to the window; Lord Willowby was still asleep in the hushed yellow-lit room. Had they been out a quarter of an hour—half an hour? It was impossible for them to say; their rapidly growing intimacy and friendly confidence took no heed of time.

"And it is very disheartening work," he added, with a sigh. "The degradation, physical and mental, you see on the faces you meet in these slums is terrible. You begin to despair of any legislation. Then the children—their white faces, their poor stunted bodies, their weary eyes—thank God you have never seen that sight. I can stand most things: I am not a very soft-hearted person: but—but I can't stand the sight of those children."

She had never heard a man's sob before. She was terrified, overawed. But the next moment he had burst into a laugh, and was talking in rather a gay and excited fashion.

"Yes," said he, "I should like to have my try at heroic legislation too. I should like to be made absolute sovereign and autocrat of this country for one week. Do you know what I should do on day number one? I should go to the gentlemen who form the boards of the great City guilds, and I would say to them, 'Gentlemen, I assure you you would be far better in health and morals if you would cease to spend your revenues on banquets at five guineas a head. You have had quite as much of that as is good for you. Now I propose to take over the whole of the property at present in your hands, and if I find any reasonable bequest in favor of fish-mongers, or skinners, or any other poor tradesmen, that I will administer, but the rest of your wealth—it is only a trifle of twenty millions or so, capitalized—I mean to use for the benefit of yourselves and your fellow-citizens.' Then, what next? I issue my edict: 'There shall be no more slums. Every house of them must be razed to the ground, and the sites turned into gardens, to tempt currents of air into the heart of the city.' But what of the dispossessed people? Why, I have got in my hands this twenty millions to whip them off to Nebraska and make of them great stock-raising communities on the richest grass lands in the world. Did I tell you, Lady Sylvia," he added, seriously, "that I mean to hang all the directors of the existing water and gas companies?"

"No, you did not say that," she answered, with a smile. But she would not treat this matter altogether as a joke. It might please him to make fun of himself; in her inmost heart she believed that if the country only gave him these unlimited powers for a single year, the millennium would *ipso facto* have arrived.

"And so," said he, after a time, "you see how I am situated. It is a poor business, this Parliamentary life. There is a great deal of mean and shabby work connected with it."

"I think it is the noblest work a man could put his hand to," she said, with a flush on her cheek that he could not see; "and the nobleness of it is that a man will go through the things you have described for the good of others. I don't call that mean or shabby work. I would call it mean or shabby if a man were building up a great fortune to spend on himself. If that was his object, what could be more mean? You go into slums and dens; you interest yourself in the poorest wretches that are alive; you give your days and your nights to studying what you can do for them; and you call all that care and trouble and self-sacrifice mean and shabby!"

"But you forget," said he, coldly, "what is my object. I am serving my apprenticeship. I want these facts for my own purposes. You pay a politician for his trouble by giving him a reputation, which is the object of his life—"

"Mr. Balfour," she said, proudly, "I don't know much about public men. You may say what you please about them. But I think I know a little about you. And it is useless your saying such things to me."

For a second he felt ashamed of his habit of self-depreciation; the courage of the girl was a rebuke—was an appeal to a higher candor.

"A man has need to beware," he said. "It is safest to put the lowest construction on your own conduct; it will not be much lower than that of the general opinion. But I did wrong, Lady Sylvia, in talking like that to you. You have a great faith in your friends. You could inspire any man with confidence in himself—"

He paused for a moment; but it was not to hear the nightingale sing, or to listen to the whispering of the wind in the dark elms. It was to gain courage for a further frankness.

"It would be a good thing for the public life of this country," said he, "if there were more women like you—ready to give generous encouragement, ready to believe in the disinterestedness of a man, and with a full faith in the usefulness of his work. I can imagine the good fortune of a man who, after being harassed and buffeted about—perhaps by his own self-criticism as much as by the opinions of others—could always find in his own home consolation and trust and courage. Look at his independence; he would be able to satisfy, or he would try to satisfy, one opinion that would be of more value to him than that of all the world besides. What would he care about the ingratitude of others, so long as he had his reward in his own home? But it is a picture, a dream."

"Could a woman be all that to a man?" the girl asked, in a low voice.

"You could," said he, boldly; and he stopped and confronted her, and took both her trembling hands in his. "Lady Sylvia, when I have dreamed that dream, it was your face I saw in it. You are the noblest woman I have known. I—well, I will say it now—I love you, and have loved you almost since the first moment I saw you. That is the truth. If I have pained you— well, you will forgive me after I have gone, and this will be the last of it."

She had withdrawn her hands, and now stood before him, her eyes cast down, her heart beating so that she could not speak.

"If I have pained you," said he, after a moment or two of anxious silence, "my presumption will bring its own punishment. 'Lady Sylvia, shall I take you back to the Hall?"

She put one hand lightly on his arm.

"I am afraid," she said; and he could but scarcely hear the low and trembling words. "How can I be to you—what you described? It is so much—I have never thought of it—and if I should fail to be all that you expect?"

He took her in his arms and kissed her forehead.

"I have no fear. Will you try?"

"Yes," she answered; and now she looked up into his face, with her wet eyes full of love and hope and generous self-surrender. "I will try to be to you all that you could wish me to be."

"Sylvia, my wife!" was all he said in reply; and indeed there was not much need for further speech between these two. The silence of the beautiful night was eloquence enough. And then from time to time they had the clear, sweet singing of the night-ingale and the stirring of the night wind among the trees.

By-and-by they went back to the Hall; they walked arm-in-arm, with a great peace and joy in their hearts; and they re-entered the dining-room. Lord Willowby started up in his easy-chair and rubbed his eyes.

"Bless me!" said he, with one of his violent smiles, "I have been asleep."

His lordship was a peer of the realm, and his word must be taken. The fact was, however, that he had not been asleep at all.

CHAPTER VII.

A CONFESSION OF FAITH.

LORD WILLOWBY guessed pretty accurately what had occurred. For a second or two his daughter sat down at the table, pale a little, silent, and nervously engaged in pulling a rose to pieces. Then she got up and proposed they should go into the drawing-room to have some tea. She led the way; but just as she had gone through, Balfour put his hand on Lord Willowby's arm and detained him.

At this juncture a properly minded young man would have been meek and apologetic; would have sworn eternal gratitude in return for the priceless gift he was going to demand; would have made endless protestations as to the care with which he would guard that great treasure. But this Hugh Balfour was not very good at sentiment. Added to the cool judgment of a man of the world, he had a certain forbidding reserve about him which was, perhaps, derived from his Scotch descent; and he knew a great deal more about his future father-in-law than that astute person imagined.

"Lord Willowby," said he, "a word before we go in. You

must have noticed my regard for your daughter; and you may have guessed what it might lead to. I presume it was not quite displeasing to you, or you would not have been so kind as to invite me here from time to time. Well, I owe you an apology for having spoken sooner than I intended to Lady Sylvia—I ought to have mentioned the matter to you first—"

"My dear fellow," said Lord Willowby, seizing his hand, while all the features of his face were suddenly contorted into what he doubtless meant as an expression of rapturous joy, "not another word! Of course she accepted you—her feelings for you have long been known to me, and my child's happiness I put before all other considerations. Balfour, you have got a good girl to be your wife; take care of her."

"I think you may trust me for that," was the simple answer.

They went into the room. Not a word was said; but Lord Willowby went over to his daughter and patted her on the back and kissed her: then she knew. A servant brought in some tea.

It was a memorable evening. The joy within the young man's heart had to find some outlet; and he talked then as no one had ever heard him talk before—not even his most intimate friend at Exeter, when they used to sit discoursing into the small hours of the morning. Lord Willowby could not readily understand a man's being earnest or eloquent except under the influence of wine; but Balfour scarcely ever drank wine. Why should he be so vehement? He was not much of an orator in the House; in society he was ordinarily cold and silent. Now, however, he had grown indignant over a single phrase they had stumbled against—"You can't make men moral by act of Parliament"— and the gray eyes under the heavy eyebrows had an intense earnestness in them as he denounced what he chose to call a pernicious lie.

"You *can* make men moral by act of Parliament—by the action of Parliament," he was insisting; and there was one there who listened with rapt attention and faith, even when he was uttering the most preposterous paradoxes, or giving way to the most violent prejudice; "and the nation will have to answer for it that proceeds on any other belief. For what is morality but the perfect adjustment of the human organism to the actual conditions of life—the observance by the human being of those unchangeable, inexorable laws of the universe, to break which is

death, physical or spiritual, as the case may be? What have all
the teachers who have taught mankind—from Moses in his day
to Carlyle in ours—been insisting on but that? Moses was only
a sort of divine vestry-man; Carlyle has caught something of the
poetry of the Hebrew prophets; but it is the same thing they
say. There are the fixed, immutable laws: death awaits the nation or the man who breaks them. Look at the lesson the world
has just been reading. A liar, a perjurer, and traitor gets up in
the night-time and cuts the throat of a nation. In the morning you find him wearing imperial robes; but if you looked
you would find the skirts of them bespattered with the blood
of the women and children he has had shot down in the street.
Europe shudders a little, but goes on its way; it has forgotten that the moment a crime is committed, its punishment
is already meted out. And what does the nation do that has
been robbed and insulted—that has seen those innocent women
and children shot down that the mean ambition of a liar might
be satisfied? It is quick to forgiveness; for it finds itself tricked
out in gay garments, and it has money put in its pocket,
and it is bidden to dance and be merry. Everything is to be
condoned now; for life has become like a masked ball, and it
does not matter what thieves and swindlers there may be in the
crowd, so long as there is plenty of brilliant lights and music
and wine. Lady Sylvia, do you know Alfred Rethel's 'Der Tod
als Feind?'—Death coming in to smite down the maskers and
the music-makers at a revel? It does not matter much who or
what is the instrument of vengeance, but the vengeance is sure.
When France was paying her penalty—when the chariot-wheels
of God were grinding exceeding hard—she cried at her enemy,
'You are only a pack of Huns.' Well, Attila was a Hun,
a barbarian, probably a superstitious savage. I don't know
what particular sort of fetich he may have worshipped — what
blurred image or idol he had in his mind of Him who is past
finding out; but, however rude or savage his notions were, he
knew that the laws of God had been broken, and the time for
vengeance had come. The Scourge of God may be Attila or another: an epidemic that slays its thousands because a nation has
not been cleanly—the lacerating of a mother's heart when in her
carelessness she has let her child cut its finger with a knife. The
penalty has to be paid; sometimes at the moment, sometimes

long after; for the sins of the fathers are visited not only on their children, but on their children's children, and so on to the end, nature claiming her inexorable due. And when I go down to the slums I have been talking to you about, how dare I say that these wretched people, living in squalor and ignorance and misery, are only paying the penalty for their own mistakes and crimes ? You look at their narrow, retreating, monkey-like forehead, the heavy and hideous jowl, the thick neck, and the furtive eye; you think of the foul air they have breathed from their infancy, of the bad water and unwholesome food they have consumed, of the dense ignorance in which they have been allowed to grow up; and how can you say that their immoral existence is anything but inevitable ? I am talking about Westminster, Lord Willowby. From some parts of these slums you can see the towers of the Houses of Parliament, glittering in gilt, and looking very fine indeed. And if I declared my belief that the immorality of these wretched people of the slums lay as much at the door of the Houses of Parliament as at their own door, I suppose people would say I was a rabid democrat, pandering to the passions of the poor to achieve some notoriety. But I believe it all the same. Wrong-doing — the breaking of the universal laws of existence, the subversion of those conditions which produce a settled, wholesome, orderly social life—is not necessarily personal; it may be national; it may have been continued through centuries, until the results have been so stamped into the character of the nation—or into the condition of a part of a nation — that they almost seem ineradicable. And so I say that you can and do make people moral or immoral by the action of Parliament. There is not an Education Bill, or a University Tests Bill, or an Industrial Dwellings Bill you pass which has not its effect, for good or ill, on the relations between the people of a country and those eternal laws of right which are forever demanding fulfilment. Without some such fixed belief, how could any man spend his life in tinkering away at these continual experiments in legislation ? You would merely pass a vote trebling the police force, and have done with it."

Whether or not this vehement and violently prejudiced young man had quite convinced Lord Willowby, it was abundantly clear that he had long ago convinced himself. His eyes were " glowering," as the Scotch say; and he had forgotten all about the tea that Lady Sylvia herself had poured out and brought to him. The fact is, Lord Willowby had not paid much attention. He was thinking of something else. He perceived that the young man was in an emotional and enthusiastic mood; and he was wondering whether, in return for having just been presented with a wife, Mr. Hugh Balfour might not be induced to become a director of a certain company in which his lordship was interested, and which was sorely in need of help at that moment.

But Lady Sylvia was convinced. Here, indeed, was a confession of faith fit to come from the man whom she had just accepted as her husband. He had for the moment thrown off his customary garb of indifference or cynicism; he had revealed himself; he had spoken with earnest voice and equally earnest eyes; and to her the words were as the words of one inspired.

"Have you any more water-color drawings to show me, Lady Sylvia?" he asked, suddenly.

A quick shade of surprise and disappointment passed over the calm and serious face. She knew why he had asked. He had imagined that these public affairs must be dull for her. He wished to speak to her about something more within her comprehension. She was hurt; and she walked a little proudly as she went to get the drawings.

"Here is the whole collection," said she, indifferently. "I don't remember which of them you saw before. I think I will bid you good-night now."

"I am afraid I have bored you terribly," said he, as he rose.

"You cannot bore me with subjects in which I take so deep an interest," said she, with some decision.

He took her hand and bade her good-night. There was more in the look that passed between these two than in a thousand effusive embraces.

"Now, Balfour," said his lordship, with unaccustomed gayety, "what do you say to changing our coats, and having a cigar in the library? And a glass of grog? — a Scotchman ought to know something about whiskey. Besides, you don't win a wife every day."

It was Lord Willowby who looked and talked as if he had just won a wife as the two men went up-stairs to the library. He very rarely smoked, but on this occasion he lit a cigarette; and he said he envied Balfour his enjoyment of that wooden pipe.

Would his guest try something hot? No? Then Lord Willow-by stretched out his legs, and lay back in the easy-chair, apparently greatly contented with himself and the world.

When the servant had finally gone, his lordship said,

"How well you talked to-night, Balfour! The flush, the ela-tion, you know—of course a man talks better before his sweet-heart than before the House of Commons. And if you and I, now, must speak of what you might call the—the business side of your marriage, well, I suppose we need not be too technical or strict in our language. Let us be frank with each other, and friendly. I am glad you are going to marry my daughter, and so doubtless are you."

The young man said nothing at all. He was smoking his pipe. There was no longer any fire of indignation or earnest-ness in his eyes.

"You know I am a very poor man," his lordship continued. "I can't give Sylvia anything."

"I don't expect it," said Balfour.

"On the other hand, you are a rich man. In such cases, you know, there is ordinarily a marriage settlement, and naturally, as Sylvia's guardian, I should expect you to give her out of your abundance. But then, Balfour," said his lordship, with a gay air and a ferocious smile, "I was thinking — merely as a joke, you know—what a rich young fellow like yourself might do to pro-duce an impression on a romantic girl. Marriage settlements are very prosaic things; they look rather like buying a wife; more-over, they have to mention contingencies which it is awkward for an unmarried girl to hear of. Wouldn't a girl be better pleased, now, if an envelope were placed on her dressing-room table the night before her marriage—the envelope containing a bank-note —say for £50,000? The mystery, the surprise, the delight— all these things would tell upon a girl's mind; and she would be glad she would not have to go to church an absolute beg-gar. Of course that is merely a joke; but can't you imagine what the girl's face would be like when she opened the enve-lope?"

Balfour did not at all respond to his companion's gayety. In the drawing-room below he had betrayed an unusual enthusiasm of speech. What man in his circumstances could fail to show a natural elation? But if Lord Willowby had calculated on this elation interfering with Mr. Balfour's very sober habit of looking at business matters, he had made a decided mistake.

Balfour laid down his pipe, and put his outstretched hands on his knees.

"I don't know," said he, coolly, "whether you mean to suggest that I should do something of the sort you describe—"

"My dear fellow!" said Lord Willowby, with an air of protest. "It was only a fancy—a joke."

"Ah! I thought so," said Balfour. "I think it is better to treat money matters simply as money matters; romance has plenty of other things to deal with. And as regards a marriage settlement, of course I should let my lawyer arrange the whole affair."

"Oh, naturally, naturally," said his lordship, gayly; but he inwardly invoked a curse on the head of this mean-spirited Scotchman.

"You mentioned £50,000," continued the younger man, speaking slowly and apparently with some indifference. "It is a big sum to demand all at once from my partners. But then the fact is, I have never spent much money myself, and I have allowed them to absorb in the business a good deal of what I might otherwise have had, so that they are pretty deep in my debt. You see, my lord, I have inherited from my father a good deal of pride in our firm, though I don't know anything about its operations myself; and they have lately been extending the business both in Australia and China, and I have drawn only what I wanted for my yearly accounts. So I can easily have £50,000 from them. That in a safe four per cent. investment would bring £2000 a year. Do you think Lady Sylvia would consider—"

"Sylvia is a mere child," her father said. "She knows nothing about such things."

"If you prefer it," said Balfour, generously, "I will make it part of the settlement that the trustees shall invest that sum, subject to Lady Sylvia's directions."

Lord Willowby's face, that had been gradually resuming its sombre look, brightened up.

"I suppose you would act as one of the trustees?" said Balfour.

His lordship's face grew brighter still. It was quite eagerly that he cried out,

"Oh, willingly, willingly. Sylvia would have every confidence in me, naturally, and I should be delighted to be able to look after the interests of my child. You cannot tell what she has been to me. I have tended her every day of her life—"

["Except when you went knocking about all over Europe without her," thought Balfour.]

"I have devoted all my care to her—"

["Except what you gave to the Seven Per Cent. Investment Company," thought Balfour.]

"She would implicitly trust her affairs in my hands—"

["And prove herself a bigger fool than I took her to be," thought this mean-spirited Scotchman.]

Lord Willowby, indeed, seemed to wake up again. Two thousand pounds a year was ample pin - money. He had no sympathy with the extravagant habits of some women. And as Sylvia's natural guardian, it would be his business to advise her as to the proper investment.

"My dear lord," cried Balfour, quite cheerfully, "there won't be the slightest trouble about that; for, of course, I shall be the other trustee."

The light on Lord Willowby's worn and sunken face suddenly vanished. But he remained very polite to his future son-in-law, and he even lit another cigarette to keep him company.

CHAPTER VIII.

MISLEADING LIGHTS.

THE two or three days Balfour now spent at Willowby Hall formed a beautiful, idle, idyllic period not soon to be forgotten either by him or by the tender - natured girl to whom he had just become engaged. Lord Willowby left them pretty much to themselves. They rode over the great dark heath, startling the rabbits; or drove along the wooded lanes, under shelter of the elms and limes; or walked through the long grass and buttercups of the park; or, in the evening, paced up and down that stone terrace, waiting for the first notes of the nightingale. It was a time for glad and wistful dreams, for tender self-confessions, and —what is more to the purpose—for the formation of perfectly ridiculous estimates of each other's character, tastes, and habits. This man, for example, who was naturally somewhat severe and exacting in his judgments, who was implacable in his contempt for meanness, hypocrisy, and pretence, and who was just a trifle too bitter and plain-spoken in expressing that contempt, had now grown wonderfully considerate to all human frailties, gentle in judgment, and good-natured in speech. He did not at all consider it necessary to tell her what he thought of her father. His fierce virtue did not prevent his promising to dine with her uncle. And he did not fancy that he himself was guilty of any gross hypocrisy in pretending to be immensely interested in the feeding of pigeons, the weeding of flower-beds, the records of local cricket-matches, and the forth-coming visit of the bishop.

During those pleasant days they had talked, as lovers will, of the necessity of absolute confidence between sweetheart and sweetheart, between husband and wife. To guard against the sad misunderstandings of life, they would always be explicitly frank with each other, whatever happened. But then, if you had reproached Balfour with concealing from his betrothed his opinion of certain of her relations, he would probably have demanded in his turn what absolute confidence was. Would life be tolerable if everything were to be spoken? A man comes home in the evening: he has lost his lawsuit—things have been bad in the City—perhaps he has been walking all day in a pair of tight boots: anyhow, he is tired, irritable, impatient. His wife meets him, and, before letting him sit down for a moment, will hurry him off to the nursery to show him the wonderful drawings Adolphus has drawn on the wall. If he is absolutely frank, he will exclaim, " Oh, get away! You and your children are a thorough nuisance !" That would be frankness ; absolute confidence could go no further. But the husband is not such a fool—he is not so selfishly cruel—as to say anything of the kind. He goes off to get another pair of shoes ; he sits down to dinner, perhaps a trifle silent ; but by-and-by he recovers his equanimity ; he begins to look at the brighter side of things, and is presently heard to declare that he is quite sure that boy has something of the artist in him, and that it is no wonder his mother takes such a pride in him, for he is the most intelligent child—etc.

Moreover, it was natural in the circumstances for Balfour to be unusually gentle and conciliatory. He was proud and pleased ;

it would have been strange if this new sense of happiness had
not made him a little generous in his judgments of others. He
was not consciously acting a part; but then every young man
must necessarily wish to make of himself something of a hero in
the eyes of his betrothed. Nor was she consciously acting a part
when she impressed on him the conviction that all her aspirations and ambitions were connected with public life. Each was
trying to please the other; and each was apt to see in the other
what he and she desired to see there. To put the case in as
short a form as may be: here was a girl whose whole nature was
steeped in Tennyson, and here was a young man who had a profound admiration for Thackeray. But when, under the shadow
of the great elms, in the stillness of these summer days, he read
to her passages from "Maud," he declared that existence had
nothing further to give than that; while she, for her part, was
eager to have him tell her of the squabbles and intrigues of Parliamentary life, and expressed her settled belief that "Vanity
Fair" was the cleverest book in the whole world.

On the morning of the day on which he was to leave, he
brought down to the breakfast-room a newspaper. He laughed
as he handed it to her.

This was a copy of the *Ballinascroon Sentinel*, which contained not only an account of the interview between Mr. Balfour,
M.P., and a deputation from his constituents, but also a leading
article on that event. The *Ballinascroon Sentinel* waxed eloquent over the matter. The Member for Ballinascroon was "a
renegade Scotchman, whose countrymen were ashamed to send
him to Parliament, and who had had the audacity to accept the
representation of an Irish borough, which had been grossly betrayed and insulted as the reward for its mistaken generosity."
There was a good deal more of the same sort of thing; it had
not much novelty for Balfour.

But it was new to Lady Sylvia. It was with flashing eyes
and a crimsoned cheek that she rose and carried the newspaper
to her father, who was standing at the window. Lord Willowby
merely looked down the column, and smiled,

"Balfour is accustomed to it," said he,

"But is it fair, is it sufferable," she said, with that hot indignation still in her face, "that any one should have to grow accustomed to such treatment? Is this the reward in store for a man

who spends his life in the public service? The writer of that shameful attack ought to be prosecuted; he ought to be fined and imprisoned. If I were a man, I would horsewhip him, and I am sure he would run away fast enough."

"Oh no, Lady Sylvia," said Balfour, though his heart warmed to the girl for that generous espousal of his cause. "You must remember that he is smarting under the wrongs of Ireland, or rather the wrongs of Ballinascroon. I dare say, if I were a leading man in a borough, I should not like to have the member representing the borough simply making a fool of it. I can see the joke of the situation, although I am a Scotchman; but you can't expect the people in the borough to see it. And if my friend the editor uses warm language, you see that is how he earns his bread. I have no doubt he is a very good sort of fellow. I have no doubt, when they kick me out of Ballinascroon, and if I can get in for some other place, I shall meet him down at Westminster, and he will have no hesitation at all in asking me to help to get his son the Governorship of Timbuctoo, or some such post."

Was not this generous? she said to herself. He might have exacted damages from this poor man. Perhaps he might have had him imprisoned and sent to the tread-mill. But no. There was no malice in his nature, no anxious vanity, no sentiment of revenge. Lady Sylvia's was not the only case in which it might have been remarked that the most ordinary qualities of prudence or indifference exhibited by a young man become, in the eyes of the young man's sweetheart, proof of a forbearance, a charity, a goodness, altogether heroic and sublime.

Her mother having died when she was a mere child, Lady Sylvia had known scarcely any grief more serious than the loss of a pet canary, or the withering of a favorite flower. Her father professed an elaborate phraseological love for her, and he was undoubtedly fond of his only child; but he also dearly liked his personal liberty, and he had from her earliest years accustomed her to bid him good-bye without much display of emotion on either side. But now, on this morning, a strange heaviness of heart possessed her. She looked forward to that drive to the station with a dull sense of foreboding; she thought of herself coming back alone—for her father was going up to town with Balfour—and for the first time in her life the solitude of the Hall seemed to her something she could not bear.

"Sylvia," said her father, when they had all got into the wagonette, "you don't look very bright this morning."

She started, and flushed with an anxious shame. She hoped they would not think she was cast down merely because she was going to bid good-bye to Mr. Balfour for a few days. Would they not meet on the following Wednesday at her uncle's?

So, as they drove over to the station, the girl was quite unusually gay and cheerful. She was no longer the serious Syllabus whom her cousin Johnny used to tease into petulance. Balfour was glad to see her looking so bright; doubtless the drive through the sweet, fresh air had raised her spirits.

And she was equally cheerful in the station; for she kept saying to herself, "*Keep up now, keep up. It is only five minutes now. And, oh! if he were to see me cry—the least bit—I should die of shame.*"

"Sylvia," said he, when they happened to be alone for a moment, "I suppose I may write to you?"

"Yes," said she, timidly.

"How often?"

"I—I don't know," said she, looking down.

"Would it bother you if you had a letter every morning?"

"Oh," she said, "you could never spare time to write to me so often as that. I know how busy you must be. You must not let me interfere in any way, now or at any time, with your real work. You must promise that to me."

"I will promise this to you," said he, taking her hand to bid her good-bye, "that my relations with you shall never interfere with my duties toward the honorable and independent electors of Ballinascroon. Will that do?"

The train came up. She dared not raise her eyes to his face as she shook hands with him. Her heart was beating hurriedly.

She conquered, nevertheless. There were several people about the station who knew Lord Willowby's daughter; and as she was rather a distinguished person in that neighborhood, and as she was pretty and prettily dressed, she attracted a good deal of notice. But what did they see? Only Lady Sylvia bidding good-bye to her papa and to a gentleman who had doubtless been his guest; and there was nothing but a bright and friendly smile in her face as she looked after that particular carriage in the receding train.

But there was no smile at all in her face as she was being

driven back through the still and wooded country to the empty Hall. The large, tender, dark-gray eyes were full of trouble and anxious memories; her heart was heavy within her. It was her first sorrow, and there was something new, alarming, awful about it. This sense of loneliness—of being left—of having her heart yearning after something that had gone away—was a new experience altogether, and it brought with it strange tremors of unrest and unreasoning anxiety.

She had often read in books that the best cure for care was hard work; and as soon as she got back to the Hall, she set busily about the fulfilment of her daily duties. She found, however, but little relief. The calm of mind and of occupation had fled from her. She was agitated by all manner of thoughts, fancies, surmises, that would not let her be in peace.

That letter of the next morning, for example—she would have to answer it. But how? She went to her own little sitting-room, and securely locked the door, and sat down to her desk. She stared at the blank paper for several minutes before she dared to place anything on it; and it was with a trembling hand that she traced out the words, "*Dear Mr. Balfour.*" Then she pondered for a long time on what she should say to him—a difficult matter to decide, seeing she had not as yet received the letter which she wished to answer. She wrote, "*My dear Mr. Balfour,*" and looked at that. Then she wrote, with her hand trembling more than ever, "*Dear H——;*" but she got no farther than that, for some flush of color mounted to her face, and she suddenly resolved to go and see the head gardener about the new geraniums. Before leaving the room, however, she tore up the sheet of paper into very small pieces.

Now, the head gardener was a soured and disappointed man. The whole place, he considered, was starved. Such flowers as he had nobody came to see; while Lord Willowby had an amazingly accurate notion of the amount which the sale of the fruit of each year ought to bring. He was curt of speech, and resented interference. On this occasion, moreover, he was in an ill humor. But, to his intense surprise, his young mistress was not to be beaten off by short answers. Was her ladyship in an ill humor too? Anyhow, she very quickly brought him to his senses; and one good issue of that day's worry was that old Blake was a great deal more civil to Lady Sylvia ever after.

"You know, Blake," said she, firmly, "you Yorkshire people are said to be a little too sharp with your tongue sometimes."

"I do not know, my lady," said the old man, with great exasperation, "why the people will go on saying I am from Yorkshire. If I have lived in a stable, I am not a hoarse. I am sure I have telled your ladyship I was boarn in Dumfries."

"Indeed you have, Blake," said Lady Sylvia, with a singular change of manner. "Really, I had quite forgotten. I think you said you left Scotland when you were a lad; but of course you claim to be Scotch. That is quite right."

She had become very friendly. She sat down on some wooden steps beside him, and regarded his work with quite a new interest.

"It is a fine country, is it not?" said she, in a conciliatory tone.

"We had better crops where I was born than ye get about the sandy wastes here," said the old man, gruffly.

"I did not mean that quite," said Lady Sylvia, patiently; "I meant that the country generally was a noble country—its magnificent mountains and valleys, its beautiful lakes and islands, you know."

Blake shrugged his shoulders. Scenery was for fine ladies to talk about.

"Then the character of the people," said Lady Sylvia, nothing daunted, "has always been so noble and independent. Look how they have fought for their liberties, civil and religious. Look at their enterprise—they are to be found all over the globe—the first pioneers of civilization—"

"Ay, and it isn't much that some of them make by it," said Blake, sulkily; for this pioneer certainly considered that he had been hardly used in these alien and unenlightened regions.

"I don't wonder, Blake," said Lady Sylvia, in a kindly way, "that you should be proud of being a Scotchman. Of course you know all about the Covenanters."

"Ay, your ladyship," said Blake, still going on with his work.

"I dare say you know," said Lady Sylvia, more timidly, "that one of the most unflinching of them—one of the grandest figures in that fight for freedom of worship—was called Balfour."

She blushed as she pronounced the name; but Blake was busy with his plants.

"Ay, your ladyship. I wonder whether that man is ever going to send the wire-netting."

"I will take care you shall have it at once," said Lady Sylvia, as she rose and went to the door. "If we don't have it by to-morrow night, I will send to London for it. Good-morning, Blake."

Blake grunted out something in reply, and was glad to be left to his own meditations. But even this shrewd semi-Scotchman, semi-Yorkshireman, could not make out why his mistress, after showing a bit of a temper, and undoubtedly getting the better of him, should so suddenly have become friendly and conciliatory. And what could her ladyship mean by coming and talking to her gardener about the Covenanters?

That first day of absence was a lonely and miserable day for Lady Sylvia. She spent the best part of the afternoon in her father's library, hunting out the lives of great statesmen, and anxiously trying to discover particulars about the wives of those distinguished men—how they qualified themselves for the fulfilment of their serious duties, how they best forwarded their husbands' interests, and so forth, and so forth. But somehow, in the evening, other fancies beset her. The time that Balfour had spent at Willowby Hall had been very pleasant for her; and as her real nature asserted itself, she began to wish that that time could have lasted forever. That would have been a more delightful prospect for her than the anxieties of a public life. Nay, more; as this feeling deepened, she began to look on the conditions of public life as so many rivals that had already inflicted on her this first miserable day of existence by robbing her of her lover. She began to lose her enthusiasm about grateful constituencies, triumphant majorities carrying great measures through every stage, the national thanksgiving awarded to the wearied statesman. It may seem absurd to say that a girl of eighteen should begin to harbor a feeling of bitter jealousy against the British House of Commons, but stranger things than that have happened in the history of the human heart.

CHAPTER IX.

LOVE'S TRIALS.

"Susan," said Master Johnny Blythe, to his sister—her name was Honoria, and therefore he called her Susan—"you have got yourself up uncommon smart to-night. I see how it is. You girls are all alike. As soon as one of you catches a fellow, you won't let him alone; you're all for pulling him off; you're like a lot of sparrows with one bit of bread among you."

"I don't know what you are talking about," said Miss Honoria, with proud indifference.

"Oh yes, you do," retorted Johnny, regarding himself in a mirror, and adjusting his white tie. "You don't catch a man like Balfour stopping down at Willowby three whole days in the middle of the session, and all for nothing. Then it was from Willowby he telegraphed he would come here to-night, after he had refused. Well, I wonder at poor old Syllabus; I thought she was a cut above a tea-and-coffee fellow. I suppose it's his £30,000 a year; at least, it would be in your case, Susan. Oh, I know! I know when you part your hair at the side you mean mischief. And so we shall have a battle royal to-night—Susan v. Syllabus—and all about a grocer!"

Those brothers! The young lady whom Master Johnny treated with so much familiarity and disrespect was of an appearance to drive the fancies of a young man mad. She was tall and slender and stately; though she was just over seventeen, there was something almost mature and womanly in her presence; she had large dark eyes, heavy-lidded; big masses of black hair tightly braided up behind to show her shapely neck; a face such as Lely would have painted, but younger and fresher and pinker; a chin somewhat too full, but round with the soft contour of girlhood. She was certainly very unlike her cousin both in appearance and expression. Lady Sylvia's eyes were pensive and serious; this young woman's were full of practical life and audacity. Lady Sylvia's underlip retreated somewhat, and gave a sweet, shy, sensitive look to the fine face; whereas Honoria Blythe's underlip was full and round and ripe as a cherry, and was in fit accordance with her frank and even bold black eye.

Mrs. Blythe came into the drawing-room. She was a large and portly person, pale, with painted eyelashes and unnaturally yellow hair. Lord Willowby had no great liking for his sister-in-law; he would not allow Sylvia to go on a visit to her; when he and his daughter came to town, as on the present occasion, they stopped at a private hotel in Arlington Street. Finally, the head of the house made his appearance. Major Blythe had all the physique that his elder brother, Lord Willowby, lacked. He was stout and roseate of face, bald for the most part, his eyes a trifle blood-shot, and his hand inclined to be unsteady, except when he was playing pool. He wore diamond studs; he said "by Gad;" and he was hotly convinced that Arthur Orton, who was then being tried, was not Arthur Orton at all, but Roger Tichborne. So much for the younger branch of the Blythe family.

As for the elder branch, Lord Willowby was at that moment seated in an easy-chair in a room in Arlington Street, reading the evening paper, while his daughter was in her own room, anxious as she never had been anxious before about her toilet and the services of the faithful Anne. Lady Sylvia had spent a miserable week. A week?—it seemed a thousand years rather; and as that portentous period had to be got through somehow, she had mostly devoted it to reading and re-reading six letters she had received from London, until every phrase and every word of these precious and secret documents was engraven on her memory. She had begun to reason with herself, too, about her hatred of the House of Commons. She tried hard to love that noble institution; she was quite sure, if only her father would take her over to Ballinascroon, she would go into every house, and shake hands with the people, and persuade them to let Mr. Balfour remain their representative when the next General Election came round; and she wondered, moreover, whether, when her lover went away on that perilous mission of his through the slums of Westminster, she could not too, as well as he, put on some mean attire, and share with him the serious dangers and discomforts of that wild enterprise.

And now she was about to meet him, and a great dread possessed her lest her relatives should discover her secret. Again and again she pictured to herself the forth-coming interview, and her only safety seemed to be in preserving a cold demeanor and a perfect silence, so that she should escape the shame of being suspected.

The Blythes lived in a small and rather poorly furnished house in Dean Street, Park Lane; Lord Willowby and his daughter had not far to drive. When they went into the drawing-room, Lady Sylvia dared scarcely look around; it was only as she was being effusively welcomed by her aunt that she became vaguely aware that Mr. Balfour was not there. Strange as it may appear, his absence seemed to her a quick and glad relief. She was anxious, perturbed, eager to escape from a scrutiny on the part of her relatives, which she more than half expected. But when she had shaken hands with them all, and when the two or three strangers present began to talk those staccato commonplaces which break the frigid silence before dinner, she was in a measure left to herself; and it was then that—not heeding in the least the chatter of Master Johnny—she began to fear. Had he already adventured on that Haroun-al-Raschid enterprise, and been stopped by a gang of thieves? There was a great outcry at this time about railway accidents; was it possible that— Or was he merely detained at the House of Commons? She forgot that the House does not sit on Wednesday evenings.

She was standing near the entrance to the room, apparently listening to Master Johnny, when she heard a knock at the door below. Then she heard footsteps on the narrow staircase which made her heart beat. Then a servant announced Mr. Balfour. Her eyes were downcast.

Now Balfour, as he came in, ought to have passed her as if she had been a perfect stranger, and gone on and addressed himself, first of all, to his hostess. But he did nothing of the kind.

"How do you do, Lady Sylvia?" said he, and he stopped and shook hands with her.

She never saw him at all. Her eyes were fixed on the floor, and she did not raise them. But she placed her trembling hand in his for a moment, and murmured something, and then experienced an infinite relief when he went on toward Mrs. Blythe.

She was glad, too, when she saw that he was to take his hostess in to dinner. Had they heard of this secret, might they not, as a sort of blundering compliment, have asked him to take her in?

As it was, she fell to the lot of a German gentleman, who knew very little English, and was anxious to practise what little he knew, but who very soon gave up the attempt on finding his companion about the most silent and reserved person whom he had ever sat next at dinner. He was puzzled, indeed. She was an earl's daughter, and presumably had seen something of society. She had a pale, interesting, beautiful face and thoughtful eyes; she must have received enough attention in her time. Was she too proud, then, he thought, to bother with his broken phrases?

The fact was, that throughout that dinner the girl had eyes and ears but for one small group of people—her cousin and Balfour, who were sitting at the farther corner of the table, apparently much interested in each other. If Lady Sylvia was silent, the charge could not be brought against Honoria Blythe. That young lady was as glib a chatterer as her brother. She knew everything that was going on. With the bright audacity of seventeen, she gossiped and laughed, and addressed merry or deprecating glances to her companion, who sat and allowed himself to be amused with much good-humored coolness. What were poor Sylvia's serious efforts to attain some knowledge of public affairs, compared with this fluent familiarity which touched upon everything at home and abroad? Sylvia had tried to get at the rights and wrongs of a question then being talked about—the propriety of allowing laymen to preach in Church of England pulpits: now she heard her cousin treat the whole affair as a joke. There was nothing that that young lady did not know something about; and she chattered on with an artless vivacity, sometimes making fun, sometimes gravely appealing to him for information. Had he heard of the old lady who became insane in the Horticultural Gardens yesterday? Of course he was going to Christie's tomorrow; they expected that big landscape would fetch twelve hundred guineas. What a shame it was for Limerick to treat Lord and Lady Spencer so! She positively adored Mr. Plimsoll. What *would* people say if the Shah did really bring three of his wives to England, and would they all go about with him?

Poor Sylvia listened, and grew sick at heart. Was not this the sort of girl to interest and amuse a man, to cheer him when he was fatigued, to enter into all his projects and understand him? Was she not strikingly handsome, too, this tall girl with the heavy-lidded eyes, and the cherry mouth, and the full round chin curving in to the shapely neck? She admitted all these things to herself; but she did not love her cousin any the more. She grew to think it shameful that a young girl should make eyes at a man like that. Was she not calling the attention of the whole table to herself and to him? Her talking, her laughing, the appealing glances of those audacious black eyes—all these things sunk deeper and deeper into the heart of one silent observer, who did not seem to be enjoying herself much.

As for Balfour, he was obviously amused, and doubtless he was pleased at the flattering attention which this fascinating young lady paid him. He had found himself seated next her by accident; but as she was apparently so anxious to talk to him, he could not well do otherwise than neglect (as Lady Sylvia thought) Mrs. Blythe, whom he had actually taken in to dinner. And was it not clear, too, that he spoke in a lower voice than she did, as though he would limit their conversation to themselves? When she asked him to tell them all that was thought among political folks of the radical victories at the French elections, why should he address the answer to herself alone? And was it not too shameless of this girl—at least so Lady Sylvia thought—who ought to have been at school, to go on pretending that she was greatly interested in General Dorregaray, the King of Sweden, and such persons, merely that she should show off her knowledge to an absolute stranger?

Lady Sylvia sat there, with a sense of wrong and humiliation burning into her heart. Not once, during the whole of that dinner, did he address a single word to her; not once did he even look toward her. All his attention was monopolized by that bold girl who sat beside him. And this was the man who, but a few days before, had been pretending that he cared for nothing in the world so much as a walk through Willowby Park with the mistress thereof; who had then no thought for anything but herself, no words or looks for any one but her.

Lady Sylvia was seated near the door, and when the ladies left the room, she was one of the first to go. You·would not have imagined that underneath that sweet and gracious carriage, which charmed all beholders except one ungrateful young man, there was burning a fierce fire of wrong and shame and indignation. She walked into the drawing-room, and went into a farther corner, and took a book—on the open page of which she did not see a single word.

The men came in. Balfour went over, and took a seat beside her.

"Well, Sylvia," said he, lightly, "I suppose you won't stay here long. I am anxious to introduce you to Lady ——; and there is to be a whole batch of Indian or Afghan princes there to-night—their costumes make such a difference in a room. When do you think you will go?"

She hesitated; her heart was full; had they been alone, she would probably have burst into tears. As it was, he never got any answer to his question. A tall young lady came sweeping by at the moment.

"Mr. Balfour," she said, with a sweet smile, "will you open the piano for me?"

And again Lady Sylvia sat alone and watched these two. He stood by the side of the piano as the long tapering fingers—Honoria had beautifully formed hands, every one admitted—began to wander over the keys; and the dreamy music that began to fill the silence of the room seemed to lend something of imagination and pathos to a face that otherwise had little in it beyond merely physical beauty. She played well too; with perfect self-possession; her touch was light, and on these dreamy passages there was a rippling as of falling water in some enchanted cave. Then down went both hands with a crash on the keys; all the air seemed full of cannonading and musketry fire; her finely formed bust seemed to have the delight of physical exercise in it as those tightly sleeved and shapely arms banged this way and that; those beautiful lips were parted somewhat with her breathing. Lady Sylvia did not think much of her cousin's playing. It was coarse, theatrical, all for display. But she had to confess to herself that Honoria was a beautiful girl, who promised to become a beautiful woman; and what wonder, therefore, if men were glad to regard her, now as she sat upright there, with the fire and passion of her playing lending something of heroism and inspiration to her face?

That men should: yes, that was right enough; but that this one man should—that was the bitter thing. Surely he had not forgotten that it was but one week since she had assigned over to him the keeping of her whole life; and was this the fashion in which he was showing his gratitude? She had looked forward to this one evening with many happy fancies. She would see him; one look would confirm the secret between them. All the torturing anxieties of absence would be banished so soon as she could reassure herself by hearing his voice, by feeling the pressure of his hand. She had thought and dreamed of this evening in the still woodland ways, until her heart beat rapidly with a sense of her coming happiness; and now this disappointment was too bitter. She could not bear it.

She went over to her father.

"Papa," she said, "I wish to go. Don't let me take you; I can get to the hotel by myself—"

"My dear child," said he, with a stare, "I thought you particularly wanted to go to —— House, after what Balfour told you about the staircase and the flowers—"

"I—I have a headache," said the girl. "I am tired. Please let me go by myself, papa."

"Not at all, child," said he. "I will go whenever you like."

Then she besought him not to draw attention to their going. She would privately bid good-night to Mrs. Blythe; to no one else. If he came out a couple of seconds after she left the room, he would find her waiting.

"You must say good-bye to Balfour," said Lord Willowby; "he will be dreadfully disappointed."

"I don't think it is necessary," said Lady Sylvia, coldly. "He is too much engaged—he won't notice our going."

Fortunately their carriage had been ordered early, and they had no difficulty in getting back to the hotel. On the way Lady Sylvia did not utter a word.

"I will bid you good-night now, papa," said she, as soon as they had arrived.

He paused for a moment, and looked at her.

"Sylvia," said he, with some concern, "you look really ill. What is the matter with you?"

"Nothing," she said. "I am tired a little, and I have a headache. Good-night, papa."

She went to her own room, but not to sleep. She declined the attentions of her maid, and locked herself in. Then she took out a small packet of letters.

Were these written by the same man? She read, and wondered, with her heart growing sorer and sorer, until a mist of tears came over her eyes, and she could see no more. And then, her grief becoming more passionate, she threw herself on the bed and burst into a wild fit of crying and sobbing, the letters being clutched in her hand as if they, at least, were one possession that could not be taken away from her.· That was a bitter night— never to be forgotten; and when the next day came, she went down—with a pale and tired face, and with dark rings under the beautiful, sad eyes—and demanded of her father that she should be allowed at once to return to Willowby Hall, her maid alone accompanying her.·

CHAPTER X.

REPENTANCE.

BALFOUR was astounded when he learned that Lord Willowby and his daughter had left without bidding him good-bye; and he was more astounded still when he found, on calling at their hotel next morning, that Lady Sylvia had gone home.

"What is the meaning of it?" said he, in amazement.

"You ought to know," said Lord Willowby. "I cannot tell you. I supposed she and you had had some quarrel."

"A quarrel!" he cried, beginning to wonder whether his reason had not altogether forsaken him.

"Well," said his lordship, with a shrug, "I don't know. She would come home last night, though I knew she had been look- ing forward to going to Lady ——'s. And, this morning, noth- ing would do but that she must get home at once. She and Anne started an hour ago."

"Oh, this is monstrous—this is unendurable!" said Balfour. "There is some mistake, and it must be cleared up at once. Come, Lord Willowby, shall we take a run down into Surrey? You will be back by four or five."

Lord Willowby did not like the notion of being dragged down into Surrey and back by an impatient lover; but he was very anxious at this time to ingratiate himself with Balfour. And when they did set out, he thought he might as well improve the occasion. Balfour was disturbed and anxious by this strange conduct on the part of his sweetheart; and he was grateful to Lord Willowby for so promptly giving him his aid to have the mystery cleared up. He was talking more than usual. What wonder, then, that in the course of conversation Lord Willowby should incidentally allude to the opportunities which a man of means had of multiplying his wealth? If he had a few thousands, for example, how could he better dispose of them than in this project for the buying of land in the suburbs of New York? It was not a speculation; it was a certainty. In 1880 the population of New York would be two millions. The value of this land for the building of handsome boulevards would be enormously increased. And so forth.

"I heard you were in that," said Balfour, curtly.

"Well, what do you think of it?" said Lord Willowby, with some eagerness.

"I don't know," answered the younger man, absently looking out of the window. "I don't think there is any certainty about it. I fancy the Americans have been overspending and over-building for some time back. If that land *were* thrown on your hands, and you had to go on paying the heavy assessments they levy out there, it would be an uncommonly awkward thing for you."

"You take rather a gloomy view of things this morning," said Lord Willowby, with one of his fierce and suddenly vanishing smiles.

"At any rate," said Balfour, with some firmness, "it is a legitimate transaction. If the people want the land, they will have to pay your price for it: that is a fair piece of business. I wish I could say as much—you will forgive my frankness—about your Seven Per Cent. Investment Association."

His lordship started. There was an ugly implication in the words. But it was not the first time he had had to practise patience with this Scotch bore.

"Come, Balfour, you are not going to prophesy evil all round?"

"Oh no," said the younger man, carelessly. "Only I know you can't go on paying seven per cent. It is quite absurd."

"My dear fellow, look at the foreign loans that are paying their eight, ten, twelve per cent.—"

"I suppose you mean the South American republics."

"Look how we distribute the risk. The failure of one particular investment might ruin the individual investor: it scarcely touches the Association. I consider we are doing an immense service to all those people throughout the country who *will* try to get a high rate of interest for their money. Leave them to themselves, and they ruin themselves directly. We step in, and give them the strength of co-operation."

"I wish your name did not appear on the Board of Directors," said Balfour, shortly.

Lord Willowby was not a very sensitive person, but this rudeness caused his sallow face to flush somewhat. What, then: must he look to the honor of his name, now that this sprig of a merchant—this tradesman—had done him the honor of proposing to marry into his family? However, Lord Willowby, if he had a temper like other people, had also a great deal of prudence and self-control, and there were many reasons why he should not quarrel with this blunt-spoken young man at present.

They had not remembered to telegraph for the carriage to meet them; so they had to take a fly at the station, and await patiently the slow rumbling along the sweetly scented lanes. As they neared the Hall, Balfour was not a little perturbed. This was a new and a strange thing to him. If the relations between himself and his recently found sweetheart were liable to be thus suddenly and occultly cut asunder, what possible rest or peace was there in store for either? And it must be said that of all the conjectures he made as to the cause of this mischief, not one got even near the truth.

Lady Sylvia was sent for, and her father discreetly left the young man alone in the drawing-room. A few minutes afterward the door was opened. Balfour had been no diligent student of women's faces; but even he could tell that the girl who now stood before him, calm and pale and silent, had spent a wakeful night, and that her eyes had been washed with tears; so that his first impulse was to go forward and draw her toward him, that he might hear her confession with his arms around her. But there was something unmistakably cold and distant in her manner that forbade his approach.

"Sylvia," he cried, "what is all this about? Your father fancies you and I have quarrelled."

"No, we have not quarrelled," she said, simply ; but there was a tired look in her eyes. "We have only misunderstood each other. It is not worth talking about."

He stared at her in amazement.

"I hear papa outside," she said; "shall we join him?"

But this was not to be borne. He went forward, took her two hands firmly in his, and said, with decision,

"Come, Sylvia, we are not children. I want to know why you left last night. I have done my best to guess at the reason, and I have failed."

"You don't know, then?" she said, turning the pure, clear, innocent eyes on his face with a look that had not a little indignation in it. It was well for him that he could meet that straight look without flinching.

"I give you my word of honor," said he, with obvious surprise, "that I haven't the remotest notion in the world as to what all this means."

"It is nothing, then?" said she, warmly, and she was going to proceed with her charge, when her pride rebelled. She would not speak. She would not claim that which was not freely given. Unfortunately, however, when she would fain have got away he had a tight grip of her hand; and it was clear from the expression on this man's face that he meant to have an explanation there and then.

So he held her until she told him the whole story—the red blood tingling in her cheek the while, and her bosom heaving with that struggle between love and wounded pride. He waited until she had spoken the very last word, and then he let her hands fall, and stood silent before her for a second or two.

"Sylvia," said he, slowly, "this is not merely a lover's quarrel. This is more serious. I could not have imagined that you knew so little about me. You fancy, then, that I am a fresh and ingenuous youth, ready to have my head turned if a schoolgirl looks at me from under long eyelashes; or, worse still, a philanderer—a professor of the fine art of flirtation. Well, that was not my reading of myself. I fancied I had come to man's estate. I fancied I had some serious work to do. I fancied I knew a little about men and women—at least I never imagined that any one would suspect me of being imposed on by a girl in her first season. Amused?—certainly I was amused—I was even delighted by such a show of pretty and artless innocence.

Could anything be prettier than a girl in her first season assuming the airs of a woman of the world? Could anything be more interesting than that innocent chatter of hers? though I could not make out whether she had caught the trick of it from her brother, or whether she had imparted to that precocious lad some of her universal information. But now it appears I was playing the part of a guileless youth. I was dazzled by the fascination of the school-girl eyes. Gracious goodness! why wasn't my hair yellow and curly, that I might have been painted as Cupid? And what would the inhabitants of Ballinascroon say if they were told *that* was my character?"

He spoke with bitter emphasis. But this man Balfour went on the principle that serious ills needed prompt and serious remedies.

"Presented to the Town-hall of Ballinascroon," he continued, with a scornful laugh, "a portrait of H. Balfour, M.P., in the character of a philanderer! The author of this flattering and original likeness—Lady Sylvia Blythe!"

The girl could stand this no longer. She burst into a wild fit of crying and sobbing, in the midst of which he put his arms round her, and hushed her head against his breast, and bade her be quiet.

"Come, Sylvia," said he, "let us have done with this nonsense at once and forever. If you wait until I give you real cause for jealousy—if you have no other unhappiness than that—your life will be a long and fairly comfortable one. Not speaking to you all through dinner? Did you expect me to bawl across the table, when you know very well your first desire was to conceal from those people the fact of our being engaged? Listening to no one but her? I hadn't a chance. She chattered from one end of the dinner to the other. But really, Sylvia, if I were you, I would fix upon some more formidable rival—"

"Please don't scold me any more," said she, with a fresh fit of crying.

"I am not scolding you," he said. "I am only talking common-sense to you. Now dry your eyes, and promise not to be foolish any more, and come out into the garden."

After the rain, the sunshine. They went out arm-in-arm, and she was clinging very closely to him, and there was a glad, bright, blushing happiness on her face.

Now this was the end of their first trouble, and it seemed a very small and trivial affair when it was over. The way was now clear before them. There were to be no more misunderstandings. But Mr. Hugh Balfour was a practical person, not easily led away by beautiful anticipations, and the more he pondered over the matter, in those moments of quiet reflection that followed his evenings at the House, the more he became convinced that the best guarantee against the recurrence of misunderstandings and consequent trouble was marriage. He convinced himself that an immediate marriage, or a marriage as early as social forms would allow, was not only desirable, but necessary; and so clear was his line of argument that he never doubted for a moment but that it would at once convince Lady Sylvia.

But his arguments did not at all convince Lady Sylvia. On the contrary, this proposal, which was to put an end to the very possibility of trouble, only landed them in a further trouble. For he, being greatly occupied at the time—the Parliamentary session having got on into June—committed the imprudence of making this suggestion in a letter. Had he been down at Willowby Hall, walking with Lady Sylvia in the still twilight, with the stars beginning to tell in the sky and the mist beginning to gather along the margin of the lake, he might have had another answer; but now she wrote to him that in her opinion so serious a step as marriage was not to be adventured upon in a hurry; and she added, too, with some pardonable pride, that it was not quite seemly on his part to point out how they could make their honey-moon trip coincide with the general autumn holiday. Was their marriage to appear to be a merely trivial or accidental thing, waiting for its accomplishment until Parliament should be prorogued ?

He got the letter very late one night, when he was sorely fatigued, harassed, and discontented with himself. He had lost his temper in the House that evening; he had been called to order by Mr. Speaker; as he walked home he was reviling himself for having been betrayed into a rage. When he saw the letter lying on the table, he brightened up somewhat. Here, at least, would be consolation—a tender message—perhaps some gentle intimation given that the greatest wish of his heart might soon be realized. Well, he opened the letter and read it. The disappointment he experienced doubtless exaggerated what he took to be the coldness of its terms. He paid no attention to the real and honest expressions of affection in it; he looked only at her refusal, and saw temper where there was only a natural and sensitive pride.

Then the devil took possession of him, and prompted him to write in reply there and then. Of course *he* would not show temper, being a man. All the same, he felt called on to point out, politely but firmly, that marriage was, after all, only one among the many facts of life; and that it was not rendered any more sublime and mysterious by making it the occasion for a number of microscopic martyrdoms and petty sacrifices. He saw no reason why the opportunity offered by the close of the session should not be made use of; as for the opinion of other people on the seemliness of the arrangement, she would have to be prepared for the discovery that neither on that point nor on any other was he likely to shape his conduct to meet the views of a mass of strangers. And so forth. It was a perfectly sensible letter. The line of argument was clear. How could she fail to see her error?

But to the poor fluttering heart down there in the country these words came with a strange chill; and it seemed to her that her lover had suddenly withdrawn from her to a great distance, leaving the world around her dark enough. Her first impulse was to utter a piteous cry to him. She sat down and wrote, with trembling fingers, these words:

"Dearest Hugh,—*I will do whatever you please, rather than have you write to me like that.*   Sylvia."

Probably, too, had she sent off this letter at once, he would have been struck by her simple and generous self-abnegation, and he would have instantly refused to demand from her any sacrifice of feeling whatsoever. But then the devil was abroad. He generally is about when two sweethearts try to arrange some misunderstanding by the perilous process of correspondence. Lady Sylvia began to recollect that, after all, something was due to her womanly pride. Would it not seem unmaidenly thus to surrender at discretion on so all-important a point as the fixing of the wedding-day? She would not have it said that they were waiting for Parliament to rise before they got married. In any case, she thought the time was far too short. Moreover, was this the tone in which a man should ask a woman to fix the day of her marriage?

So she answered the letter in another vein. If marriage, she said, was only one of the ordinary facts of life, she at least did not regard it in that light at all. She cared for tittle-tattle as little as he; but she did not like the appearance of having her wedding trip arranged as if it were an excursion to Scotland for grouse-shooting. And so forth. Her letter, too, was clever— very clever indeed, and sharp. Her face was a little flushed as she sealed it, and bade the servant take it to the post-office the first thing in the morning. But apparently that brilliant piece of composition did not afford her much satisfaction afterward, for she passed the night, not in healthful sleep, but in alternate fits of crying and bitter thinking, until it seemed to her that this new relationship into which she had entered with such glad anticipations was bringing her sorrow after sorrow, grief after grief. For she had experienced no more serious troubles than these.

When Hugh Balfour received this letter he was in his bedroom, about eight o'clock in the evening; and he was dressed for the most part in shabby corduroy, with a wisp of dirty black silk round his neck. His man Jackson had brought up from the kitchen some ashes for the smearing of his hands and face. A cadger's basket stood on the table hard by.

<hr>

CHAPTER XI.

DE PROFUNDIS.

A MORE ruffianly-looking vagabond than the honorable member for Ballinascroon could not have been found within the area of London on that warm June evening. And yet he seemed fairly pleased with himself as he boldly took his way across the Green Park. He balanced his basket jauntily over the dirty seal-skin cap. He whistled as he went.

It was his third excursion of the sort, and he was getting to be quite familiar with his *rôle*. In fact, he was not thinking at all at this moment of tramps' patter, or Covent Garden, or any thing connected with the lodging-house in which he had already spent two nights. He whistled to give himself courage in another direction. Surely it was not for him, as a man of the world, occupied with the serious duties of life, and, above all, hard-headed and practical, to be perturbed by the sentimental fantasy of a girl. Was it not for her interest, as well as his own, that he should firmly hold out? A frank exposition of their relations now would prevent mistakes in the future. And as he could not undertake to play a Cupid's part, to become a philanderer, to place a mysterious value on moods and feelings which did not correspond with the actual facts of life, was it not wiser that he should plainly declare as much?

And yet this scoundrelly-looking hawker derived but little consolation from his gay whistling. He could not but think of Lady Sylvia as she wrote the letter now in his pocket; and in his inmost consciousness he knew what that tender-hearted girl must have suffered in penning the cold, proud lines. She had none of his pressing work in which to escape from the harassing pain of such a discussion. He guessed that weary days and sleepless nights were the result of such letters as that he now carried with him. But then, she was in the wrong. Discipline was wholesome. So he continued his contented trudge and his whistling.

He crossed St. James's Park, passed through Queen Anne's Gate, and finally plunged into a labyrinth of narrow and squalid streets and lanes with which he seemed sufficiently familiar. It was not a pleasant quarter on this warm night; the air was close and foul; many of the inhabitants of the houses—loosely dressed women, for the most part, who had retreating foreheads, heavy jowls, and a loud laugh that seemed scarcely human—had come out to sit on the door-step or the pavement. There were not many men about. A few hulking youths — bullet-headed, round-shouldered, in-kneed—lounged about the doors of the public-houses, addressing each other in the most hideous language apropos of nothing.

The proprietor of the common lodging-house stood at the entry in his shirt-sleeves. He took no notice of Balfour, except that, on his approach, he went along the passage and unlocked a door, admitted him, and shut the door again: this door could not be reopened on the other side, so that there was no chance of a defaulter sneaking off in the night without paying his fourpence.

Balfour went up-stairs. The doors of the various rooms and the rickety little windows were all wide open. The beds—of coarse material, certainly, but clean — were all formally made. There was not a human being in the place.

He had a room to himself—about eight feet square, with two beds in it. He placed his basket on the bed; and then went down-stairs again, and out into the backyard. The only occupant of the yard was a grizzled and feeble old man, who was at this moment performing his ablutions in the lavatory, which consisted of three pails of dirty water standing on a bench in an open shed. The man dried his face, turned, and looked at Balfour with a pair of keen and ferrety eyes, said nothing, and walked off into the kitchen. Balfour was left in sole occupation of the yard, with its surroundings of tumble-down out-houses and dilapidated brick walls. He lit a pipe, and sat down on a bench.

It was not a good time of the year for these researches, the precise-object of which he had formerly explained to Lady Sylvia. The summer weather draws tramps, hawkers, and other branches of our nomadic population into the country, where they can cadge a bit for food, and where, instead of having to pay for a bed in a hot room, they can sleep comfortably enough beneath an empty cart, or by a hedge-row, or in a new drain-pipe. Nevertheless, a good many strange people turned into this lodging-house of a night; and Balfour, on his first appearance, had rather ingratiated himself with them by pretending to have had a drop too much, and insisting on standing beer all round. As he muttered his determination to fight any man who refused to drink with him —and as there was a brawny and bony look about the build of his shoulders—the various persons present overcame their natural modesty, and drank the beer. Thereafter the new-comer relapsed into a gloomy silence; sat on a bench in a corner which was hidden in shadow; and doubtless most of his companions, as they proceeded to talk of their experiences of unions, guardians, magistrates, and the like—the aristocracy, of course, preferring to talk of the money they had made in by-gone times, when their particular trade or lay had not been overrun with competition— imagined he was asleep.

On the following night he was well received; and now he entered a little more into conversation with them, his share in it being limited to occasional questions. But there was one man there who, from the very first, regarded him with suspicion; and he knew that from the way in which this man followed him about with his watchful eyes. This was an old man called Fiddling Jack, who, with a green shade over his eyes, went about Lambeth as a blind man, accompanied by his daughter, a child of nine or ten, who played the violin and collected the coppers. Whether his care of the child was parental or merely prudential, he always brought her back to the lodging-house, and sent her to bed by nine o'clock; the rest of the evening he spent in the great kitchen, smoking a black clay pipe. From the very first Balfour knew that this old man suspected something; or was it that his eyes, being guarded from the light all day, seemed preternaturally keen when the green shade was removed?

But the man whom Balfour most feared was another old man, who in former days had been the owner of a large haberdashery business in the King's Road, Chelsea, and who had drunk himself down until he now earned his living by selling evening papers on one of the river piers. His brain, too, had given way; he was now a half-maudlin, amiable, harmless old man, whose fine language and courteous manners had got for him the title of "Mr." Now Mr. Sturt excelled in conversation, and he spoke with great propriety of phrase, so that again and again Balfour found himself on the point of replying to this old gentleman as he would have done to a member of the House of Commons. In fact, his only safeguard with respect to Mr. Sturt lay in complete silence.

But indeed, on this third evening of his explorations, his heart was not in his work at all. As he walked up and down the squalid yard, occasionally noticing a new-comer come in, his mind was filled, not with any social or political problem, but with a great compunction and yearning. He dared not take Lady Sylvia's letter from his pocket, but he tried to remember every word in it; and he pondered over this and the other phrase to see if it could not somehow be construed into an expression of affection. Then he began to compose his answer to it; and that, he determined, would be a complete abandonment of the position he had taken up. After all, was not a great deal to be granted to the woman one loved? If she was unreasonable, it was only the privilege of her sex. In any case, he would argue no longer; he would try the effect of a generous surrender.

Having come to this decision, which afforded him some internal comfort, he bethought himself of his immediate task; and accordingly he walked into the kitchen, where a number of the *habitués* had already assembled. An excess of courtesy is not the order of the day in a common lodging-house, and so he gave no greeting and received none. He sat down on a rickety stool in the great dusky den; and while some of the odd-looking folks were having their supper, he lit another pipe. But he had not sat there five minutes when he had formed a distinct opinion that there was an alteration in the manner of those people toward him. They looked at him askance; they had become silent since the moment of his entrance. Moreover, the new-comers, as they dropped in, regarded him curiously, and invariably withdrew to the farther end of the big apartment. When they spoke, it was among themselves, and in a low voice.

So conscious did he in time become of all this that he resolved he would not spoil the evening of these poor folks; he would go up to that small room above. Doubtless some secret wish to re-read Lady Sylvia's letter had some influence on this decision; at any rate, he went out into the yard, took a turn up and down with his hands in his pockets; and then, with apparent carelessness, went up-stairs. He sat down on the edge of the small and rude bed, and took out the letter.

He had not been there five minutes when a woman rushed into the room, greatly excited. She was a stalwart woman, with an immensely broad bust, keen gray eyes, and a gray mustache that gave a truculent look to her face.

"For God's sake, get out o' this, sir!" she said, hurriedly, but not loudly. "The boys have been drinking at the Blue Tun, and they're coming down on you. Look sharp, sir. Never mind the basket; run for it—"

"But what's the matter, Mrs. Grace?" said he, stubbornly, refusing to rise. He could not submit to the ignominy of running without knowing why.

"It's all along o' that Fiddling Jack—by the Lord, I'll pay him out!" said the woman, with an angry look. "He's been about saying you was a buz-man—"

"A what?"

"He says it was you got Billy Rowland a lifer; and the boys are saying they'll do for you this very night. Get away now, sir. It's no use talking to them; they've been drinking."

"Look here, Mrs. Grace," said he, calmly, as he removed a false bottom from the basket beside him, and took out a six-chambered revolver, "I am a peaceable person ; but if there's a row, I'll play ducks and drakes with some of them."

"For God's sake, don't show them that, or you're a dead man," said the woman. "Now, sir, off you go."

He seemed in no great hurry ; but he put the pistol into his breast-pocket, put on his cap, and went down-stairs. There was no sound at all—no unusual excitement. He got the proprietor to unlock the dividing door, and went along the passage. He called a good-night to Mrs. Grace.

But he had no sooner got to the street than he was met by a great howl, like the roaring of wild beasts ; and then he saw before him a considerable crowd of people who had just come along, and were drawing round the entrance in a semicircle. He certainly turned pale for a moment, and stood still. It was only in a confused sort of way that he perceived that this hoarsely murmuring crowd was composed chiefly of women — viragoes with bare heads and arms—and louts of lads about nineteen or twenty. He could not distinguish their cries ; he only knew that they were mingled taunts and menaces. What to do he knew not, while to speak to this howling mass was on the face of it useless. What was all this about "Billy Rowland," "Scotland Yard," "Spy," "Buz-man," and the rest ?

"What is it you want with me ?" he called aloud ; but of what avail was his single voice against those thousand angry cries ?

A stone was flung at him and missed him. He saw the big lout who threw it dodge back into the crowd.

"You cowardly scoundrel !" he shouted, making an involuntary step forward. "Come out here and I'll fight you—I'll fight any one of you. Ah ! skulk behind the women, do !"

At this moment he received a stinging blow on the side of the head that sent him staggering for a yard or two. A woman had crept up by the side of the houses and pitched a broken piece of tile at him. Had she thrown it, it must have killed him ; as it was, it merely cut him, so that instantaneously the side of his head and neck was streaming with blood.

He recovered his footing ; the stinging pain awoke all the Celtic ferocity in him ; he drew out his revolver, and turned to the spot from whence his unexpected assailant had attacked him.

There was one terrible moment of hesitation. Had it been a man, he would have shot him dead. As it was, he paused; and then, with a white face, he threw his revolver on the pavement.

He did not quite know what happened next, for he was faint from loss of blood, and giddy. But this was what happened. The virago who had pitched the piece of tile at him, as soon as she saw the pistol lying on the pavement, uttered a screech of joy, and sprung forward to seize it. The next moment she received a stinging blow on the jaw, which sent her reeling senseless into the gutter; and the next moment Mrs. Grace had picked up the revolver, while with her other hand she caught hold of Balfour as with the grip of a vise, and dragged him into the passage.

"Run!" she said. "The door is open! Through the yard—there is a chair at the wall. Don't stop till you're at the Abbey!"

She stood at the narrow entrance and barred the way, the great brawny arm gripping the revolver.

"Swelp me," she shouted—and she knew how to make herself heard—"swelp me Gŏd, if one of you stirs a foot nearer, there'll be murder here this night! I mean it. My name's Sal Grace; and by the Lord there's six of you dead if you lift a hand against me!"

At the same moment Balfour, though he felt giddy, bewildered, and considerably weak about the knees, had bolted down the backyard until he came to the brick wall. Here he found a rickety cane-bottomed chair, and by its aid he managed to clamber over. Now he was in an open space of waste ground—it had just been bought by the Government for some purpose or other—and, so far as he could see, it was closely fenced all round. At length, however, he descried a hole in the paling that some children had made, and through that he managed to squeeze himself. Presently he was making his way as fast as he could through a series of slums; but his object was less to make straight for the Abbey than to rout out the policemen on his way, and send them back to the relief of his valiant defender, and this he most luckily and successfully accomplished. He had managed, too, during his flight, to partly mop up the blood that had streamed from the wound in his head.

Then he missed his way somehow, for otherwise a very few minutes' running and walking must have taken him either to the

Abbey or the Embankment; and now, as he felt faint, he staggered into a public-house.

"Well, my man, what's the matter with you?" said the burly publican, as he saw this new-comer sink down on a bench.

"Some water—some brandy," said Balfour, involuntarily putting his hand up to the side of his head.

"Good Lord! you've 'ad the worst of it, my lad," said the publican—he was familiar with the results of a free fight. "Here, Jim, get a pail o' water, and let this chap put his 'ead in it. Don't you let that blood get on the floor, my man."

The cool water applied to his head, and the glass of brandy, vile as it was, that he drank, pulled Balfour together. He rose, and the publican and the pot-boy were astonished to find the difference in the appearance of this coster's face produced by the pail of water. And when, on leaving, he gave the pot-boy half a crown for his attention, what were they to make of it?

By some means or other he finally managed to wander into Victoria Street; and here, with some difficulty, he persuaded a cabman to drive him up to Piccadilly. He was secure himself, and he had little fear for the safety of Mrs. Grace. He knew the authority wielded over the neighborhood by that stalwart Amazon; and in any case he had sent her sufficient police aid.

He got his man to wash that ugly cut along the side of his head before sending for a surgeon to have it properly dressed.

"Will you look at your letters, sir?"

"No, not to-night," he said, for he was feeling tired.

But on second thoughts he fancied he might as well run his eye over the envelopes. He started on finding there one from Lady Sylvia. Had she then written immediately after the despatch of her last?

"*Dearest Hugh*," the girl wrote. "*It will be when you please. I cannot bear quarrelling with you. Your Sylvia.*"

As he read the simple words—he was weak and feverish—his eyes became moist. This girl loved him.

CHAPTER XII.

HAVEN AT LAST.

THE cut Balfour had received was merely a flesh-wound, and not at all serious; but of course when Lady Sylvia heard of the adventure in Westminster, she knew that he must have been nearly murdered, and she would go to him at once; and her heart smote her sorely that she should have been selfishly thinking of her own plans and wishes when this noble champion of the poor was adventuring his very life for the public good. She knew better than to believe the gibing account of the whole matter that Balfour sent her. He was always misrepresenting himself—playing the part of Mephistopheles to his own Faust—anxious to escape even from the loyal worship and admiration freely tendered him by one loving heart.

But when she insisted on at once going up to London, her father demurred. At that moment he had literally not a five-pound note he could lay his hands on ; and that private hotel in Arlington Street was an expensive place.

"Why not ask him to come down here for a few days?" Lord Willowby said. "Wouldn't that be more sensible? Give him two or three days' rest and fresh air to recover him."

"He wouldn't come away just now, papa," said Lady Sylvia, seriously. "He won't let anything stand between him and his public duties."

"His public duties!" her father said, impatiently. "His public fiddle-sticks! What are his public duties?—to shoot out his tongue at the very people who sent him into Parliament!"

"He has no duties to *them*," she said, warmly. "They don't deserve to be represented at all. I hope at the next General Election he will go to some other constituency. And if he does," she added, with a flush coming to her cheeks, "I know one who will canvass for him."

"Go away, Sylvia," said her father, with a smile, "and write a line to the young man, and tell him to come down here. He will be glad enough. And what is this nonsense about a house in this neighborhood?—don't you want to see about that, if you are going to get married in August? At the same time, I think you are a couple of fools."

"Why, papa?" she demanded, patiently.

"To throw away money like that! What more could you want than that house in Piccadilly? It could be made a charming little place. And this nonsense about a cottage down here— roses and lilies, I suppose, and a cuckoo clock and a dairy; you have no right to ask any man to throw away his money like that."

Lord Willowby showed an unusual interest in Mr. Balfour's affairs; perhaps it was merely because he knew how much better use he could have made of this money that the young people were going to squander.

"It is his own wish, papa."

"Who put it into his head?"

"And if I did," said Lady Sylvia, valiantly, "don't you think there should be some retreat for a man harassed with the cares of public life? What rest could he get in Piccadilly? Surely it is no unusual thing for people to have a house in the country as well as one in town; and of course there is no part of the country I could like as much as this part. So you see you are quite wrong, papa; and I am quite right—as I always am."

"Go away and write your letter," said her father.

Lady Sylvia went to her room, and sat down to her desk. But before she wrote to Balfour she had another letter to write, and she seemed to be sorely puzzled about it. She had never written to Mrs. Grace before; and she did not know exactly how to apologize for her presumption in addressing a stranger. Then she wished to send Mrs. Grace a present; and the only thing she could think of was lace—for lace was about the only worldly valuable which Lady Sylvia possessed. All this was of her own undertaking. Had she consulted her father, he would have said, "Write as you would to a servant." Had she consulted Balfour, he would have shouted with laughter, at the notion of presenting that domineering landlady of the Westminster slums with a piece of real Valenciennes. But Lady Sylvia set to work on her own account; and at length composed the following message out of the ingenuous simplicity of her own small head:

"WILLOWBY HALL, *Tuesday morning.*

"MY DEAR MRS. GRACE,—I hope you will pardon the liberty I take in sending you these few lines, but I have just heard how nobly and bravely you rendered assistance, at great risk to yourself, to Mr. Balfour, who is a particular friend of my father's and mine, and I thought you would not be offended if I wrote to say how very heartily we thank you. And will you please accept from us the accompanying little parcel? It may remind you occasionally that though we have not the pleasure of your personal acquaintance, we are none the less most deeply grateful to you.

"I am, my dear Mrs. Grace, yours very sincerely,

"SYLVIA BLYTHE."

Little did Balfour know of the packet which he forwarded to his valiant friend down in Westminster; but Happiness Alley speedily knew of it, and knows of it to this day. For at great times and seasons, when all the world has gone out to see the queen drive to the opening of Parliament, or to look at the ruins of the last great fire, or to welcome the poor creatures set free by a jail delivery, and when Mrs. Grace and her friends have got back to the peace of their own homes, and when pipes have been lit and jugs of ale placed on the window-sill to cool, then with a great pride and vainglory a certain mahogany casket is produced. And if the uses of a fichu are only to be guessed at by Mrs. Grace and her friends, and if the precise value of Valenciennes is unknown to them, what matters? It is enough that all the world should know that this article of attire was presented to Mrs. Grace by an earl and an earl's daughter, in proof of which the casket contains—and this Mrs. Grace regards as the highest treasure of all—a letter written in the lady's own hand. She does not show the letter itself. She does not wish to have it fingered about and dirtied. But at these high times of festivity, when the lace is taken out with an awful and reverent care, the envelope of the letter may at least be exhibited; and that is stamped with an earl's coronet.

In due time Balfour went down to Willowby, and now at last it seemed as if all the troubles and sorrows of these young people were over. In the various glad preparations for the event to which they both looked forward, a generous unanimity of feeling prevailed. Each strove to outdo the other in conciliation. And

Lady Sylvia's father smiled benignly on the pair, for he had just borrowed £300 from Balfour to meet some little pressing emergency.

It was a halcyon time indeed, for the year was at its fullest and sweetest, and the member for Ballinascroon was not hampered by the services he rendered to his constituents. One brilliant June day after another shone over the fair Surrey landscapes; beech, ash, and oak were at their greenest; the sunlight warmed up the colors of the pink chestnut and the rose-red hawthorn, and sweet winds played about the woods. They drove to picturesque spots in that line of hill that forms the backbone of Surrey; they made excursions to old-fashioned little hamlets on the Thames; together they rode over the wide commons, where the scent of the gorse was strong in the air. Balfour wondered no. longer why Sylvia should love this·peaceful and secluded life. Under the glamour of her presence idleness became delightful for the first time in the existence of this busy, eager, ambitious man. All his notions of method, of accuracy, of common-sense even, he surrendered to this strange fascination. To be unreasonable was a virtue in a woman, if it was Lady Sylvia who was unreasonable. He laughed with pleasure one evening when, in a strenuous argument, she stated that seven times seven were fifty-six. It would have been stupid in a servant to have spilled her tea, but it was pretty when Lady Sylvia's small wrist was the cause of that mishap. And when, with her serious, timid eyes grown full of feeling, she pleaded the cause of the poor sailor sent to sea in rotten ships, he felt himself ready then to go into the House and out-Plimsoll Plimsoll in his enthusiasm on behalf of so good a cause.

It was not altogether love in idleness. They had their occupations. First of all, she spent nearly a whole week in town choosing wall-colors, furniture, and pictures for that house in Piccadilly, though it was with a great shyness she went to the various places and expressed her opinion. During that week she saw a good deal more of London and of London life than commonly came within her experience. For one thing, she had the trembling delight of listening, from behind the grill, to Balfour making a short speech in the House. It was a terrible ordeal for her; her heart throbbed with anxiety, and she tore a pair of gloves into small pieces unknowingly. But as she drove home she convinced herself with a high exultation that there was no man in the House looked so distinguished as that one, that the stamp of a great statesman was visible in the square forehead and in the firm mouth, and that if the House knew as much as she knew, it would be more anxious to listen for those words of wisdom which were to save the nation. Balfour's speech was merely a few remarks made in committee. They were not of great importance. But when, next morning, she eagerly looked in the newspapers, and found what he had said condensed into a sentence, she was in a wild rage, and declared to her father that public men were treated shamefully in this country.

That business of refurnishing the house in Piccadilly had been done perforce; it was with a far greater satisfaction that she set about decorating and preparing a spacious cottage, called The Lilacs, which was set in the midst of a pretty garden, some three miles from Willowby Park. Here, indeed, was pleasant work for her, and to her was intrusted the whole management of the thing, in Balfour's necessary absence in town. From day to day she rode over to see how the workmen were getting on. She sent up business-like reports to London. And at last she gently hinted that he might come down to see what had been done.

"Will you ride over or drive?" said Lord Willowby to his guest, after breakfast that morning.

"I am sure Mr. Balfour would rather walk, papa," said Lady Sylvia, "for I have discovered a whole series of short-cuts that I want to show him—across the fields. Unless it will tire you, papa?"

"It won't tire me at all," said Lord Willowby, with great consideration, "for I am not going. I have letters to write. But if you walk over, you must send Lock to the cottage with the horses, and ride back."

Although they were profoundly disappointed that Lord Willowby could not accompany them, they set out on their walk with an assumed cheerfulness which seemed to conceal their inward grief. It was July now; but the morning was fresh and cool after the night's rain, and there was a pleasant southerly breeze blowing the fleecy clouds across the blue sky, so that there was an abundance of light, motion, and color all around them. The elms were rustling and swaying in the park; the rooks were cawing; in the distance they saw a cloud of yellow smoke arise from the road as the fresh breeze blew across.

She led him away by secret paths and wooded lanes, with here and there a stile to cross, and here and there a swinging gate to open. She was anxious he should know intimately all the surroundings of his future home, and she seemed to be familiar with the name of every farm-house, every turnpike, every clump of trees, in the neighborhood. She knew the various plants in the hedges, and he professed himself profoundly interested in learning their names. They crossed a bit of common now; he had never known before how beautiful the flowers of a common were —the pale lemon-colored hawk-weed, the purple thyme, the orange and crimson tipped bird's-foot trefoil. They passed through waving fields of rye; he had never noticed before the curious sheen of gray produced by the wind on those billows of green. They came in sight of long undulations of wheat; he vowed he had never seen in his life anything so beautiful as the brilliant scarlet of the poppies where the corn was scant. The happiness in Lady Sylvia's face, when he expressed himself delighted with all these things, was something to see.

They came upon a gypsy encampment, apparently deserted by all but the women and children. One of the younger women immediately came out and began the usual patter. Would not the pretty lady have her fortune told? She had many happy days in store for her, but she had a little temper of her own, and so forth. Lady Sylvia stood irresolute, bashful, rather inclined to submit to the ordeal for the amusement of the thing, and looking doubtfully at her companion as to whether he would approve. As for Balfour, he did not pay the slightest heed to the poor woman's jargon. His eye had been wandering over the encampment, apparently examining everything. And then he turned to the woman, and began to question her with a directness that startled her out of her trade manner altogether. She answered him simply and seriously, though it was not a very direful tale she had to tell. When Balfour had got all the information he wanted, he gave the woman half a sovereign, and passed on with his companion; and of course Lady Sylvia said to herself that it was the abrupt sincerity, the force of character, in this man that compelled sincerity in others, and she was more than ever convinced that the like of him was not to be found in the world.

"Well, Sylvia," said he, when they reached The Lilacs, and had passed through the fragrant garden, "you have really made it a charming place. It is a place one might pass one's life away in—reading books, smoking, dreaming day-dreams."

"I hope you will always find rest and quiet in it," said she, in a low voice.

It was a long, irregular, two-storied cottage, with a veranda along the front; and it was pretty well smothered in white roses. There was not much of a lawn; for the ground facing the French windows had mostly been cut up into flower-beds—beds of turquoise blue forget-me-nots, of white and speckled clove-pinks that sweetened all the air around, of various-hued pansies, and of white and purple columbine. But the strong point of the cottage and the garden was its roses. There were roses everywhere —rose-bushes in the various plots, rose-trees covering the walls, roses in the tiny hall into which they passed when the old housekeeper made her appearance. "I'll tell you who ought to live here, Sylvia," said her companion. "That German fellow you were telling us about who lives close by—Count Von Rosen. I never saw such roses in my life."

Little adornment indeed was needed to make this retreat a sufficiently charming one; but, all the same, Lady Sylvia had spent a vast amount of care on it, and her companion was delighted with the skill and grace with which the bare materials of the furniture which he had only seen in the London shops had been arranged. As they walked through the quaint little rooms they did not say much to each other; for doubtless their minds were sufficiently busy in drawing pictures of the happy life they hoped to spend there.

Of course all these nice things cost money. Balfour had been for some time drawing upon his partners in a fashion which rather astonished those gentlemen; for they had grown accustomed to calculate on the extreme economy of the young man. One morning the head clerk in the firm of Balfour, Skinner, Green, & Co., in opening the letters, came upon one from Mr. Hugh Balfour, in which that gentleman gave formal notice that he would want a sum of £50,000 in cash on the 1st of August. When Mr. Skinner arrived, the head clerk put the letter before him. He did not turn pale, nor did he nervously break the paper-knife he held in his hand. He only said, "Good Lord!" and then he added, "I suppose he must have it."

It was in the second week in August that Mr. Hugh Balfour,

M.P. for Ballinascroon, was married to Lady Sylvia Blythe, only daughter of the Earl of Willowby, of Willowby Hall, Surrey; and immediately after the marriage the happy pair started off to spend their honey-moon in Germany.

CHAPTER XIII.

FIVE-ACE JACK.

WE will now let Mr. Balfour and his young and charming bride go off together on their wedding trip—a trip that ought to give them some slight chance of becoming acquainted with each other, though a certain profound philosopher, resident in Surrey, would say that the glamour of impossible ideals was still veiling their eyes—and we will turn, if you please, to a very different sort of traveller, who just about the same time was riding along a cattle trail on the high-lying and golden-yellow plains of Colorado. This was Buckskin Charlie, so named from the suit of gray buckskin which he wore, and which was liberally adorned with loose fringes cut from the leather. Indeed, there was a generally decorative air about this herdsman and his accoutrements which gave him a half-Mexican look, though the bright sun-tanned complexion, the long light-brown hair, and the clear blue eyes were not at all Mexican. There was a brass tip to the high pommel in front of him, round which a lasso was coiled. He wore huge wooden stirrups, which looked like sabots with the heels cut out. The rowels of his spurs were an inch and a half in diameter. And the wiry little pony he rode had both mane and tail long and flowing.

It is a pleasant enough morning for a ride, for on these high-lying plains the air is cool and exhilarating even in the glare of the sunshine. The prospect around him is pleasant too, though Buckskin Charlie probably does not mind that much. He has long ago got accustomed to the immeasurable breadth of billowy prairie land, the low yellow-brown waves of which stretch away out into the west until they meet with the range of the Rocky Mountains—a wall of ethereal blue standing all along the western horizon, here and there showing a patch of shining white. And he is familiar enough, too, with the only living objects visible — a herd of antelope quietly grazing in the shadow of some distant and low-lying bluffs; an occasional chicken-hawk that lifts its heavy and bespeckled wings and makes away for the water in the nearest gully; and everywhere the friendly little prairie-dog, standing up on his hillock like a miniature kangaroo, and coolly staring at him as he passes. Buckskin Charlie is not hungry, and therefore takes no interest in natural history.

It is a long ride across the plains from Eagle Creek Ranch to New Minneapolis, but this important place is reached at last. It is a pretty little hamlet of wooden cottages, with a brick school-house, and a small church of the like material. It has a few cotton-wood trees about. It is irrigated by a narrow canal which connects with a tributary of the South Platte.

Buckskin Charlie rides up to the chief shop of this hamlet and dismounts, leaving his pony in charge of a lad. The shop is a sort of general store, kept by one Ephraim J. Greek, who is also, as a small sign indicates, a notary public, conveyancer, and real-estate agent. When Buckskin Charlie enters the store, Mr. Greek—a short, red-faced, red-haired person, who is generally addressed as Judge by his neighbors—is in the act of weighing out some sugar for a small girl who is at the counter.

"Hello, Charlie!" says the Judge, carelessly, as he continues weighing out the sugar. "How's things at the ranch? And how is your health?"

"I want you to come right along," says Charlie, without further ceremony. "The boss is just real bad."

"You don't say!"

Charlie looks for a second or two at the Judge getting the brown-paper bag, and then he says, impatiently,

"He wants you to come right away, and he won't stand no foolin'—you bet."

But the Judge is not to be hurried. He asks his small customer what else her mother wants, and then he turns leisurely to the sun-tanned messenger.

"'Tain't the fooist time, Charlie, the Colonel has been bad like that. Oh, I know. I knowed the Colonel before you ever set eyes on him—yes, sir. I knowed him in Denver, when he was on'y Five-Ace Jack. But now he's the boss, and no mistake. Reckon he's doin' the big Bonanza business, and none o' your pea-nut consarns—"

Here Buckskin Charlie broke in with a number of words which showed that he was intimately familiar with Scripture, and might have led one to suppose that he meant to annihilate the dilatory Judge, but which, as it turned out, were only intended to emphasize his statement that the Colonel had branded 1800 calves at the ranch last year, and had also got up 2000 head from Texas. By the time this piece of information had been delivered and received, the wants of the small girl in front of the counter had been satisfied; and then the Judge, having gone out and borrowed a neighbor's pony, set forth with his impatient companion for Eagle Creek Ranch.

On the way they had a good deal of familiar talk about the boss, or the Colonel, as he was indifferently called; and the Judge, now in a friendly mood, told Buckskin Charlie some things he did not know before about his master. Their conversation, however, was so saturated with Biblical lore that it may be advisable to give here a simpler and plainer history of the owner of Eagle Creek Ranch. To begin with, he was an Englishman. He was born in Cumberland, and as a young fellow achieved some little notoriety as a wrestler; in fact, that was all the work his parents could get out of him. It was in vain that they paid successive sums to have him apprenticed to that business, or made a partner in this; Jack Sloane was simply a ne'er-do-well, blessed with a splendid physique, a high opinion of his own importance, and a distinguished facility in wheedling people into lending him money. Such was his position in England when the rush to California occurred. Here was Jack's opportunity. His mother wept bitter tears when she parted with him; but nobody else was affected to the same extent.

As a gold-digger Jack was a failure, but he soon managed to pick up an amazing knowledge of certain games of cards, insomuch that his combined luck and skill got for him the complimentary title of Five-Ace Jack. Whether he made money or not at this profession does not appear, for at this point there is a gap in his history. When his relatives in England—among whom, I regret to say, was a young lady incidentally alluded to in the first chapter of this story—next heard of him he was in Texas, employed at a ranch there. No one ever knew what had made the social atmosphere of San Francisco rather too sultry for Five-Ace Jack.

Then the Pike's Peak craze occurred, in 1859, and once again Jack was induced to join the general rush. He arrived at Denver just as the bubble had burst. He found a huge multitude of people grown mad with disappointment, threatening to burn down the few wooden shanties and canvas tents that then constituted the town, and more especially to hang incontinently an esteemed friend of the present writer, who had just issued the first numbers of the *Rocky Mountain News*. Then the great crowd of bummers and loafers, not finding the soil teeming with nuggets, stampeded off like a herd of buffalo, leaving a few hardy and adventurous spirits to explore the neighboring cañons, and find out by hard work whether or not gold existed there in paying quantities. Jack Sloane remained behind also—in Denver. He started what was called a whiskey saloon in a tent, but what was really a convenient little gambling hell for those who had grown reckless. Times grew better. Rumors came down from the mountains that the gulch and placer mines which had been opened were giving a fair yield; here and there—as, for example, in the Clear Creek Cañon—a vein of rotten quartz had been struck containing free gold in surprising richness. Now was Jack's time. He opened a keno and faro bank in a wooden shanty, and he charged only ten per cent. on the keno winnings. He was an adept at euchre and poker, and was always willing to lend a hand, his chief peculiarity being that he invariably chose that side of the table which enabled him to face the door, so that he might not be taken unawares by an unfriendly shot. He drove a rousing trade. The miners came down from "the Rockies" with their bags of gold-dust ready open to pay for a frolic, and Five-Ace Jack received a liberal percentage from the three-card-monte men who entertained these innocent folks. But for a sad accident Jack might have remained at Denver, and become an exemplary member of society. He might have married one of the young ladies of accommodating manners who had even then managed to wander out to that Western town. He and she might at the present moment have been regarded as one of the twelve "Old Families" of Denver, who, beginning for the most part as he began, are now demonstrating their respectability by building churches like mad, and by giving balls which, in the favored language of the place, are described as "quite the toniest things-going." But fortune had a grudge against Jack.

There was an ill-favored rascal called Bully Bill, who was coming in from the plains one day, when he found two Indians following him. To shoot first, and ask the Indians' intentions afterward, was the rule in these parts; and accordingly Bully Bill fired, bringing one Indian down, the other riding off as hard as he could go. The conqueror thought he would have the scalp of his enemy as a proof of his valor; but he was a bad hand at the business, and as he was slowly endeavoring to get at the trophy, he found that the other Indian had mustered up courage, and was coming back. There was no time to lose. He simply hewed the dead Indian's head off, jumped on his pony, and, after an exciting chase, reached the town in safety. Then he carried the head into Five-Ace Jack's saloon; and as there were a few of the boys there, ready for fun, they got up an auction for that ghastly prize. It was knocked down at no less a sum than two hundred dollars—a price which so fired the brain of Bully Bill that he went in wildly for playing cards. But Five-Ace Jack never played cards wildly, and he was of the party. He observed that not only did Bully Bill lose steadily, but also that his losses seemed to vex him much; and, in fact, just as the last of the two hundred dollars was disappearing, he was surprised and deeply pained to find that Bully Bill was trying to cheat. This touched Jack's conscience, and he remonstrated; whereupon there was a word or two, and then Jack drew his shooter out and shot Bully Bill through the head. They respectfully placed the body on two chairs, and Jack called for some drinks.

This incident ought to have caused no great trouble; for at that time there was no Union Pacific Railroad Company—a troublesome body which has ere now impeached judge, jury, and prisoner, all in a lump, for a conspiracy to defeat the ends of justice, when some notorious offender has got off scot-free. But Bully Bill had three brothers up in the mountains; and Jack was of opinion that if he remained in Denver his mind would be troubled with many cares. However, he had amassed a good deal of money in this gambling hell of his; and so he was able to persuade a few of his meaner dependents to strike their tents along with him, and go out into the wilderness. He wandered over the plains until he saw a good place for a ranch — not a stock-raising ranch, but a place to accommodate the droves of pilgrims who were then slowly and laboriously making their way

to the West. He built his ranch about a hundred yards back
from the wagon route, and calmly awaited custom.

But even in these peaceful solitudes, if all stories be true—and
we in England heard nothing of Jack Sloane for many years—he
did not quite desist from his evil ways. Finding, first of all, that
many of the wagon parties went by without calling in at his
ranch, he and his men dug a large pit right across the route, so
that the drivers had perforce to turn aside and come right up to
his hostelry. Then he stationed a blacksmith a mile or two
down the road, for the greater convenience of the travellers who
were always glad to have the feet of their mules and oxen exam-
ined. It was very singular, however, that between the blacksmith's shop and Jack's ranch so many of the animals should go
lame; but what did that matter, when Jack was willing to exchange a perfectly fresh team for the tired team, a little consideration of money being added? It is true that the lame oxen
became rapidly well so soon as they were left in Jack's possession; but was not that all the more lucky for the next comers,
who were sure to find something wrong with their teams between
the blacksmith's shop and Eagle Creek Ranch?

Another peculiarity of this part of the plains was that the
neighborhood seemed to be infested with Indians, who, whether
they were Utes or Arrapahoes, showed a surprising knowledge as
to which wagon trains were supplied with the most valuable cattle, and never stampeded an indifferent lot. These attacks were
made at night, and doubtless the poor travellers, stunned by the
yells of the red men and the firing of guns and revolvers, were
glad to escape with their lives. But on one occasion, it is ru-
mored, an Indian would appear to have been hurt, for he was
heard to exclaim, in a loud voice, "*Holy Jabers! me fut! me
fut!*" Neither the Utes nor the Arapahoes, it was remembered, pronounce the word "foot" in that fashion, even when
they happen to know English, and so it came about that always
after that there were ugly rumors about Eagle Creek Ranch and
the men who lived there. But not even the stoutest bull-whacker who ever crossed the plains would dare to say a word on this
subject to Five-Ace Jack; he would have had a bullet through
his head for his pains.

And now we take leave of "Five-Ace Jack," for in his subsequent history he appears as "Colonel Sloane," "the Colonel," or

"the boss." As he grew more rich, he became more honest, as has happened in the case of many worthy people. His flocks and his herds increased. He closed the ranch as a place of entertainment — indeed, people were beginning now to talk of all sorts of other overland routes; but he made it the centre of a vast stock-rearing farm, which he superintended with great assiduity. He was an imperious master with his herders—the physical force that was always ready to give effect to his decisions was a weapon that stuck upright in the south-east corner of his trousers; but he was a just master, and paid his men punctually. Moreover, by-gones being by-gones, he had made an excursion or two up into "the Rockies," and had become possessed of one or two mines, which, though they were now only paying working expenses, promised well. Time flies fast in the West; people come and go rapidly. When Colonel Sloane stopped at the Grand Central of Denver, and drank petroleum-champagne at four dollars a bottle at that pretentious, dirty, and disagreeable hostelry, there was no one to recognize him as Five-Ace Jack. He was cleanly shaved; his linen was as brilliant as Chinese skill and Colorado air could make it, and could have helped to build a church with any of them. But somehow he never cared to remain long within the precincts of Denver; he was either up at Idaho, looking after his mines, or out at the ranch, looking after his herdsmen.

It was toward this ranch that Buckskin Charlie and Judge Greek were now riding, on this cool, clear, beautiful morning. All around them shone the golden-yellow prairie, an immeasurable sea of grass and flowers; above them shone the clear sky of Colorado; far away on their right the world was inclosed by the pale, transparent blue of the long wall of mountains. Eagle Creek Ranch was a lonely-looking place as they neared it. The central portion of the buildings spoke of the times when the Indians—the real Indians, not Five-Ace Jack and his merry men— were in the habit of scouring the plains; for it was a block-house, built of heavy logs of pine. But from this initial point branched out all sorts of buildings and enclosures—sheds, pens, stables, and what not, some of them substantially erected, and others merely made of cotton-wood fence. Out there they speak disrespectfully of cotton-wood, because of its habit of twisting itself into extraordinary shapes. It is admitted, however, by the settlers that this very habit defeats the most perverse ingenuity on the part of a hog; for the hog, intent on breaking away, fancies he has got outside the fence, whereas, owing to the twisting of the wood, he is still inside of it.

The Colonel lay in his bed, thinking neither of his hogs nor of his pens, nor yet of his vast herds of cattle roaming over the fenceless prairie land. The long, muscular, bony frame was writhing in pain; the black, dishevelled hair was wet with perspiration; the powerful hands clutched and wrung the coarse bedclothing. But the Colonel had all his wits about him; and when Mr. Greek, approaching him, began to offer some expressions of sympathy, he was bidden to mind his own business in language of quite irrelevant force. Buckskin Charlie was ordered to bring in his master's writing-desk, which was the only polished piece of furniture in the ranch. Then the Colonel, making a powerful effort to control his writhings, proceeded to give his instructions.

He was not going to die yet, the Colonel said. He had had these fits before. It was only a tough antelope steak, followed by a hard ride and a consuming thirst too hastily quenched. But here he was, on his back; and as he had nothing else to do, he wanted the Judge to put down on paper his wishes and intentions with regard to his property. The Colonel admitted that he was a rich man. Himself could not tell what head of cattle he owned. He had two placer mines in the Clear Creek Cañon; and he had been offered twelve thousand dollars for the celebrated Belle of St. Joe, up near Georgetown. He had a house at Idaho Springs. He had a share in a bank at Denver. Now the Colonel, in short and sharp sentences, interrupted by a good deal of writhing and hard swearing, said he would not leave a brass farthing—a red cent was what he actually mentioned—to any of his relatives who had known him in England, for the reason that they knew too much about him, and would be only too glad that he was gone. But there was a young girl who was a niece of his. He doubted whether she had ever seen him; if she had, it must have been when she was a child. He had a photograph of her, however, taken two or three years before, and she was a good-looking lass. Well, he did not mind leaving his property to her, under one or two conditions. There he paused for a time.

Five-Ace Jack was a cunning person, and he had brooded over this matter during many a lonely ride over the plains. He did not want his money to go among those relatives of his, who doubtless — though they heard but little about him — regarded him as a common scoundrel. But if he could get this pretty niece of his to come out to the far West with her husband, might they not be induced to remain there, and hold and retain that property that had cost the owner so much trouble to pull together? If they disliked the roughness of the ranch, could anything be more elegant than the white wooden villa at Idaho, with its veranda and green blinds? Then he considered that it was a long way for her to come. If she had children—and she might have, for it was two or three years since he heard she was married—the trouble and anxiety of bringing them all the way from England would dispose her to take a gloomy view of the place. Surely it was not too hard a condition that, in consideration of their getting so large a property, this young Bell and her husband should come out, free from encumbrances of all sorts, to live one year in Colorado, either at Idaho or at Eagle Creek Ranch, just as they chose?

Both the Colonel and the Judge were bachelors; and it did not occur to either of them, when that condition was put down on paper, that a young woman on this side of the water could be so foolish as to get up with flashing eyes and say—as actually happened in less than a year afterward—that not for all the cattle in Colorado, and not for all the gold in the Rocky Mountains, and not for twenty times all the diamonds that were ever gotten out of Golconda, would she leave her poor, dear, darling, defenceless children for a whole year. Just as little did they think, when this memorandum was finally handed over to the Judge to be drawn out in proper form, that any proceeding on the part of Five-Ace Jack, of Eagle Creek Ranch, could have the slightest possible influence on the fortunes of Lady Sylvia Balfour. Jack was a Colorado ranchman; Lady Sylvia was the daughter of an English earl.

CHAPTER XIV.

FIRST EXPERIENCES.

MARRIAGE is in legal phrase the "highest consideration;" even the cold and unromantic eye of the law perceives that the fact of a woman giving herself up, body and soul, to a man, is more than an equivalent for any sort of marriage settlement. But at no period of the world's history was it ever contemplated that a woman's immediate duty, on becoming a wife, was forthwith to efface her own individuality. Now this was what Lady Sylvia deliberately set about doing in the first flush of her wifely devotion. As she had married the very source and fountain-head of all earthly wisdom, what use was there in her retaining opinions of her own? Henceforth she was to have always at her side the law-giver, the arbiter, the infallible authority; she would surrender to his keeping all her beliefs, just as she implicitly surrendered her trunks. She never thought twice about her new dresses: what railway guard could withstand that terrible, commanding eye?

Now, little has been said to the point in these pages about Balfour if it has not been shown that he was a man of violent prejudices. Perhaps he was not unlike other people in that respect, except in so far as he took little pains to conceal his opinions. But if there was anything likely to cure him of prejudices, it was to see them mimicked in the faithful and loving mirror now always by his side; for how could he help laughing at the unintentional distortions? He had been a bitter opponent of the Second Empire while that bubble still glittered in the political atmosphere; but surely that was no reason why Lady Sylvia should positively refuse to remain in Paris?

"Gracious goodness!" said he, "have you acquired a personal dislike for thirty millions of people? You may take my word for it, Sylvia, that as all you are likely to know about the French is by travelling among them, they are the nicest people in the world, so far as that goes. Look at the courtesy of the officials!

look at the trouble a working-man or a peasant will take to put you in the right road! Believe me, you may go farther and fare worse. Wait, for example, till you make your first plunge into Germany. Wait till you see the Germans on board a Rhine steamer—their manners to strangers, their habits of eating—"

"And then?" she said; "am I to form my opinion of the Germans from that? Do foreigners form their opinion of England by looking at a steamer-load of people going to Margate?"

"Sylvia," said he, "I command you to love the French."

"I won't," she said.

But this defiant disobedience was only the curious result of a surrender of her own opinions. She was prepared to dislike thirty millions of human beings merely because he had expressed detestation of Louis Napoleon. And when he ended the argument with a laugh, the laugh was not altogether against her. From that moment he determined to seize every opportunity of pointing out to her the virtues of the French.

Of course it was very delightful to him to have for his companion one who came quite fresh to all those wonders of travel which lie close around our own door. One does not often meet nowadays with a young lady who has not seen, for example, the Rhine under moonlight. Lady Sylvia had never been out of England. It seemed to her that she had crossed interminable distances, and left her native country in a different planet altogether, when she reached Brussels, and she could not understand her husband when he said that in the Rue Montagne de la Cour he had always the impression that he had just stepped round the corner from Regent Street. And she tried to imagine what she would do in these remote places of the earth if she were all by herself — without this self-reliant guide and companion, who seemed to care no more for the awful and mysterious officials about railway-stations and the entrances to palaces than he would for the humble and familiar English policeman. The great deeds of chivalry were poor in her eyes compared with the splendid battle waged by her husband against extortion; the field of Waterloo was nearly witnessing another fearful scene of bloodshed all because of a couple of francs. Then the Rhine, on the still moonlight night, from the high balcony in Cologne, with the colored lights of the steamers moving to and fro—surely it was he alone who was the creator of this wonderful scene. That he was the creator of some of her delight in it was probable enough.

Finally, they settled down in the little village of Rolandseck; and now, in this quiet retreat, after the hurry and bustle of travelling was over and gone, they were thrown more directly on each other's society, and left to find out whether they could find in the companionship of each other a sufficient means of passing the time. That, indeed, is the peril of the honey-moon period, and it has been the origin of a fair amount of mischief. You take a busy man away from all his ordinary occupations, and you take a young girl away from all her domestic and other pursuits, while as yet neither knows very much about the other, and while they have no common objects of interest—no business affairs, nor house affairs, nor children to talk about—and you expect them to amuse each other day after day, and day after day. Conversation, in such circumstances, is apt to dwindle down into very small rills indeed, unless when it is feared that silence may be construed into regret, and then a forced effort is made to pump up the waters. Moreover, Rolandseck, though one of the most beautiful places in the world, is a place in which one finds it desperately hard to pass the time. There is the charming view, no doubt, and the Balfours had corner rooms, whence they could see, under the changing lights of morning, of mid-day, of sunset, and moonlight, the broad and rushing river, the picturesque island, the wooded and craggy heights, and the mystic range of the Drachenfels. But the days were still, sleepy, monotonous. Balfour, seated in the garden just over the river, would get the *Kölnische* or the *Allgemeine*, and glance at the brief telegram headed "Grossbritannien," which told all that was considered to be worth telling about his native country. Or, together, they would clamber up through the warm vineyards to the rocky heights by Roland's Tower, and there let the dreamy hours go by in watching the shadows cross the blue mountains, in following the small steamers and the greater rafts as they passed down the stream, in listening to the tinkling of the cattle bells in the valley below. How many times a day did Balfour cross over by the swinging ferry to the small bathing-house on the other side, and there plunge into the clear, cold, rushing green waters? Somehow the days passed.

And, on the whole, they passed pleasantly. In England there

was absolutely nothing going on that could claim any one's attention; the first absolute hush of the recess was unbroken even by those wandering voices that, later on, murmur of politics in unfrequented places. All the world had gone idling; if a certain young lady had wished to assume at once the *rôle* she had sketched out for herself—of becoming the solace and comfort of the tired legislator—there was no chance for her in England at least. Perhaps, on the whole, she was better occupied here in learning something about the nature of the man with whom she proposed to spend a lifetime. And here, too, in these quiet solitudes, Balfour occasionally abandoned his usual bantering manner, and gave her glimpses of a deep undercurrent of feeling, of the existence of which not even his most intimate friends were aware. When they walked alone in the still evenings, with the cool wind stirring the avenues of walnut-trees, and the moonlight beginning to touch the mists lying about Nonnenwerth and over the river, he talked to her as he had never talked to any human being before. And curiously enough, when his love for this newly found companion sought some expression that would satisfy himself, he found it in snatches of old songs that his nurse, a Lowland Scotchwoman, had sung to him in his childhood. He had never read these lyrics. He knew nothing of their literary value. It was only as echoes that they came into his memory now; and yet they satisfied him in giving something of form to his own fancies. He did not repeat them to her; but as he walked with her, these old phrases and chance refrains seemed to suggest themselves quite naturally. Surely it was of her that this was written:

> " Oh, saw ye my wee thing, and saw ye my ain thing,
>   And saw ye my true love down on yon lea?
> Crossed she the meadow yestreen at the gloaming,
>   Sought she the burnie where flowers the haw-tree?
> Her hair it is lint white, her skin it is milk white,
>   Dark is the blue o' her saft-rollin' e'e,
> Red, red her ripe lips, and sweeter than roses—
>   Where could my wee thing wander frae me?"

Or this, again:

> " Her bower casement is latticed wi' flowers,
>   Tied up wi' siller thread,
> And courtly sits she in the midst,
>   Men's langing eyes to feed;

> She waves the ringlets frae her cheek
>   Wi' her milky, milky han';
> And her cheeks seem touched wi' the finger o' God,
>   ' My bonnie Lady Ann."

He forgot that he was in the Rhine-land—the very cradle of lyrical romance. He did not associate this fair companion with any book whatever; the feelings that she stirred were deeper down than that, and they found expression in phrases that had years and years ago become a part of his nature. He forgot all about Uhland, Heine, and the rest of the sweet and pathetic singers who have thrown a glamour over the Rhine Valley; it was the songs of his boyhood that occurred to him.

> "Like dew on the gowan lying
>   Is the fa' o' her fairy feet;
> And like the winds in summer sighing,
>   Her voice is low and sweet."

The lines are simple enough. Perhaps they are even commonplace. But they sufficed.

It must be said, however, that Balfour was the reverse of an effusive person, and this young wife very speedily discovered that his bursts of tender confidences were likely to be few and far between. He was exceedingly chary of using endearing phrases, more especially if there was a third person present. Now she had been used to elaborate and studied expressions of affection. There was a good deal of histrionics about Lord Willowby. He got into violent rages with his servants about the merest trifles; but these rages were as predetermined as those of the First Napoleon are said to have been; he found that it answered his purpose to have his temper feared. On the other hand, his affection for his daughter was expressed on all occasions with profuse phraseology—a phraseology that was a trifle mawkish and artificial when heard by others, but which was not so to the object of it. She had grown accustomed to it. To her it was but natural language. Doubtless she had been taught to believe that all affection expressed itself in that way.

Here, again, she tried to school herself. Convinced, by these rare moments of self-disclosure, that the love he bore her was the deepest and strongest feeling of his nature, she would be content to do without continual protestation of it. She would have no lip-service. Did not reticence in such matters arise from the feeling that there were emotions and relations too sacred to be continually flaunted before the public gaze? Was she to distrust the man who had married her, because he did not prate of his affection for her within the hearing of servants?

The reasoning was admirable; the sentiment that prompted it altogether praiseworthy. But before a young wife begins to efface her personality in this fashion, she ought to make sure that she has not much personality to speak of. Lady Sylvia had a good deal. In those Surrey solitudes, thrown greatly in on herself for companionship, she had acquired a certain seriousness of character. She had very definite conceptions of the various duties of life; she had decided opinions on many points; she had, like other folks, a firmly fixed prejudice or two. For her to imagine that she could wipe out her own individuality, as if it were a sum on a slate, and inscribe in its stead a whole series of new opinions, was mere folly. It was prompted by the most generous of motives, but it was folly none the less. Obviously, too, it was a necessary corollary of this effort at self-surrender, or rather self-effacement, that her husband should not be made aware of it; she would be to him, not what she was, but what she thought she ought to be.

Hypersubtleties of fancy and feeling? the result of delicate rearing, a sensitive temperament, and a youth spent much in solitary self-communion? Perhaps they were; but they were real for all that. They were not affectations, but facts—facts involving as important issues as the simpler feelings of less complex and cultivated natures. To her they were so real, so all-important, that the whole current of her life was certain to be guided by them.

During this pleasant season but one slight cloud crossed the shining heaven of their new life. They had received letters in the morning; in the evening, as they sat at dinner, Lady Sylvia suddenly said to her husband, with a sort of childish happiness in her face,

"Oh, Hugh, how delightful it must be to be a very rich person! I am eagerly looking forward to that first thousand pounds —it is a whole thousand pounds all at once, is it not? Then you must put it in a bank for me, and let me have a check-book."

"I wonder what you will do with it," said he. "I never could

understand what women did with their private money. I suppose
they make a pretence of paying for their own dress ; but as a
matter of fact they have everything given them — jewellery,
flowers, bonnets, gloves—"

"I know," said she, with a slight blush, "what I should like to
do with my money."

"Well ?" said he. Of course she had some romantic notion in
her head. She would open a co-operative store for the benefit
of the inhabitants of Happiness Alley, and make Mrs. Grace the
superintendent. She would procure "a day in the country" for
all the children in the slums of Seven Dials. She would start a
fund for erecting a gold statue to Mr. Plimsoll.

"You know," said she, with an embarrassed smile, "that papa
is very poor, and I think those business matters have been harassing him more than ever of late. I am sure, Hugh dear, you are
quite right about women not needing money of their own — at
least, I know I have never felt the want of it much. And now
don't you think it would please poor papa if I were to surprise
him some morning with a check for a whole thousand pounds?
I should feel myself a millionnaire."

He showed no surprise or vexation. He merely said, in a cold
way,

"If it would please you, Sylvia, I see no objection."

But immediately after dinner he went out, saying he meant to
go for a walk to some village on the other side of the Rhine—
too distant for her to go. He lit a cigar, and went down to the
ferry. The good-natured ferry-man, who knew Balfour well, said
"'n Abend, Herr." Why should this sulky-browed man mutter
in reply, "The swindling old heathen !" It was quite certain that
Balfour could not have referred to the friendly ferry-man.

He walked away along the dusty and silent road, in the gathering twilight, puffing his cigar fiercely.

"At it already," he was saying to himself bitterly. "He
could not let a week pass. And the child comes to me with her
pretty ways, and says, 'Oh, won't you pity this poor old swin-
dler ?' And of course I am an impressionable young man ; and
in the first flush of conjugal gratitude and enthusiasm I will do
whatever she asks ; and so the letter comes within the very first
week ! By the Lord, I will stop that kind of thing as soon as I
get back to London !"

He returned to the hotel about ten o'clock. Lady Sylvia had gone to her room; he went there, and found her crying bitterly. And as she would not tell him why she was in such grief, how could he be expected to know? He thought he had acted very generously in at once acceding to her proposal; and there could not be the slightest doubt that the distance to that particular village was much too great for her to attempt.

CHAPTER XV.

A NEW ACQUAINTANCE.

AT breakfast next morning, Lady Sylvia appeared as cheerful as possible. She was quite talkative, and was more charmed than ever with the beauties of the Rhine. No reference was made to that little incident of the previous evening.

She had been schooling herself as usual. Was it not natural for him to show some resentment at this foolish school-girl notion of presenting a £1000 bank-note to her father? Her husband could not be expected to share in her romantic notions. He was a man of the world. And had he not shown his generosity and unfailing consideration in not only assenting to her proposal, but in going off to conceal his natural disapproval? Her woman's eyes had been too quick; that was all.

On the other hand, Balfour, delighted to find his young wife in such good spirits, could not think of reviving a matter which might lead to a quarrel. She might give her father the thousand pounds, and welcome. Only he, Balfour, would take very good care, as soon as he got back to England, that that was the last application of the kind.

Now, the truth was, there had been no such application. Lord Willowby had written to his daughter, and she had received the letter; but there was not in it a single word referring to money matters. A simple inquiry and a simple explanation would have prevented all this unpleasantness, which might leave traces behind it. Why had not these been forth-coming? Why, indeed! How many months before was it that Balfour was urging his sweetheart to fix an early day for their wedding, on the earnest plea that marriage was the only guarantee against misunderstandings? Only with marriage came perfect confidence. Marriage was to be the perpetual safeguard against the dangers of separation, the interference of friends, the mischief wrought by rumor. In short, marriage was to bring about the millennium. That is the belief that has got into the heads of a good many young people besides Mr. Hugh Balfour and Lady Sylvia Blythe.

But as they were now quite cheerful and pleased with each other, what more was wanted? And it was a bright and beautiful day; and soon the steamer would be coming up the river to take them on to Coblentz, that they might go up the Moselle. As they stood on the small wooden pier, Lady Sylvia, looking abroad on the beautiful panorama of crag and island and river, said to her husband, in a low voice,

"Shall we ever forget this place? And the still days we spent here?"

"I will give you this advice, Sylvia," said he. "If you want to remember Rolandseck, don't keep any photograph of it in England. That will only deaden and vulgarize the place; and you will gradually have the photograph dispossessing your memory picture. Look, now, and remember. Look at the color of the Rhine, and the shadows under the trees of the island there, and the sunshine on those blue mountains. Don't you think you will always be able to remember?"

She did not look at all. She suddenly turned away her head, for she did not wish him to see that her eyes had filled. It was not the last time she was to look at Rolandseck—or rather at the beautiful picture that memory painted of it—through a mist of tears.

"Hillo!" cried her husband, as they were stepping on board the *Kaiser Wilhelm,* "I'm hanged if there isn't Billy Bolitho!"

"Who is he?" said she, timidly. Her first impulse was to shrink from meeting any stranger.

"Oh, the best fellow in the world," said Balfour, who appeared to be greatly pleased. "He is a Parliamentary agent. Now you will hear all that's been going on. Bolitho knows everybody and everything; and, besides, he is the best of fellows himself."

Mr. Bolitho, with much discretion, did his utmost to avoid running against these two young people; but that was of no use.

Balfour hunted him up, and brought him along to introduce him to Lady Sylvia. He was an elderly gentleman, with silvery white whiskers, a bland and benevolent face, and remarkably shrewd and humorous eyes. He was very respectful to Lady Sylvia. He remarked to her that he had the pleasure of knowing her father; but, as Balfour put in, it would have been hard to find any one whom Mr. Bolitho did not know.

And how strange it was, after these still days in the solitude by the Rhine, to plunge back again into English politics! The times were quiet enough in England itself just at the moment; but great events had recently been happening, and these afforded plenty of matter for eager discussion and speculation. Lady Sylvia listened intently: was it not part of her education? She heard their guesses as to the political future. Would the prime minister be forced to dissolve before the spring? Or would he not wait to see the effect on the country of the reconstruction of the cabinet, and appear in February with a fascinating budget, which would charm all men's hearts, and pave the way for a triumphant majority at the General Election? All this she could follow pretty well. She was puzzled when they spoke of the alleged necessity of the prime minister seeking re-election on assuming the office of chancellor of the exchequer; and she did not quite know what league it was that was likely to oppose— according to rumor—the re-election at Birmingham of a statesman who had just been taken into the cabinet. But all this about the chances of a dissolution she could understand pretty well; and was it not of sufficient interest to her, considering that her husband's seat in the House was in peril?

But when they got into the *personnel* of politics she was lost altogether. There were rumors of a still further reconstruction of the ministry; and the chances of appointments falling to such and such people brought out such a host of details about the position of various men whose names even were unknown to her that she got not a little bewildered. And surely this garrulous, bland old gentleman talked with a dreadful cynicism about public affairs, or rather about the men engaged in them. And was not his talk affecting her husband too? Was it true that these were the real objects which caused this man to pose as a philanthropist and the other to preside at religious meetings? She began to find less and less humor in these remarks of Mr. Bolitho.

She would like to have carried her husband away from the sphere of his evil influence.

"I suppose now, Balfour," said he, "you have been taking a look round? You know, of course, that Ballinascroon will make short work of you?"

"Yes, I know that," said the other.

"Well," said Mr. Bolitho, "they say that we sha'n't know what the Government mean to do until Bright's speech in October. I have a suspicion that something besides that will happen in October. They may fancy a bold challenge would tell. Now, suppose there was a dissolution, where would you be?"

"Flying all over the country, I suppose—Evesham, Shoreham, Woodstock, Harwich, anywhere—seeing where I could get some rest for the sole of my foot."

"If I were you," said Mr. Bolitho, "I would not trust to a postponement of the dissolution till the spring. I would take my measures now."

"Very well, but where? Come, Bolitho, put me on to a good thing. I know you have always half a dozen boroughs in your pocket."

"Well," said Mr. Bolitho to Lady Sylvia, with a cheerful smile, "your husband wishes to make me out a person of some importance, doesn't he? But it is really an odd coincidence that I should run across him to-day; for, as it happens, I am going on to Mainz to see Eugy Chorley, and that is a man of whom you might fairly say that he carries a borough in his pocket—Englebury."

"That's old Harnden's place. What a shame it would be to try to oust the old fellow!" said Balfour.

"Oh, he is good for nothing," said Mr. Bolitho, gayly. "He ought to be in a Bath-chair, at Brighton. Besides, he is very unpopular; he has been spending no money lately. And I suppose you have got to oust somebody somewhere if you mean to sit in the House."

"But what are his politics?" said Lady Sylvia to this political pagan.

"Oh, nothing in particular. Formerly, if there was a free fight going on anywhere, he was sure to be in it—though you never could tell on which side. Now he limits himself to an occasional growl."

"And you would have my husband try to turn out this poor old gentleman?" said Lady Sylvia, with some indignation.

"Why not?" said Mr. Bolitho, with a charming smile. "How many men has Harnden turned out in his time, I wonder? Now, Lady Sylvia, you could be of great use to your husband if you and he would only come straight on with me to Mainz. Mr. Chorley and his wife are at the —— Hotel. He is a solicitor at Englebury; he is the great man there, does all the parochial business, is a friend of the duke's—in short, he can do what he likes at Englebury. Your husband would have to conciliate him, you know, by putting a little business in his way—buying a few farms or houses on speculation and selling them again. Or, stay, this is better. Eugy wants to sell a few acres of land he himself has. I believe he stole the piece from the side of an out-of-the-way common—first had a ditch cut for drainage, then put up a few posts, then a wire to keep children from tumbling in, then, a couple of years after, he boldly ran a fence round and cleared the place inside. I suppose no one dared to interfere with a man who had the private affairs of every one in the parish in his hands. Well, I think Mr. Chorley, when he sees all this fuss going on about enclosures, sometimes gets uneasy. Now your husband might buy this land of him."

"For what purpose, pray?" demanded Lady Sylvia, with some dignity. "Do I understand you that this land was stolen from the poor people of the village?"

"Yes," said Mr. Bolitho, coolly. "And your husband could give it back to them—make a public green of it, and put up a gymnasium. That would have to be done after the election, of course."

"And how do you propose that I should aid my husband?" asked Lady Sylvia. Balfour, who was listening in silent amusement, could not understand why she grew more and more chill in her demeanor.

"Oh," said Mr. Bolitho, with a shrewd smile, "you will have to conciliate Mrs. Chorley, who is much the more terrible person of the two. I am afraid, Lady Sylvia, you don't know much about politics."

"No," said Lady Sylvia, coldly.

"Of course not—not to be expected. She won't be hard in her catechising. But there are one or two points she is rather fierce about. You will have to let the English Church go."

"To let the English Church go ?" said Lady Sylvia, doubtfully.

"I mean as a political institution."

"But it is not a political institution," said Lady Sylvia, firmly.

"I mean as a political question, then," said Mr. Bolitho, blandly. "Pray don't imagine that I am in favor of disestablishment, Lady Sylvia. It is not my business to have any opinions. I dare not belong either to the Reform or to the Carlton. I was merely pointing out that if Mrs. Chorley speaks about disestablishment, it would not be worth your while to express any decided view, supposing you were not inclined to agree with her. That is all. You see, Mrs. Chorley is the daughter of the great Quakeress, Mrs. Dew—of course you have heard of her?"

"No, I have not," said Lady Sylvia.

"Dear me! Before your time, I suppose. But she was a delightful old woman—the dearest little old lady! How well I remember her! She used to live in Bloomsbury Square, and she had supper parties every Tuesday and Friday evening; it is five-and-thirty years ago since I went to those parties. Mrs. Dew was a widow, you know, and she presided at the table; and when supper was over she used to get up and propose a series of toasts in the most delightful prim and precise manner. She was a great politician, you must understand. And many men used to come there of an evening who became very celebrated persons afterward. Dear me, it's a long time since then! But I shall never forget the little woman standing up with a glass of toast and water in her hand—she did not drink wine—and giving the health of some distinguished guest, or begging them to drink to the success of a bill before the House; and we always drank her health before we left, and she used to give us such a pretty little old-fashioned courtesy. Mrs. Chorley," added Mr. Bolitho, with a grim smile, "is not quite such another."

"But do you mean," said Lady Sylvia, with some precision, "that because Mrs. Chorley is the daughter of a Quakeress, I am to pretend to wish for the destruction of the Church of England —my own Church ?"

"My dear Lady Sylvia!" cried Mr. Bolitho, with a sort of paternal familiarity, "you must not put it in that way."

But here Balfour interposed; for he perceived that she was becoming a trifle warm, and a young husband is anxious that his wife should acquit herself well before his friends.

"Look here, Sylvia," he said, good-humoredly, "I suppose neither you nor I have very keen personal interest in.that question. No doubt the Church of England will be disestablished in time, and before that time comes it will be well to prepare for the change, so that it may be effected with as little harm and as little harshness as possible. But the severance of the connection between Church and State has nothing to do with the destruction of the Church; it is a political question; and if Mrs. Chorley or anybody else is so constituted as to take a frantic interest in such a thing, why should any other person goad her by contradiction? The opinions of Mrs. Chorley won't shift the axis of the earth."

"You mistake me altogether, Hugh," said Lady Sylvia. "I have not the slightest intention of entering into any discussion on any topic whatsoever with Mrs. Chorley."

Of course not. She already regarded Mrs. Chorley, and all her views and opinions, no matter what they were, with a sovereign contempt. For was it not this unholy alliance into which her husband seemed inclined to enter that was the cause of his speaking in a slighting, indifferent manner about subjects which ought to have been of supreme importance to him? And the cheerful and friendly face of Mr. Bolitho pleased her no longer.

"Are we going on to Mainz, then?" she asked of her husband.

"I think we might as well," said he. "There can be no harm in seeing this potentate, at all events. And we can go up the Moselle another time."

So he abandoned, at a moment's notice, that voyage up the beautiful river to which she had been looking forward for many a day, merely that he should go on to see whether he could bribe a solicitor into betraying a constituency. She knew that her noble husband could never have done this but under the malign influence of this godless old man, whose only notion of the British Constitution was that it offered him the means of earning a discreditable livelihood. And she, too, was to take her part in the conspiracy.

"You know, Lady Sylvia," said Mr. Bolitho, with a pleasant smile, "there is one thing will conciliate Mrs. Chorley more than your agreeing with her about politics; and that is the fact that you are your father's daughter."

She did not quite understand at first. Then it dawned upon her that they hoped to bring Mrs. Chorley into a friendly mood

by introducing that political termagant to the daughter of an earl.
Lady Sylvia, who had retired into her guide-book, and would listen no more to their jargon of politics, resolved that that introduction would be of such a nature as Mrs. Chorley had never experienced before in the whole course of her miserable, despicable,
and ignominious life.

CHAPTER XVI.

THE CONSPIRATORS.

It was late when they arrived at Mainz, and there was some
little delay about getting supper ready, because, a quarter of an
hour after it was ordered, they heard the squealing of a young
cock outside, that being the animal destined for their repast.
Moreover, when the fowl appeared, he turned out to be a tough
little beast, only half cooked; so they sent him away, and had
something else. For convenience' sake they supped in the great,
gaunt, empty Speise-saal. It was about ten o'clock when they
went up to the sitting-room on the first floor which they had ordered.

There was thus plenty of time for Lady Sylvia to have got
over the first fierce feeling of wrath against Mr. and Mrs. Chorley,
which had been begotten by the cynicism of Mr. Bolitho and the
indifference of her husband. Surely those large and tender blue-
gray eyes—which her husband now thought had more than ever
of the beautiful liquid lustre that had charmed him in the days
of her sweet maidenhood—were never meant as the haunt of an
incontrollable rage? And, indeed, when Mr. and Mrs. Chorley,
who had been wandering about the town on foot, were brought
up to the apartment at that late hour of the night by Mr. Bolitho,
and introduced to Mr. and Lady Sylvia Balfour, there was nothing hideous or repellent about the political Gorgon, nothing calculated to awaken dismay or disgust. On the contrary, Mrs.
Chorley, who was a tall, motherly-looking woman, with a fresh-
colored face, gray hair, thin and decided lips, and blue eyes that
stared a tone over her silver spectacles, was more than friendly
with the young girl. She was almost obsequious. She was sure

Lady Sylvia must be so tired; would not Lady Sylvia have a cup of tea now? She would be so pleased if she could do anything for Lady Sylvia. Lady Sylvia sat proud and cold. She did not like to be fawned upon. She was listening, in indignant silence, for the first efforts of her husband and Mr. Bolitho to cajole this mercenary solicitor into betraying an English constituency.

One thing she might have been sure of — that her husband would not be guilty of any tricks of flattery or hypocrisy to gain his end. His faults lay all the other way — in a bluntness and directness that took too small account of the sensitiveness of other people. And on this evening he was in very good spirits, and at once attacked Mr. Eugenius Chorley with a sort of gay and friendly audacity. Now, Mr. Chorley was a little, dapper, horsey-looking man, with shrewd, small eyes, a face wrinkled and red as a French rennet, accurately clipped whiskers, and a somewhat gorgeous necktie, with a horseshoe in emeralds in it. He was shrewd, quick, and clever; but he was also very respectable and formal, and he disliked and distrusted jokes. When Balfour gayly asked him what price Englebury put upon itself, he only stared.

"My friend Bolitho," continued Balfour, with a careless smile, "tells me you've got some land there, Mr. Chorley, of no particular use to you. If I were to buy that, and turn it into a public garden, wouldn't the inhabitants of Englebury be vastly grateful to me?"

Here Mr. Bolitho struck in, very red in the face.

"Of course you understand, Chorley, that is mere nonsense; we were having a joke about it on the steamer. But really now, you know, we may have a General Election in October; and Mr. Balfour is naturally anxious to fix on some borough where he may have a reasonable chance, as Ballinascroon is sure to bid him good-bye; and I have heard rumors that old Harnden was likely to retire. You, as the most important man in the borough, would naturally have great influence in selecting a candidate."

It was a broad hint—a much franker exposition of the situation than Mr. Bolitho at all liked; but then the reckless audacity of this young man had compromised him.

"I see," said the small, pink-faced solicitor, with his hands clasping his knee; and then he added, gravely—indeed, solemnly

—"You are doubtless aware, Mr. Balfour, that your expressed intention of giving the inhabitants a public garden would become a serious matter for you in the event of there being a petition ?"

"Oh," said Balfour, with a laugh, "I sha'n't express any intention. You would never think of repeating a private chat we had one evening by the Rhine. The people of Englebury would know nothing about it till long after the election ; it would only be a reward for their virtuous conduct in returning so admirable a representative as myself."

Mr. Chorley did not like this fashion of treating so serious a matter ; in the conduct of the public affairs of Englebury he was accustomed to much recondite diplomacy, caucus meetings, private influence, and a befitting gravity.

"There is a number of our people," said he, cautiously, "dissatisfied with Mr. 'Arnden."

"Parliament really wants some fresh blood in it," urged Mr. Bolitho, who would have been glad to see a General Election every three months ; for his Parliamentary agency was not at all confined to looking after the passage of private bills.

"And his connection with Macleary has done him harm," Mr. Chorley again admitted.

"Oh, that fellow !" cried Balfour. "Well, I don't think a man is responsible for the sins of his brother-in-law ; and old Harnden is an honest and straightforward old fellow. But Macleary ! I know for a fact that he received £300 in hard cash for talking out a bill on a Wednesday near the end of this very session. Let him charge me with libel, and I will prove it. Thank goodness, I am free in that respect. I am not hampered by having a blackguard for a brother-in-law—"

He stopped suddenly, and Lady Sylvia, looking up, was surprised by the expression of his face, in which a temporary embarrassment was blended with a certain angry frown. He hurried on to say something else ; she sat and wondered. What could he mean by this allusion to a brother-in-law ? He had no brother-in-law at all. She was recalled from these bewildered guesses by the assiduous attentions of Mrs. Chorley, who was telling Lady Sylvia about all the beautiful places which she must visit, although Lady Sylvia treated these attentions with but scant courtesy, and seemed much more deeply interested in this electioneering plot.

For it was as a plot that she distinctly regarded this proposal; and she was certain that her husband would never have been drawn into it but for the evil influence of this worldling, this wily serpent, this jester. And what was this that they were saying now?—that Englebury had no politics at all; that it was all a matter of personal preference; that the Dissenters in that remote and rustic paradise had not even thought of raising the cry of disestablishment; and that Balfour, if he resolved to contest the seat, would have a fair chance of success. Balfour had grown a trifle more serious, and was making inquiries. It appeared that Mr. Chorley was not much moved by political questions; his wife was a Dissenter, but he was not. Very probably Mr. Harnden would resign. And the only probable rival whom Balfour would in that case encounter was a certain Reginald Key, who was a native of the place, and had once represented a neighboring borough.

"Confound that fellow!" said Mr. Bolitho; "is he back in England again? It doesn't matter which party is in power, they can't get him killed. They've sent him, time after time, to places that invalid every Englishman in a couple of years; and the worse the place is, the better he thrives—comes back smiling, and threatens to get into Parliament again if they don't give him a better appointment. What a nuisance he used to be in the House! But certainly the feeblest thing I ever knew done by a Liberal government was their sending him out to the Gold Coast—as if twenty Gold Coasts could kill that fellow! Don't you be afraid of him, Balfour. The Government will get him out of the way somehow. If they can't kill him, they will at least pack him out of England. So you think, Chorley, that our friend here has a chance?"

Mr. Chorley looked at his wife: so far the oracle had not spoken. She instantly answered that mute appeal.

"I should say a very good chance," she observed, with a friendly smile, "a very excellent chance; and I am perhaps in a better position to sound the opinions of our people than my husband is, for, of course, he has a great deal of business on his hands. No doubt it would be a great advantage if you had a house in the neighborhood. And I am sure Lady Sylvia would soon become very popular: if I may say so, I am sure she would become the popular candidate."

Surely all things were going well. Had this important ally been secured, and not a word said about disestablishment? It was Lady Sylvia who now spoke.

"I must beg you," said the girl, speaking in clear tones, with her face perhaps a trifle more proud and pale than usual—"I must beg you to leave me out of your scheme. I must say it seems to me a singular one. You meet us, who are strangers to you, by accident in a foreign country; and without consulting the gentleman who is at present your member, and without consulting any of the persons in the town, and without asking a word about my husband's opinions or qualifications, you practically invite him to represent the constituency in Parliament. All that happens in an hour. Well, it is very kind of you; but it seems to me strange. Perhaps I ought not to ask why you should be so kind. There has been a talk about presenting a public green to the people; but I cannot suppose you could be influenced by so paltry a bribe. In any case, will you be so good as to leave me, at least, out of the scheme?"

All this was said very quietly, and it was with a sweet courtesy that she rose and bowed to them and left the room; but when she had gone they looked as if a thunder-bolt had fallen in the midst of them. Balfour broke the silence; he was as surprised as the others, but he was far more deeply vexed.

"That shows the folly," said he, with an angry look on his face, "of allowing women to mix themselves up in politics—I mean unmarried women—I mean young women of no experience, who take everything *au grand sérieux*. I am sure, Mrs. Chorley, you will allow me to apologize for my wife's conduct; she herself will be sorry enough when she has time to reflect."

"Pray don't say another word, Mr. Balfour," Mrs. Chorley replied; but all the bright friendliness had gone from her face, and she spoke coldly. "I have no doubt Lady Sylvia is a little tired by travelling—and impatient; and, indeed, my husband and myself ought not to have intruded ourselves upon her at so late an hour. I have no doubt it is eleven o'clock, Eugenius?"

Her husband rose, and they left together. Then Mr. Bolitho put his hands into his pocket and stretched out his legs.

"The fat's in the fire," said he.

For a second Balfour felt inclined to pick a fierce quarrel with this man. Was it not he who had led him into this predicament? and what did he care for all the constituencies and solicitors and agents that ever were seen as compared with this desperate business that had arisen between him and his young wife?

But he controlled himself. He would not even show that he was vexed.

"Women don't take a joke," said he, lightly. "Besides, she knows little about actual life. It is all theory with her; and she has high notions about what people should be and do. It was a mistake to let her know anything about election affairs."

"I thought she was deeply interested," said Mr. Bolitho. "However, I hope no harm is done. You will see old Chorley to-morrow before they leave; he is a decent sort of fellow; he won't bear a grudge. And from what he says, it appears clear to me that Harnden does really mean to resign; and Chorley could pull you through if he likes—his wife being favorable, that is. Only, no more at present about the buying of that land of his. I am afraid he felt that."

Bolitho then went, and Balfour was left alone. He began pacing up and down the room, biting the end of a cigar which he did not light. He could not understand the origin of this outburst. He had never suspected that placid, timid, sensitive girl of, having such a temper. Where had she got the courage, too, that enabled her to speak with such clear decision? He began to wonder whether he had ever really discovered what the character of this girl was during those quiet rambles in the by-gone times.

He went into her room and found her seated in an easy-chair, reading by the light of a solitary candle. She put the book aside when he entered. He flattered himself that he could deal with this matter in a gentle and friendly fashion: he would not have a quarrel in their honey-moon.

"Sylvia," said he, in a kindly way, "I think you have successfully put your foot in it this time."

She did not answer.

"What made you insult those people so?"

"I hope I did not insult them," she said.

"Well," he said, with a laugh, "it was getting close to it. I must say, you might have shown a little more consideration to friends of mine—"

"I did not regard them as friends of yours. I should be sorry to do that."

"They were, at all events, human beings; they were not black beetles. And I think you might have considered my interest a little bit, and have remained silent, even if you had conjured up some imaginary cause of offence—"

"How could I remain silent?" she suddenly said, with vehemence. "I was ashamed to see you in the society of such people; I was ashamed to see you listening to them; and I was determined that I, for one, would not be drawn into their unblushing conspiracy. Is it true, Hugh, that you mean to bribe that man? Does he really mean to accept that payment for betraying his trust?"

"My dear child," said he, impatiently, "you don't understand such things. The world is the world, and not the paradise of a school-girl's essay. I can assure you that if I were to buy that bit of land from Chorley—and so far it has only been spoken of as a joke—that would be a very innocent transaction as things go; and there could be no bribing of the constituency, for they would not know of the public green till afterward. Bribery? There was more bribery in giving Mrs. Chorley the honor of making your acquaintance—"

"I know that," said the girl, with flushed cheeks. "I gathered that from the remarks of your friend Mr. Bolitho. And I was resolved that I, at least, would keep out of any such scheme."

"Your superior virtue," said Balfour, in a matter-of-fact way, "has asserted itself most unmistakably. I shall not be surprised to find that you have killed off the best chance I could have had of getting into the next Parliament."

"I should be sorry to see you get into any Parliament by such means," she said; for her whole soul was in revolt against this infamous proposal.

"Well, at all events," said he, "you must leave me to be the best judge of such matters, as far as my own conduct is concerned."

"Oh, I will not interfere," she said, with a business-like air, though her heart was throbbing cruelly. "On the contrary. If you wish to get back soon, in order to look after this borough, I will go whenever you please. There will be plenty for me to do at The Lilacs while you are in London."

"Do you mean," said he, regarding her with astonishment, "when we return to England, do you mean that you will go down to Surrey, and that I should remain in Piccadilly?"

There was a voice crying in her heart, "*O my husband — my husband!*" but she would pay no heed to it. Her face had got pale again, and she spoke calmly.

"If that were convenient to you. I should not wish to be in the way if you were entertaining your friends—I mean the friends who might be of use to you at Englebury. I should be sorry to interfere in any way with your chances of getting the seat, if you consider it right and honorable that you should try."

He paused for a moment, and then he said, sadly enough, "Very well."

CHAPTER XVII.

THE HOME-COMING.

OF course they did not quarrel. We live in the nineteenth century. Tolerance of opinion exists in the domestic circle as well as elsewhere; and no reasonable man would like his wife to be that vague and colorless reproduction of her husband which Lady Sylvia, all unknown to Balfour, had striven to be. She ought to have her own convictions; she ought to know how to govern her own conduct; nay, more, he would allow her to do as she pleased. There was but one condition attached. "You shall have your own way in everything," said the man in the story to his wife; "but you can't expect to have my way too." Lady Sylvia was welcome to act as she pleased; but then he reserved the same liberty for himself.

This decision he came to without any bitterness of feeling. He was quite anxious to make all possible excuses for her. Doubtless she preferred Surrey to Piccadilly. It is true, he had looked forward to her being a valuable helpmeet to him in his political life; but it was perhaps expecting too much of her that she should at once interest herself in the commonplace incidents of an election. He would be well content if this beautiful, tender-eyed creature, whose excessive sensitiveness of conscience was, after all, only the result of her ignorance of the world, were to wait for him in that sylvan retreat, ready to receive him and cheer him with the sweet solicitude of her loving ways. And in the mean time he would try to make their companionship as pleasant as possible; he would try to make this journey one to be remembered with pride and gratitude. If there were one or two subjects which they avoided in conversation, what of that?

And as soon as Lady Sylvia heard that the Chorleys and Mr. Bolitho had left Mainz, she became more tender and affectionate than ever toward her husband, and would do anything to meet his wishes. Learning that certain of his political friends were at the moment at Lucerne, she offered to go thither at once, so that he might have something to interest him apart from the monotony of a wedding trip; and although, of course, he did not accept the offer, he recognized her intention, and was grateful to her. Was it not enough occupation for him to watch the effect on this ingenuous mind of the new wonders that she saw, as they went on to Schaffhausen, and the Tyrol, and Verona, and Venice?

In their hotel at Venice, Balfour ran against a certain Captain Courtenay, with whom he had a slight acquaintance. They had a chat in the evening in the smoking-room.

"Seen Major Blythe lately?" said Balfour, among other things.

"No," answered the other, somewhat coldly.

"You don't know, I suppose," asked Balfour, quite unconcernedly, "how that business at the C—— Club came off?"

The young man with the fair mustache eyed him narrowly. It is not a safe thing to tell a man evil things of his relatives, unless you know how they stand with regard to each other.

"Yes, I do know—eh—an unfortunate business—very. Fact is, Blythe wouldn't explain. I suppose there was some delay about the posting of that letter; and—and—I have no doubt that he would have paid the money next day if he had not been bullied about it. You see, a man does not like to be challenged in that way, supposing he has made a trifling mistake—"

"Yes," said Balfour, nodding his head in acquiescence; "but how was it settled?"

"Well," said the other, with some embarrassment, "the fact is —well, the committee, don't you know? had to enforce the rules —and he wouldn't explain—and, in fact, he got a hint to resign—"

"Which he took, of course."

"I believe so."

Balfour said nothing further; but in his mind he coupled a

remark or two with the name of Major the Honorable Stephen Blythe which that gentleman would have been startled to hear.

Then he went up-stairs to the sitting-room, and found Lady Sylvia at the open casement, looking out on the clear, blue-green, lambent twilight.

"Well, good wife," said he, gayly, "are you beginning to think of trudging home now? We ought to see a little of The Lilacs before all the leaves are gone. And there won't be much to keep me in London now, I fancy; they are getting more and more certain that the Government won't bring on the dissolution before the new year."

She rose, and put a hand on each of his shoulders, and looked up into his face with grateful and loving eyes.

"That is so kind of you, Hugh. It will be so pleasant for us to get to know what home really is—after all these hotels. And you will be in time for the pheasants: I know several people will be so glad to have you."

Of course the merest stranger would be delighted to have so distinguished a person as Mr. Balfour come and shoot his pheasants for him; failing that, would she not herself, like a loyal and dutiful wife, go to her few acquaintances down there and represent to them the great honor they might have of entertaining her husband?

"I see there is to be a demonstration on the part of the agricultural laborers," said he, "down in Somersetshire. I should like to see that—I should like to have a talk with some of their leaders. But I am afraid we could not get back in time."

"My darling," she protested, seriously, "I can start at five minutes' notice. We can go to-night, if you wish."

"Oh no, it isn't worth while," said he, absently. And then he continued: "I'm afraid your friends the clergymen are making a mistake as regards that question. I don't know who these leaders are; I should like to know more precisely their character and aims; but it will do no good to call them agitators, and suggest that they should be ducked in horse-ponds—"

"It is infamous!" said Lady Sylvia. She knew nothing whatever about it. But she would have believed her husband if he had told her that St. Mark's was made of green cheese.

"I mean that it is unwise," said he, without any enthusiasm. "Christ meant his church to be the church of the poor. The rich man has a bad time of it in the Gospels. And you may depend on it that if you produce among the poorer classes the feeling that the Church of England is on the side of the rich—is the natural ally of the squires, landlords, and other employers—you are driving them into the hands of the Dissenters, and hastening on disestablishment."

"And serve them right too," said she, boldly, "if they betray their trust. When the Church ceases to be of the nation, let it cease to be the national church."

This was a pretty speech. How many weeks before was it that Lady Sylvia was vowing to uphold her beloved Church against all comers, but more especially against a certain malignant iconoclast of the name of Mrs. Chorley? And now she was not only ready to assume that one or two random and incautious speeches represented the opinion of the whole of the clergymen of England, but she was also ready to have the connection between Church and State severed in order to punish those recusants.

"I am not sure," said Balfour, apparently taking no notice of this sudden recantation, "that something of that feeling has not been produced already. The working-man of the towns jeers at the parson; the agricultural laborer distrusts him, and will grow to hate him if he takes the landlord's side in this matter. Now, why does not the Archbishop of Canterbury seize the occasion? Why does not he come forward and say, 'Hold a bit, my friends. Your claims may be just, or they may be exorbitant—that is a matter for careful inquiry—and you must let your landlords be heard on the other side. But, whatever happens, don't run away with the notion that the Church has no sympathy with you; that the Church is the ally of your landlord; that it is the interest of your parson to keep you poor, ill fed, ill lodged, and ignorant. On the contrary, who knows so much about your circumstances? Who more fitting to become the mediator between you and your landlord? You may prefer to have leaders from your own ranks to fight your battles for you; but don't imagine that the parson looks on unconcerned, and, above all, don't expect to find him in league with your opponents.' Some mischief could be avoided that way, I think."

"Hugh," said she, with a sudden burst of enthusiasm, "I will go down to Somersetshire with you."

"And get up on a chair and address a crowd," said he, with a smile. "I don't think they would understand your speech, many of them."

"Well," said she, "perhaps I shall be better employed in making The Lilacs look very pretty for your return. And I shall have those slippers made up for you by that time. And, oh, Hugh—I wanted to ask you—don't you think we should have those cane rocking-chairs taken away from the smoking-room, now the colder evenings are coming in, and morocco easy-chairs put in their stead?"

"I am sure whatever you do will be right," said he.

"And papa will be back from Scotland then," said she. "And he writes me that my uncle and his family are going down for a few days; and it will be so pleasant to have a little party to meet us at the station—"

The expression of his face changed suddenly.

"Did you say your uncle?" said he, with a cold stare.

"Yes," said she, with innocent cheerfulness; "it will be quite pleasant to have some friends to welcome us, after our long stay among strangers. And I know papa will want us to go straight to the Hall, and dine there; and it will be so nice to see the dear old place—will it not?"

"No doubt," said he. And then he added, "Sylvia, if any invitation of that sort reaches you, you may accept for yourself, if you wish, but please leave me out of it."

She looked up and perceived the singular alteration in his look; he had become cold, reserved, firm.

"What do you mean, Hugh?" she cried.

"Only this," said he, speaking distinctly. "I prefer not to dine at Willowby Hall if your uncle is there. I do not wish to meet him."

"Why?" she said, in amazement.

"I am not a tale-bearer," he answered. "It is enough for me that he is not the sort of person with whom I wish to sit down at table. More than that—but I am only expressing an opinion, mind; I don't wish to control your conduct—I think it might be better if you were to allow your acquaintance with your uncle's family quietly to drop."

"Do you mean," said she, with the pale face becoming slightly flushed, "that I am to resolve not to see those relatives of mine any more—without having a word of reason for it?"

"I wished to spare you needless pain," said he, in quite a gentle way. "If you want to know, I will tell you. To begin with, I don't think your uncle's dealings in regard to money matters are characterized by that precision—that—that scrupulous accuracy—"

"I understand," she said, quickly, and the color in her face deepened. "But I did not expect you, of all men in the world, to reproach any one for his poverty. I did not expect that. My uncle is poor, I know—"

"Pardon me, Sylvia, I never made your uncle's lack of money a charge against him : I referred to a sort of carelessness—forgetfulness, let us say—as regards other people's money. However, let that pass. The next thing is more serious. As I understand, your uncle has been involved in some awkward business—arising from whist-playing—at the C—— Club ; and I hear this evening that he has resigned in consequence."

"Who told you that ?"

"Captain Courtenay."

"The gentleman who is staying in this hotel ?"

"Yes."

"Have you anything else to say against my uncle ?" she demanded.

"I think I have said enough ; I would rather have said nothing at all."

"And you ask me," she said, with some indignation in her voice, "to cut myself adrift from my relatives because you have listened to some story told by a stranger in a coffee-room. What do I know about Captain Courtenay ? How can he tell what explanation my uncle may have of his having resigned that club ? I must say, Hugh, your request is a most extraordinary one."

"Now, now, Sylvia," he said, good-naturedly. "You know I made no request ; I do not wish to interfere in the slightest way with your liberty of action. It is true that I don't think your uncle and his family are fit people for you to associate with ; but you must act as you think best. I, for one, don't choose to be thrown into their society."

Now, Lady Sylvia never had any great affection for her aunt, and she was not likely to hold her cousin Honoria in dear remembrance ; but, after all, her relatives were her relatives, and she became indignant that they should be spoken of in this way.

"Why did you make no objection before? Why did you go and dine at their house?"

He laughed.

"It suited my purpose to go," said he, "for I expected to spend a pleasant evening with you."

"You saw nothing wrong in my visiting them then."

"Then I had no right to offer you advice."

"And now that you have," said she, with a proud and hurt manner, "what advice do I get? I am not to see my own relations. They are not proper persons. But I suppose the Chorleys are: is that the sort of society you wish me to cultivate? At all events," she added, bitterly, "my relatives happen to have an *h* or two in their possession."

"Sylvia," said he, going over and patting her on the shoulder, "you are offended—without cause. You can see as much of your uncle's family as you please. I had no idea you were so passionately attached to them."

That ended the affair for the moment; but during the next few days, as they travelled by easy stages homeward, an ominous silence prevailed as to their plans and movements subsequent to their reaching England. At Dover she found a telegram awaiting her at the hotel; without a word she put it before her husband. It was from Lord Willowby, asking his daughter by what train she and her husband would arrive, so that the carriage might be waiting for them.

"What shall I say?" she asked, at length.

"Well," said he, slowly, "if you are anxious to see your relatives, and to spend some time with them, telegraph that you will be by the train that leaves Victoria at 5.15. I will take you down to The Lilacs; but I must leave you there. It will suit me better to spend a few days in town at present."

Her face grew very pale.

"I don't think," she said, "I need trouble you to go down with me. I can get to Victoria by myself. 5.15, I think you said?"

She rung for a blank telegraph form.

"What are you going to do?" said Balfour, struck by something peculiar in her manner.

"I am going to telegraph to papa to meet me at the station, as I shall be alone."

"You will do nothing of the kind," said he, gently, but firmly. "You may associate with what people you please, and welcome; only there must be no public scandal as regards the relations between you and me. Either you will go on with me to Piccadilly, and remain there, or I go down with you to The Lilacs, and leave you to go over to the Hall, if you wish to do so."

She telegraphed to her father that they had postponed their return to The Lilacs, and would remain in town for the present. She bought a shilling novel at the station, and silently and assiduously cried behind it the greater part of the journey up to town. Arrived in London, the poor martyr suffered herself to be dragged away to that lonely house in Piccadilly. It was a sorrowful home-coming.

Then the cup of her sorrows was not yet full. With an inhuman cruelty, her husband (having had his own ends served) sought to make light of the whole matter. All that evening he tried to tease her into a smile of reconciliation; but her wrongs lay too heavily upon her. He had even the brutality to ask her whether she could invite the Chorleys to dine with them on the following Friday, and whether they had not better get a new dessert service for the occasion. He did well, she thought, to mention the Chorleys. These were the people he considered it fit that she should meet: her own relatives he would debar.

CHAPTER XVIII.

THE SOLITUDES OF SURREY.

PARLIAMENT was not dissolved that autumn, and there was no need that Englebury and its twin electors, Mr. and Mrs. Chorley, should interfere with the happiness of Mr. and Lady Sylvia Balfour. Both the young people, indeed, would have scouted the notion that any fifteen dozen of Chorleys could have possessed that power. Surely it was possible for them to construct a sufficiently pleasant *modus vivendi*, even if they held somewhat different views about political matters.

But long before the crisis of a General Election occurred, Hugh Balfour had managed to think out very seriously several questions regarding the relations between himself and his young wife. He was determined that he would be largely generous and considerate to her. When he saw how tenderly devoted to him she was; when he got to know more of those clear perceptions of duty and obedience and unhesitating unselfishness that governed her conduct; when he saw how that sweetness and strange sincerity of manner of hers charmed every one who was introduced to her, surely he had every reason to be generously considerate. It is true that he had dreamed some sentimental dream of a helpmeet who would be constantly at his side in the rough work of the world; but was not that his own folly? It was a pretty notion, doubtless; but look at the actual facts. Was it desirable that this tenderly nurtured, sensitive girl should plunge into the animosities and anxieties of political life? Her first slight acquaintance, for example, with the ways of a borough election had only shocked and pained her; nay, more, it had very nearly produced a quarrel between him and her. This kind of risk was quite unnecessary. He laughed at the notion of her being an enthusiast for or against the Birmingham League. How could she be deeply interested in the removal of Shrewsbury School, or in Lord Kimberley's relations with the Pacific Railway, or in the expedition of the Dutch against Acheen? Would he gain any more knowledge of the working of the London vestries, supposing he dragged her dainty little feet through the hideous slums of the great city? At this moment he was going off for a riding excursion, after the manner of Cobbett, through Somersetshire. He wanted to find out for himself—for this man was no great enthusiast in politics, but had, on the other hand, a patient desire to satisfy himself as to facts—what were the actual conditions and aspirations of agricultural life there; and he wanted to find out, too, what would be the chances of a scheme of sanitary reform for the rural districts. Now, of what possible good could Lady Sylvia be in inspecting piggeries? The thing was absurd. No, no. Her place was in the roomy phaeton he had brought down from town for her, behind the two beautiful black horses which she drove with admirable nerve and skill. She formed part of a pretty picture as we used to see her in these moist and blustering November days. Black clouds behind the yellow elms; the gusty south wind whirling the ruddy leaves from the branches; a wild glare of light shining along the wet road until it gleamed like a canal of brilliant silver; and in the midst of this dazzling radiance, the small figure perched high on the phaeton, clad all in furs, a scarlet feather in her hat, and the sweetest of smiles for known passers-by on the fresh young face. Was it any wonder that he left her to her familiar Surrey lanes, and to the amusement of ordering her small household of The Lilacs, and to the snugness of her father's library in the evening, he going off by himself to that humdrum business of prying about Somersetshire villages?

He was away for about ten days in Somersetshire. Then he wrote to her that he would return to London by way of Englebury; and she was not to expect him very soon, for he might be detained in London by a lot of business. It would not be worth her while to come up. His time would be fully occupied, and she was much better down in Surrey, enjoying the fresh air and exercise of the country.

He had not the slightest doubt that she was enjoying herself. Since her marriage she had not at all lived the secluded life she had led at the Hall. Many a night there were more carriages rolling along the dark and muddy lanes toward The Lilacs than had driven up to the Hall in the previous month. Balfour was the most hospitable of men, now that he had some one to take direction of his dinner-parties; and as these parties were necessarily and delightfully small, there was nothing for it but to have plenty of them. The neighbors were convinced there never had been a more fortunate match. Happiness shone on the face of the young house-mistress as she sat at the top of the table which had been florally decorated with her own hands. Her husband was quite openly proud of her; he took not the slightest pains to conceal the fact, as most young husbands laboriously and ineffectually do. And then the wonderful way in which he professed to be interested about those local matters which form, alas! the staple of talk at rural dinner-parties! You would have thought he had no care for anything beyond horses, dogs, and pheasants. He was grieved to hear that the parson's wife would not countenance the next charity concert, but he was quite sure that Lady Sylvia would win her over. He hoped it was not true that old Somebody or other was to be sold out of Something farm, after having occupied it for forty years, but feared it was too true that he had taken to drink. And one night, when he heard that a neighboring master of harriers had intimated that he would cease to hunt if he were not guaranteed a sum of £2000 a year, Balfour declared that he would make up whatever deficit the subscription might show.   He became popular in our neighborhood. He never talked about politics, but gave good dinners instead.

Indeed, there were one or two of us who could not quite reconcile Mr. Balfour's previous history with his present conduct. You would have thought, to hear him speak, that his highest notion of human happiness was shooting rabbits on Willowby Heath, although, as every one knew, he was a very indifferent shot.   Then the fashion in which he drove round with his wife, paying afternoon calls!   Gentlemen who pay afternoon calls are ordinarily more amiable than busy; and how this man, with all his eager ambitions and activities, could dawdle away the afternoon in a few dull drawing-rooms in the country, was a strange thing to some of us.   Was he so proud of this young wife of his that he was never tired of showing her off?   Or was it—seeing that by-and-by he would be away in the hurry and worry of an election, and perhaps locked up for six months in the close atmosphere of the House of Commons—was it that he wished Lady Sylvia to have as many friends as possible down in these rural solitudes, so as to lighten the time for her?

At all events, she seemed to enjoy her married life sufficiently well.   This neighborhood had always been her home.   She was within easy driving or riding distance of the Hall, and could see that things were going straight there.   She had many friends. When her husband left her for a week or two to her own devices, he had no doubt at all but that her time would be fully occupied, and that her life was passing as pleasantly as could be desired.

When Lady Sylvia got that letter, saying he would return from Somersetshire by way of Englebury, and would remain a few days in London, she was sitting at one of the French windows of The Lilacs, looking out on a dismal December afternoon, the rain slowly drizzling down on the laurels and the wet gravel-paths.   She took it from the servant, and opened it with much composure.   She had been schooling herself for some time back.

She read the letter through with great calmness, and folded it again, and put it in her pocket.   Then she thought she would go

and get some needle-work, for it was a melancholy business this
staring out at the rain. But as she rose to pass through the
room, the sensitive lips began to tremble strangely; and suddenly, with a passionate abandonment of despair and grief, she threw
herself on a couch, and hid her face in the cushion, and burst
into a long and bitter fit of crying. The proud, hurt soul could
no longer contain itself. It was in vain that she had been training herself to play the part which he had seemingly allotted her.
She saw her husband being removed further and further from
her; his interests and occupations and hopes were becoming
more and more a matter personal to himself; their lives were
divided, and the barrier was daily growing more hopelessly obvious and impassable. Was this, then, the end of those beautiful
dreams of what marriage was to make their future life together?
Was she already a widow, and forsaken?

Then this wild fit of despair and grief took another turn, and
her heart grew hot with anger against those things that had come
between her husband and herself. Once or twice, in her court-
ship days, she had entertained a passing feeling of resentment
against the House of Commons, for that it took away from her
so much of her lover's thoughts; but now a more vehement jealousy possessed her, and she regarded the whole business of public
life as a conspiracy against domestic happiness. The Chorleys?
No, not the Chorleys. These people were too contemptible to
come between her husband and herself. But they were a part,
and an ugly representative part, of that vulgarizing, distracting,
hateful political life, which was nevertheless capable of drawing
a man away from his wife and home, and filling his mind with
gross cares and mean ambitions. The poor, spoiled, hurt child
felt in her burning heart that the British Constitution had cruelly wronged her. She regarded with a bitter anger and jealousy
the whole scheme of representative government. Was it not
those electioneering people, and the stupid laborers of Somersetshire, and the wretched newspapers that were writing about doz-
ens of subjects they did not understand, who had robbed her of
her husband?

A servant tapped at the door. She jumped up, and stood there
calm and dignified, her back to the window, so that her face was
scarcely visible in the shadow. The man only wanted to put
some coals on the fire. After he was gone, Lady Sylvia dried

her eyes, sat down once more at the window, and began to consider, her lips a trifle more firmly put together than usual.

After all, there was a good deal of womanly judgment and decision about this girl, in spite of all the fanciful notions and excess of sensitiveness that had sprung from her solitary musings. Was it seemly that she should fret like a child over her own unhappiness? Her first duty was her duty as a wife. If her husband believed it to be better that he should fight his public life alone, she would do her best in the sphere to which she had been relegated, and make his home as pleasant for him as she could. Crying because her husband went off by himself to Englebury? She grew ashamed of herself. She began to accuse herself with some indignation. She was ready to say to herself that she was not fit to be anybody's wife.

Full of a new and eager virtue, she hastily rung the bell. The man did not fall down in a fit when she said she wanted the phaeton sent round as soon as possible, but he gently reminded her ladyship that it was raining, and perhaps the brougham— But no ; her ladyship would have the phaeton, and at once. Then she went up-stairs to get dressed, and her maid produced all sorts of water-proofs.

Why so much haste? Why the eager delight of her face? As she drove briskly along the wet lanes, the rain-drops were running down her cheeks, but she looked as happy and comfortable as if it had been a breezy day in June. The horses splashed the mud about ; the wheels swished through the pools. In the noise, how could the man behind her hear his young mistress gayly humming to herself,

> "Should he upbraid,
> I'll own that he'll prevail ?"

He thought she had gone mad, to go out on a day like this, and no doubt made some remarks to himself when he had to jump down into the mud to open a certain iron gate.

Now, there was in this neighborhood a lady who had for many a day been on more or less friendly terms with Lady Sylvia, but who seemed to become even more intimate with her after her marriage. The fact is, Mr. Balfour appeared to take a great liking to this person, and was continually having his wife and her brought together. Those who know her well are familiar with her tricks of manner and thinking—her worship of bishops, her scorn of husbands in general, and her demeanor of awful dignity, which has gained for her the style and title of Our Most Sovereign Lady Five-foot-three; but there is no denying the fact that there is about her eyes a certain pathetic, affectedly innocent look that has an odd power over those who do not know her well, and that invites those people to an instant friendliness and confidence. Well, this was the person whom Lady Sylvia now wished to see; and after she had taken off her wet water-proofs in the hall and dried her face, she went straight into the drawing-room, and in a minute or two was joined by her friend.

"My dear Lady Sylvia," cried her Most Gracious Majesty, kissing the young thing with maternal fondness, what could have brought you out on such a day—and in the phaeton, too?"

Lady Sylvia's cheeks were quite rosy after the rain. Her eyes were bright and glad. She said, blithely,

"I came out for the fun of it. And to beg you to give me a cup of tea. And to have a long chat with you."

Surély these were sufficient reasons; at least, they satisfied the elder woman, who rung for the tea, and got it, and then assumed a wise and confidential air, in order to hear the confessions of this gushing young creature. Had she formed some awful project of going up to London on a shopping excursion, in the absence of her husband? or had the incorrigible Blake been grumbling, as usual, and threatening to leave?

Nothing of the kind. It was the elder woman who was to be lectured and admonished — on the duty of wives, on the right of husbands to great consideration, and so forth, and so forth. Of course the lecture was introduced by a few playful and preliminary bits of gossip, so as to remove from the mind of the listener the notion that it had been premeditated; nevertheless, Lady Sylvia seemed to be very earnest on this matter. After all, said she, it was the lot of women to suffer. Those who seemed to be most fortunately placed in the world had doubtless their secret cares; there was nothing for it but to bear them with a brave heart. A wife could not lessen the anxieties of her husband by sharing them; she would more probably increase them by her womanly fear and exaggeration. It was not to be expected that a woman should be constantly intermeddling in affairs of which she could not possibly be a fair judge. A great many wives thought they were neglected, when it was only their excessive vanity that was wounded : that was foolish on the part of those wives. *U. s. w.* Lady Sylvia talked bravely and gladly. She was preaching a new gospel; she had the eagerness of a convert.

Her listener, who, notwithstanding that sham dignity of hers, has a great deal of womanly tact and tenderness, merely listened, and smilingly agreed. But when Lady Sylvia, after refusing repeated entreaties that she should stay to dinner, drove away in the dusk and the rain to her solitary home, it was observed that her friend was unusually thoughtful. She scarcely said anything at all during dinner; although once, after an interval of profound silence, she startled us all by asking, abruptly,

"Why does not Mr. Balfour take Lady Sylvia up to his house in Piccadilly?"

CHAPTER XIX.

THE CANDIDATE.

On that same afternoon Mr. Hugh Balfour was also out driving—in a dog-cart—and his companion was Mr. Bolitho, whom he had picked up at an out-of-the-way station, and was conducting to Englebury. It was a dismal drive. There was not the rain here that there was in Surrey, but in its place there was a raw, damp, gray mist that hung about the woods and fields, and dripped from the withered briers in the hedges, and covered the thick top-coats of the two men with a fur of wet. Neither cigar nor pipe would keep alight in this cold drizzle. Balfour's left hand, the fingers closed on the spongy reins, was thoroughly benumbed. Even the bland and cheerful Billy Bolitho had no more jokes left.

"I suppose," said Balfour, at last, amidst the clatter of the cob's hoofs on the muddy road—"I suppose we might as well go up and see the Chorleys'this evening?"

"I would rather say the morning," answered Mr. Bolitho, looking mournfully out from between the points of his coat collar at the black stump of his cigar. "Chorley is one of those uncomfortable people who dine about five and have prayers at nine."

It was wrong of Mr. Bolitho to make this random charge against the Englebury solicitor, for he knew absolutely nothing about the matter. He was, however, thoroughly uncomfortable. He was cold, damp, and hungry. He had visions of the "Green Man" at Englebury, of an ample dinner, a warm room, and a bottle of port-wine. Was he going to adventure out again into this wretched night, after he had got thoroughly dry and comfortable, all because of a young man who seemed to pay no heed to the requirements of digestion?

It was quite dark when they at last drove over the bridge and up into the main thoroughfare of Englebury, and right cheerful looked the blazing shops of the small town. They passed under the sign of the "Green Man" into the spacious archway; the great bell summoned the hostler from out of the gloom; they jumped down and stamped their feet; and then they found themselves face to face with a very comely damsel, tall and slender and dark of face, who, in the absence of her sister, the landlady, wanted to know if the gentlemen would order dinner before going up-stairs to their rooms. As she made the suggestion, she glanced up at a goodly row of joints and fowls that were suspended from the roof of the central hall, outside the capacious, shining, and smiling bar.

"You order the dinner, Bolitho," said Balfour. "I'm going to see that the cob is looked to."

"Confound the cob!" said the other; but Balfour had already disappeared in the darkness. So he turned with great contentment to the distinguished-looking and gracious young person, and entered into a serious consultation with her. Mr. Bolitho was not in the habit of letting either cobs or country solicitors stand in the way of his dinner.

And a very sound and substantial dinner it was that they had in the snug little room on the first floor, after they had got on some dry clothing and were growing warm again. There was a brisk fire blazing in the grate; there were no fewer than four candles in the room, two on the table and two on the mahogany sideboard. Balfour laughed at the business-like manner in which Mr. Bolitho ploughed his way through the homely feast; but he was sharply hungry himself, and he so far departed from his ordinary habits as to call for a tankard of foaming stout. The agreeable young lady herself waited on them, although she did not know as yet that one of the strangers wished to represent her native town in Parliament? She seemed a little surprised, however, when, at the end of dinner, the younger gentleman asked whether she could send him up a clay pipe, his own wooden one having gone wrong. She had overheard the two friends talking about very great persons indeed as though they were pretty familiar with them, and a fourpenny cigar from the bar would, she considered, have been more appropriate. But the other gentleman redeemed himself in her eyes by ordering a bottle of the very best port-wine they had in the house.

"Gracious goodness!" cried Balfour, with a loud laugh, "what do you mean, Bolitho?"

"I mean to make myself comfortable," said the other, doggedly.

"Oh, it is comfortable you call it," remarked the younger man. "Well, it is a good phrase."

"Yes, I mean to make myself comfortable," said Mr. Bolitho, when he had drawn in his chair to the fire, and lit a cigar, and put a glass of port on the mantel-piece, "and I also mean to give you some advice—some good and excellent advice—which is all the more appropriate since you may be said to be beginning to-day your canvass of the borough of Englebury. Well, I have had to do with a good many candidates in my time; but I will say this for you, that you are just about the last man in the world I would choose to run for a seat if I had any choice."

"That is cheerful, at any rate," said Balfour, who had lit his long clay, and was contentedly stretching out his legs to the fire. "Go on."

"I say it deliberately. If you get in at all, it won't be through any action on your own part. I would almost rather fight the election for you in your absence. Why, man, you have no more notion of conciliating anybody than an arctic bear has. Don't you know you are asking a great favor when you ask people to return you to Parliament? You don't suppose you can cheek every constituency as you cheeked those poor wretches at Ballinascroon?"

"My dear philosopher and friend," said the culprit, "I am not aware of having ever addressed a word to any elector of Englebury, barring your Mr. Chorley."

"I don't mean here or now," said Bolitho, who thought he would read this young man a sound lesson when he was about it.

"I mean always and everywhere. A man cannot get on in politics who blurts out his opinions as you do yours. You can't convince a man by calling him a fool. You have been spoiled. You got your first seat too easily, and you found yourself independent of the people who elected you. If you had had to conciliate your constituency as some men have, it would have been useful practice for you. I tell you a member of Parliament cannot afford to be continually declaring his opinions, as if he had all the wisdom in the world—"

Here the culprit, far from being meek and attentive, burst out laughing.

"The fact is, Bolitho, all this harangue means that you want me to be civil to Chorley. Doesn't it, now?"

Mr. Bolitho, being in a pleasant humor, suffered a shrewd, bland smile to appear about the corners of his mouth.

"Well," said Balfour, frankly, "I mean to be enormously civil to old Chorley—so long as he doesn't show up with some humbug. But mind you, if that old thief, who wants to sell the borough in order to get a good price for his filched common, begins to do the high virtuous business, then the case becomes altered. Civil? Oh yes, I shall be civil enough. But you don't expect me to black his boots?"

"You see," said Bolitho, slowly, "you are in rather an awkward position with regard to these two people—I will tell you that honestly. You have had no communication with them since you first saw them in Germany?"

"No, none."

"Well, you know, my gay young friend, you pretty nearly put your foot in it by your chaffing old Chorley about selling the piece of green. Then, no sooner had they got over that than Lady Sylvia— You know what I mean."

Balfour looked a bit annoyed.

"Leave Lady Sylvia out of it," said he. "She does not want to interfere in these things at all."

"No," said Mr. Bolitho, cautiously; "but you see there is the effect of that—that remark of hers to be removed. The Chorleys may have forgotten; they will make allowances—"

"They can do as they like about that," said Balfour, bluntly; "but Lady Sylvia won't trouble them again. Now as to the bit of common?"

"Well, if I were you, I would say nothing about it at present."

"I don't mean to, nor in the future either."

"You don't intend to make him an offer?"

"Of course not."

Mr. Bolitho looked at the young man. Had he been merely joking when he seemed to entertain seriously the project of bribing Mr. Chorley by purchasing his land from him? Or had some new and alien influence thwarted his original purpose? Mr. Bolitho instantly thought of Lady Sylvia.

"Perhaps you are right," said he, after a second or two. "Chorley would be shy of taking an offer, after you had directly described the thing as bribing the town. But, all the more, you should be conciliatory to him and his wife. Why should they fight for you?"

"I don't know."

"What have you to offer them?"

"Nothing."

"Then, you are asking a great favor, as I said before."

"Well, you know, Bolitho, Englebury has its duty to perform. You shouldn't make it all a matter of private and personal interchange of interests. Englebury has its place in the empire; it has the proud privilege of singling out a faithful and efficient person to represent it in Parliament; it has its relations with the British Constitution; and when it finds that it has the opportunity of returning so distinguished a person as myself, why shouldn't it jump at the chance? You have no faith in public virtue, Bolitho. You would buy land, and bribe. Now, that is wrong."

"It's all very well for you to joke about it," said Mr. Bolitho, rather gloomily, "but you'll sing a different tune if you find yourself without a seat after the next General Election."

On the following morning they walked up through the town which Mr. Balfour aspired to represent, toward Mr. Chorley's house. It was a bright morning after the rain, the sun shining pleasantly on the quaint old town, with its huddled red-and-white houses, its gray church, its high-arched bridge that spanned a turbidly yellow river. Mr. Chorley's house stood near the top of the hill—a plain, square, red brick building, surrounded by plenty of laurels and other evergreens, and these again enclosed by a high brick wall. They were ushered into a small drawing-room, stuffed full of ornaments and smelling of musk. In a few moments Mr. and Mrs. Chorley entered together.

Surely nothing could be more friendly than the way in which they greeted the young man. The small, horsey-looking solicitor was prim and precise in his manner, it is true; but then he was always so. As for Mrs. Chorley, she regarded the young man with a pleasant look from over her silver spectacles, and begged him and Mr. Bolitho to be seated, and hoped they had had an agreeable drive on that bright morning. And when Mr. Bolitho explained that they had arrived on the previous evening, and had put up at the "Green Man," she was good enough to express her regret that they had not come right on and accepted the hospitality of herself and her husband for the night.

"But perhaps," said she, suddenly, and with an equally sudden change in her manner—"perhaps Lady Sylvia is with you?"

"Oh dear, no!" said Balfour, and he instantly changed the subject by beginning to talk about his experiences down in Somersetshire, and how he had heard by accident that Mr. Bolitho was in the neighborhood of Englebury, and how he had managed to pick him up. That alarming look of formality disappeared from Mrs. Chorley's face. Mr. Chorley suggested some sherry, which was politely declined. Then they had a talk about the weather.

But Balfour was not a timid man, and he disliked beating about the bush.

"Well, Mr. Chorley," said he, "how are your local politics? Government very unpopular? Or, rather, I should ask—as interesting me more nearly—is old Harnden still unpopular?"

"Mr. 'Arnden is not very popular at present," said Mr. Chorley, with some caution. "He does his duty well in Parliament, no doubt; but, after all, there are—certain courtesies which—which are due to one's constituents—"

"Exactly," said Balfour. "I have discovered that in the case of the place I represent. The courtesies that pass between me and the people of Ballinascroon are almost too beautiful. Well, what about the chance of a vacancy at the next General Election?"

In reply to this blunt question, Mr. Chorley regarded the young man with his shrewd, watchful, small blue eyes, and said, slowly,

"I don't know, sir, that Mr. 'Arnden has any intention at present of resigning his seat."

This guardedness was all thrown away on Balfour.

"What would be my chances," said he, curtly, "if I came down and contested the seat?"

Here Mrs. Chorley broke in. From the moment they had begun to speak of the next election, the expression of her face had changed. The thin lips were drawn more firmly together. Instead of the beaming maternal glance over her spectacles, there was a proud and cold look that was at once awful and ominous.

"If I may be allowed to speak, Mr. Balfour," said she, in lofty accents, "I would say that it is rather strange that you should mention any such proposal to us. When we last spoke of it, you will remember that some remarks were applied to us by Lady Sylvia which were never apologized for—by her, at least. Have you any explanation to make?"

There was a sudden flash of fire in the deep-set gray eyes. Apologize for his wife to such people as these?

"Explanation?" said he; and the tone in which he spoke caused the heart of Mr. Bolitho to sink within him. "If Lady Sylvia spoke hastily, that only convinced me the more of the folly of allowing women to interfere in politics. I think the business of an election is a matter to be settled between men."

There was a second or two of awful silence. A thunder-bolt seemed to have fallen. Mrs. Chorley rose.

"I, at least," said she, in majestic accents, and with an indescribable calm, "will not interfere in this election. Gentlemen, good-morning. Eugenius, the chaise is at the door."

With that she walked in a stately manner out of the room, leaving the burden of the situation on her unfortunate husband. He looked rather bewildered; but nevertheless he felt bound to assert the dignity of the family.

"I must say, Mr. Balfour," said he, rather nervously, "that your language is—is unusual. Mrs. Chorley only asked for—for an expression of regret—an apology which was only our due after the remarks of—of Lady Sylvia."

By this time Balfour had got on his feet, and taken his hat in his hand. All the Celtic blood in his veins was on fire.

"An apology!" he said. "Why, man, you must be mad! I tell you that every word my wife said was absolutely true. Do you expect her to send you a humble letter, begging for your forgiveness? I apologized for her hastiness at the time; I am sorry I did. For what she said then, I say now—that it is quite monstrous you should suddenly propose to use your influence in the borough on behalf of a man who was an absolute stranger to you; and if you imagined that I was going to bribe you by buying that waste land, or going to bribe the borough by giving them a public green, then get that notion out of your head as soon as possible. Good-morning, Mr. Chorley. Pray tell Mrs. Chorley that I am very sorry if I have hurt her feelings; but pray tell her too that my wife is not conscious of having said anything that demands an apology."

And so this mad young man and his companion went out, and walked down the main street of Englebury in the pleasant sunshine. And it was all in vain that Mr. Bolitho tried to put in his piteous prayers and remonstrances. The borough? He would see the borough sink into the bottomless pit before he would allow his wife to apologize for a speech that did her infinite honor! The election? He would fight the place if there were ten thousand Chorleys arrayed against him!

"I tell you you have gone stark staring mad," said the despairing Mr. Bolitho. "Chorley will immediately go over to Harnden—you will see. His wife will goad him to it. And how can you think of contesting the seat against Harnden and Chorley combined?"

Nature had not conferred a firm jaw on Mr. Hugh Balfour for nothing.

"I tell you, in turn," said the young man, who was neither to hold nor to bind, simply because something had been said about his wife—"I tell you, in turn, that I mean to contest the seat all the same; and, what is more, by the Lord Harry, I mean to win it!"

CHAPTER XX.

AT A CERTAIN CLUB.

"Bolitho," said Mr. Hugh Balfour, as the two companions were preparing to leave for the London train, "when you see my wife, don't say anything to her about this affair. She would only be annoyed to think that she was in any way connected with such a wretched wrangle. Women are better out of these things."

Now, Mr. Bolitho was somewhat vexed. The guiding principle in life of this bland, elderly, easy-going gentleman was to make friends everywhere, or, at least, acquaintances, so that you could scarcely have mentioned to him a borough in England in which he did not know, more or less slightly, some man of influence. And here he had been involved in a quarrel—all because of the impetuous temper of this foolish young man—with the ruling politician of Englebury!

"I don't think," said he, with a wry smile, "that I am likely to see Lady Sylvia."

"What do you mean?" Balfour asked, as they set out to walk to the station.

"Oh, well, you know," replied the astute Parliamentary agent, with this sorry laugh still on his face, "I have a strong suspicion—you will correct me if I am wrong—that Lady Sylvia looks on me as a rather dangerous and disreputable person, who is likely to lead you into bad ways—bribery and corruption, and all that. I am quite sure from her manner to me at Mainz that she considered me to be the author of an abominable conspiracy to betray the people of Englebury."

"Yes, I think she did," Balfour said, with a laugh, "and I think she was right. You were the author of it, no doubt, Bolitho. But then it was all a joke; we were all in it, to the extent of talking about it. What I wish to impress on your young mind is, that women don't understand jokes of that sort, and—and it would have been wiser to have said nothing about it before Lady Sylvia. In fact," he added, with more firmness, "I don't wish my wife to be mixed up in any electioneering squabble."

"Quite right, quite right," responded Mr. Bolitho, with grave suavity; but he knew very well why Mr. Hugh Balfour had never asked him to dine at The Lilacs.

"Now," said Balfour, when they had reached the station and got their tickets, "we shall be in London between six and seven. What do you say to dining with me? I shall be a bachelor for a few evenings, before going down to the country."

Mr. Bolitho was nothing loath. A club dinner would be grateful after his recent experience of rural inns.

"At the Oxford and Cambridge, or the Reform? Which shall it be?" asked the young man, carelessly.

But Mr. Bolitho regarded it as a serious matter. He was intimately acquainted with the cooking at both houses—in fact, with the cooking at pretty nearly every club in the parish of St. James's. After some delay, he chose the Reform; and he was greatly relieved when he saw his companion go off to telegraph to the steward of the club to put down his guest's name in the books. That showed forethought. He rather dreaded Mr. Balfour's well-known indifference about such matters. But if he was telegraphing to the steward, surely there was nothing to fear.

And when at length they reached London, and had driven straight on to the club, the poor man had amply earned his dinner. He had been cross-examined about this person and that person, had been driven into declaring his opinion on this question and that, had been alternately laughed at and lectured, until he thought the railway journey was never going to end. And now as they sat down at the small white table, Mr. Balfour was in a more serious mood, and was talking about the agricultural laborer. A paper had just been read at the Farmers' Club which would doubtless be very valuable as giving the employers' side of the question; did Mr. Bolitho know where a full report of that address could be got?

Mr. Bolitho was mutely staring at the framed bill of fare that the waiter had brought to the table. Was it possible, then, that Balfour had ordered no dinner at all? Was he merely going to ask—in flagrant violation of the rules of the club—for some haphazard thing to take the place of a properly prepared dinner?

"Will you have some soup? Do you ever take soup?" asked his host, absently; and his heart sunk within him.

"Yes, I will take some soup," said he, gloomily.

They had the soup. Mr. Balfour was again plunged in the question of agricultural labor. He did not notice that the waiter was calmly standing over them.

"Oh," said he, suddenly recalling himself—"fish? Do you ever take fish, Bolitho?"

"Well, yes, I will take some fish," said Mr. Bolitho, somewhat petulantly: at this rate of waiting they would finish their dinner about two in the morning.

"Bring some fish, waiter—any fish—salmon," said he, at a

venture; for he was searching in a handful of papers for a letter he wished to show his guest. When he was informed that there was no salmon, he asked for any fish that was ready, or any joint that was ready; and then he succeeded in finding the letter.

They had some fish too. He was talking now about the recently formed association of the employers of labor. He absently poured out a glass of water and drank some of it. Mr. Bolitho's temper was rising.

"My dear fellow," Balfour said, suddenly observing that his guest's plate was empty, "I beg your pardon. You'll have some joint now, won't you?" They always have capital joints here; and it saves so much time to be able to come in at a moment's notice and have a cut. I generally make that my dinner. Waiter, bring some beef, or mutton, or whatever there is. And you were saying, Bolitho, that this association might turn out a big thing?"

Mr. Bolitho was now in a pretty thorough-going rage. He had not had a drop of anything to drink. In fact, he would not drink anything now—not even water. He would sooner parch with thirst. But if ever, he vowed to himself—if ever again he was so far left to himself as to accept an invitation to dine with this thick-headed and glowering-eyed Scotchman, then he would allow them to put strychnine in every dish.

If Mr. Bolitho had not got angry over the wretched dinner he was asked to eat, he would frankly have reminded his host that he wanted something to drink. But his temper once being up, he had grown exceedingly bitter about the absence of wine. He had become proud. He longed for a glass of the water before him, but he would not take it. He would wait for the satisfaction of seeing his enemy overcome with shame when his monstrous neglect was revealed to him.

Temper, however, is a bad substitute for wine when a man is thirsty. Moreover, to all appearance, this crass idiot was likely to finish his dinner and go away without any suspicion that he had grievously broken the laws of common decency and hospitality. He took a little sip of water now and again as innocently as a dipping swallow. And at length Mr. Bolitho could bear it no longer. Thirst and rage combined were choking him.

"Don't you think, Balfour," said he, with an outward calm that revealed nothing of the wild volcano within—"don't you think one might have a glass of wine of some sort?"

Balfour, with a stare of surprise, glanced round the table. There certainly was no wine there.

"My dear fellow," said he, with the most obvious and heartfelt compunction, "I really beg your pardon. What wine do you drink? Will you have a glass of sherry?"

Bolitho was on the point of returning to his determination of drinking nothing at all; but the consuming thirst within was too strong for him. He was about to accept this offer sulkily, when the member for Ballinascroon seemed to recollect that he was entertaining a guest.

"Oh no," he said, anxiously; "of course you will have some champagne. Waiter, bring the wine list. There you are, Bolitho; pick out what you want, like a good fellow. It was really very forgetful of me."

By this time they had got to the celery and cheese. Mr. Bolitho had scarcely had any dinner; his thirst had prevented his eating, and his anger had driven him into a most earnest and polite attention to his companion's conversation. But when the champagne arrived, and he had drunk the first glass at a draught, nature revived within him. The strained and glassy look left his eyes; his natural bland expression began to appear. He attacked the cheese and celery with vigor. The wine was sound and dry, and Mr. Bolitho had some good leeway to make up. He began to look on Balfour as not so bad a sort of fellow, after all; it was only his tremendous earnestness that made him forgetful of the smaller things around him.

"And so," said he, with a dawning smile breaking over his face, "you mean to go, unaided and alone, and fight the whole paction of your enemies in Englebury—the Chorleys, old Harnden, Reginald Key, and the hunting parson—all together?"

"Well," said Mr. Balfour, cheerfully, "I sha'n't try it if I can see an easier chance elsewhere. But I am not afraid. Don't you see how I should appeal to the native dignity of the electors to rise and assert itself against the political slavery that has been imposed on the borough? Bolitho, Englebury shall be free. Englebury shall suffer no longer the dictation of an interested solicitor."

"That's all very well," said Mr. Bolitho; "but Chorley owns half the *Englebury Mercury*."

"I will start the *Englebury Banner*."

"And suppose Harnden should resign in favor of Key?"

"My dear friend, I have heard on very good authority that there is not the least chance of Key being in England at that time. The Government are sure to try the effect of some other malarious place. I have heard several consulships and island governorships suggested; but you are quite right—he is a hard man to kill; and I believe their only hesitation so far has been owing to the fact that there was no sufficiently deadly place open. But they will be even with him sooner or later. Then as for your hunting parson—I could make friends with him in ten minutes. I never saw a hunting parson; but I have a sneaking liking for him. I can imagine him — a rosy-cheeked fellow, broad-shouldered, good-humored, a famous judge of horse-flesh and of port-wine, generous in his way, but exacting a stern discipline in exchange for his blankets and joints at Christmas. He shall be my ally—not my enemy."

"Ah," said Mr. Bolitho, with a sentimental sigh, "it is a great pity you could not persuade Lady Sylvia to go down with you. When a candidate has a wife—young, pretty, pleasant-mannered—it is wonderful what help she can give him."

"Yes, I dare say," said Balfour, with a slight change in his manner. "But it is not Lady Sylvia's wish—and it certainly isn't mine—that she should meddle in any election. There are some women fitted for that kind of thing (doubtless excellent women in their way), but she is not one of them, and I don't particularly care that she should be."

Mr. Bolitho felt that he had made a mistake, and he resolved in future not to mention Lady Sylvia at all. This wild adoration on the part of the young man might pass away; it might even pass away before the General Election came on, in which case Balfour might not be averse from having her pretty face and serious eyes win him over a few friends. In the mean time, Mr. Bolitho hinted something about a cigar, and the two companions went up-stairs.

Now, when Balfour drove up that night to his house in Piccadilly, he was surprised to see an unnecessary number of rooms dimly lighted. He had telegraphed to the house-keeper, whom they always left there, to have a bedroom ready for him, as he intended to have his meals at his club during his short stay in town. When he rung, it was Jackson who opened the door.

"Hallo, Jackson," said he, "are you here?"

"Yes, sir. Her ladyship sent us up two days ago to get the house ready. There is a letter for you, sir, up-stairs."

He went up-stairs to his small study, and got the letter. It was a pretty little message, somewhat formal in style, to be sure, but affectionate and dutiful. Lady Sylvia had considered it probable he might wish to have some gentlemen friends to dine with him while in town, and she had sent the servants up to have everything ready, so that he should not have to depend entirely on his club. She could get on very well with Anne, and she had got old Blake over from the Hall to sleep in the house. She added that as he might have important business to transact in connection with his visit to Englebury, he was on no account to cut short his stay in London prematurely. She was amusing herself very well. She had called on So-and-so and So-and-so. Her papa had just sent her two brace of pheasants and any number of rabbits. The harriers had met at Willowby Clump on the previous Saturday. The School-board school was to be finished on the following week—and so forth.

He put the letter on the table, his eyes still dwelling on it thoughtfully; and he lit his pipe, and sunk into a big easy-chair.

"Poor old Syllabus," he was thinking—for he caught up this nickname from Johnny Blythe—"this is her notion of duty, that she should shut herself up in an empty house!"

And, indeed, as he lay and pondered there, the house in which he was at this moment seemed very empty too; and his wife, he felt, was far away from him, separated from him by something more than miles. It was all very well for him to grow proud and reserved when it was suggested to him that Lady Sylvia should help him in his next canvass; it was all very well for him to build up theories to the effect that her pure, noble, sensitive mind were better kept aloof from the vulgar traffic of politics. But even now he began to recall some of the dreams he had dreamed in his bachelor days—in his solitary walks home from the House, in his friendly confidences with his old chum at Exeter, and most of all when he was wandering with Lady Sylvia herself on those still summer evenings under the great elms of Willowby Park. He had looked forward to a close and eager companionship, an absolute identity of interests and feelings, a mutual and constant help-giving which had never been realized. Suddenly he jumped to his feet, and began to walk up and down the room.

He would not give himself up to idle dreams and vain regrets. It was doubtless better as it was. Was he a child, to long for sympathy when something unpleasant had to be gone through? She herself had shown him how her quick, proud spirit had revolted from a proposal that was no uncommon thing in public life; better that she should preserve this purity of conscience than that she should be able to aid him by dabbling in doubtful schemes. The rough work of the world was not for that gentle and beautiful bride of his; but rather the sweet content and quiet of country ways. He began to fret about the engagements of the next few days to which he had pledged himself. He would rather have gone down at once to The Lilacs, to forget the babble and turmoil and vexations of politics in the tender society of that most loving of all friends and companions. However, that was impossible. Instead, he sat down and wrote her an affectionate and merry letter, in which he said not one word of what had happened at Englebury, beyond recording the fact of his having been there. Why should he annoy her by letting her suppose that she had been mixed up in a squabble with such a person as Eugenius Chorley?

<hr>

CHAPTER XXI.

HIS RETURN.

IT was with a buoyant sense of work well done that Balfour, on a certain Saturday morning, got into a hansom and left Piccadilly for Victoria Station. He had telegraphed to Lady Sylvia to drive over from The Lilacs to meet him, and he proposed that now he and she should have a glad holiday-time. Would she run down to Brighton for the week preceding Christmas? Would she go over to Paris for the New-year? Or would she prefer to spend both Christmas and New-year among the evergreens of her English home, with visits to neighboring friends, and much excitement about the decoration of the church, and a pleased satisfaction in giving away port-wine and flannels to the properly pious poor? Anyhow, he would share in her holiday. He would ride with her, drive with her, walk with her; he would shoot Lord Willowby's rabbits, and have luncheon at the Hall; in the evening, in the warm, hushed room, she would play for him while he smoked, or they would have confidential chatting over the appearance and circumstances and dispositions of their friends. What had this tender and beautiful child to do with politics? She herself had shown him what was her true sphere; he would not have that shy and sensitive conscience, that proud, pure spirit, hardened by rude associations. It is true, Balfour had a goodly bundle of papers, reports, and blue-books in his bag. But that was merely for form's sake — a precaution, perhaps, against his having to spend a solitary half hour after she had gone to bed at nights. There could be no harm, for example, in his putting into shape, for future use, the notes he had made down in Somersetshire, just as occasion offered. But he would not seek the occasion.

And all things combined to make this reunion with his wife a happy one. It was a pleasant omen that, whereas he had left London in a cold gray fog, no sooner had he got away from the great town than he found the country shining in clear sunlight. Snow had fallen overnight; but while the snow in Buckingham Palace Road was trampled into brown mud, here it lay with a soft white lustre on the silent fields and the hedges and the woods. Surely it was only a bridal robe that Nature wore on this beautiful morning—a half-transparent robe of pearly white that caught here and there a pale tint of blue from the clear skies overhead. He had a whole bundle of weekly newspapers, illustrated and otherwise, in the carriage with him, but he never thought of reading. And though the wind was cold, he let it blow freely through the open windows. This was better than hunting through the rookeries of London.

He caught sight of her just as the train was slowing into the station. She was seated high in the phaeton that stood in the roadway, and she was eagerly looking out for him. Her face was flushed a rose-red with the brisk driving through the keen wind; the sunlight touched the firmly braided masses of her hair and the delicate oval of her cheek; and as he went out of the station-house into the road, the beautiful, tender, gray-blue eyes were lit up by such a smile of gladness as ought to have been sufficient welcome to him.

7*

"Well, old Syllabus," said he, "how have you been? Crying your eyes out?"

"Oh no, not at all," she said, seriously. "I have been very busy. You will see what I have been doing. And what did you mean by sending the servants down again?"

"I did not want to have you starve, while I had the club to fall back on. Where the—"

But at this moment the groom appeared with the packages he had been sent for. Balfour got up beside his wife, and she was about to drive off, when they were accosted by a gentlemanly-looking man who had come out of the station.

"I beg your pardon—Mr. Balfour, I believe?"

"That is my name."

"I beg your pardon, I am sure; but I have an appointment with Lord Willowby—and—and I can't get a fly here—"

"Oh, I'll drive you over," said Balfour, for he happened to be in an excellent humor: had he not been, he would probably have told the stranger where to get a fly at the village. The stranger got in behind. Perhaps Lady Sylvia would, in other circumstances, have entered into conversation with a gentleman who was a friend of her father's; but there was a primness about his whiskers and a certain something about his dress and manner that spoke of the City, and of course she could not tell whether his visit was one of courtesy or of commerce. She continued to talk to her husband so that neither of the two people behind could overhear.

And Balfour had not the slightest consciousness of caution or restraint in talking to this bright and beautiful young wife of his. It seemed to him quite natural now that he should cease to bother this loving and sensitive companion of his about his anxieties and commonplace labors. He chatted to her about their favorite horses and dogs; he heard what pheasants had been shot in Uphill Wood the day before; he was told what invitations to dinner awaited his assent; and all the while they were cheerfully whirling through the keen, exhilarating air, crossing the broad bars of sunlight on the glittering road, and startling the blackbirds in the hedges, that shook down the powdery snow as they darted into the dense holly-trees.

"You have not told me," said Lady Sylvia, in a somewhat measured tone, though he did not notice that, "whether your visit to Englebury was successful."

"Oh," said he, carelessly, "that was of no importance. Nothing was to be done then. It will be time enough to think of Englebury when the General Election comes near."

Instead of Englebury, he began to talk to her about Brighton. He thought they might drop down there for a week before Christmas. He began to tell her of all the people whom he knew who happened to be at Brighton at the moment. It would be a pleasant variety for her; she would meet some charming people.

"No, thank you, Hugh," she said, somewhat coldly; "I don't think I will go down to Brighton at present. But I think you ought to go."

"I?" said he, with a stare of amazement.

"Yes; these people might be of use to you. If a General Election is coming on, you cannot tell what influence they might be able to give you."

"My dear child," said he, fairly astonished that she should speak in this hard tone about certain quite innocent people in Brighton, "I don't want to see these people because they might be of use to me. I wanted you to go down to Brighton merely to please you."

"Thank you, I don't think I can go down to Brighton."

"Why?"

"Because I cannot leave papa at present," she said.

"What's the matter with him?" said Balfour, getting from mystery to mystery.

"I cannot tell you now," she said, in a low voice. "But I don't wish to leave The Lilacs, so long as he is at the Hall; and he has been going very little up to London of late."

"Very well; all right," said Balfour, cheerfully. "If you prefer The Lilacs to Brighton, so do I. I thought it might be a change for you—that was all."

But why should she seem annoyed because he had proposed to take her down to Brighton? And why should she speak despitefully of a number of friends who would have given her a most hearty welcome? Surely all these people could not be in league with the British House of Commons to rob her of her husband.

In any case, Balfour took no heed of these passing fancies of hers. He had registered a mental vow to the effect that, whenever he could not quite understand her, or whenever her wishes clashed with his, he would show an unfailing consideration and kindness toward this tender soul who had placed her whole life in his hands. But that consideration was about to be put to the test of a sharp strain. With some hesitation she informed him, as they drove up to the Hall, that her uncle and aunt were staying there for a day or two. Very well; there was no objection to that. If he had to shake hands with Major the Honorable Stephen Blythe, was there not soap-and-water at The Lilacs? But Lady Sylvia proceeded to say, with still greater diffidence, that probably they would be down again in about ten days. They had been in the habit of spending Christmas at the Hall; and Johnny and Honoria had come too; so that it was a sort of annual family party. Very well; he had no objection to that either. It was no concern of his where Major Blythe ate his Christmas dinner. But when Lady Sylvia went on to explain, with increasing hesitation, that herself and her husband would be expected to be of this Christmas gathering, Mr. Balfour mentally made use of a phrase which was highly improper. She did not hear it, of course. They drove up to the Hall in silence; and when they got into the house, Balfour shook hands with Major Blythe with all apparent good-nature.

Lord Willowby had wished the stranger to follow him into the library. In a few moments he returned to the drawing-room. He was obviously greatly disturbed.

"You must excuse me, Sylvia; I cannot possibly go over with you to lunch. I have some business which will detain me half an hour at least—perhaps more. But your uncle and aunt can go with you."

That was the first Balfour had heard of Major Blythe and his wife having been invited to lunch at his house; but had he not sworn to be grandly considerate? He said nothing. Lady Sylvia turned to her two relatives. Now, had Lord Willowby been going over to The Lilacs, his brother might have ventured to accompany him; but Major Blythe scarcely liked the notion of thrusting his head into that lion's den all by himself.

"My dear," said the doughty warrior to his wife, "I think we will leave the young folks to themselves for to-day—if they will kindly excuse us. You know I promised to walk over and see that mare at the farm."

Balfour said nothing at all. He was quite content when he

got into the phaeton, his wife once more taking the reins. He bade good-bye to Willowby Hall without any pathetic tremor in his voice.

"Hugh," said Lady Sylvia, somewhat timidly, "I think you are prejudiced against my uncle; I am very sorry—"

"I don't look on your uncle," said Balfour, with much coolness, "as being at all necessary to my existence, and I am sure I am not necessary to his. We each of us can get on pretty well without the other."

"But it is dreadful to have members of one family in—in a position of antagonism or dislike to each other," she ventured to say, with her heart beating a trifle more rapidly.

"Well, yes," he said, cheerfully. "I suppose Major Blythe and I are members of the same family, as we are all descended from Adam. If that is what you mean, I admit the relationship; but not otherwise. Come, Sylvia, let's talk about something else. Have you seen the Von Rosens lately?"

For an instant she hesitated, eager, disappointed, and wistful; but she pulled her courage together, and answered with seeming good-will.

"Oh yes," she said. "Mr. Von Rosen called yesterday. And the strangest thing has happened. An uncle of his wife has just died in some distant place in America, and has left a large amount of property to Mrs. Von Rosen, on condition she goes out there some time next year, and remains for a year at the house that has been left her. And she is not to take her children with her. Mrs. Von Rosen declares she won't go. She won't leave her children for a whole year. They want her to go and live in some desert place just below the Rocky Mountains."

"A desert!" he cried. "Why, don't you know that the neighborhood of the Rocky Mountains has been my ideal harbor of refuge whenever I thought of the two worst chances that can befall one? If I were suddenly made a pauper, I should go out there and get a homestead free from the Government, and try my hand at building up my own fortunes. Or if I were suddenly to break down in health, I should make immediately for the high plains of Colorado, where the air is like champagne; and I would become a stock-raiser and a mighty hunter in spite of all the bronchitis or consumption that could attack one. Why, I know a lot of fellows out there now; they live the rudest life all day long—riding about the plains to look after their herds, making hunting excursions up into the mountains, and so forth ; and in the evening they put on dress-coats to dinner, and have music, and try to make themselves believe they are in Piccadilly or Pall Mall. Who told her it was a desert ?"

"I suppose it would be a desert to her without her children," said Lady Sylvia, simply.

"Then we will go over after lunch and reason with that mad creature," said he. "The notion of throwing away a fortune because she won't go out and live in that splendid climate for a single year !"

What the result of this mission of theirs was need not be stated at present. Enough that Balfour and his wife, having spent the best part of the afternoon with these neighboring friends of theirs, went home to dine by themselves in the evening. And Balfour had been looking forward during this past fortnight to the delight of having his wife all to himself again ; and he had pictured the still little room, her seated at the piano, perhaps, or perhaps both seated at the fire, and all troubles and annoyances hunted out into the cold winter night. This was the new plan. When he looked at her—at the true, sweet, serious, trusting eyes, and at the calm, pensive, guileless forehead—he began to wonder how he could ever, in his selfish imaginations, have thought of having her become a sort of appanage of himself in his public life. Would he wish her to become a shifting and dexterous wire-puller, paying court to this man, flattering another, patronizing a third, all to further her husband's interests ? That, at all events, was not what he wished her to be now. He admired her for her courageous protest against that suggested scheme for the bribing of Englebury. Not for a hundred seats in Parliament would he have his wife make interested professions of friendship for such people as the Chorleys. The proper place for the high-souled young matron was the head of her own table, or a seat by the fire in her own drawing-room ; and it was there that he hoped to gain rest, and sweet encouragement, and a happy forgetfulness of all the vulgar strife of the outside world.

"Sylvia," he said, suddenly, at dinner, "why do you look so depressed ? What is the matter with you ?"

"Oh, nothing," she said, rousing herself, and making an effort —not very successful—to talk about this American trip. Then she relapsed into silence again, and the dinner was not a cheerful feast.

"Are you tired?" he asked again. "Perhaps you had better go and lie down for a while."

No, she was not tired. Nor did she go, as was her wont after dinner, into the next room and begin to play a few of the airs and pieces that he liked. She sat down by the fire opposite him. Her face was troubled, and her eyes distant and sad.

"Come, Sylvia," he said, as he lit his pipe, "you are vexed about something. What is it? What is the trouble?"

"I am not vexed, really. It is no matter," she again answered.

Well, as his motto was "Live and let live," he was not bound to goad her into confidences she was unwilling to make; and as the enforced silence of the room was a rather painful and lugubrious business, he thought he might as well have a look at one or two of the papers he had brought down. He went and fetched his bag. He sat down with his back to the light, and was soon deep in some report as to the water supply of London.

Happening to look up, however, he found that his wife was silently crying. Then he impatiently threw the book on the table, and demanded to know the cause. Perhaps there was some roughness in his voice; but, at all events, she suddenly flung herself down before him, and buried her face on his knees, and burst into a fit of wild sobbing, in which she made her stammering confession. It was all about her father. She could not bear to see him suffering this terrible anxiety. It was killing him. She was sure the man who had come down in the train had something to do with these pecuniary troubles, and it was dreadful to her to think that she and her husband' had all they could desire, while her father was driven to despair. All this, and more, she sobbed out like a penitent child.

Balfour put his hand gently on her soft brown hair.

"Is that all, Sylvia?" he said. "If it is only money your father wants, he can have that. I will ask him."

She rose—her eyes still streaming with tears—and kissed him twice. And then she grew gayer in spirit, and went and played some music for him while he smoked his pipe. But as he smoked he thought, and his thoughts were rather bitter about a man who, wanting money, had not the courage to ask for it, but had degraded his daughter into the position of being a beggar for it.

And as Mr. Balfour was a business-like person, though he had not been trained up to commerce, he determined to ascertain exactly how Lord Willowby's affairs stood before proffering him this promised help.

CHAPTER XXII.

FRIENDS AND NEIGHBORS.

THERE was a brisk fire in the breakfast-room at The Lilacs, and the frosty December sunlight, streaming through the window, touched the white table-cloth with a ruddy and cheerful glow. A man of about thirty, tall, stalwart-looking, with a huge brown mustache and a partially cropped beard, light-blue eyes, and a healthy complexion, stood on the hearth-rug with his hands complacently fixed in his pocket. This was Count—or rather, as he had dropped his courtesy title since settling down in England, Mr.—Von Rosen, who had served as lieutenant in the Franco-German war, and had subsequently fallen in love with and married a young English lady, who had persuaded him to make England his home. He was a young man of superfluous energy, of great good-humor and good spirits, who made himself a nuisance to the neighborhood in which he lived by the fashion in which he insisted on other people joining him in his industrious idleness. For example, he had on this very morning, at seven o'clock, sent a letter to Mr. Hugh Balfour, of whose arrival at The Lilacs he had only heard on the previous night, urging him to join a certain shooting party. Lady Sylvia was to drive over with them, and spend the day with two ladies whom she knew. He himself would call at nine. And so he stood here with his hands in his pocket, apparently quite contented, but nevertheless wondering why English people should be so late with their breakfast.

"Ah," said he, with his face brightening, as Balfour entered the room. "You are ready to go? But I have to beg your pardon very much. My man says you were not awake when he brought the letter; it was stupid of him to send it to your room."

"On the contrary," said Balfour, as he mechanically took up a handful of letters that were lying on the table, "I have to beg your pardon for keeping you waiting. I thought I would put on my shooting-boots before coming down. Lady Sylvia will be here presently. Come, what do you say to having some breakfast with us?"

He was scanning the outside of the various envelopes with something of an absent air. There was nothing meditative about the German ex-lieutenant. He had once or twice allowed his highly practical gaze to fall on a certain game pie.

"A second breakfast?" said he. "Yes, perhaps it is better. My first breakfast was at six. And in these short days it is foolishness to waste time at the luncheon. Oh yes, I will have some breakfast. And in the mean time why do you not read your letters?"

"Well, the fact is," said Balfour, "my wife thinks I should have a clear holiday down here, and I have been wondering whether it is any use—"

But quite mechanically, while he was speaking, he had opened one of the letters, and he paused in his speech as he read its contents.

"By Jove," said he, partly to himself and partly to his companion, "they must be pretty certain that I shall be in the next Parliament, or they would not offer to put this in my hands! Perhaps they don't know that I am sure to be kicked out of Ballinascroon."

At this moment Lady Sylvia entered the room, and that young lady went up to the German lieutenant in the most winning and gracious way—for he was a great friend of hers—and thanked him very prettily for the trouble he had taken about this invitation.

"Trouble?" he said, with a laugh. "No, no. It is a good drive over to Mr. Lefevre's, and I shall have nice company. And you will find him such a fine fellow—such a good, fine fellow—if you will meet him some night at our house, Lady Sylvia; and your husband will see, when we begin the shooting, that there is no selfishness in him at all—he will prefer that his friends have more shooting than himself, and his keepers they know that too —and my wife she says if you will be so good as to stay with her all the day, we will come back that way in the afternoon— and it is better still, a great deal better, if you and Mr. Balfour will stay to dine with us."

Lady Sylvia was very pleased and grateful. Apart from her personal liking for these friends of hers, she was glad to find her husband taking to the amusements and interests of this country-life. She said that Mr. Von Rosen's plan would be very agreeable to her if it suited her husband; and then she turned to him. He was still regarding that letter.

"What did you say, Hugh?" she asked.

"Oh yes," he answered, as if startled out of some reverie. "That is very kind of you, Von Rosen. It would be a delightful day. The fact is, however, I am not quite sure that I ought to go, though nothing would give me greater pleasure, as I have just got an offer here that is rather flattering to a young member who has not done much work in the House. It is rather an important measure they propose to put into my hands. Well, I suppose I shall only be sort of junior counsel to Lord ——; but at least I could get up his case for him. Well, now, I must see these two men at once. Sylvia," he continued, turning to his wife, "if I ask these two friends of mine to run down here to-morrow to dinner, I suppose you could put them up for the night?"

All the glad light had gone from her face. They had sat down at the table by this time; and before answering him, she asked Mr. Von Rosen whether he would not help himself to something or other that was near him. Then she said, in a somewhat precise fashion,

"I think it would look rather singular to ask two strangers down here for a single night at the present time."

"Why singular?" said he, with a stare.

"So near Christmas," she continued, in the same proud and cold way, "people are supposed to have made up their family parties. It is scarcely a time to invite strangers."

"Oh, well," said he, with a good-natured laugh, "I did not mean to offend you. I dare say you are right; an evening devoted to talking about this bill would not have been lively for you. However, I must see my two patrons, and that at once. Von Rosen, would you mind saying to Mr. Lefevre how much I thank him for his friendly offer? I fear I must let you have your drive over by yourself."

It was by the merest accident that he happened to notice his wife's face. When he saw the look of pain and disappointment that passed over it, he did not quite know what he had done to produce that feeling, but he altered his determination in a second.

"By-the-way," said he, "I might as well go up to London to-morrow. Yes, that will be better. I will telegraph to them to dine with me at the club; and to-day I can give up to your first-rate little arrangement. Come, Von Rosen, you have not finished already?"

"I do not wish to waste time," said that inveterate idler. "The daylight is very short now. You have finished too?"

And so they set out, Lady Sylvia having promised to go over to Mrs. Von Rosen during the day, and remain until the evening. As they drove off in the dog-cart, Balfour seemed rather preoccupied. When he remarked, "Things have come to a bonny cripus!" what was his companion to make of that absurd phrase? Von Rosen did not know the story of the small boy in Northern parts who was found bitterly sobbing, and digging his knuckles into his eyes; and who, on being asked what was the matter, replied, in language which has to be softened for Southern ears, "Things have come to a bonny cripus; I only called my father an old fool, and he went and kicked me behind." It was the introductory phrase of this insulted boy that Balfour used. "Things have come to a bonny cripus," said he.

They drove along the crisp and crackling road. The hoar-frost on the hedges was beginning to melt; the sunlight had draped the bare twigs in a million of rainbow jewels; the copper-colored sun shone over the black woods and the dank green fields.

"Women are strange creatures," said Balfour again; and this was a more intelligible remark.

"Why do you say that?" asked the simple lieutenant, who had noticed nothing at breakfast beyond the coffee and the game pie.

"I do believe," said Balfour, with a smile which was not altogether a glad one, "that my wife is beginning positively to hate everybody and everything connected with Parliament and politics; and that is a lively lookout for me. You know I can't go on staying down here. And yet I shouldn't wonder if, when Parliament meets, she refused to go up to London."

"No, no, no," said the lieutenant; "there you are very wrong. It is not reasonable—not at all reasonable. She may like the country better; but it is not reasonable. That is what I tell my wife now. She declares she will not go to live in America for a year, and leave her children; and I say to her, 'You will think again about that. It is a great trouble that you will leave your children, it will be a great sorrow for a time; but what will you think of yourself after, if you do not do what is right for them? When they grow up, when they want money, what will you think if you have thrust away all that property—and only for a single year's absence?'"

"And has your wife proved reasonable? has she consented to go?" asked Balfour.

Von Rosen shrugged his shoulders.

"No—not yet. But I will not argue with her. I will leave her to think. Oh, you do not know what a woman will do, if she thinks it is for the good of her children. At present it is all 'Oh, never, never! Leave my darling little girl, so that she won't know me when I come back? Not for all the money in America!' Well, that is natural too, though it is foolishness. You would not like to have your wife with too hard a heart. And I say to her, 'Yes, I will not ask you. We are not so very poor that you must suffer great pain. If you will give up the American property, give it up, and no more to be said.' But I know. She is reasoning with herself now. She will go."

"Do you think she will?" said Balfour, thoughtfully, "Do you think she will give up so much of her own feeling if she thinks it right?"

"Know?" said the tall young German, with one of his hearty laughs. "Yes, I know that very well. Oh, there is no one so sensible as my wife—not any one that I know anywhere—if you can show her what is right. But if you ask me what I think of her uncle, that will cause so much trouble all for his nonsense, then I think he was a most wretched fellow—a most wretched and pitiable fellow."

Here occurred an unintelligible growl, whether in German or English phraseology his companion could not say; but doubtless the muttered words were not polite. Another man would probably have given additional force to this expression of feeling by twitching at the reins; but Von Rosen never vented his rage on a horse.

They had a capital day's sport, although Balfour, who was evidently thinking of anything in the world rather than pheasants, rabbits, and hares, shot very badly indeed. Their luncheon was brought to them at a farm-house, the mistress of the farm giving them the use of her sacred parlor, in which all the curiosities of ornament and natural history contributed by three generations were religiously stored. They got back to Von Rosen's house about six; just in time for a cup of tea and a chat before dressing for an early country dinner.

Surely, one or two of us who were sitting round the table that evening must have thought—surely these two young people ought to have been happy enough, if outward circumstances have anything to do with content of mind. There was he, in the prime of youthful manhood, with strength written in every outline of the bony frame and in every lineament of the firm, resolute, and sufficiently handsome head, rich beyond the possibilities of care, and having before him all the hopefulness and stimulus of a distinguished public career; she, young, high-born, and beautiful, with those serious and shy eyes that went straight to the heart of the person she addressed, and secured her friends everywhere, also beyond the reach of sordid cares, and most evidently regarded by her husband with all affection and admiration. What trouble, other than mere imaginary nonsense, could enter into these linked lives? Well, there was present at this dinner that Cassandra of married life who was mentioned in the first chapter of this highly moral and instructive tale, and she would have answered these questions quickly enough. She would have assumed—for she knew nothing positive about the matter—that these two were now beginning to encounter the bitter disillusionizing experience of post-nuptial life. The husband was beginning to recognize the fact that his wife was not quite the glorious creature he had imagined her to be; he was looking back with a wistful regret to the perfectly false ideal of her he had formed before marriage; while she, having dreamed that she was marrying a lover, and having woke up to find she had only married a husband, was suffering untold and secret misery because she found her husband's heart transferred from her real self to that old ideal picture of herself which he had drawn in the dream-like past. This was what she would have said. This was what she was always preaching to us. And we generally found it best in our neighborhood to give her Most Gracious Majesty her own way; so that this theory, as regarded the conjugal relations of nearly everybody we knew, was supposed to be strictly accurate. At least, nobody had the temerity to question it.

"Lady Sylvia," said this very person, "why don't you ever go up to London? Mr. Balfour must think he is a bachelor again when he is all by himself in Piccadilly."

"I don't like London much," said Lady Sylvia, with great composure. "Besides, my husband is chiefly there on business matters, and I should only be in the way."

"But you take a great interest in politics," observed this monitress, who doubtless considered that she was administering some wholesome discipline.

"My wife may take some interest in politics," said Balfour, "but she has no great love for politicians. I confess they are not picturesque or interesting persons, as a rule. I am afraid their worldly wisdom, their callousness, is a trifle shocking."

"Well, at all events," said our Most Gracious Lady—for she was determined to put in a little bit of remonstrance, though she would gravely have rebuked anybody else for daring to do so— "you have not much political work to distract your attention at present, Parliament not sitting, and all that excitement about a dissolution having passed away."

"My dear Mrs. ——," said he, with a laugh, "now is the worst time of all; for a good many of us don't know whether we shall be in the next Parliament, and we are trying what we can do to make our calling and election sure. It is a disagreeable business, but necessary. To-morrow, for example, I am going to town to see two gentlemen about a bill they propose I should introduce; but I shall have to ask them first what is the betting about my being able to get into Parliament at all. My present constituents have proved very ungrateful, after the unfailing attention and courtesy I have lavished upon them."

Here the German ex-soldier burst into a great roar of laughter, as if there were anything amusing in a young man's throwing contumely on a number of persons who had done him the honor of returning him to the House of Commons.

But, after all, it was not our business at this little dinner-party to speculate on the hidden griefs that might accompany the outward good fortune of these two young people. We had more palpable trouble near at hand, as was revealed by an odd little accident that evening. Our hostess had a great affection for two boisterous young lads, who were the sons of the august little woman just referred to, and she had invited them to come into the dining-room after dessert. Surely a mother ought to teach these brats not to make remarks on what does not concern them? Now, as we were talking in an aimless fashion about the Ashan-

tee war, the recent elections, and what not, a sudden sound outside stilled us into silence. It was the children of the church
choir who had come up to sing us a Christmas carol; and the
sound of their voices outside in the still night recalled many a
vivid recollection, and awoke some strange fancies about the coming year. What were most of us thinking of then? This young
ass of a boy all at once says, "Oh, Auntie Bell, where will you be
next Christmas? And do they sing Christmas carols far away in
America?" And Auntie Bell, being taken rather aback, said she
did not know, and smiled; but the smile was not a glad one, for
we knew that sudden tears had started to the soft and kindly
eyes. We were not quite so happy as we went home that night.
And when some one remarked to the mother of those boys—
But there, it is no use remonstrating with women.

<hr>

CHAPTER XXIII.

A CONFESSION.

On the morning of his departure for London, Balfour would
take no notice of the marked disfavor with which Lady Sylvia
regarded his setting out. It was hard on the poor child, no
doubt, that he should leave her in the midst of these few Christmas holidays, and all for the sake of some trumpery Parliamentary business. He might have remonstrated with her, it is true;
might have reminded her that she knew what his life must be
when she married him; might have recalled her own professions
of extreme interest in public affairs; might have asked her if a
single day's absence—which he had tried to avert by a proposal
which she had rejected—was, after all, such a desperate business.
But no. He had no wish to gain an argumentative victory over
his beautiful young wife. He would allow her to cherish that
consolatory sense of having been wronged. Nay, more; since
she had plainly chosen to live in a world apart from his, he
would make her life there as happy as possible. And so, as he
kissed her in bidding her good-bye, he said,

"By-the-way, Sylvia, I might as well go round by the Hall and
see your father. If he is in all that trouble—this is Christmas-
time, you know—perhaps he will let me help him."

Well, she did look a little grateful.

"And I shall be down as soon as I can to-morrow forenoon," he added.

But as he drove away from The Lilacs in the direction of Willowby Hall, he did not at all feel so amiably disposed toward his wife's father, whom he conjectured—and conjectured quite wrongly—to have been secretly soliciting this help from Lady Sylvia. But, at all events, Balfour said to himself, the relations between himself and his wife were of more importance than his opinion of Lord Willowby. The sacrifice of a few thousand pounds was not of much concern to him; it was of great concern to him that his wife should not remain unhappy if this matter of money could restore her usual cheerfulness.

When he reached the Hall, he found that Major and Mrs. Blythe had left the day before, but would return for Christmas. Lord Willowby was smoking an after-breakfast cigarette in the library. He looked surprised when Balfour entered; his son-in-law had not often paid him a visit unaccompanied by Lady Sylvia.

"The fact is," said Balfour, coming straight to the point, "Sylvia is rather distressed at present because she imagines you are in some trouble about business matters. She thinks I ought to ask you about it, and see if I can help you. Well, I don't like interfering in any one's affairs, especially when I have not been solicited to interfere; but really, you know, if I can be of service to you—"

"Ah! the good girl—the dear girl!" said Lord Willowby, with that effusiveness of tone that his daughter had learned to love as the only true expression of affection. "I can see it all. Her tender instinct told her who that man was whom you drove over the day before yesterday; she recognized my despair, my shame, at being so beset by a leech, a blood-sucker, a miserable wretch who has no more sense of honor—"

And at this point Lord Willowby thought fit to get into a hot and indignant rage, which in no measure imposed on his son-in-law. Balfour waited patiently until the outburst was over. Perhaps he may have been employing his leisure considering how a man could be beset by a leech; but inadvertently he looked out of window at his horses, and then he thought of his train.

"And indeed, Balfour," said his lordship, altering his tone, and appealing in a personal and plaintive way to his son-in-law, "how could I speak to you about these matters? All your life you have been too well off to know anything about the shifts that other men have sometimes to adopt."

"My dear Lord Willowby," said Balfour, with a smile, "I am afraid it is those very shifts that have led you into your present troubles."

"If you only knew—if you only knew," said the other, shaking his head. "But there! as my dear girl is anxious, I may as well make a clean breast of it. Will you sit down?"

Balfour sat down. He was thinking more of the train than of his father-in-law's affairs.

"Do you know," said Lord Willowby, with something of a pathetic air, "that you are about the last man in the world to whom I should like to reveal the cause of my present anxieties. You are—you will forgive me for saying so—apt to be harsh in your judgments; you do not know what temptations poverty puts before you. But my dear girl must plead for me."

Balfour, who did not at all like this abject tone, merely waited in mute attention. If this revelation was to be protracted, he would have to take a later train.

"About a year and a half ago," said his lordship, letting his eyes rest vaguely on the arm of Balfour's easy-chair, "things had gone very badly with me, and I was easily induced into joining a speculation, or rather a series of speculations, on the Stock Exchange, which had been projected by several friends of mine who had been with me in other undertakings. They were rich men, and could have borne their previous losses; I was a poor man, and—and, in short, desperate. Moreover, they were all business men, one or two of them merchants whose names are known all over the world; and I had a fair right to trust to their prudence—had I not?"

"Prudence is not of much avail in gambling," said Balfour. "However, how did you succeed?"

"Our operations (which they conducted, mind you) were certainly on a large scale—an enormous scale. If they had come out successfully, I should never have touched a company, or a share, or a bond, for the rest of my life. But instead of that, everything went against us; and while one or two of us could have borne the loss, others of us must have been simply ruined.

Well, it occurred to one or two of these persons—I must beg you to believe, Balfour, that the suggestion did not come from me—that we might induce our broker, by promises of what we should do for him afterward, to assume the responsibility of these purchases and become bankrupt."

A sudden look of wonder—merely of wonder, not yet of indignation—leaped to the younger man's face.

"My dear fellow," pleaded Lord Willowby, who had been watching for this look, "don't be too rash in condemning us—in condemning me, at all events. I assure you I at once opposed this plan when it was suggested. But they had a great many reasons to advance against mine. It was making one man bankrupt instead of several. Then on whom would the losses fall? Why, on the jobbers, who are the real gamblers of the Stock Exchange, and who can easily suffer a few losses when pitted against their enormous gains."

"But how was it possible?" exclaimed Balfour, who had not yet recovered from his amazement. "Surely the jobbers could have appealed to the man's books, in which all your names would have been found."

"I assure you, Balfour," said his lordship, with a look of earnest sincerity, "that so much was I opposed to the scheme that I don't know how that difficulty was avoided. Perhaps he had a new set of books prepared, and burned the old ones. Perhaps he had from the outset been induced to enter his own name as the purchaser of the various stocks."

"But that would have been worse and worse—a downright conspiracy to swindle from the very beginning. Why, Lord Willowby, you don't mean to say that you allowed yourself to be associated with such a—well, perhaps I had better not give it a name."

"My dear Balfour," said his lordship, returning to his pathetic tone, "it is well for you that you have never suffered from the temptations of poverty. I feared your judgment of my conduct would be harsh. You see, you don't think of the extenuating circumstances. I knew nothing of this plan when I went into the copartnership of speculation—I cannot even say that it existed. Very well: when my partners came to me and showed me a scheme that would save them from ruin, was I openly to denounce and betray them merely because my own conscience did not exactly approve of the means they were adopting?"

"To condone a felony, even with the purest and highest motives—" said Balfour; and with that Lord Willowby suddenly rose from his chair. That single phrase had touched him into reality.

"Look here, Balfour—" said he, angrily.

But the younger man went on with great calmness to explain that he had probably been too hasty in using these words before hearing the whole story. He begged Lord Willowby to regard him (Balfour) as one of the public: what would the public, knowing nothing of Lord Willowby's private character, think of the whole transaction? And then he prayed to be allowed to know how the affair had ended.

"I wish it *was* ended," said Lord Willowby, subsiding into his chair again, and into his customary gloomy expression. "This man appears to consider us as being quite at his mercy. They have given him more money than ever they promised, yet he is not satisfied. He knows quite well that the jobbers suspected what was the cause of his bankruptcy, though they could do nothing to him; now he threatens to disclose the whole business, and set them on us. He says he is ruined as far as is practicable; and that if we don't give him enough to retire on and live at his ease, he will ruin every one of us in public reputation. Now do you see how the case stands?"

He saw very clearly. He saw that he dared not explain to his wife the story he had been told; and he knew she would never be satisfied until he had advanced money in order to hush up a gigantic fraud. What he thought of this dilemma can easily be surmised; what he said about it was simply nothing at all.

"And why should he come at me?" said Lord Willowby, in an injured way. "I have no money. When he was down here the day before yesterday, he used the plainest threats. But what can I do?"

"Prosecute him for attempting to obtain money by threats."

"But then the whole story would come out."

"Why not—if you can clear yourself of all complicity in the matter?"

Surely this was plain, obvious good sense. But Lord Willowby had always taken this young man to be a person of poor imagination, limited sympathies, and cold, practical ways. It was all very well for him to think that the case lay in a nutshell.

He knew better. He had a sentiment of honor. He would not betray his companions. In order to revenge himself on this wretched worm of a blood-sucker, would he stoop to become an informer, and damage the fair reputations of friends of his who had done their best to retrieve his fallen fortunes?

He did not frankly say all this, but he hinted at something of it.

"Your generosity," said Balfour, apparently with no intention of sarcasm, "may be very noble; but let us see exactly what it may lead to. What does this man propose to do if he is not paid sufficient money?"

"Oh, he threatens everything—to bring an action against us, to give the jobbers information which will enable them to bring an action, and so forth."

"Then your friends, at all events, will have to pay a large sum; and both you and they will be ruined in character. That is so, isn't it?"

"I don't know about character," said this poor hunted creature. "I think I could make some defence about that."

"I don't think your defence would affect the public verdict," said this blunt-spoken son-in-law.

"Well, be it so!" said his lordship, in desperation. "Let us say that the general voice of business men—who, of course, never employ any stratagems to get out of predicaments in their own affairs—will say that we conspired to commit a fraud. Is that plain enough language? And now perhaps you will say that the threat is not a sufficiently serious one?"

"I will say nothing of the kind," said Balfour, quietly. "The whole case seems much more serious than any one could have imagined. Of course, if you believe you could clear yourself, I say again, as I said before, bring an action against the man, and have the whole thing out, whoever suffers. If you are disinclined to take that course—"

"Well, suppose I am?"

"In that case," said Balfour, rising, "will you give me a day or two to think over the affair?"

"Certainly; as many as you like," said Lord Willowby, who had never expected much from the generosity of this son-in-law of his.

And so Balfour got into his trap again and drove on to the

station. Nothing that had happened to him since his marriage had disturbed him so much as the revelation of this story. He had always had a certain nameless, indefinable dislike to Lord Willowby; but he had never suspected him capable of conduct calculated to bring dishonor on the family name. And oddly enough, in this emergency, his greatest apprehension was that he might not be able to conceal the almost inevitable public scandal from Lady Sylvia. She had always loved her father. She had believed in his redundant expressions of affection. In the event of this great scandal coming to her ears, would she not indignantly repudiate it, and challenge her husband to repudiate it also?

That evening, by appointment, Balfour's two friends dined with him at his club; and they had a more or less discursive chat over the bill which it was proposed he should introduce in the case of his being reseated at the following General Election. Strangely enough, he did not enter into this talk with any particular zest. He seemed abstracted, absorbed; several times he vaguely assented to an opinion which he found it necessary to dispute directly afterward. For, what the member for Ballinascroon was really saying to himself was this: "To-morrow I go down again to the country. My wife will want to know what I am going to do about her father's affairs. I shall be thrown a good deal during the next few days into the society of Lord Willowby and his brother. And on Christmas-day I shall have the singular felicity of dining in the company of two of the most promising scoundrels in this country."

<hr>

CHAPTER XXIV.

CHRISTMAS SENTIMENT.

THERE is no saying what a man, even of the strictest virtue, will do for the sake of his wife. But, curiously enough, when Hugh Balfour found himself confronted by these two disagreeable demands, that he should lend or give a sum to Lord Willowby in order that a very disgraceful transaction should be hushed up, and that he should dine on Christmas evening with that peer of doubtful morals and his still more disreputable brother, he found far more difficulty in assenting to the latter than to the former proposition. That was a matter of a few moments—the writing a few figures on a check; this was spending a whole evening, and Christmas evening too, in the company of people whom he despised and detested. But what will not a man do for his wife?

Either concession was a sufficiently bitter draught to drink. He had always been keenly scrupulous about money matters, and impatiently harsh and contemptuous in his judgment of those who were otherwise. He had formed a pronounced antipathy against Lord Willowby, and a man does not care to strain his conscience or modify his creed for a person whom he dislikes. Then, there was the possibility of a public disclosure, which would probably reveal the fact that he had lent Lord Willowby this money. Could he defend himself by saying that he had counselled Lord Willowby, before lending him the money, to go into court and clear himself? He would not do that. When he gave that advice with mock humility, he knew perfectly that Lord Willowby was only prevaricating. He knew that this precious father-in-law of his was hopelessly entangled in a fraud which he had either concocted or condoned. If this money were to be lent at all, it was frankly to be lent in order that the man who threatened to inform should be bought over to hold his peace. But then what is it that a young and devoted husband will not do for his wife?

Moreover, the more distressing of the two demands had to be met first. Lord Willowby told him that his partners in that scheme of cheating the jobbers had resolved to meet on the first of the new year to consider what was to be done; so that in the mean time Balfour could allow his conscience to rest, so far as the money was concerned. But in the mean time came Christmas; and he told his wife that he had no objection to joining that family party at the Hall. When he said that he had no objection, he meant that he had about twenty dozen, which he would overrule for her sake. And indeed Lady Sylvia's delight at his consent was beautiful to see. She spent day after day in decorating Willowby Hall with evergreens; she did not altogether neglect The Lilacs, but then, you see, there was to be no Christmas party there. She sung at her work; she was as busy as she could be; she even wished—in the fulness of her heart— that her cousin Honoria were already arrived to help her. And

Balfour? Did he assist in that pretty and idyllic pastime? Oddly enough, he seemed to take a greater interest than ever in the Von Rosens and some neighbors of theirs. He was constantly over among us; and that indefatigable and busy idler, the German ex-lieutenant, and he were to be seen every day starting off on some new business—a walking-match, a run with the thistle-whippers, a sale of hay belonging to the railway; in fact, anything that did not lead those two in the direction of Willowby Hall. On one occasion he suddenly said to our Queen T——,

"Don't you think Christmas is a terribly dull business?"

"We don't find it so," said that smiling person; "we find it terribly noisy—enough to ruin one's nerves for a week."

"Ah," said he, "that is quite different. I can understand your enjoying Christmas when you have a children's party to occupy the evening."

"I am sure," said our Sovereign Mistress, who, to do her justice, is always ready with little kindnesses—"I am quite sure we should all be so glad if you and Lady Sylvia would come over and spend the evening with us; we would make Lady Sylvia the presiding fairy to distribute the gifts from the Christmas-tree. It is the most splendid one we have ever had—"

"You are very kind," said he, with a sigh. I wish I could. There is other joy in store for me. I have to dine with some of my father-in-law's relatives, and we shall have an evening devoted to bad wine and the Tichborne case."

And at length Christmas-day came round; and then it appeared that Mr. Balfour was expected to go from church to Willowby Hall and remain there until the evening. This, he considered, was not in the bond. He had managed to make the acquaintance of a certain clergyman in the neighborhood of Englebury; and this worthy person had just forwarded him the proof-sheets of an essay on some public question or other, with a meek request that Mr. Balfour would glance over it and say whether the case of the enemy had been fairly and fully stated. This was courageous and honest on the part of the parson, for Mr. Balfour was on the side of the enemy. Now, as this article was to be published in a monthly magazine, was it not of great importance that the answer should be returned at once? If Lady Sylvia would go on to the Hall with her papa, he, Balfour, would return to The Lilacs, get this bit of business over, and join the gay family party in the evening. Lady Sylvia seemed rather disappointed that this clergyman should have deprived her husband of the pleasure of spending the whole day in the society of her relatives; but she consented to the arrangement, and Balfour, with much content, spent Christmas-day by himself.

And then, in the hush of the still and sacred evening, this happy family party met round the Christmas board. It was a pleasant picture—for the bare dining-room looked no longer bare when it was laden with scarlet berries and green leaves, and Lord Willowby could not protest against a waste of candles on such a night. Then, with his beautiful young wife presiding at the head of the table—herself the perfect type of gentle English womanhood—and Honoria Blythe's merry black eyes doing their very best to fascinate and entertain him, why should this ungrateful Scotch boor have resolved to play the part of Apemantus? Of course he was outwardly very civil—nay, formally courteous; but there was an air of isolation about him, as if he were sitting there by an exercise of constraint. He rarely took wine anywhere; when he did, he almost never noticed what he drank: why was it, therefore, that he now tasted everything, and put the glass down as if he were calculating whether sudden death might not ensue? And when Major Blythe, after talking very loudly for some time, mentioned the word "Tichborne," why should this man ejaculate—apparently to himself—"O good Lord!" in a tone that somehow or other produced a dead silence.

"Perhaps it is no matter of concern to you," said Major Blythe, with as much ferocity as he dared to assume toward a man who might possibly lend him money, "that an innocent person should be so brutally treated?"

"Not much," said Balfour, humbly.

"I dare say you have not followed the case very closely, Balfour," said his lordship, intervening to prevent a dispute.

"No, I have not," he said. "In fact, I would much rather walk the other way. But then," he added, to Miss Honoria, who was seated by him, "your papa must not imagine that I have not an opinion as to who the Claimant really is."

"No!" exclaimed Honoria, with her splendid eyes full of theatrical interest. "Who is he, then?"

"I discovered the secret from the very beginning. The old

prophecies have been fulfilled. The ravens have flown away. Frederick Barbarossa has come back to the world at last."

"Frederick Barbarossa?" said Miss Honoria, doubtfully.

"Yes," continued her instructor, seriously. "His other name was O'Donovan. He was a Fenian leader."

"Susan," called out her brat of a brother, "he's only making a fool of you!" but at any rate the sorry jest managed to stave off for a time the inevitable fight about the fat person from the colonies.

It was a happy family gathering. Balfour was so pleased to see a number of relatives enjoying themselves together in this manner that he would not for the world have the party split itself into two after dinner. Remain to drink madeira when the ladies were going to sing their pious Christmas hymns in the other room? Never! Major Blythe said by gad he wasn't going into the drawing-room just yet; and poor Lord Willowby looked helplessly at both, not knowing which to yield to. Naturally, his duties as host prevailed. He sat down with his brother, and offered him some madeira, which, to tell the truth, was very good indeed, for Lord Willowby was one of the men who think they can condone the poisoning of their guests during dinner by giving them a decent glass of wine afterward. Balfour went into the drawing-room and sat down by his wife, Honoria having at her request gone to the piano.

"Why don't you stay in the dining-room, Hugh?" said she.

"Ah," said he, with a sigh, "Christmas evenings are far too short for the joy they contain. I did not wish the happiness of this family gathering to be too much flavored with Tichborne. What, is your cousin going to sing now—

> Oh, how sweet it is to see
> Brethren dwell in enmity!

or some such thing?"

She was hurt and offended. He had no right to scoff at her relatives; because if there was any discordant element in that gathering, it was himself. They were civil enough to him. They were not quarrelling among themselves. If there was any interference with the thoughts and feelings appropriate to Christmas, he was the evil spirit who was disturbing the emotions of those pious souls.

Indeed, she did not know what demon had got possession of

him. He went over to Mrs. Blythe, a woman whom she knew he heartily disliked, and sat down by that majestic three-decker, and paid her great and respectful attention. He praised Honoria's playing. He asked to what college they meant to send Johnny when that promising youth left school. He was glad to see the major looking so well and hearty: did he take his morning ride in the Park yet? Mrs. Blythe, who was a dull woman, nevertheless had her suspicions; but how could she fail to be civil to a gentleman who was complaisance personified?

His spirits grew brighter and brighter; he was quite friendly with Lord Willowby and his younger brother when they came in from the dining-room. Lady Sylvia deeply resented this courtesy, because she thought it arose from a sarcastic appreciation of the incongruity of his presence there; whereas it was merely the result of a consciousness that the hour of his release was at hand. He had done his duty; he had sacrificed his own likings for the sake of his wife; he had got through this distasteful dinner; and now he was going back to a snug room at The Lilacs, to a warm fire, an easy-chair, a pipe, and a friendly chat.

But who can describe the astonishment of these simple folks when a servant came in to say that Mr. Balfour's carriage was at the door? Only ten o'clock—and this Christmas night!

"Surely there is some mistake, Hugh?" said his young wife, looking at him with great surprise. "You don't wish to go home now?"

"Oh yes, child," said he, gravely. "I don't want to have you knocked up. It has been a long day for you to-day."

She said not another word, but got up and went to the door.

"Come, Sylvia," said her father, who had opened the door for her, "you must give us another hour, anyway: you are not very tired? Shall I tell him to take the horses out again?"

"No, thank you," said she, coldly. "I think I will go now."

"I am sorry," said Balfour, when she had gone, "to break up your charming Christmas party; but the fact is, Sylvia has been very fatigued ever since she put up those evergreens; and I am rather afraid of the night air for her."

He did not explain what was the difference between the night air of ten o'clock and the night air of eleven o'clock; for presently Lady Sylvia came down-stairs again wrapped up in furs, and she was escorted out to the carriage with great ceremony by her father. She was silent for a time after they drove away.

"Hugh," she said, abruptly, by-and-by, "why do you dislike my relatives so? And if you do dislike them, I think you might try to conceal it, for my sake."

"Well," said he, "I do think that is rather ungrateful. I thought I went out of my way to be civil to them all round to-night. I think I was most tremendously civil. What was it, then, that displeased you?"

She did not answer; she was oppresséd by bitter thoughts. And when he tried to coax her into conversation, she replied in monosyllables. In this manner they reached The Lilacs.

Now, before leaving home that evening he had given private instructions that a pretty little supper was to be prepared for their return; and when Lady Sylvia entered, she found the dining-room all cheerfully lit up, a fire blazing, and actual oysters (oysters don't grow on the hedge-rows of Surrey, as some of us know) on the table. This was how he thought he and she might spend their first Christmas evening together, late as the hour was; and he hastened to anticipate even the diligent Anne in helping his wife to get rid of her furs.

"Now, Syllabus," said he, "come in and make yourself comfortable."

"Thank you," said she, "I am a little tired. I think I will go up-stairs now."

"Won't you come down again?"

"I think not."

And so, without any great sense of injury, and forgetting altogether the supper that was spread out on the table, he shut himself up alone in the still dining-room, and lit his pipe, and took down a book from the library. Soon enough these temporary disappointments were forgotten; for it was a volume of Keats he had taken down at hap-hazard, and how could a man care what happened to him on the first Christmas evening of his married life, if he was away in the dream-land of "Endymion," and removed from mortal cares?

Major Blythe and his family remained at Willowby Hall for some few days; Lady Sylvia never went near them. Nay, she would not allow the name of one of her relations to pass her lips. If her husband mentioned any one of them, she changed the conversation; and once, when he proposed to drive over to the Hall, she refused to go.

On the other hand, she endeavored to talk politics to her husband, in a stiff and forced way, which only served to distress him. He remonstrated with her gently—for, indeed, he was rather disappointed that his honest endeavors to please her had borne so little fruit—but she only grew more reserved in tone. And he could not understand why she should torture herself by this compulsory conversation about politics, foreign and domestic, when he saw clearly that her detestation of everything connected with his public life increased day by day, until—merely to save her pain—he could have wished that there was no such place as Englebury on the map of England.

He told her he had spoken to her father about these pecuniary troubles, and offered to assist him. She said that was very kind, and even kissed him on the forehead, as she happened to be passing his chair; but not even that would induce her to talk about her father or anything belonging to him. And, indeed, he himself could not be very explicit on the point, more especially as everything now pointed to his having to lend Lord Willowby money, not to hush up a fraud, but to defend a criminal prosecution.

About the third week in January all England was startled by the announcement that there was to be an immediate dissolution of Parliament, and that a General Election would shortly follow. Balfour did not seem so perturbed as might have been expected; he even appeared to find some sense of relief in the sudden news. He at once grew active, bright, eager, and full of a hundred schemes, and the first thing he did was, of course, to rush up to London, the centre of all the hurry and disturbance that prevailed. Lady Sylvia naturally remained in Surrey; he never thought for a moment of dragging her into that turmoil.

CHAPTER XXV.

VICTORY !

THERE was not a moment to lose. All England was in confusion—local committees hastily assembling, Parliamentary agents
down in Westminster wasting their substance on shilling telegrams, wire-pullers in Pall Mall pitifully begging for money to
start hopeless contests in the interest of the party, eager young
men fresh from college consulting their friends as to which im-
pregnable seat they should assault with a despairing courage, and
comfortable and elderly members dolefully shaking their heads
over the possible consequences of this precipitate step, insomuch
that the luncheon claret at their club had no longer any charms
for them. And then the voluble partisans, the enthusiasts, the
believers in the great liberal heart of England, how little did they
reck of the awful catastrophe impending! The abolition of the
income tax would rally wavering constituencies. The recent re-
verses at the poll were only the result of a temporary irritation;
another week would give the Government an overwhelming majority. Alas! alas! These confident professions were balm to
many an anxious heart, this or the other luckless wight seeking
all possible means of convincing himself that his constituents
could not be so cruel as to oust him; but they did not prevent
those constituents from arising and slaying their representative,
transforming him from a living and moving member of Parliament into a wandering and disconsolate voice.

Balfour had to act and think for himself in this crisis; Mr.
Bolitho was far too busy to attend to such a paltry place as Englebury, even if he had been willing to join in what he regarded
as a Quixotic adventure. And now a strange thing happened.
Balfour had long been of opinion that his wife's notions of what
public life should be were just a little too romantic and high-
strung to be practicable. It was well she should have them; it
was well that her ignorance of the world allowed her to imagine
them to be possible. But, of course, a man living in the denser
and coarser atmosphere of politics had to take human nature as

he found it, and could not afford to rule his conduct by certain theories which, beautiful enough in themselves, were merely visionary.

Oddly enough, however, and probably unconsciously, he did at this moment rule his conduct by Lady Sylvia's sentiments. It is true that, when he first talked about that business of buying the filched common from Mr. Chorley and subsequently presenting it to the Englebury people, he appeared to treat the whole affair as a joke; but, all the same, he had expressed no great disapproval of the scheme. It was only after Lady Sylvia's indignant protest that he came to consider that proposal as altogether detestable. Further, when Bolitho suggested to him that he should try to oust the member then sitting for Englebury, he saw no reason why he should not try to do so. Had not Harnden himself led similar assaults on seats deemed even more a personal perquisite than his own? Harnden was used up, was of no good to either party, had spoken of retiring: why should not the seat be contested? This was Balfour's opinion at the time, and he himself could not have told when he had altered it. All the same, as he now hurried up to London, he felt it would be mean to try to oust this old gentleman from his seat: if Harnden did not mean to resign, he, Balfour, would make a rush at some other place —Evesham, Shoreham, Woodstock, any quarter, in fact, that was likely to covet the glory of returning so distinguished and independent a person as himself.

And in his straightforward fashion he went direct to this old gentleman, whom he found in a little and old-fashioned but famous club in St. James's Street. The member for Englebury had once been a fine-looking man, and even now there was something striking about the firm mouth, aquiline nose, keen eyes, fresh color, and silvery hair; but the tall form was bent almost double, and the voice was querulous and raucous. He came into the small side room with Balfour's card in his hand; he bowed slightly and stiffly; and in that second had keenly studied his adversary's face, as if he would read every line of the character impressed on it.

"Sit down," said he.

Balfour sat down, and appeared to consider for a second or so how he would open the conversation. The two were familiar with each other's appearance in the House, but had never spoken.

"I suppose you know, Mr. Harnden, that they mean to turn me out of Ballinascroon."

"Yes, I do—yes," said the old gentleman, in a staccato fashion. "And you want to turn me out of Englebury? Yes—I have heard that too."

"I thought of trying," said Balfour, frankly. "But now I have made up my mind not to stand unless there is a vacancy. There was a talk of your resigning. I have called now to ask you whether there was any truth in the rumor; if not, I will let Englebury alone."

"Ay," said the elder man, with gruff emphasis; "Chorley—that fool Chorley—told you, didn't he? You are in league with Chorley, aren't you? Do you think that fellow can get my seat for you?"

"I tell you I don't mean to try, sir, unless you intend to give it up of your own free-will. Chorley? Oh no; I am not in league with Chorley; he and I had a quarrel."

"I didn't hear about that," said the old gentleman, still regarding his enemy with some reserve. "I haven't been down there for a long time now. And so Chorley was humbugging you, was he? You thought he had put you in for a good thing, eh? Don't you believe that ass. Why, he made some representations to me some time ago—"

At this point Mr. Harnden suddenly stopped, as if some new light had struck him.

"Ha, that was it, was it? You quarrelled with him, did you?" he said, glancing at Balfour a quick, shrewd look.

"Yes, I did," said Balfour, "and I swore I would fight him, and you, and everybody all round, and win the seat in spite of any coalition. That was vaporing. I was in a rage."

Mr. Harnden stroked his hands on his knees for some little time, and then he laughed and looked up.

"I believe what you have told me," he said, staring his enemy full in the face. "I see now why that presumptuous fellow, Chorley, made overtures to me. To tell you the truth, I thought he wanted me to spend more money, or something of that sort, and I sent him about his business. Well, sir, you've done the best thing you could have thought of by coming straight to me, because I will tell you a secret. I had prepared a nice little plan for dishing both you and Chorley."

And here the old gentleman laughed again at his own smartness. Balfour was glad to find him in this pleasant humor: it was not every one, if all stories be true, that the member for Englebury received so pleasantly.

"I like the look of you," said Mr. Harnden, bluntly. "I don't think you would play any tricks."

"I am very much obliged to you," said Balfour, dryly.

"Oh, don't you be insulted. I am an old man: I speak my mind. And when you come to my time of life—well, you'll know more about electioneering dodges. So you've quarrelled with Chorley, have you?"

"Yes."

"H'm. And you believed he would have given you my seat?"

"I thought with his help I might have won it—that is, if his representations were true. I was told you weren't very popular down there, Mr. Harnden."

"Perhaps not—perhaps not," said the old man. "They grumble because I speak the truth, in Parliament and out. But don't you make any mistake about it—all that would disappear if another man were to contest the seat. They'll stick to me at an election, depend on that, sir."

"Then you propose to remain in Parliament," said Balfour, rising. "In that case I need not waste your time further."

"Stay a minute," said the old man, curtly. "I told you I meant to dish you and Chorley."

"Yes."

"You and I might dish Chorley, and you might have the seat."

Balfour was not an emotional person, but he was a young man, and desperately anxious about his chances of being returned; and at this abrupt proposal his heart jumped.

"There is something about that fellow that acts on me like a red rag on a bull," continued this irascible old man. "He is as cunning as a fox and as slippery as an eel; and his infernal twaddle about the duties of a member of Parliament—and his infernal wife too! Look here: you are a young man; you have plenty of energy. Go down at once to Englebury; issue an address; pitch it high and strong about corrupt local influence and intimidation; denounce that fellow, and call on the electors to free themselves from the tyranny of dictation—you know the sort of buncombe. That will drive Chorley over to me."

"You are excessively kind, sir," said Balfour, who, despite his disappointment, could not help bursting out into a laugh. "I have no doubt that would be excellent sport for you. But, you see, I want to get into Parliament. I can't go skylarking about Englebury merely to make a fool of Mr. Chorley."

"There's a good deal of the greenhorn about you," said the old gentleman, testily, for he did not like being laughed at; "but that is natural at your age. Of course I mean to resign. I had thought of resigning in favor of that boy of Lord S——'s, who is a clever lad, if he would give up French radicals and atheism. But I will resign in your favor, if you like—at the last moment —after Chorley has been working for me like the hound he is. And what do you say to that, young man?"

Mr. Harnden rose, with a proud smile on his face. He was vain of his diplomacy; perhaps, too, it pleased him to patronize this young man, to whom a seat in the House was of such infinite consequence.

"Do I understand, sir, that you meant to give up your seat in any case?" Balfour asked.

"Certainly I did," said the other. "If I wished to retain it, do you think I should be afraid of you—I mean, of any candidate that Chorley could bring forward? No, no; don't you believe any such stuff. The people of Englebury and I have had our quarrels, but we are good friends at bottom. It will be a very disgraceful thing if they don't give me a handsome piece of plate when I retire."

"My dear sir," said Balfour, with saturnine simplicity, "*I* will take care of that."

"And I am not going to spend a penny in a bogus contest, mind that. But that is not your business. Now go away. Don't tell anybody you have seen me. I like the look of you. I think you have too many opinions; but as soon as you get into some small office—and the Government might do worse, I will say— you will get cured of that. Good-day to you."

There is a telegraph office at the foot of St. James's Street. Balfour walked right down there, and sent a message to his friend Jewsbury at Oxford: "*Come down at once to the 'Green Fox,' Englebury. Some fun going on.*" Then, finding he could just catch the afternoon train, he jumped into a hansom and drove to Paddington Station. He arrived at Englebury without even a tooth-brush; but he had his check-book in his pocket.

The Rev. Mr. Jewsbury arrived the next day, and the business of the election began at once. Jewsbury was in the secret, and roared with laughter as he heightened the pungency of the paragraphs which called on the electors of Englebury to free themselves from political slavery. And Balfour laughed as heartily when he found himself lashed and torn to pieces every morning by the *Englebury Mercury*, because he looked forward to the time when the editor of that important organ might have to change his tune, in asking the sitting member to obtain the Government advertisements for him.

It was a fierce fight, to be sure; and Mr. and Mrs. Chorley had such faith in their time-honored representative that they called on their fellow-townsmen to raise a sum to defray Mr. Harnden's expenses. Then, on the night before the election, the thunderbolt fell. Mr. Harnden attended a meeting of his friends and supporters. He thanked them most cordially for all they had done on his behalf. The weight of years, he said, was beginning to tell on him; nevertheless, he had been loath to take his hand from the plough; now, however, at the last moment, he felt it would be a mistake to task their kindness and forbearance longer. But he felt it a privilege to be able to resign in favor of an opponent who had throughout treated him with the greatest courtesy—an opponent who had already made some mark in the House—who would do credit to the borough. That the constituency was not divided in its opinions they would prove by voting for Mr. Balfour like one man. He called for three cheers for his antagonist; and the meeting, startled, bewildered, but at the same time vaguely enthusiastic, positively roared. Whether Mr. Chorley, who was on the platform, joined in that outburst could not well be made out. Next day, as a matter of course, Mr. Hugh Balfour was elected member of Parliament for the borough of Englebury; and he straightway telegraphed off this fact to his wife. Perhaps she was not looking at the newspapers.

Well, he was only a young man, and he was no doubt proud of his success as he hastened down to Surrey again. Then everything promised him a glad home-coming; for he had learned, in passing through London, that the charge against Lord Willowby and his fellow-speculators had been withdrawn—he supposed the richer merchants had joined to buy the man off. And as he drove over to The Lilacs he was full of eager schemes. Lady

Sylvia would come at once to London, and the house in Piccadilly would be got ready for the opening of Parliament. It would
be complimentary if she went down with him to Englebury, and
called on one or two people whose acquaintance he had made
down there. Surely she would be glad to welcome him after his
notable victory ?

But what was his surprise and chagrin to find that Lady Sylvia's congratulations were of a distinctly formal and correct character, and that she did not at all enter into his plans for leaving
The Lilacs.

"Why, Sylvia," said he, "surely you don't hate Englebury simply because you disliked the Chorleys? Chorley has been my sworn
enemy all through this fight, and I have smote him hip and thigh."

"I scarcely remember anything about the Chorleys," she said,
indifferently.

"But why would you rather live down here?" said he, in
amazement.

"You know you will be every night at the House," she said.

"Not more than other members," he remonstrated. "I shall
have three nights a week free."

"And then you will be going out among people who are altogether strangers to me—who will talk about things of which I
know nothing."

"My dear child," said he, "you don't mean to say you intend
to live down here all by yourself during the time Parliament is
sitting? You will go mad."

"I have told you before, Hugh," said she, "that I cannot leave
papa while he is so poorly as he is at present. You will have
plenty of occupation and amusement in London without me; I
must remain here."

There was a flash of angry light in the deep-set gray eyes.

"If you insist on remaining here," said he, "because your father chooses to go pottering about after those rabbits—"

Then he checked himself. Had he not vowed to himself again
and again that he would be tenderly considerate to this gentle-
souled creature who had placed the happiness of her life in his
hands ? If she had higher notions of duty than he could very
well understand, ought he not at least to respect them ?

"Ah, well, Sylvia," said he, patting her on the shoulder, "perhaps you are right. But I am afraid you will find it very dull."

CHAPTER XXVI.

THE CRISIS.

THINGS had indeed "come to a bonny cripus;" and he was altogether unaware of it. He was vaguely conscious, it is true, that his married life was not the married life he had looked forward to; and he was sorry that Lady Sylvia should insist on moping herself to death in that solitary house in Surrey. But then if her sense of duty to her ailing father demanded the sacrifice, he could not interfere; and there was some compensation for her in the beauty of the summer months that were now filling her garden with flowers. As for himself, he let no opportunity slip of paying her small and kindly attentions. He wrote to her every day. When he happened to have an idle forenoon, he would stroll into Christie's and buy some knick-knack for her. Lady Sylvia had never had the chance of gratifying her womanly passion for old china; but now that Balfour had discovered her weakness for such things, she had them in abundance. Now it was a Dresden milk jug, now a couple of Creil plates, again a Sèvres jardinière, that was sent as a little token of remembrance; while he scarcely ever went down on Saturday morning without carrying with him some similar bit of frail treasure, glad that he knew of something that would interest her. In the mean time he was intensely busy with his Parliamentary work; for, not having been in office, and having no hope of office, the tremendous overthrow of his party at the General Election had in no way damped his eager energy.

When the blow fell, it found him quite unprepared. One afternoon he received a telegram from his wife asking him if he could go down that evening. It was a most unusual summons; for she was scrupulously careful not to interfere with his Parliamentary duties; but of course he immediately hastened down to The Lilacs. He was more surprised than alarmed.

He went into the drawing-room, and found his wife standing there, alone. The light of the summer evening was somewhat dimmed by the multitude of leaves about the veranda; but his first glance told him that she was deadly pale, and he saw that she was apparently supporting herself by the one hand that caught the edge of the table.

"Sylvia," said he, in dismay, "what is the matter?"

"I am sorry to have troubled you to come down," she said, in a voice that was strangely calm, "but I could bear this no longer. I think it is better that we two should separate."

He did not quite understand at first; he only felt a little cold about the heart. The next moment she would have fallen backward had he not caught her; but she quickly recovered herself, and then gently put his hands away from her.

"Sylvia," said he again, "what is the matter with you?"

He stared at the white face as if it were that of a madwoman.

"I mean what I say, Hugh," she answered. "I have thought it over for months back. It is no hasty wish or resolve."

"Sylvia, you must be out of your senses," he exclaimed. "To separate! Why? For what reason? Is it anything that I have done?"

He wished to take her hand; she withdrew a step.

"The sooner this pain is over, the better for both of us," she said; and again the trembling hand sought the support of the table. "We have been separated—we are separated now—except . in name. Our married life has been a mistake. I do not think it is either your fault or mine; but the punishment is more than I can bear. I cannot any longer suffer this—this pretence. Let us separate. We shall both be free to live our own lives, without pretending to the world to be what we are not—"

"My darling!" he exclaimed; but somehow the warmth of his protest was chilled by that impassive demeanor: it was no outburst of temper that had summoned him down from London. "Sylvia! why won't you tell me your reasons? What is it you want altered? I have tried in every way to make your life just as you wished it—"

"I know you have," she said; "you have been kindness itself. But it is not a thing to be reasoned about. If you do not know already how far we are apart, how can I tell you? We ought never to have married. We have not a single thought or feeling, a single opinion, occupation, or interest, in common. I have tried to bear it—God knows how I have tried, night and day, to school myself into believing that it was only the natural way of the world. I cannot believe it; I cannot believe that any other woman has suffered what I have suffered, and now I must speak. Your life is in your work. I am only an encumbrance to you— a something apart from yourself and your interests, that demands attentions which are paid by you as a duty. I wish to release you and to release myself from a life of hypocrisy which I cannot any longer bear. Have I said enough?"

He stood for a moment or two absolutely silent: he never forgot those moments during his life.

"You have said enough," he answered, calmly; and then he absently turned to the window. The daylight was going; the hush of the evening had fallen over the birds; there was not a leaf stirring. "Yes, you have said enough. You cannot expect me to answer what you have said at once. Apparently, you have been thinking about it for some time. I must think about it too."

He took up his hat, which he had mechanically placed on the table beside him, and passed out into the garden. His face had a strange, gray look on it; the eyes were sunken and tired. Probably he himself scarcely knew that he opened the great wooden gate, went out into the road, and then by-and-by chose a familiar path across the fields where he was not likely to meet any one. He did not seem to care whither his wandering steps led him. His head was bent down, and at first he walked slowly, with the gait of one who was infirm or ailing; but presently he quickened his pace, his manner became more nervous and excited, occasionally he uttered a word as if he were addressing some one in an imaginary conversation.

The woods grew darker; the first stars came out. Far away there was the sound of a cart being driven home in the dusk, but all around him was still.

Then he came to a stone bridge over a small river; and here he paused for a time, leaning his arms on the parapet, and staring down—without seeing anything—at the black water. How could he see anything? For the first time since he had reached manhood's estate he was crying bitterly.

He was now a good many miles from home, but his wanderings had brought him no relief. It was all a mystery to him; he knew not what to do. How could he move by any piteous appeal that cold resolve? It was no mere whim or fancy he had to deal with, but something at once strong and subtle, a conviction of slow growth, a purpose that despair had rendered inflexible. But the origin of it? His brain refused to act; he wondered whether he, too, were going mad.

Now, a short distance from this river there stood a house that he knew; and as he aimlessly began to retrace his steps, he passed the gate. There was a light burning in one of the rooms; the window was open; he heard a faint sound of music. Suddenly it occurred to him: surely, Lady Sylvia, before she had come to this terrible resolve, must have spoken, in however indirect a fashion, of her manner of life, to some sympathetic woman friend; and to whom more likely than this kind person for whom she had professed so great an admiration and love? He went nearer to the house. She was alone in the room, playing some sufficiently sorrowful melody to herself. In his desperation and bewilderment, he determined that he would demand the counsel of this kind friend, who would at least understand a woman's nature, even supposing that she was not in Lady Sylvia's confidence. He was too anxious and perturbed to think twice. He entered the house, was at once shown into the drawing-room, and there and then told the whole story to his startled listener.

And it was with a great interest and sympathy that she heard the story, for she could not fail to observe that once or twice tears started to the young man's eyes as he tried to find some excuse in his own conduct for Lady Sylvia's resolve; and, moreover, she had a great liking for the young wife whose griefs and troubles had just been revealed to her. But what was the young man's surprise to find that this gentle and kindly lady, as he hurriedly told his brief story, began to grow monstrously angry, and when he had finished, was quite wrathful and indignant. There were no tears in her eyes, but there were tears in her voice—of proud and pathetic remonstrance.

"The cause of it!" she exclaimed, with the beautiful dark eyes, it must be owned, a trifle moist. "If she had some real sorrow to think of, she would have no room in her head for these morbid notions. Look at the other young wife who is our neighbor— my greatest friend and companion—who has bravely made up her mind to go and live for a whole year in America without those young children that are the very life of her life. That is a trial, that is a sorrow that demands some sympathy; and if Lady Sylvia had some real grief of that kind to undergo, depend on it, she would not be torturing herself and you with her imaginary disappointments. Her disappointments! What is the truth? She is too well off. She has been too carefully kept aside from any knowledge of the real misery that is in the world. Her notion of human life is that it should become just what everybody wants it to be. And her cure for her fancied troubles is separation from her husband? Very well. Let her try it."

And here, of course, she did cry a bit, as a woman must; but Balfour did not at all resent her angry vehemence, although it was far from complimentary to his young and unhappy wife.

"Yes," said she, with a passionate indignation, "let her try it. You cannot argue her out of her folly; let her have her will. Oh, I know the dreams that young girls have; and that is her excuse—that she has never known what life is. It is to be all rose-color. Well, let her try her own remedy. Perhaps she would like to see what real trouble is: a young mother tearing herself away from her children, and going to a distant country, where she cannot hear for weeks if one of them were to die. I can tell you, if she came with us, it might be possible to show her something of what human beings have really to suffer in this world—the parting of emigrants from their home and their kindred, the heart-breaking fight for money—"

"But why should she not go with you?" he said, eagerly. "Do you mean that you are going with the Von Rosens?"

She paused; and the nimble wit within the beautiful little head was busy with its quick imaginings. She had not thought of this as a practical proposal when she held it out as a wild threat. But why not—why not? This woman was vehement in her friendships when they were once formed. What would she not do to purge the mind of this young wife of fancies begotten of indolence and too good fortune? There was some color in her face. Her breath came and went a trifle quickly.

"Why not, to be sure?" said she; and she regarded the young man with a strange compassion in her eyes. "I do think if you trusted her to us for a time—if she would go with us—we could do her some good. I think we could show her some things. I think she might be glad enough to alter her decision—yes, glad enough."

"But a year is a long time," said he, staring absently at the open window and the black night and the stars outside.

"But we are not going for a year," said she; and it was clear that now she was most anxious to attempt this soul-cure. "We are only going to accompany our friends on their outward trip, and see them comfortably settled — comfortably, indeed! when that poor girl has to leave her children behind! If there was any righteousness in the law, they would give her the land and the money at once, and pay no attention to that ridiculous will. Oh no, Mr. Balfour, we shall only be going for a three months' trip or so; but we shall see many things in that time, and I think I could speak a little now and again to Lady Sylvia. Distance does a great deal. I don't think she will be sorry when we turn and begin to get home again to England. I don't think you will ever hear another word as long as you live about separation."

His face had brightened wonderfully.

"Do you know what a great favor it is you are offering me?" he said.

"Oh no, not at all," said she, eagerly. "We are going for a pleasure excursion. It is a mere holiday. We shall have a sharp wrench when we bid good-bye to the Von Rosens, but Lady Sylvia will have nothing to do with that. And she will see plenty to amuse her, and the change will do her health good."

Well, this young man was grateful enough to her; but he was not at all aware of what she had done for his sake. What had become of all those pet theories of hers about the false ideals formed before marriage, and of the inevitable disappointment on the discovery of the truth after marriage? This—if the humiliating confession must be made to the indulgent reader—was the identical Surrey prophetess and seer who used to go about telling us that nearly everybody who was married was wretched. The man had dowered his sweetheart with qualities she never possessed; after marriage he learned the nature of the woman who was to be his life companion, and never ceased to look back with an infinite longing and sadness to that imaginary woman with whom he had fallen in love. The girl, on the other hand, married her lover with the notion that he was to be always heroic and her lover; whereas she woke up to find that she had only married a husband, who regarded her not as life itself, but as only one of the facts of life. These we knew to be her pet theories. When this young man came to tell her of his troubles, why did not this

Frau Philosophin, as we called her, fall back on her favorite theories, as affording all the explanation that he needed? The fact is—though it requires a good deal of courage to put the words down—the heart of this person was much more trustworthy than her head. It was a very lovable and loving heart, answering quickly to any demand for sympathy, and most firmly tenacious of friendships. When she was told that Lady Sylvia was in trouble—when she saw that this young husband was in trouble—her fiddle-stick theories went to the winds, and her true woman's heart gave prompt and sure answer. She was a little nettled and indignant, it is true, for she had had, for some evenings before, mysterious fits of crying in quiet corners of the house over this journey we were about to undertake; but her indignation had only made her frank, and she had spoken bravely and honestly to Hugh Balfour. Yes, he had more to thank her for than he imagined, though his gratitude was quite sufficiently sincere and warmly expressed.

The tender-hearted little woman held his hand for a moment at the door.

"I shall not speak a word of this to any human being," said she—just as if she had no husband to whom she had sworn allegiance—"until you tell me that I may, and then I hope to hear that Lady Sylvia has accepted my offer. Don't argue with her; you might drive her into a sort of verbal obstinacy. Don't ask her to change her decision; she has not come to it without much heart-rending, and she cannot be expected to abandon it for the sake of a few sentences. Accept it; the cure will be more permanent."

"Thank you, and God bless you!" said he; and then he disappeared in the night.

"What if she should object?" he asked himself, as he hurried on through the darkness, his only guidance being from the stars. He had been so stunned and bewildered by the announcement of her resolve that he had never even thought of what she would do further—whether she would prefer to go back to Willowby Hall, or to remain in sole possession of The Lilacs. Either alternative seemed to him to be a sufficiently strange ending to the dreams that these two had dreamed together as they walked on that lonely terrace of a summer night, listening for the first notes of the nightingale, and watching the marshalling of the innumerable hosts of heaven. To go back to her father: to be left alone in that Surrey cottage.

He found her in the same room, calm and apparently self-possessed; but he saw from her eyes that she had given way to passionate grief in his absence.

"Sylvia," said he, "if I thought you had sent for me from any hasty impulse, I should ask you to let me reason with you. I see it is not so. You have made up your mind, and I must respect your wish. But I don't want to have any public scandal attaching either to your name or mine; and I believe—whether you believe it or not—that you will repent that decision. Now I am going to ask a favor of you. The ——s mean to accompany their friends the Von Rosens to their new home in America, and will then return—probably they will be away about three months. They have been good enough to offer to take you with them. Now, if you really believe that our relations are altogether so wrong that nothing is left but separation, will you consent to try three months' separation first? I will not seek to control your actions in any way; but I think this is reasonable."

The mention of her friend's name brought some color to the pale, thoughtful, serious face, and her bosom heaved with her rapid breathing, as he put this proposal before her.

"Yes," she said, "I will do what you wish."

"And your father?"

"I have not spoken to my father. I hope you will not. It is unnecessary."

CHAPTER XXVII.

THE ISOBARS.

It was an eager and an anxious time with our women-folk, who began to study the weather charts in the newspapers, and to draw from thence the most dismal forebodings. The air was full of isobars: we heard their awful tread. Areas of low pressure were lying in wait for us; the barometer curves assumed in imagination the form of mountainous waves, luring us to our doom. And then we had a hundred kind friends writing to warn us against this line and that line, until it became quite clear that, as we were to be drowned anyhow, it did not matter a brass farthing which line we selected. And you—you most amiable of persons, who gave us that piece of advice about choosing a starboard berth—our blessings on you! It was an ingenious speculation. When two vessels meet in mid-Atlantic—which they are constantly doing, and at full speed too—it is well known that they are bound to port their helm. Very well, argued our sympathetic adviser, porting the helm will make your steamer sheer off to starboard, and the other vessel, if there is to be a collision, will come crashing down on the port side: hence take your berth on the starboard side, for there you will be at least a trifle safer. It was a grain of comfort.

But there was one of us who feared none of these things, and she was to be the commander and comptroller of the expedition. She would have faced a dozen of the double-feathered arrows that appeared in the weather charts. "Beware the awful isobar!" we said to her. "Beware the awful fiddle-sticks!" she flippantly answered. And on the strength of her having done a bit of yachting now and again, she used solemnly to assure Lady Sylvia—on those evenings she spent with us then, talking about the preparations for the voyage—that there was nothing so delightful as life on the sea. The beautiful light and changing color, the constant whirling by of the water, the fresh breezes tingling on the cheek—all these she described with her eyes aglow; and the snug and comfortable evenings, too, in the ruddy saloon, with the soft light of the lamps, and cards, and laughter. Here ensued a battle royal. The first cause of this projected trip of ours was a dear friend and near neighbor called Mrs. Von Rosen—though we may take the liberty of calling her Bell in these pages—and in the days of her maidenhood she once made one of a party who drove from London to Edinburgh by the old coach-road, stopping at the ancient inns, and amusing themselves not a little by the way. This young lady now stoutly contested that life in a yacht was nothing to life in a phaeton; and for her part she declared there was nothing half so beautiful as our sunny English landscapes, far away in the heart of the still country, as one drove through them in the sweet June days. It was the rude-spoken German ex-lieutenant who brought ridicule on this discussion by suggesting that the two modes of travelling might be combined: apply to Father Neptune, livery-stable keeper, Atlantic.

Lady Sylvia was indeed grateful to her kind friend for all the attentions shown her at this time. Of course it was as a mere pleasure-excursion that we outsiders were permitted to speak of this long journey by land and sea. We were not supposed to know anything of that cure of a sick soul that our sovereign lady had undertaken. Balfour was busy in Parliament. Lady Sylvia was very much alone, and she had not been looking well of late. These her friends happened to have to make this trip to America: the opportunity of the double sea-voyage and of the brisk run through the continent on the other side was not to be thrown away. This was the understood basis of the agreement. We were not supposed to know that a courageous little woman had resolved to restore the happiness of two wedded lives by taking this poor petted child and showing her the kingdoms of the earth, and the hardship and misery of human life, and what not. As for Lord Willowby, no one knows to this day whether that reticent peer suspected anything or not. He was kind enough to say, however, that he was sure his daughter was in good hands, and sure, too, that she would enjoy herself very much. He deeply regretted that he could not ask to be allowed to join the party. We deeply regretted that also. But we had to conceal our grief. After all, it was necessary his lordship should stay at home to keep down the rabbits.

The command went forth—a proclamation from the admiral-in-chief of the expedition that all ceremonies of leave-taking were to be performed within-doors and at home, and that she would on no account allow any friend or relative of any one of the party to present himself or herself at Euston Square Station, much less to go on with us to Liverpool. She was very firm on this point, and we guessed why. It was part of her never-failing and anxious thoughtfulness and kindness. She would have no formal parting between Balfour and his wife take place under the observation of alien eyes. When Lady Sylvia met us at the station down in Surrey, she was alone. She was pale and very nervous; but she preserved much outward calmness, and professed to be greatly pleased that at last we had fairly started. Indeed, we had more compassion for the other young wife who was with us—who was being torn away from her two children and sent into banishment in Colorado for a whole long year. Our poor Bell could make no effort to control her grief. The tears were running hard down her face. She sat in a corner of the carriage, and long after we had got away from any landmark of our neighborhood that she knew, she was still gazing southward through these bewildering tears, as if she expected to see, somewhere over the elms, in the roseate evening sky, some glorified reflection of her two darlings whom she was leaving behind. Her husband said nothing, but he looked more savage than ever. For the past week, seeing his young wife so desperately distressed, he had been making use of the most awful language about Colonel Sloane and his flocks and herds and mines. The poor Colonel had done his best. He had left his wealth to this girl simply because he fancied she knew less about his life than most of her other relatives, and might cherish some little kindly feeling of gratitude toward him. Instead of paying for masses for his soul, he only asked that this young niece of his should remember him. Well, there is no saying what her subsequent feelings with regard to him may have been, but in the mean time the feelings of her husband were most pronounced. If he prayed for the soul of Five-Ace Jack, it was in an odd sort of language.

The homeless look about that big hotel in Liverpool! the huge trunks, obviously American, in the hall and round the doors! the unsettled people wandering around the rooms, all intent on their own private schemes and interests! What care had they for the childless mother and the widowed wife, who sat—a trifle mute, no doubt—at our little dinner-table, and who only from time to time seemed to remember that they were starting away on a pleasure-excursion? The manager of the trip did her best to keep us all cheerful, and again and again referred to the great kindness of the owners of our noble ship, who had taken some little trouble in getting for us adjacent cabins.

The next day was hot and sultry, and when we went down to the side of the river to have a look at the ship that was to carry our various fortunes across the Atlantic, we saw her through a vague silvery haze that in no way diminished her size. And, indeed, as she lay there out in mid-stream, she seemed more like a floating town than a steamer. The bulk of her seemed enormous. Here and there were smaller craft—wherries, steam-launches, tenders, and what not; and they seemed like so many flies hovering on the surface of the water when they came near that majestic ship. Our timid women-folk began to take courage. They did not ask whether their berths were on the starboard side. They spoke no more of collisions. And as Queen T——, as some of us called her, kept assuring them that their apprehensions of sea-sickness were entirely derived from their experiences on board the wretched and detestable little Channel boats, and that it was quite impossible for any reasonable Christian person to think of illness in the clean, bright, beautiful saloons and cabins of a first-class transatlantic steamer, they plucked up their spirits some-what, and did not sigh more than twice a minute.

It was about three in the afternoon that we stepped on board the tender. There was a good deal of cerebral excitement abroad among the small crowd. People stared at each other in a ner-vous, eager manner, apparently trying to guess what had brought each other to such a pass. Leaving out of view the cheery com-mercial traveller, who was making facetious jokes and exchang-ing pocket-knives and pencils with his friends, there was scarcely a face on board that did not suggest some bit of a story, and often that seemed to be tragic enough. There was a good deal of covert crying. And there was a good deal of boisterous racket in our quarter, chiefly proceeding from our young German friend, who was determined to distract the attention of his wife and of her gentle companion from this prevailing emotional busi-ness, and could think of no better plan than pretending to be an-gry over certain charges in the hotel bill, the delay in starting the tender off, and a dozen other ridiculous trifles.

Then we climbed up the gangway, and reached the deck of the noble and stately ship, passing along the row of the stewards, all mustered up in their smart uniforms, until we made our way into the great saloon, which was a blaze of crimson cloth and shining gold and crystal.

"And this is how they cross the Atlantic!" exclaimed Queen T——, who treasured revengeful feelings against the Channel steamers.

But that was nothing to her surprise when we reached our three cabins, which we found at the end of a small corridor. The yellow sunlight—yellowed by the haze hanging over the Mersey—was shining in on the brightly painted wood, the pol-ished brass, the clean little curtains of the berths; and altogether showed that, whatever weather we might have in crossing, nothing was wanting to insure our comfort—not even an electric bell to each berth—so far as these snug and bright little cabins were concerned. Von Rosen was most anxious that we should continue our explorations of these our new homes. He was most anxious that we should at once begin unpacking the contents of our smaller bags and placing them in order in our respective cabins. What had we to do on deck? We had no relatives or friends to show over the ship. There was nothing but a crowd up there—staring all over the place. We ought to make those preparations at once; so that we should have plenty of time subsequently to secure from the purser good seats at the dinner table, which should remain ours during the voyage.

A loud bell rung up on deck.

"Confound it!" cried the lieutenant, as if he would try to drown the noise with his own voice. "I have brought my latch-key with me! What do I want with a latch-key in America?"

But when that bell rung, our Queen T—— turned—just for a moment—a trifle pale.

"Lady Sylvia," said she, "would you not like to go up on deck to see the ship get up her anchor?"

We knew why she wanted the young wife to go on deck, and were inwardly indignant that the poor thing should be subjected to this gratuitous cruelty. Was she not suffering enough herself, that she should be made the spectator of the sufferings of others? But she meekly assented, and we followed too.

It was a strange scene that this crowd on deck presented, now that the ringing of another bell had caused a good many of the friends and relatives of passengers to leave the large ship and take their stand on the paddle-boxes of the tender. At first sight it seemed rather a merry and noisy crowd. Messages were being called out from the one vessel to the other; equally loud jokes were being bandied; missiles, which turned out to be keepsakes, were being freely hurled through the air, and more or less deftly caught. But this was not the aspect of the crowd that the monitress of Lady Sylvia wished to put before her eyes. There were other ceremonies going on. The mute hand-shake, the last look, the one convulsive tremor that stopped a flood of tears with a heart-breaking sob—these were visible enough. And shall we ever forget the dazed look in the face of that old man with the silvery hair as he turned away from bidding good-bye to a young woman, apparently his daughter? He did not seem quite to understand what he was doing. One of the officers assisted him by the arm as he stepped on to the gangway; he looked at him in a vague way, and said, "Thank you—thank you. Good-bye," to him. Then there was a middle aged man with a bit of black cloth round his hat. But why should one recall these moments of extreme human misery? If it was necessary that Lady Sylvia should drink this bitter draught—if it was necessary that she should have pointed out to her something of what real and definite sorrows and agonies have to be borne in life—why should these things be put before any one else? The case of Lady Sylvia, as every woman must perceive, was quite exceptional. Is it for a moment to be admitted that there could be in England any other woman, or, let us say, any small number of other women, who, being far too fortunately circumstanced, must needs construct for themselves wholly imaginary grievances and purely monomaniacal wrongs, to the distress equally of themselves and their friends? The present writer, at all events, shrinks from the responsibility of putting forward any such allegation. He never heard of any such women. Lady Sylvia was Lady Sylvia; and if she was exceptionally foolish, she was undergoing exceptional punishment.

Indeed, she was crying very bitterly, in a stealthy way, as the great ship on which we stood began to move slowly and majestically down the river. The small and noisy tender had steamed back to the wharf, its occupants giving us many a farewell cheer so long as we were within ear-shot. And now we glided on through a thick and thundery haze that gave a red and lurid tinge to the coast we were leaving. There was a talk about dinner; but surely we were to be allowed time to bid good-bye to England? Farewell! farewell! The words were secretly uttered by many an aching heart.

It was far from being a joyful feast, that dinner, though Von Rosen talked a great deal, and was loud in his praises of everything—of the quick, diligent service and pleasant demeanor of the stewards, of the quality of the hock, and the profusion of the *carte*. The vehement young man had been all over the ship, and seemed to know half the people on board already.

"Oh, the captain!" said he. "He is a famous fellow—a fine fellow—his name is Thompson. And the purser, too, Evans—he is a capital fellow; but he is in twenty places at once. Oh, do you know, Lady Sylvia, what the officers call their servant who waits on them?"

Lady Sylvia only looked her inquiry: the pale, beautiful face was dazed with grief.

"Mosquito!—I suppose because he plagues them. And you can have cold baths—salt-water—every morning. And there will be a concert, in a few evenings, for the Liverpool Seaman's Home. —Bell, you will sing for the concert?"

And so the young man rattled on, doing his best to keep the women-folk from thinking of the homes they were leaving behind. But how could they help thinking, when we got up on deck after dinner, and stood in the gathering dusk! England had gone away from us altogether. There was nothing around us but the rushing water, leaden-hued, with no trace of phosphorescent fire in it; and the skies overhead were dismal enough. We stayed on deck late that night, talking to each other—about everything except England.

<hr>

CHAPTER XXVIII.

THE LAST LOOK.

ALL around us the great unbroken circle of the sea, overhead the paler color of the morning sky, and this huge floating palace of 4500 tons crashing its way through the rolling waves of a heavy ground-swell—that was what we found when we stepped out on to the white and sunlit deck.

"What cheer, Madame Columbus? And how goes the log?" cried the lieutenant, making his appearance at the top of the companion-way.

Madame Columbus had been up betimes—in order to make sure of her bath—and was now engaged in private conversation with Lady Sylvia.

"We are a point west by north of Ben Nevis," she answered, promptly, "but the Irish coast is not yet in sight."

The latter half of her statement was true, anyhow; there was not even the faint cloud of an island visible all around the dark-blue horizon. And so we set out on our march up and down the deck, which had been strictly enjoined upon us by our admiral-in-chief, but which was occasionally interfered with by a lurch that sent this or that couple flying toward the hand-rail. And we were all full of our new experiences; of the strange sensation of plunging through the night at this terrible speed, of the remarkable ease with which articles could be taken out of portmanteans, and of the absolute impossibility of getting them put in again so as to secure something like order in our respective cabins. It was a brilliant morning, with a fresh and delightful breeze; but so blue was the sky, and so blue was the sea, that the eyes, becoming accustomed to this intense blue, saw everything on board the ship as of a glowing brown or red, while the human faces we looked at in passing were simply a blaze of crimson. Then we went below to breakfast, and instituted a sort of formal acquaintance with two or three folks who had been, the previous evening at dinner, absolute strangers to us.

That forenoon, as we sat on deck with our books, which were seldom looked at, we could not understand why Queen T——— was so fiercely opposed to our going ashore at Queenstown for an hour or two. As the pale line of coast now visible on the horizon came nearer and more near, she seemed to regard both Ireland and the Irish with great disfavor, though we knew very well that ordinarily she had a quite remarkable affection for both.

"What is Queenstown?" said she. "A squalid little place, filled with beggars and tradespeople that prey on the ignorance of Americans. They give you baskets of fruit, with brown paper filling up half. They charge you—"

"Why, you have never been there in your life!" exclaimed our Bell, with staring eyes.

' "But I know, all the same!" was the retort. "Haven't Americans told me again and again of their first experiences of Irish hospitality? And what is the use of being at all that trouble of going ashore to look at a miserable little town?"

"Madame," said the lieutenant, with a loud laugh, "I do think you are afraid we will not come back if we once are on the land. Do you think we will run away? And the company—will they give us back our passage-money?"

She relapsed into a proud and indignant silence; we knew not how Queenstown had managed so grievously to offend her.

And now we drew near the point at which we were to bid

a real farewell to our native land; and as we slowly glided into the broad, bright bay, Queenstown gave us an Irish welcome of laughter shining through tears, of sunlight struggling through fleecy clouds of rain, and lighting up the beautiful green shores. There was a beautiful green, too, in the water of the bay, which was rippled over by a light westerly breeze. Well, we remained on board, after all. We were informed by our admiral-in-chief that now, when the ship was almost empty, and certainly still, was an excellent opportunity for setting our cabins to rights, and putting away everything we should not require on the voyage. What was there to see by remaining on deck? A quiet bay, a green shore, and some white houses—that was all. Those of us who rebelled, and insisted on remaining on deck, she treated with silent scorn. She was successful, at least, in carrying Lady Sylvia with her below.

And yet it must be confessed that we were all of us glad to get away from Queenstown. We wished to feel that we had really started. Wasting time in waiting for mails is not an exciting occupation, at Queenstown or elsewhere. When, therefore, the tender came out from the shore, and discharged her human and other cargo, and when the order was given to let go the gangway, we were glad enough—all of us, perhaps, except one; for what meant that slight exclamation, and the inadvertent step forward, as this last means of communication was withdrawn? But there was a friendly hand on her arm. The child looked on in mute despair as the great vessel began to move through the water. There was a good deal of cheering as we now, and finally, set out on our voyage; she did not seem to hear it.

And now we were out on the Atlantic, the land gradually receding from sight, the great ship forging ahead at full speed through the rushing waves, the golden glory of the afternoon shining on her tall masts. They were getting out some sail, too; and as the string of men were hauling up the heavy gaff of the mizzen try-sail, one tall fellow, the leader of the choir, was singing so that all could hear,

> " Oh, it's Union Square as I chanced for to pass,
> Yo, heave, ho !
> Oh, it's there I met a bonnie young lass :"

while the idiotic refrain,

> " Give a man time to roll a man down,"

sounded musically enough with its accompaniment of flapping canvas and rushing waves. And there were rope-quoits got out, too, and the more energetic shovel - board; while those who scorned such vain delights were briskly promenading the deck with an eye to dinner. And then, at dinner, the sudden cry that made every one start up from the table and crowd round the nearest port-hole to look out on that extraordinary sunset—the sea a plain of dark and rich purple, almost hard in its outline against the sky; the sky a pure, dazzling breadth of green—a sort of olive green, but so dazzling and clear that it burned itself into the memory, and will forever remain there—with a few lines of still more lambent gold barred across the west. That fire of color had blinded all eyes. When we returned to our seats we could scarcely see each other.

"What a beautiful night we shall have!" said Lady Sylvia, who was doing her best to be very brave and cheerful—because, you see, it was our common duty, she considered, to cheer up the spirits of the young mother who had left her two children behind her—"and what a pity it is, my dear Mrs. Von Rosen, that you did not bring your guitar with you! Half of the charm of the voyage will be lost. And you know it will be moonlight to-night—you might have sung to us."

"I am like Mrs. S——'s little girl," said our Bell, "whom they used to bother so before visitors. She said, one day, in the most pathetic voice, 'I wish I didn't know no songs; and then I shouldn't have to sing none.' But the guitar has been put away for a long time now. That belonged to the days of romance. Do you know any Scotch songs, Lady Sylvia? I have gone mad about them lately."

"I believe it was once remarked of you, Bell," says one of us, "that your heart was like a magnetized needle, always turning toward the north. But what we want to know is where you are going to stop. Cumberland ballads used to be enough for you; then you got to the Borders; then to the Lowlands; and now you are doubtless among the clans. Does anybody know if there are stirring tunes in Iceland, or any *Volkslieder* to be picked up about the north pole? Nevertheless, we will take what you like to give us. We will pardon the absence of the guitar. When the moon comes out, we will take up the rugs

on deck, and get into a nice shadowy corner, and—and what is
that about 'Above—below—all's well?'"

"We are indeed well off," says our grave monitress, "that we
have nothing to think about but moonlight and singing. What
I am thankful for is that the clear night will lessen the chances
of our running down any unfortunate small vessel. Ah! you
don't know, Lady Sylvia, how often that happens—and nobody
ever hears of it. A huge ship like this would simply cut down
one of these smaller vessels to the water's edge and go clean over
her. And of course the greatest danger of our doing so is near
land. Think of the poor men, after being months at sea, perhaps, and within a day or so of meeting their wives and families
again, finding this huge monster crashing down on them! I
tremble when I hear people speak of the vessels anchored on the
Newfoundland Banks, and the fogs there, and the great steamers
going on through the night. A collision is nothing to us—I
suppose we should scarcely feel any shock at all—but it is certain death to the unhappy wretches who are out there at the
fishing. Well, it is part of the risk of their calling. They
have to support their families somehow; and I suppose their
wives know each time they leave the land that they may
never be heard of again. I wonder whether these poor men
ever think that they are hardly used in life. No doubt they
would prefer to belong to a fine club; .and their wives would
like to drive about in carriages. But I suppose they have
their compensations. The home-coming must be pleasant
enough."

"But do we go right on through a fog all the same?" asked
our Bell, in some alarm.

"At a reduced speed, certainly; and people say that the
booming of the fog-horn at night is one of the most horrid
sounds in the world."

"You never thought of that danger, Lady Sylvia," said Bell,
with a smile, "when your—when Mr. Balfour and you used to
speak of going round the world in a steam-yacht. By-the-way, I
suppose that steam-yacht that came out with us has got back to
Queenstown by this time."

Queen T—— glanced quickly and nervously at her.

"I hope so," said Lady Sylvia. "It was very friendly of the
people to escort us a bit on our way. I suppose they knew some

one on board. But I did not see any one waving a good-bye to them when they left."

"Oh," said Queen T——, carelessly, "I have no doubt they only came out for a run."

When we went on deck we found the last glow of the twilight fading out of the north-western skies. We were all alone on the moving world of waters, the huge metallic-hued waves breaking over in masses of white foam that were clearly visible in the semi-darkness. But by this time we had grown so accustomed to the monotonous sound of the rushing waves that it was almost the equivalent of silence; so that any other sound—the striking of the bells every half-hour in the steering-room, for example, and the repetition by the man at the lookout—was startlingly clear and distinct. We got our chairs brought together, and the shawls spread out, and formed a little group by ourselves, whose talking, if we were so inclined, could not well be overheard. But there was not much talking, somehow. Perhaps that monotonous rushing of the water had a drowsy effect. Perhaps we were trying to find out the names of the pale, clear stars overhead, far beyond the tall masts that kept swaying this way and that as the vessel rose and fell on the long waves. Or were we wondering whether the man at the lookout, whose form was duskily visible against the clear, dark sky, could make out some small and distant speck —some faint glimmer of a light, perhaps—to tell us that we were not quite alone in this awful world of waters?

Then the stars grew paler; for a new glory began to fill the lambent skies, and the white deck began to show black shadows that moved on the silvery surface as the ship rose to the waves.

"Do you remember that moonlight night at Grasmere?" says Queen T—— to her friend. "And won't you sing us 'The Flowers of the Forest?'"

It was quite another song that she sung—in a low voice that mingled curiously with the monotonous, melancholy rush of the waves. It was about the bonnie young Flora who "sat sighing her lane, the dew on her plaid an' the tear in her e'e." Why should she have picked out this ballad of evil omen for our very first night on the Atlantic?

> "She looked at a boat wi' the breezes that swung
> Away on the wave like a bird o' the main;
> An' aye as it lessened she sighed an' she sung,
> 'Farewell to the lad I shall ne'er see again.'"

Perhaps her conscience smote her.   Perhaps she thought it was
hardly fair to suggest to this poor young thing who was thrown
on our care that the cruel parting she had just undergone was a
final one.   At all events, as she began to sing this other song, it
seemed to some of us that she was taking a clear leap across a
long interval of time, and imagining herself somehow as already
returning to English shores.   For she sung—

> "Rest, ye wild storms, in the caves of your slumbers!
>   How your dread howling a lover alarms!
> Wauken, ye breezes, row gently, ye billows,
>   And waft my dear laddie ance mair to my arms!
> But oh! if he's faithless, and minds na his Nannie,
>   Flow still between us, thou wide roaring main!
> May I never see it, may I never trow it,
>   But, dying, believe that my Willie's my ain!"

Perhaps it was only our idle fancy, on this beautiful and pensive
night, that coupled Bell's selections with the fortunes of our
guest; but, all the same, one of us — who is always tenderly
thoughtful in such small matters—suddenly called out,

"Come, Bell, we shall have no more sad songs.   Who was it
that used to sing 'The Braes o' Mar' with a flushed face, as if all
the clans from John O'Groat's to Airlie were marshalling under
her leadership?"

Bell is an obliging person.   She sung that song, and many
another; and there was an attempt at a modest duet or two;
while the ceaseless roar of the waves went on, and we watched
the moonlight quiver and gleam on the hurrying waters.

"Oh, my dear," says Queen T——, putting her hand on the
head of her old friend and companion, who was nestled at her
feet, "this is not at all like crossing the Channel, is it?"

"Not much," says Bell.   "I am already convinced that my
ancestors were Vikings."

Nor was it at all like crossing the Channel when we went below
for the night—passing the great ruddy saloon, with its golden
lamps and hushed repose—and sought out the privacy of our
quiet and neat little cabins.   But here an act of retributive justice
had to be administered.   There were two people standing alone
in one of these cabins, amidst a wild confusion of slippers,
dressing bags, and clothes-brushes.   Says the one to the other,
sternly,

"What did you mean by that suspicious glance when the steam-yacht was mentioned ?"

"What steam-yacht?" says she, innocently ; but in the dusky light of the lamp her face is seen to flush.

"You know very well."

Here her fingers become somewhat nervous, and a piteous and guilty look comes into the eyes.

"Do you mean to deny that Balfour was in that boat, that you knew he was to be in it, and that you dared to keep the knowledge from his wife ?"

"And if he was," says she, with her lips beginning to quiver, "how could I tell her? It would have driven the poor thing mad with pain. How could I tell her ?"

"I believe you have a heart as hard as the nether millstone."

And perhaps she had ; but it was certainly not her own sorrows that were making the tears run down her face, as she pretended to be busy over a portmanteau.

CHAPTER XXIX.

MID-ATLANTIC.

THOSE glad days !—each one a new wonder as our tremendous speed drove us into successive and totally different worlds of light and color. The weather prophets were all at fault. Each morning was a surprise. There might have been, for example, a plunging and roaring during the night, that told us there was a bit of sea on; but who could have imagined beforehand the brilliant and magnificent beauty of this westerly gale—the sea rolling along in mountainous waves, the wild masses of spray springing high into the air from the bows of the ship, the rapid rainbows formed by the sunlight striking on those towering clouds, then a rattle as of musketry fire as they fell on the sunlit and streaming decks ? And if there were two obstinate young creatures who would not at all consent to stand in the huddled companion-way—if they would insist on having their morning march up and down the plunging decks, with the salt-water running down their reddened faces— had they not their reward ? They were the discoverers of the fact that we were running a race. What were those black objects that leaped clear into the sunlight, and went head-foremost again into the rushing waves? One after the other the merry dolphins sprung into the air and vanished again, and we were grateful to them for this friendly escort. They were sociable fellows, those dolphins—not like the whales, which generally kept away somewhere near the horizon, where they could only be made out by the recurrent jet of white foam.

And then, again, it might have been the very next morning that we found the world of water and sky grown still and dream-like, pervaded by a mystic calm. The sea like vast folds of silk, dull, smooth, and lustreless, a waste of tender and delicate grays, broken only by the faintest shadows where the low waves rolled; the sky lightly clouded over and also gray, with lines of yellowish light that grew narrower and narrower as they neared the horizon; and here the only bit of color in the vague and shadowy picture—a sharp, bold, clear line of blue all round the edge of the world, where the pale sea and the pale sky met.

And so we went on day after day, and the bells tolled the half-hours, and the gong sounded for meals, and the monotonous chorus of the sailors—

> "So now farewell,
> My bonnie young girl,
> For I'm bound for the Rio Gran'"—

told us of the holy-stoning of the decks. There was rather more card-playing than reading; there was a good deal of perfunctory walking; sometimes there was a song or two in the long saloon of an evening. And by this time, too, people had got to know each other, and each other's names and circumstances, in a most surprising manner. The formal "Good-morning" of the first day or two had developed into "And how are you this morning, Mr. ——?" The smallest civility was sufficient warranty for the opening of an acquaintanceship. Ladies freely took any proffered arm for that inevitable promenade before dinner—all except one, and she the most remarked of all. What was it, then, that seemed to surround her, that seemed to keep her apart? A certain look in her face?—she was not a widow. Her manner? —she was almost anxiously courteous to every one around her. All sorts and conditions of men were eager to bring her chair, or pick up her dropped book, or bid other passengers stand aside to let her pass through the companion-way; and all the elderly women—to judge by their looks—seemed to bless her in their hearts for her sweet face, and all the young women appeared to be considerably interested in her various costumes; but somehow she made no familiar acquaintances. They might challenge our bright-faced Bell to make up a side at rope-quoits; and that brave lass, though she seldom landed more than two out of the dozen of quoits on the peg, would set to work with a will, her eyes bluer than ever with the blue light from the sea, the sunlight touching the constant gladness of her face. But when our beautiful, pale, sad guest came near to look on, they only moderated their wild laughter somewhat. They did not challenge her. It was not she whom they expected to pencil down the score on the white paint of the ventilation shaft. But there was not one of these brisk and active commercial gentlemen (who were the most expert performers) who would not instantly stop the game in order to dart away and get a chair for her: that modest smile of thanks was sufficient reward.

There was a young lady who sat near us at dinner, a very pretty young lady, who had come all the way from San Francisco, and was returning home after a lengthened stay in Europe. It was quite evident that she and her friends must have stayed some time in Geneva, and that they had succumbed to the temptations of the place. She seemed to be greatly struck by Lady Sylvia's appearance, and for the first day or two paid more attention to her than to her meals. Now on the third day, imagine our astonishment—for small things become great on board ship—on finding the pretty young San Franciscan come in to breakfast without a scrap of jewellery either round her neck or on her hands. She had even discarded the forefinger ring—an opal surrounded with diamonds—which we had unanimously declared to be beautiful. Moreover, she never wore any jewellery during the rest of that voyage. Why was this? Wearing jewellery, even Genevan jewellery, is a harmless foible. Is there any magnetism radiating from a human being that is capable of destroying bracelets and finger-rings, or, at least, of rendering them invisible? These are the mysteries of life.

But indeed we had more serious matters to think about, for we had with us a stern monitress, who did not fail to remind us that existence, even on board a transatlantic steamer, is not all composed of dry champagne and rope-quoits. She had made the acquaintance of the purser, and from him she had obtained particulars regarding some of the many emigrants on board. The piteous tales she told us may have received a touch here and there from an imagination never of the dullest, but they sounded real enough, and it was very clear that they went straight to Lady Sylvia's heart. Was it not possible, she anxiously asked, to do something for this poor man who was dying of consumption, and who, conscious of his doom, was making a struggle to have a look at his two sons out in Montana before the sunken eyes finally closed? What we had to do for him, a day or two afterward, was to attend his funeral. The weighted corpse, wrapped round with a union-jack, was borne along by the sailors to the stern of the ship, and there a number of the passengers congregated, and stood with uncovered head to hear the short burial-service read. It was not a pathetic scene. The man was unknown to us, but for that brief hint of his dying wish. The wild winds and the rushing waves drowned most of the words of the service. And yet there was something strange in the suddenness with which the corpse plunged down and disappeared, and in the blank loneliness of the sea thereafter. The man had neither friend nor relative on board.

There was an open space on the lower deck into which, for the freer air, the emigrants often came; and there they followed their domestic pursuits, as unconscious as bees of being looked down upon from above. Surely it was with no impertinent curiosity that our Queen T—— taught her gentle friend to regard these poor people; rather it was with a great sympathy and friendliness. One morning she drew her attention to a young woman, who appeared to be also a young mother, for she had a couple of children dawdling about her heels; and Lady Sylvia was greatly distressed that those young things should be so dirty and obviously neglected. She was for sending for the invaluable Mr. Evans, and begging him to take some little present to the mother.

"But why should they be dirty? And why should they be neglected?" demanded that fierce social philosopher, whose height is five feet three. "Look at the mother; look at her tawdry ribbons, her unkempt hair, her dirty face. She is a woman who has got no womanly pride. If she has a husband, God help him! Fancy what his home must be. If he has got rid of her, I should imagine he must be glad; he could keep the house cleaner without her. But look at that young woman over there—I know she has a young family too, for I saw them this morning. See how she has tucked up her dress, so that she can go over the wet decks; see how she has carefully braided her hair; and do you see how all those tin things she has been washing are shining bright? and look at her now, polishing that knife, and putting the cloth up on the rope to dry. For my part, I have no sympathy for women who are squalid and dirty. There is no reason in the world why they should be so. A woman, and especially a wife, ought to make the best of her circumstances; and if her husband does drink and ill-use her, she won't make him any the more ashamed of himself by becoming a slattern, and driving him away from a dirty house. I am going down to speak to that young woman who is polishing the tin jugs."

And she did, too, and became acquainted with all the young wife's circumstances. These were not at all dreadful or pathetic. She was a brisk and active young Irishwoman, who was very proud that her husband in New York had at last saved up enough money to send for her and her children; and her only fear was that, New York being such a big place, there might be a chance of missing her husband on going ashore. Queen T—— wholly reassured her on this point, and begged to be allowed to make the acquaintance of her children; and of course she gave them a keepsake all round, with a whole heap of frnit and sweets obtained by illicit means from the chief saloon steward.

On—on—on, night and day, with this tremendous speed. Even our women-folk now had dismissed all fear of being ill. On one morning, it is true, during a pretty stiff gale in the "Devil's Hole," or "Rolling Forties," they were remarkably abstemious at breakfast, but not one of them succumbed; and now that we were getting near the Newfoundland Banks, they waxed valiant. They declared that crossing the Atlantic was mere child's play compared to crossing the Channel. Bell grew learned about square-sails and try-sails, and had picked up all the choruses of the sailors. "Give a man time to roll a man down," is not at all a proper sentiment for a young lady; but a great deal is admissible at sea.

Then we had a dolorous day of rain, and there were more huddled groups than ever in the smoking-room playing poker, and more disconsolate groups than ever at the top of the companion-way, looking out on the leaden sky and the leaden sea. Moreover, as the day waned, fog came on; and that evening, as we sat in the saloon, there was ominous conversation aboard. We heard the dull booming of the fog-horns as we sped through the night. Was not our course somewhat too northerly? What about icebergs? Toward morning should we not be dangerously near Cape Race—not dangerously for ourselves, but for the anchored schooners and smacks on the Great Bank, any one of which would be ploughed down by this huge vessel, with only perhaps one shriek of agony to tell what had happened? It was a gloomy evening.

But then, the next morning! Where was the fog? A dome of clear blue sky; a sea of dark blue, with the crisp white crests of the running waves; a fresh, invigorating westerly breeze. And now surely we were getting out of the region of unknown and monotonous waters into something definite, human, approachable; for it was with a great interest and gladness that the early risers found all around them the anchored schooners, and it was with even a greater interest that we drew near and passed a rowing-boat full of men, whose bronzed faces were shining red in the sun.

"These are the poor fellows I told you about," said our admiral and commander-in-chief to her friend. "Think of the danger they must be in on a foggy night—think of their wives and children at home. I should not wonder if their wives were glad to see them when they got back to shore!"

"It is dreadful—dreadful," said Lady Sylvia; and perhaps it was the new excitement of seeing these strange faces that made her eyes moist.

We had to pass still another long, beautiful day, with nothing around us visible but the blue sea and the blue sky; but if the honest truth must be told, we were not at all impatient to find before us the far, low line of the land. Indeed, we looked forward to leaving this life on board ship with not a little regret. We were going farther, perhaps to fare worse. We had become a sort of happy family by this time, and had made a whole host of friends, whom we seemed to have known all our lives. And one of us was rather proud of her skill at rope-quoits, and another was mad on the subject of sea-air, and another—his initials were Oswald Von Rosen—was deeply interested in the raffles and betting of the smoking-room. What would the next day's run be? What would the number of the pilot be? Would that ancient mariner have a mustache or not? There was a frightful amount of gambling going on.

The next morning our admiral insisted that there was a strong odor of sea-weed in the air, and seemed proud of the fact.

"Madame Columbus," said our German friend, seriously, "it is a happy omen. I do not think you could prevent a mutiny much longer—no; the men say there is no such place as America; they will not be deceived; they will return to Spain. The crew of the *Pinta* are in revolt. They do not care any more for the presence of those birds—not at all. If we do not see land soon, they will kill you and go home."

But the confidence which we placed in our admiral was soon to be justified. Far away on the southern horizon we at length descried a pilot-boat flying the flag of proffered assistance. We hailed with joy the appearance of this small vessel, which the savage inhabitants of the nearest coast had doubtless sent out to welcome the pioneers of civilization; and we regarded with awe and reverence the sublime features of Madame Columbus, now irradiated with triumph. As for the wretched creatures who had been mutinous, it is not for this hand to chronicle the sudden change in their manner: "They implored her," says a great historian, "to pardon their ignorance, incredulity, and insolence, which had created so much unnecessary disquiet, and had so often obstructed the prosecution of her well-concerted plan; and passing, in the warmth of their admiration, from one extreme to another, they now pronounced her whom they had so lately reviled and threatened, to be a person inspired by Heaven with sagacity and fortitude more than human, in order to accomplish a design so far beyond the ideas and conceptions of all former ages."

Stranger still, the native whom we took on board this friendly boat was found to be clothed, and he spoke a language which, although not English, was intelligible. We regarded him with great curiosity; but there was nothing savage or uncouth in his manners. He had rings in his ears, and he smoked a short clay pipe.

Of course our excitement all that day was great, and there was a wild scene in the smoking-room in the evening—a mock trial by jury having produced a good many bottles of whiskey in the way of fines. The songs were hearty and hoarse. We raffled a rug.

On the following morning there was something to make one rub one's eyes. It was a long, faint, pale-blue thing, stretching along the western horizon, and having the appearance of a huge whale lying basking in the mist of the early sunlight. We called aloud to those who were below. That blue line in the yellow mist was—America!

CHAPTER XXX.

LANDED!

THERE was excitement enough, to be sure. Every one was on deck, eagerly regarding the land that was momentarily drawing nearer. And who were these ladies whom we now saw for the first time? Surely they could not have been ill all the way across the Atlantic? Or had they not rather given way to an abject terror of the sea, and hidden themselves close in their berths in order to get a sort of ostrich safety? And the gentlemen who attended them, too—whence had they procured such a supply of tall hats? We resented the appearance of that ungainly article of costume. We had grown accustomed to the soft and delicate colors of sea and cloud; this sudden black patch struck a blow on the eye; it was an outrage on the harmonious atmospheric effects all around us.

For now we were slowly steaming over the bar, in the stillness of the summer morning; and the beautiful olive-green of the water, and the great bay before us, and the white-sailed schooners, and the long semicircle of low green hills were all softened together with a mist of heat. The only sharp point of light was close at hand, where the promontory of Sandy Hook, blazing in sunlight, jutted out into the rippling water. It was all like a dream as we slowly glided along. The pale hills looked spectral and remote: we preferred not to know their name. And then, as we drew near the Narrows, our blue-eyed Bell could not conceal her astonishment and delight. Surely, she said, we had

missed our way somewhere, and got back to the wrong side of
the Atlantic! The wooded hills coming close to the sea; the
villas on the slopes, half hidden in soft green foliage; the long
line of sandy shore; the small yachts riding at anchor in the
clear and rippling water—why, surely, surely, she said, we had
just come down the Clyde, and had got to Dunoon, or Inellan, or
the Kyles of Bute. We knew quite well that one of these yachts
was the *Aglaia.* We knew perfectly that if we were walking
along the shore there, we should meet a thick-set little man in
smart blue uniform, who would say,

"Ay, ay, mem, and will you be going for a sail to-day, mem?
Mr. ——, it is away up the hills he is to-day; and he will be
penting all the day; and the wind it is ferry good to-day, mem,
for a run down to the Cumbraes and back, mem."

And what would our Bell answer? She would say,

"Dear Captain Archie, we will go on board the *Aglaia* at
once, and go to the Cumbraes, and farther than that. We will
leave Mr. —— painting up in the hills for ever and ever, until
he comes down a Rip Van Winkle. We will go far beyond the
Cumbraes, to Loch Ranza and Kilbranan Sound, to the Sound of
Jura and Loch Buy, and we will listen to the singing of the mermaid of Colonsay. And I pledge you my word, Captain Archie,
that we will never once in all the voyage begin to cry because
we are not bound for Idaho."

But these idle dreams, begotten of the morning mist and the
sunlight, were soon dispelled. We came to anchor off Staten
Island. We regarded the natives who boarded us from the small
steamer with great interest and wonder; they were as like ordinary human beings as possible, and did not seem at all depressed
by having to live in a place some three thousand miles away from
anywhere—which was our first notion of America. Then we had
to go down into the saloon, and go through the form of swearing we had no forbidden merchandise in our luggage. It was
a tedious process; but we did not fail to admire the composure
of one stout little gentleman, who passed the time of waiting in
copying out on a large sheet of paper a poem entitled " Love."

" The love that sheds its mortal ray,"

the verses began. He had stumbled across them in a book out of
the saloon library, and they had been too much for his kindly

10

heart. Happily he had his copy completed before the great ship was got into the dock.

And now the dusky, steepled mass of New York lay before us, and experts were eagerly naming the principal buildings to strangers, and the sun was beating fiercely on us with a heat we had never experienced at sea. There was a little black crowd of people on the wharf; this great floating palace seemed bearing down on the top of them. And surely it was preposterous that handkerchiefs should be waved already.

Now the people who had warned us of the awful isobars, and generally recommended us to say our prayers before stepping on board a transatlantic steamer, had also harrowed our souls with a description of the difficulties of landing. Two sovereigns was the least tip to be slipped into the hands of the custom-house officer, and even then he might turn upon us with a fiendish malignity and scatter our innocent wardrobes all about the wharf. Then what about getting to a hotel in a city that has no cabs? Should we get into a labyrinth of tram-way cars, and end by getting back to the steamer and demanding that we should be taken to Liverpool forthwith? Well, we never quite knew how it was all managed; but there was no scrimmage, and no tipping of any sort, and nothing but the most formal opening of one portmanteau out of a dozen; and such remarkable civility, swiftness, and good arrangement that, before we could wholly understand it, we were being whirled away in a huge hotel omnibus that had high springs like a George IV. chariot, and that ploughed through the thick dust, and then sprung up on the tram-way rails with a bound that flung us about like pease in a bladder.

"Gracious goodness!" cried Queen T——, clinging on to the window, so that she should not be flung out on the other side; "this is more dangerous than crossing a dozen Atlantics!"

"Madame," said our German companion, with his teeth clinched, and his hands keeping a tight grip of about a dozen bags, umbrellas, and shawls, "the Americans suffer a great deal from liver-complaint; that is why they keep their streets so."

But what was the use of his talking about America? A booby could have seen we were not in America at all. We had expected to find New York a sort of overgrown Liverpool; but here we were—in Paris! Paris everywhere—in the green casements of the window, the plaster-fronted houses with Mansard-roofs, the acacia-looking ailanthus along the pavements, the trailing creepers about the balconies, the doors of carved wood with white metal handles. Paris, Paris everywhere—in the hot dry air and the pale and cloudless sky, in the gaudy shop fronts and restaurants with Parisian lettering on the signs. And surely this, too, is a Parisian hotel that we enter—the big and gilt saloons, the bedrooms heavily furnished in dark-red velvet, an odor of tobacco everywhere, and blue clouds and pink Cupids decorating the staircase!

And already we are involved in our first quarrel, for that vehement German has been insisting on the Irish porters bringing up all our luggage at once; and as there has been a sort of free fight below, he comes fuming up-stairs.

"Ah, it is true," says he, "what an American did once tell me. He said, 'You think it is all equality in my country? No, no; that is a great mistake. The obsequiousness,' said he, 'that marks the relations between the waiter at a hotel and the guest at a hotel, that is shocking—shocking. But then,' said he, 'the obsequiousness is all on the side of the guest.'"

We did not believe for a moment that any such American ever existed, though all nations, except the Scotch, have a common trick of saying evil things of themselves. We believed that this young man had impudently invented the story to excuse his overbearing and blustering treatment of three poor down-trodden sons of Erin, who, when they did bring up our portmanteaus, showed how they revolted against this ignoble slavery by pitching them down anyhow. They had our respectful sympathy; but we dared not offer them the common consolation of a piece of money. They were doubtless, as their bearing showed them to be, the descendants of kings.

There is one distressing peculiarity of American hotels which has never been remarked upon by any traveller, and that is their extreme instability of foundation. As we were engaged in opening our portmanteaus to get some costumes more suitable for the prevailing heat, those French-looking bedrooms, with their tall and narrow windows sheltered by white casements, and their solid couches and easy-chairs all covered with that crimson velvet which is a sweet solace in July—our bedrooms, I say, kept oscillating this way and that, so that we could scarcely keep our feet. The passages, too! After a great deal of knocking and calling, we mustered up our party to go down to luncheon, and then we found the long lobby swaying hither and thither far more violently than the saloon of the big ship had done in the " Rolling Forties." We dared not go down the stairs without clinging on to each other. We began to believe that the city of New York must be built like a water-hen's nest, which rises and falls with the rise and fall of the stream. It seemed very hard, indeed, that we should have successfully crossed the Atlantic without experiencing any discomfort, only to find ourselves heaved about in this fashion. It was observed, however, that this strange conduct on the part of the hotel gradually ceased as we sat at luncheon, so that we were happily allowed to examine the characteristics of the American family at the next table—the first distinctive group of natives we had seen on shore. They fully bore out all we had heard about this country. The eldest daughter was rather pretty, but sallow and unhealthy, and she drank a frightful quantity of iced water. The mamma was shrunken and shrivelled—all eyes, like a young crow—and seemed afflicted with a profound melancholy. The papa devoted himself to his newspaper and his toothpick. And there were one or two younger children, noisy, turbulent, petted, and impertinent. All these well-known characteristics we perceived at a glance. It is true, we afterward discovered that the family was English ; but that was of little account.

We went for a drive in the hot, clear, brilliant afternoon. Paris—Paris—Paris everywhere. Look at the cafés, with their small marble tables ; look at the young men in straw hats, who are continually chewing the end of a damp cigar that won't keep alight ; look at the showy nettings of the small, wiry, long-tailed horses, and the spider-wheeled vehicles that spin along to the Bois de—to the Central Park, that is. Of course when we meet one of those vehicles we keep to the right hand—anybody could have foretold that. And here is the Park itself — a very beautiful park indeed, with green foliage, winding roads, ornamental waters, statues, fountains. There is a band playing down there in the shade of the trees. And here is a broad paved thoroughfare —a promenade—with a murmur of talking, and a prevailing odor of cigarettes. Of course it is Offenbach the band is playing ; and it is pleasant enough to take a seat at this point of the Bois and look at the people, and listen to the music, and observe the glare of the sunlight on the greensward beyond and on the crystal shoots of the fountains. And the plashing drops of the fountains have a music of their own. What is it they are singing and saying and laughing?

> "Tant qu'on le pourra, larirette,
>   On se damnera, larira !
>   Tant qu'on le pourra,
>   L'on trinquera,
>   Chantera,
>   Aimera
>   La fillette.
>   Tant qu'on le pourra, larirctte,
>   On se damnera, larira !"

"How do you like being in Paris?" says Lady Sylvia, with a gentle smile, to her companion, thc German ex-lieutenant.

"I do not like thinking of Paris at all," said he, gravely. "I have not seen Paris since I saw it from Versailles. And there are two of my friends buried at Versailles."

And what was making our glad-faced Bell so serious too? She had not at all expressed that admiration of the thoroughfares we had driven through which was fairly demanded by their handsome buildings. Was she rather disappointed by the French look of New York? Would she rather have had the good honest squalor and dirt and smoke of an English city? She was an ardent patriot, we all know. Of all the writing that ever was written, there was none could stir her blood like a piece that was printed in a journal called the *Examiner*, and that begins:

> "First drink a health, this solemn night,
>   A health to England, every guest;
> That man's the best cosmopolite
>   Who loves his native country best."

Was it because she had married a German that she used to repeat, with such bitterness of scorn, that bitterly scornful verse that goes on to say:

> "Her frantic city's flashing heats
>   But fire, to blast, the hopes of men.
> · Why change the titles of your streets?
>   You fools, you'll want them all again !"

But it was surely not because she had married a German that, when she came to the next appeal, the tears invariably rushed to her eyes:

> "Gigantic daughter of the West,
> 　We drink to thee across the flood;
> We know thee and we love thee best,
> 　For art thou not of British blood?
> Should war's mad blast again be blown,
> 　Permit not thou the tyrant powers
> To fight thy mother here alone,
> 　But let thy broadsides roar with ours!
> 　　Hands all round!
> 　God the tyrant's cause confound!
> To our dear kinsmen of the West, my friends,
> 　And the great name of England round and round!"

And was our poor Bell grieved at heart, now that she had crossed the three thousand miles of the Atlantic, to find that the far daughter of the West had forsaken the ways of her old-fashioned mother, and had taken to French finery and to singing—

> "Tant qu'on le pourra, larirette,
> 　On se damnera, larira!"

"My dear child," it is necessary to say to her, "why should you be so disappointed? They say that New York changes its aspect every five years; at present she has a French fit on. London changes too, but more slowly. Twenty years ago every drawing-room was a blaze of gilt and rose-color; people were living in the time of Louis XIV. Five years ago Kensington and St. John's Wood had got on to the time of Queen Anne; they fixed you on penitential seats, and gave you your dinner in the dark. Five years hence Kensington and St. John's Wood will have become Japanese—I foresee it—I predict it; you will present me with a pair of gold peacocks if it isn't so. And why your disappointment? If you don't like Paris, we will leave Paris. To-morrow, if you please, we will go up the Rhine. The beauty of this Paris is that the Rhine flows down to its very wharves. Instead of taking you away out to Chalons, and whipping you on to Bar-le-duc and Nancy, and making you hop across the Vosges—the Vogesen, I beg your pardon—we will undertake to transport you in about twenty minutes for the trifling sum of ten cents. Shall it be so?"

"I am not so stupid as to be disappointed with New York yet," said our Bell, rather gloomily.

She called it New York. And she still believed it was New

York, though we went in the evening to a great hall that was all lit up with small colored lamps; and the band was playing Lecocq; and the same young men in the straw hats were promenading round and round and smoking cigarettes, and smart waiters were bringing glasses of beer to the small tables in the boxes. Then we got back to the hotel, not a little tired with the long, hot, parching day; and we went to bed—perchance to dream of cool English rains and our Surrey hedges, and the wet and windy clouds blowing over from the sea.

———————

CHAPTER XXXI.

GHOSTS AND VISIONS.

OF course we did not run away from New York merely because our good Bell was of opinion that the city had something too much of a French look. We had many excellent friends pressing their hospitalities on us; we had many places to visit; and then Queen T—— must needs insist on telegraphing to England that letters should be sent out to us by a particular steamer. Letters! No doubt when Columbus landed on the shores of San Salvador, and found a whole new world awaiting his explorations, his first impulse was to sit down and cry because he could not hear whether his mother-in-law's cold was better.

She was most economical, too, about that telegram. She would not have Lady Sylvia send a separate message.

"A couple of words extra will do," she said, "and they will understand to go over to the Hall and let your father—and Mr. Balfour too—know that you have arrived safely. Why should you send a separate message?"

Why, indeed! The young wife was grateful to this kind friend of hers for so considerately throwing dust in our eyes. Why should she send a separate message to her husband, when the expense would be so desperate?

And although Queen T—— lavished her time on writing letters to her boys at home, she always did that in the privacy of her own room, and rather strove to hide or to make little of these communications with England. Columbus himself, when the king and queen asked him to give an account of his travels, could not have been more particular than this new discoverer in describing the wonderful things she had seen. The amount of information conveyed to those boys — who would much rather have had a sovereign sewed up between two cards — was enormous. On one occasion she was caught giving them a precise account of the Constitution of the United States, obviously cribbed from Mr. Nordhoff's "Politics for Young Americans." But then these budgets were generally written at night, and they were never paraded next day. When, before Lady Sylvia, she spoke of England, she treated it as a place of little account. Our necessary interests were in the things around us. One could not always be looking back and indulging in sentiment. That was more to be pardoned—and as she said this, the small philosopher was down at the Battery, her tender eyes gazing wistfully at a certain archway which barred our view of the sea beyond—that was more to be pardoned to the thousands upon thousands of sad-hearted men and women who had landed at this very point, who had passed through that archway, with their hopes of the New World but feebly compensating them for their loss of home and kindred and friends. This, said she, was the most interesting spot in all America, and the most pathetic. And as she had been two whole days on this continent, we calmly acquiesced.

And at length the arrival of our letters, which contained a vast amount of important news about nothing at all, relieved the anxious hearts of the two mothers, and set us free. We bid farewell to this Atlantic Paris, with its hot pavements, its green ailanthus-trees, its dry air, and intolerable thirst; and at about three o'clock on a strangely still and sultry day we drive down to the wharf and embark on a large and curiously constructed steamer. But no sooner have we got out on to the broad bosom of the river than we find how grateful are these spacious saloons, and lofty archways, and cool awnings, for now the swift passage of the boat produces something like a breeze, and for a time we cease to brood on iced drinks. Under the pleasant awning we have our chairs and books and fruit; but the books are not much regarded, for, as we noiselessly and swiftly steam up against the current, it appears more and more certain that we have got into some mystic dream-land which can in no wise be any part of America, and that this river is not only neither the Hudson nor the Rhine, but wholly unlike any river seen out of a vision of the night. What is the meaning of the extraordinary still haze that kills our natural colors, and substitutes for them the mere phantasmagoria of things? The low and wooded hills that here bound the river ought to be green; they are, on the contrary, of a pale opalesque blue and white. The blue sky is faintly obscured; we can only catch glimpses of white villas in these dusky woods; all around is a sort of slumberous, strangely hued mist; and the only definite color visible is the broad pathway of sunlight on the stream, and that is of a deep and ruddy bronze where the ripples flash. We begin to grow oppressed by this strange gloom. Is it not somewhere in this neighborhood that the most "deevilish cantrips" are still performed among the lonely hills, while the low thunder booms, and unearthly figures appear among the rocks? Should we be surprised if a ghostly barge put off from that almost invisible shore, bringing out to us a company of solemn and silent mariners, each with his horn of schnapps, and his hanger, and his ancient beard? Will they invite us to an awful carouse far up in the sombre mountains, while our hair turns slowly gray as we drink, and the immeasurable years go sadly by as we regard their wild faces? "Bell! Bell!" we cry, "exorcise these Dutch fiends! Sing us a Christian song! Quick—before the thunder rolls!" And so, in the midst of this dreadful stillness, we hear a sweet and cheerful sound, and our hearts grow light. It is like the ringing of church bells over fields of yellow corn:

> "Faintly as tolls the evening chime—"

the sound is low, but it is clear and sweet as the plashing of a fountain—

> "Our voices keep tune, and our oars keep time."

And, indeed, there are two voices now humming the subdued melody to us—

> "Soon as the woods on shore look dim,
> We'll sing at St. Ann's our parting hymn."

Surely the mists begin to clear, and the sun is less spectral over those dusky hills? Hendrick Hudson — Vanderdecken — whatever in the devil's name they call you — be off, you and your ghastly crew! We will not shake hands; but we wish you a

safe return to your gloomy rocks, and may your barrels of
schnapps never be empty! We can see them retire; there is no
expression on their faces; but the black eyes glitter, and they
stroke their awful beards. The dark boat crosses the lane of
bronzed sunshine; it becomes more and more dusky as it nears
the shore; it vanishes into the mist. And what is this now,
close at hand?—

> "Saint of this green isle, hear our prayers—
> Oh, grant us cool heavens and favoring airs!"

Vanderdecken, farewell! There will be solemn laughter in the
hills to-night.

But there is no romance about this German ex-lientenant, who
exhibits an unconscionable audacity in talking to anybody and
everybody, not excepting the man at the wheel himself; and of
course he has been asking what this strange atmospheric phenomenon meant.

"Ha!" he says, coming along, "do you know what it is, this
strange mist? It is the forests on fire—for miles and miles and
miles—away over in New Jersey and in Pennsylvania, and it has
been going on for weeks, so that the whole air is filled with the
smoke. Do you smell it now? And there is not enough wind
to carry it away; no, it lies about here, and you think it is a
thunder-storm. But it is not always—I mean everywhere; and
the captain says there is not any at West Point, which is very
good indeed. And it is very beautiful there, every one says; and
the hotel is high up on the hill."

In the mean time this mystical river had been getting broader,
until it suddenly presented itself to us in the form of a wide and
apparently circular lake, surrounded with mountains, the wooded
slopes of which descended abruptly to the shores, and were there
lost in a wilderness of rocks and bushes. Do you wonder that
Bell called out,

"It is the Holy Loch! Shall we go ashore at Kilmun?"

And then the river narrowed again, and the waters were very
green; and of course we bethought ourselves of the Rhine, flowing rapidly along its deep gorge.

Or was it not rather one of the shores of the Lake of Geneva?
Look at the picturesque little villas stuck over the rocks, amidst
the bushes and trees, while the greens seem all the more intense

that the sun out there in the west has become a rayless orb of
dusky and crimson fire—as round and red and dull a thing as
ever appeared in a Swiss lithograph. It never seemed to occur
to any of us that, after all, this was not the Holy Loch, nor the
Rhine, nor the Lake of Geneva, but simply the river Hudson.

And yet we could not help reverting to that Rhine fancy when
we landed on the little wooden pier, and entered a high hotel omnibus, and were dragged by two scraggy horses up an exceedingly
steep and dusty road to a hotel planted far above the river, on
the front of a plateau and amidst trees. It was a big, wide hotel, mostly built of wood, and with verandas all round; and there
were casements to the bedroom windows; and everywhere in the
empty and resounding corridors an odor as of food cooked with
a fair amount of oil. We threw open one of these casements.
There was a blaze of fire in the west. The wooded hills were of
a dark green. Far below us flowed the peaceful river, with a faint
mist gathering on it in the shadows.

Then by-and-by we descended to the large, bare-walled, bare-
floored, but brilliantly lighted saloon, in which the guests were assembling for dinner; and now it was no longer the Rhine, for
the first object that struck the eye was the sharp contrast between the dazzling white of the tables and the glossy, black faces
and heads of the waiters. From this time forward, it may here
be said, we began to acquire a great liking for those colored folk,
not from any political sympathy, for we were but indifferently
fierce politicians, but simply because we found Sambo, so far as
we had the honor of making his acquaintance, remarkably good-
natured, attentive, cheerful, and courteous. There was always an
element of surprise about Sambo, the solemn black bullet-head
suddenly showing a blaze of white teeth, as he said "Yes, sah!"
and "Yes, mahm!" and laughingly went off to execute orders
which he had never in the least understood. There was so much
of the big baby about him, too. It is quite certain that Queen
T—— deliberately made the most foolish blunders in asking for
things, in order to witness the suppressed and convulsive amusement of these huge children; and that, so far from her being annoyed by their laughing at her, she was delighted by it, and cov-
ertly watched them when they thought they were unobserved.
She was extremely tickled, too, by the speech of some of them,
which was a great deal nearer that of Mr. Bones, of St. James's

Hall, than she had at all expected it would be. In fact, in the privacy of her own chamber she endeavored once or twice— But this may be read by her boys, who have enough of their mother's wicked and irreverent ways.

Then, after dinner, we went out to the chairs on the wide and wooden balcony, high up here over the still-flowing river, in the silence of the hot, still, dark night. A gray haze lay along the bed of the stream ; the first stars overhead were becoming visible. Far away behind us stretched those dusky hills into which the solemn Dutchmen had disappeared. Were they waiting now for the first glimmer of the moon before coming out to begin their ghostly carouse? Could we call to them, over the wide gulf of space, and give them an invitation in our turn? "Ho! ho! Vanderdecken—Hendrick Hudson—whatever they call you —come, you and your gloomy troop, down the hill-sides and through the valleys, and we will sing you a song as you smoke your clays! The dogs shall not bark at you ; and the children are all in bed; and when you have smoked and drank deep, you will depart in peace! Ho! ho! Ho! ho!"

Could we not hear some echo from those mystic hills?—a rumble of thunder, perhaps?

"Listen !" called out our Bell—but it was not the hoarse response of Vanderdecken that she heard—"there it is again, in among the trees there. Don't you hear it? Katy-did! Katy-did! Katy-did !"

And by-and-by, indeed, the hot, still night air became filled with these calls in the dark ; and as we watched the moon rise over the hills, our fancies forsook the ghostly Dutchmen, and were busy about that mysterious and distant Katy, whose doings had so troubled the mind of this poor anxious insect. What was it, then, that Katy did that is never to be forgotten? Was it merely that she ran away with some gay young sailor from over the seas, and you, you miserable, envious, censorious creature, you must needs tell all the neighbors, and give the girl no peace? And when she came back, too, with her husband, the skipper, and her five bonny boys, and when they both would fain have settled down in their native village, she to her spinning-wheel, and he to his long clay and his dram, you would not even then let the old story rest. Katy-did! Katy-did! And what then? Peace, you chatterer, you tell-tale, you scandal-monger! or we will take you to be the imprisoned spirit of some deceased and despicable slanderer, condemned forever to haunt the darkness of the night with your petulant, croaking cry.

* * * * * * *

Ho! ho! Vanderdecken! Cannot you send us a faint halloo? The moon is high over the hills now, and the wan light is pouring down into the valleys. Your dark figures, as you come out from the rocks, will throw sharp shadows on the white roads. Why do you draw your cowls over your face? The night is not chilly at all, and there is no one to see you as you pass silently along. Ho! ho! Vanderdecken! The night is clear. Our hands shall not tremble as we lift the bowl to you. Cannot you send us a faint halloo?

* * * * * * *

> "Saint of this green isle, hear our prayers—
> Oh, grant us cool heavens and favoring airs!
> Blow, breezes, blow! the stream runs fast,
> The rapids are near, and the daylight's past!"

Or is it the tinkling of the sheep-bells on our Surrey downs, with the sunlight shining on the spire of the church, and the children walking between the hedges, the blue sky over all? Or is it the clear, sweet singing of the choir that we hear, falling on the grateful sense like the cool plashing of running water? Gloomy phantoms have no place on our Surrey downs; the air is bright there; there is a sound as of some one singing.

* * * * * * *

Katy-did! Katy-did! Was it on such a night as this that she stole away from her home, and looked pale and troubled as she fled along the lonely road to the side of the stream? See how the moon lights up the dusky sides of the hills, and touches the rounded foliage of the woods, and flashes a bold line of silver across the broad, smooth river! There are other lights down there, too—the colored lights of moving boats. And will she step on board with a quick, hurried, trembling foot, and hide her pale face and streaming eyes in her lover's arms? Farewell, farewell to the small, empty room and its flowers; farewell to the simple life and the daily task; for the great, eager, noisy world lies all ahead, unknown and terrible. Swiftly speeds the boat through the moonlight and the mist — there is no sound as it goes — not even a faint and parting cheer from Vanderdecken and his merry men as they solemnly gaze down from the hills.

*   *   *   *   *   *   *

It is the lieutenant who rouses us from our dreams.

"Lady Sylvia," says he, "you know the Rhine—were you ever at Rolandseck? Do not you think this place is very like Rolandseck?"

For a second or two she could not answer. Had she ever been to Rolandseck on the Rhine!

CHAPTER XXXII.

OUR RANCH-WOMAN.

FAR away in the north, where the sea is—the real sea, not the decoction of chalk we have around most of our southern English shores—the small boy sits on the rocks, over the clear deep, and carefully baits his hook (five a penny from the village grocer). As soon as he has hidden the blue barb with a crisp white bit of cockle, or with a slice from a spout-fish, or with a mussel of tawny orange and brown, he lowers it into the beautiful water, where nothing is as yet visible but the wavering outline of the rocks, and the moving purple of the sea-weed, and mayhap the glimmer of a star-fish on the sand at unknown depths below. Then suddenly, from the liquid darkness around, comes sailing in, with just one wave of its tail, a saithe ! and the eager eyes of the fisherman follow every movement of his prey, ready to prompt the sudden twitch. But now the fish begins to play the hypocrite. He does not at all make straight for the tempting morsel suspended there, but glides this way and that by the side of it, and under it and over it, pretending all the while to pay no attention to it whatsoever. Occasionally he seems to alter his mind; he makes a dart at the bait, coming right on with his eyes staring and his mouth agape, and then, again, the youthful fisherman says something about *vich-an-dhiaoul* as he sees the narrow green back of the saithe shoot down again into the deeps. But the doom is near and certain.

Now this was the way in which our Bell proceeded to take

possession of that tempting property that was waiting for her at Colorado. She was never tired of suggesting that we should go to this place and that place, rather than that her legitimate curiosity should be satisfied as to her new home. Her eyes went down to New Orleans, and then went up to Montreal, but were scarcely ever turned due west. And when we, who rather feared that she was proposing these diversions for our sakes alone, remonstrated with her, and pointed out that she would have ample opportunity of visiting the great lakes and Canada on her way back at the expiry of her year of banishment, you should have seen the light that came suddenly into her face. She seemed already to imagine herself free.

"Take a roundabout way home?" exclaimed the young matron, with proud eyes. "I think not. The moment my year is out, you will see if I don't come home straighter than any crow that ever flew. If I could only go up to the top of the mountains—and spread my wings there—and make one swoop across the plains, and another swoop across the Atlantic—"

"Stopping at New York, of course, for a biscuit."

"—you would see how soon I should be in England. Just fancy the first evening we shall spend all together again! Lady Sylvia, you will come to us that evening?"

"I hope so," said Lady Sylvia, with a startled look—she had been dreaming.

And so, in pursuit of these idle vagaries we left West Point and ascended the Hudson a bit by boat, and then landed and got into a train which most kindly kept by the side of the river as it whirled us along. The carriage was a comfortable one, with armchairs on pedestals by the windows, and with small tables for our books, fruit, and what not; and while the lieutenant had passed along to the smoking-car to have a cigar and some iced drink on this blazing hot day, the women-folk amused themselves by spreading out on the table a whole store of trinkets belonging to a youthful merchant attached to the car, and by selecting a vast number of perfectly useless presents for people at home. It was an agreeable occupation enough, to connect the names of those who were far away with those bits of ivory, and photograph frames, and puzzles; and Queen T—— faithfully undertook to deliver all these little gifts with appropriate messages. The representation that they were going to carry those trumpery things about with them all over America, that their boxes would be encumbered, that the things themselves would be broken, and that the proper time for purchasing presents was just before sailing from New York, met with that absolute indifference which was generally accorded to the advice of a person who had by this time subsided into the position of being a mere chronicler of the doings of the party, and who had found out that in this land of liberty it was as unsafe for him to open his mouth as it was in his own home in England.

"My dear Lady Sylvia," said Queen T——, as this Swiss-looking railway-car was rumbling along toward Saratoga through a dusty and wooded country that look parched enough under the blue sky, "I guess I feel just real mean."

Lady Sylvia's eyes asked what this extraordinary language meant.

"Don't you?" she continued. "Here are we going into Saratoga in the company of a ranch-woman, a farmeress, a stock-raiser, a bowie-knifer. What was it the judge said in New York about Saratoga?—that we should find there 'a blaze of wealth, beauty, and culture such as was not to be found in any capital in Europe?' and of course it would have been bad enough in any case for us simple country-folk to go into such a whirl of fashionable life; but with one of the wild desperadoes of Colorado—what will they think of us?"

"I guess you want a tarnation lickin'," said the stock-raiser, calmly. "Buffalo Jack, where's my cowhide?"

Buffalo Jack, being immersed in time-tables, would pay no heed to her nonsense; but Lady Sylvia was heard to say that the conduct of a ranch-woman in coming to Saratoga was deserving of respect rather than ridicule, for she would no doubt learn something of manners before going back to her bowie-knives and cattle.

What, then, was this big, busy town through which we drove, with its broad thoroughfares, deep dust, green trees, and huge hotels?

We looked at the jewellers' shops, and the cafés, and the promenaders, and one cries out, "Baden-Baden!"

We catch a glimpse of some public gardens and colored lamps and avenues, and another calls out, "It is Kreuznach, and the band is playing!"

We whirl along another spacious thoroughfare, and a third calls out, "It is the Boulevard Poissonnière!" when it is mildly suggested that, after all, this may be no more Kreuznach than the Hudson was the Rhine, and that it might be better, on the whole, to call it Saratoga.

It was with great diffidence that we ascended the steps of the monster hotel, and found ourselves in a large central hall. We were conscious that we were travel-stained, and had scarcely sufficient moral courage to ask the clerk for rooms. We knew that the smart young men standing around were regarding us; and oh! so snowy were their white neckties, which they wore in the middle of the day. And then, to make matters worse, this pernicious ranch-woman had donned in the morning a costume of light-blue serge, in which she had done some yachting the year before; and we knew, though we dared not look, that there must be stains of the salt-sea foam on it. Finally, our inward rage and humiliation were complete when, having been furnished with our keys, we entered the lift to be conveyed to the floors above; for here we found ourselves confronted by three young ladies—but the human imagination refuses to recall the splendor of the attire of these angels in human form. Each of them had a jeweller's shop on her hands.

However, we dried our eyes in secret, and made as brave an appearance as possible when we assembled together in the saloon below.

"Look here, child," said Queen T—— to our ranch-woman, as she lifted a white object from the table. "Do you see that? That is a fork. You take it in your left hand, and you lift your food to your mouth with it, instead of with your fingers, as you have been accustomed."

"It's a thorough good lickin' you want," said this child of nature, doggedly. It was all we could get out of her.

· Then we went out for a drive; and a mighty fine show we made, with our green gauze curtains to keep out the dust, and *with our two horses.* The lieutenant was perched up beside the driver. Occasionally he disappeared from our sight altogether, hidden away by the dense clouds of brown dust that came rolling in the wake of some carriage. And the farther we went out into the country, the deeper the dust in the roads appeared to become, until our German friend had assumed the guise of a baker, and there was scarcely any difference between the color of his hat, his beard, and his coat. But we came to our journey's end at last, for we reached a series of deep gullies in the sand ; and in each of these gullies, which were a good bit apart, were some more or less temporary buildings, mostly of wood ; and at each of them we found a gentleman in a tall black hat, who in the most courteous manner offered us a glass of the saline water he was prepared to sell, informed us of its chemical qualities, presented us with a prospectus of his company, and was generally most affable. It was a terrible temptation. We might have remained there all day, drinking gallons of the water—for nothing. And indeed we began to pride ourselves on our connoisseurship ; and if the present writer had only the various prospectuses by him at present, he could pick out the particular spring which we unanimously declared to be the finest. We had to tear ourselves away.

"After all," said Bell, with a sigh, "they manage these things better at Carlsbad."

Then we drove away again through the thick sand, and in process of time found ourselves on the broad, bare avenue which leads out to Saratoga Lake. And here we found ourselves still further ashamed, notwithstanding our two horses, by the fashion in which the people shot by us in their light little carioles, their toes perched up, their swift little trotters apparently running away with them. In spite of the dust, we could see the diamonds flashing on the fingers and shirts and neckties of the brown-faced, brown-bearded gentlemen who appeared to have come right up from California. We reached the lake, too—a large, calm extent of silvery gray water, becoming somewhat melancholy in the evening light. We gathered some flowers, and bethought ourselves of another lake, set far away among lonely woods, that we had seen in the by-gone days.

"Once upon a time," says Queen T——, as we are standing on the height, and looking abroad over the expanse of water, "I can remember there were two young people sailing out on a lake like this in a small boat in the moonlight. And one of them proposed to give up his native country in order that he might marry an English girl. And I think it is the same girl that has now to give up her native country—for a time—for the sake of her children. Were you ever at Ellesmere, Lady Sylvia ?"

Lady Sylvia had never been to Ellesmere, but she guessed why these things were spoken of. As for Bell, she was putting the gathered flowers in a book; they were for her children.

We drove back to dine in the large saloon, with its flashing lights and its troop of black waiters. We were more than ever impressed by the beautiful attire and the jewellery of the ladies and gentlemen who were living in Saratoga; and in the evening, when all the doors of the saloons were thrown open, and when the band began to play in the square inside the hotel, and when these fashionable people began to promenade along the balcony which runs all round the intramural space of grass and trees, we were more than ever reminded of some evening entertainment in a Parisian public garden. Our plainly dressed women-folk were out of place in this gay throng that paced up and down under the brilliant lamps. As for our ranch-woman, she affected to care nothing at all for the music and this bright spectacle of people walking about the balcony in the grateful coolness of the summer night, but went down the steps into the garden, and busied herself with trying to find out the whereabouts of a katy-did that was sounding his incessant note in the darkness. What was it they played? Probably Offenbach; but we did not heed much. The intervals of silence were pleasanter.

But was it not kind of those two gentlemen, both of whom wore ample frock-coats and straw hats, to place their chairs just before us on the lawn, so that we could not but overhear their conversation? And what was it all about?

"Pennsylvania's alive — jest alive," said the elder of the two. "The miners are red-hot — yes, *sir!* You should have heerd me at Mauch Chunk — twenty thousand people, and a barbecue in the woods, and a whole ox roasted — biggest thing since 'Tippecanoe and Tyler too.' When I told 'em that the bloated bond-holders robbed 'em of their hard-earned wages, to roll in wealth, and dress in purple and fine linen, like Solomon in all his glory, and the lilies of the valley, you should have heerd 'em shout. I thought they would tear their shirts. The bond is the sharp-p'inted stick to poke up the people."

"And how about Philadelphy?" says the other.

"Well, I was not quite so hefty there. There's a heap of bonds in Philadelphy; and there's no use in arousing prejudices — painful feelings — misunderstandings. It ain't politics. What's good for one sile ain't good for another sile. You sow your

seed as the land lays; that's politics. Where people hain't got
no bonds, there's where to go in heavy on the bond-holders.
But in Philadelphy I give it to 'em on reform, and corruption,
and the days of the Revolution that tried men's souls, and that
sort o' thing — and wishin' we had Washington back again.
That's always a tremendous p'int, about Washington; and when
people are skittish on great questions, you fall back on the Father of his Country. You see—"

"But Washington's dead," objected the disciple.

"Of course he's dead," said the other, triumphantly; "and
that's why he's a living issue in a canvass. In politics the deader
a man is, the more you can do with him. He can't talk back."

"And about Massachusetts, now ?" the humble inquirer asked.

"Well, those Yankees don't take too much stock in talk. You
can't do much with the bonds and corruption in Massachusetts.
There you touch 'em up on whiskey and the nigger. The evils
of intemperance and the oppressions of the colored brother, those
are the two bowers in Massachusetts."

"Rhode Island ?"

"Oh, well, Rhode Island is a one-horse State, where everybody
pays taxes and goes to church; and all you've got to do is to
worry 'em about the Pope. Say the Pope's comin' to run the
machine."

Then these two also relapsed into silence, and we are left free
to pursue our own speculations.

And indeed our chief manageress and monitress made no secret of her wish to leave Saratoga as soon as possible. We had
taken it *en route* out of mere curiosity; it was obvious to her that
she could gain no moral here to preach at the head of her poor
pupil. These lights and gay costumes and languid quadrilles
were the mere glorification of idleness; and she had brought
this suffering one to America to show her, in our rapid transit
from place to place, something of the real hardships that human nature had to fight against and endure, the real agony that
parting and distance and the struggle for life could inflict on the
sons and the daughters of men. Saratoga was not at all to her
liking. There was no head for any discourse to be got out of it.
Onward, onward, was her cry.

So it was that on the next day, or the next again, we bade
farewell to this gay haunt of pleasure, and set out for grimmer

latitudes. We were bound for Boston. Here, indeed, was a fruitful theme for discourse; and during the long hours, as we rolled through a somewhat Bavarian-looking country — with white wooden houses set amidst that perpetual wooden forest that faded away into the hills around the horizon—we heard a great deal about the trials of the early settlers and their noble fortitude and self-reliance. You would have fancied that this lecturess was a passionate Puritan in her sympathies; though we who knew her better were well aware that she had a sneaking liking for gorgeous ritual, and that she would have given her ears to be allowed to introduce a crucifix into our respectable village church. That did not matter. The stern manners and severe discipline of the refugees were, at the moment, all she could admire, and somehow we began to feel that if it had not been for our gross tyranny and oppression the *Mayflower* would never have sailed.

But a graver lesson still was to be read to us. We could not understand why, after a time, the train was continually being stopped at short intervals, and we naturally grew impatient. The daylight left us, and the lights in the carriage were not bright enough to allow us to read. We were excessively hungry, and were yet many miles away from Boston. We had a right to speak bitterly of this business.

Then, as the stoppages became more lengthened, and we had speech of people on the line, rumors began to circulate through the carriages. An accident had happened to the train just ahead of ours. There was a vague impression that some one had been killed, but nothing more.

It was getting on toward midnight when we passed a certain portion of the line; and here the place was all lit up by men going about with lanterns. There was a sound of hammering in the vague obscurity outside this sphere of light. Then we crept into the station, and there was an excited air about the people as they conversed with each other.

And what was it all about? Queen T—— soon got to know. Out of all the people in the train, only one had been killed— a young girl of fifteen: she was travelling with her father and mother; they had not been hurt at all. The corpse was in a room in the station; the parents were there too. They said she was their only child.

We went on again; and somehow there was now no more
complaining over the delay. It was past midnight when we
reached Boston. The streets looked lonely enough in the darkness. But we were thinking less of the great city we had just
entered than of the small country station set far away in the silent forest, where that father and mother were sitting with the
dead body of their child.

CHAPTER XXXIII.

AN INROAD OF PALE-FACES.

But we were not always to be preached at by this miniature
Madame Solomon. We had not come three or four thousand
miles to be lectured up hill and down dale. Even our stern
teacher herself forgot her moralities when, after a long night's
rain, Boston received us with breezy blue skies, cool winds, and a
flashing sunlight that broke on the stirring trees., We breathed
once more, after the heat of New York and the dust of Saratoga.
We walked along the pavements, and, as we had always been told
that Boston was peculiarly English, we began to perceive an English breadth of frame on the part of the men, an English freshness of complexion on the part of the women. We shut our
eyes to the fact that the shops were more the shops of Brussels
than of Brighton. Surely these were English clouds that swiftly
crossed the sky; English trees and parks that shone fair in their
greenness; an English lake that was rippling in waves before
the brisk breeze? And then, again, away down in the business
part of the city, amidst tall warehouses and great blocks of stores,
how could we fail to notice that that was the Atlantic itself which
we suddenly caught glimpses of at the end of the thoroughfares,
just as if some one, tired of the perpetual gray and red of the
houses, had taken a huge brush and dashed in a stroke of brilliant cobalt across the narrow opening?

"Ships go from here to England, do they not?" asked Lady
Sylvia once, as we were driving by a bit of the harbor.

"Certainly."

She was looking rather wistfully at the blue water, and the
moored steamers, and the smaller craft that were sailing about.

"In a fortnight one could be back in Liverpool?"

"Doubtless."

But here our Bell broke in, laying her hand gently on the hand of her friend.

"You must not think of going back already, Lady Sylvia," she said, with a smile. "We have got to show you all the wonders of our Western country yet. How could you go back without seeing a buffalo-hunt?"

"Oh," said she, hastily — and the beautiful pale face flushed somewhat—"I was not thinking of that. It was a mere fancy. It seems so long since we left England, and we have come so great a way, that it is strange to think one could be back in Surrey in a fortnight."

"We cannot allow you to play truant, you know," said Queen T——, in her gentle way. "What would every one say if we allowed you to go back without seeing Niagara?"

"I assure you I was not thinking of such a thing," said Lady Sylvia, seriously, as if she were afraid of grievously offending Niagara. "Would not every one laugh if I were to show homesickness so soon?"

But, all the same, we could see that she never looked at these blue waters of the Atlantic without a certain wistfulness; and, as it happened, we were pretty much by the sea-side at this time. For first of all we went down to Manchester—a small, scattered, picturesque watering-place overlooking Massachusetts Bay, the Swiss-looking cottages of wood dotted down anywhere on the high rocks above the strand. And when the wild sunset had died out of the western skies — the splendid colors had been blinding our sight until we turned for refuge to the dark, intense greens of the trees in shadow—we had our chairs out on the veranda, up here on the rocks, over the sea. We heard the splashing of the waves below. We could vaguely make out the line of the land running away out to Cape Cod; and now the twin lights of the Sisters began to shoot their orange rays into the purple dusk. Then the moon rose; and the Atlantic grew gray; and there was a pale radiance on the rocks around us. Our good friends talked much of England that long, still, beautiful night; and now it seemed a place very far apart from us, that we should scarcely be able to recognize when we saw it again.

Then we went to see some other friends at Newport, arriving

just in time to get a glimpse of the afternoon drive before the people and their smart little vehicles disappeared into those spacious gardens in which the villas were partly hidden. The next morning we drove round by the sea; and now the sun was burning on the almost smooth water, and there was a fresh smell of sea-weed, and the tiny ripples curled crisp and white along the pebbly bays. Our Bell began to praise the sea. Here was no churned chalk, but the crystal sea-water of the northern shores that she loved. And when she turned her eyes inland, and found occasional glimpses of moorland and rock, she appealed to Lady Sylvia to say if she did not think it was like some part of Scotland, although, to be sure, there was no heather here.

"I have never been in Scotland," said Lady Sylvia, gently, and looking down. "I—I almost thought we should have gone this year."

There was no tremor at all in her voice; she had bravely nerved herself on the spur of the moment.

"You must go next year. Mr. Balfour will be so proud to show his native country to you," said Queen T——, very demurely; but we others could see some strange meaning in her eyes—some quick, full expression of confident triumph and joy.

And how is it possible to avoid some brief but grateful mention of the one beautiful day we spent at Cambridge—or, rather, outside Cambridge—in a certain garden there? It was a Sunday, fair and calm and sweet-scented, for there were cool winds blowing through the trees, and bringing the odors of flowers into the shadowed veranda. Was not that bit of landscape over there, too—the soft green hill with its patches of tree, the hedges and fields, the breezy blue sky with its floating clouds of white—a pleasant suggestion of Surrey? There was one sitting with us there who is known and well beloved wherever, all over the wide world, the English tongue is spoken; and if that gracious kindliness which seemed to be extended to all things, animate and inanimate, was more particularly shown to our poor stricken patient, who could wonder who had ever seen her sensitive mouth and pathetic eyes? Of whom was it written:

> "Soft as descending wings fell the calm of the hour on her spirit;
> Something within her said, 'At length thy trials are ended?'"

If she could not quite say that as yet, her sorrows were for the moment at least forgotten, and she sat content and pleased and grateful. And then we had dinner in an old-fashioned room of the old-fashioned house, and much discourse of books; the mute listener, having won the favor of all, being far more frequently addressed than anybody else. The full moon was shining on the trees when we went out into the clear night. It was shining, too, on the Charles River, when we had driven on along the white road; and here, of course, we stopped to look at the wonderful picture. For beyond this flashing of silver on the rippling water, the river was bounded by a mass of houses that were black as midnight in the shadow; and here and there a dusky spire rose solemnly into the lambent sky, while down below there was a line of lamps burning in the dark like a string of ruddy jewels. These were the only points of color, those points of orange; all else was blue and silver—a dream of Venice.

What more is to be said about Boston before we leave it for the mystic woods and lakes of Chingachgook, whose ghost we hope to see emerge from the dim forest, in company with that of the simple-minded Deerslayer? Well, a word must be said about the great thoughtfulness of our good friends there, who took us to see every place and thing of note—except Bunker's Hill. They most scrupulously avoided all mention of Bunker's Hill, just as a Scotchman would rather die than mention Bannockburn in the South; and, to tell the truth, we never saw the place at all. This is much to be regretted; for the visiting of such scenes is most useful in refreshing one's knowledge of history; and indeed this courtesy on the part of our Boston friends led to a good deal of confusion afterward. For, one evening up in Canada, when Bell had been busy with her maps, she suddenly cried out,

"Why, we never went to see Bunker's Hill!"

"Neither we did," was the reply.

"And it is close to Boston!"

"Assuredly."

She remained in deep reflection for a moment or two; and then she said, in absolute innocence,

"I do wonder that a nation that fought so well, North and South, should show such a sensitiveness as that. They never said a word about Bunker's Hill when we were at Boston. You would have thought the humiliation of that small defeat was quite forgotten by this time; for I am quite sure the South would not speak about it, and I am quite sure the North is as proud of Stonewall Jackson now as the South can be."

Stonewall Jackson?—Bunker's Hill?

"What do you mean?" said Queen T——, severely; for she thought the young wife had taken leave of her senses.

"Well," said she, simply, and rather ungrammatically, "if the North was beaten, they fought well enough afterward; and when they can point to such battles as Gettysburg, they need not be afraid of the South remembering Bunker's Hill against them."

This was too awful. She was the mother of two children. But we wrote to our friends in Boston, begging them in the future not to let any of their English friends go through the town without telling them what Bunker's Hill was all about.

Next, a word about the singular purity of the atmosphere: at mid-day, as we stood in the street or walked across the Common, we could make out with the naked eye the planet Venus, shining clear and brilliant in the blue overhead.

Finally, a word as to a certain hotel. We had gone there partly because it was conducted on the European plan, and partly because it was said to be the best in America, and we naturally wanted to see what America could do in that way. We came to the conclusion that this hotel was probably the best in America a generation ago, and that its owners, proud of its reputation, had determined that it should never be interfered with—not even by an occasional broom. It was our friend the Uhlan who waxed the most ferocious. He came down in a towering rage the first morning after our arrival.

"The best hotel in America!" he cried. "I tell you, we have no room at all; it is a box; it is a miserable hole, without light; it is full of mosquitoes; it looks into a sort of well, over the kitchen, and it is hotter than an oven; and the noise of the quarrelling in the kitchen; and I think a woman dying of—what do you call it? asthma?—in the next room— No, I will not stay here another night for a thousand pounds!"

However, we pacified him, and he did stay another night, and was richly rewarded. He came down on the second morning with a pleased air. He had a sheet of writing-paper in his hand, on which were displayed a number of strange objects.

"Ha!" said he, with a proud smile, "it is so kind of them to let us know the secrets of the American ladies. These things lie thick all over the room ; but they are very small, and you cannot easily see them for the dust. But they are very strange — oh, very strange. Did you ever see hair-pins so small as these?"

He showed us a beautiful variety of these interesting objects, some of them so minute as almost to be invisible to the naked eye. Almost equally minute, too, were certain India-rubber bands. Then that tiny brush, tipped with black; what was that for? Surely the thousand virgins of Cologne must have in turn inhabited this room, to have left behind them so many souvenirs.

"You have no business with those things!" said Bell, angrily. "They don't belong to you!"

"To whom, then?" said he, meekly. "To the Crown? Is it treasure-trove? But one thing I know very well. When we go away from this pretty hotel—from this, oh! very charming hotel —we will not shake the dust from our feet, because that would be quite unnecessary. They have enough; don't you think so?"

And then we set out on our travels once more; and during a long and beautiful day went whirling away northward through a rough, hilly, and wooded country, intersected by deep ravines, and showing here and there a clear stream running along its pebbly bed. Here and there, too, on the hills the woods were already beginning to show a yellow tinge ; while at rare intervals we descried a maple that had anticipated the glowing colors of the Indian summer, and become like a flame of rose-red fire among the dark green of the pines. It was a picturesque country enough—this wilderness of rocks and streams and forests; and it might have been possible to begin and imagine the red men back again in this wilderness that they once haunted, but that, from time to time, we suddenly came on a clearing that showed a lot of bare wooden shanties, and the chances were that the place rejoiced in some such name as Cuttingsville. Cuttingsville! But perhaps, after all, there is a fitness in things ; and it would have been a worse sort of desecration to steal one of the beautiful Indian names from some neighboring stream and tack it on to this tag-rag habitation of squatters.

The evening sun was red behind the dark green of the trees when, at Glenn's Falls, we left the railway, and mounted on the top of a huge coach set on high springs. Away went the four horses; and we found ourselves swinging this way and that as if we were being buffeted about by the five tides that meet off the

Mull of Cantire. It was a pleasant ride, nevertheless; for it was now the cool of the evening, and we were high above the dust, and we were entering a country not only beautiful in itself, but steeped in all sorts of historical and romantic tradition. Far over there on the right—the last spur of the Adirondacks—was the mountain held by the French artillery to command the military road through these wilds, and bearing the name of French Mountain to this day. Ahead of us, hidden away in the dark woods, was the too famous Bloody Pond. And Fort William Henry?—of a surety, friend, these lovely damsels shall be safely housed to-night, and the dogs of Mingoes may carry the news to Montcalm that his prey has escaped him!

It was a plank-road that carried us away into the forest, and the monotonous fall of the horses' hoofs was the only sound that broke the stillness of the night and of the woods. The first stars came out in the pale gray overhead. Our lamps were lit now; and there was a golden glory around us—a blaze in the midst of the prevailing dusk.

And now the forest became still more dense, and the road wound in an intricate fashion through the trees. For our part, we could see no path at all. The horses seemed perpetually on the point of rushing headlong into the forest, when lo! a sharp turn would reveal another bit of road, it also seeming to disappear in the woods. And then the pace at which this chariot, with its blazing aureole, went flashing through the darkness! Mile after mile we rattled on, and the distant lake was nowhere visible. Not thus did the crafty Hurons steal through these trees to dog the footsteps of the noble Delawares. We were almost ashamed to think that there was no danger surrounding us, and that our chief regard was about supper.

Suddenly there was a wild yell ahead, and at the same moment a black object dashed across the heads of our leaders. Then we caught sight of a vehicle underneath the lamps; and there was a shout of laughter as it flew onward after that narrow escape. The sharp turn in the road had very nearly produced another massacre of pale-faces in the neighborhood of Fort William Henry.

"Do you remember that night at Keswick?" our Uhlan said, with a laugh. "That was near, too; was it not, madame? And now this great coach—we should have run clean over that wagonette, as you described the big steamers running over a small schooner; and the driver, did you see how smart he was in taking his leaders off the planks? It was very well done—very well done; he is a smart fellow, and I will give him another cigar, if it does not annoy you, Lady Sylvia."

"It is very pleasant in the night air," said our courteous guest. "And indeed I am accustomed at home to the smell of pipes—which is a great deal worse."

And so The Lilacs was still her home? She betrayed no embarrassment in speaking of the nest she had forsaken; but then she was sheltered by the darkness of the night.

Then at last the long, delightful drive was done; and there was a great blaze of lamps over a broad flight of stairs and a spacious hall. We turned before we entered. Down there in the dusk, and hemmed around by shadowy hills, lay the silent waters of Lake George.

CHAPTER XXXIV.

A COMPLETE HISTORY OF CANADA.

THERE were two people standing at a window and looking abroad over the troubled waters of Lake George—or Lake Horicon, as they preferred to call it—on this colorless and cheerless morning. The scene was a sad one enough. For far away the hills were pale under the clouded sky, and there were white mists stealing over the sombre forests, and the green islands lay desolate in the midst of the leaden sea that plashed coldly on their stony shores. Were they thinking—these two—as they watched the mournful grays of the morning change and interchange with the coming and going of the rain-clouds, that the great mother Nature was herself weeping for her red children gone away forever from this solitary lake and these silent woods? This was their domain. They had fished in these waters, they had hidden in these dense forests from the glare of the sun, for ages before the ruthless invader had come from over the seas. Or was it of a later race that these two were thinking—of persons and deeds that had first become familiar to them in the pleasant summertime, as the yacht lay becalmed on the golden afternoons, with the mountains of Skye grown mystical in the perfect stillness? Was it of Judith Hutter, for example, and Hurry Harry, and the faithful Uncas, who had somehow got themselves so mixed up with that idling voyage that one almost imagined the inhabitants of Tobermory would be found to address one as a pale-face when the vessel drew near the shore? One of the two spoke.

"I think," said she, slowly — but there was a peculiar proud light in her eyes—"I think I might this very minute telegraph to Mr. Balfour to come right over by the next steamer."

The companion of this person was not in the habit of expressing surprise. He had got accustomed to the swift and occult devices of her small and subtle brain. If the member for Englebury had at that moment arrived by coach, and walked up the front steps of the hotel, he would have betrayed no astonishment whatever. So he merely said, "Why?"

"You will see," she continued, "that her first thought about this lake will be its likeness to some other lake that she has known. She is always looking back to England. Last night she spoke quite cheerfully about going home. If Mr. Balfour were suddenly to meet us at Montreal—"

"Have you telegraphed to him?" demands the other, sternly; for he is never sure as to the madness of which this woman is capable.

"No."

"Nor written to him?"

"No."

"Then don't be a fool. Do you mean to say that two people who find their married life so unbearable that they must needs separate, are at once to be reconciled because one of them takes a trip across the Atlantic? Is that your remedy for married misery, your salt-water cure — thirty guineas return, with three pounds a head for the wine bill?"

"It was only one of them who wished for a separation," says this gentle schemer, with a happy smile, "and already she knows a little of what separation is like. Don't I see it? And the farther we go, the more varied things we see. I know that her heart is yearning all the more to go back to its home. She speaks now of New York as if it were continents and continents away. It is not a question of time—and of your thirty guineas;

it is a question of long days and nights, and solitary thinking, and strange places and strange people, and the thought of the increasing labor of one's going back. And just fancy when we have gone away across the wide prairies—oh, I know! You will see the change in her face when we turn toward England again!"

Her companion is not at all carried away by this burst of enthusiasm.

"Perhaps," he observes, "you will be good enough to say at what point Mr. Balfour is suddenly to appear, like a fairy in a pantomime, or a circus-rider through a hoop."

"I never said he was to appear anywhere," is the petulant reply.

"No; and therefore he is all the more likely to appear. At Niagara? Are we to increase the current with a flood of tears?"

"I tell you I have neither telegraphed nor written to him," she says. "I don't know where he is, and I don't care."

"Then we are determined to have our cure complete? 'Lady Sylvia Balfour before three months of moral scolding: the same after the three months: the recipe forwarded for eighteen-pence in postage-stamps. Apply to Professor Stickleback, on the top of Box Hill, Surrey.' There is one thing quite certain—that if you are the means of reconciling these two, they will both of them most cordially hate you for the rest of their life."

"I cannot help that," is the quiet answer. "One must do what good one can. It isn't much, at the best."

We were almost the only occupants of the steamer that left the small pier and proceeded to cut its way through the wind-swept waters of the lake. And now, sure enough, these people began to talk about Loch Lomond, and Killarney, and Windermere, and all sorts of other places, just as if they wished to pander to this poor creature's nostalgia; it was of no use to remind them that the lake was an American lake, with associations of its own, and these far from uninteresting. Very gloomy, however, was the aspect in which Lake Horicon now presented itself to us; for the clouds seemed to come closer down, and the low and wooded hills became of a heavier purple, and darker still became the water that was dashed in hurrying waves on the sandy and rocky shore. Then we got into the narrows, and were near enough the hills to see where the forest had been on fire, the charred stems of the trees appearing in the distance like so many vine stems washed white. The lake opened out again, and on we steamed, the mountains far ahead of us growing of a still deeper purple, as if a fearful storm were impending over them. Suddenly Lady Sylvia uttered a light cry. She had by accident turned. And, lo! behind us there was a great blaze of sunlight, falling on the hills and the water—the lake a sheet of dazzling silver, the islands of a brilliant and sunny green, one keen flash of blue visible among the floating clouds. And it was then, too, we saw an eagle slowly sailing over the russet woods—the only living thing visible in this wilderness of water and forest. The sunlight spread. There were glimmerings of silver in the heavy clouds lying over the region of the Adirondacks. A pale glow crossed from time to time our drying decks. When we landed to undertake the short railway journey between Lake George and Lake Champlain, we found ourselves in hot sunshine.

Lake Champlain, too, was fair and sunny and green, and the waters that the steamer churned were as clear as those of Schaffhausen, while the windy shreds of cloud that floated by the Adirondacks were of the lightest and fleeciest. But there were storms brewing somewhere. As the day waned, we had sudden fits of purple darkness, and dashes of rain went sweeping along the lake. In the evening there was a wild smoke of red in the west behind the pallid hills, and this ruddy glare here and there touched the gray-green waters of the lake with a dusky fire, and made the hull of one boat which we could see in the distance gleam like some crimson stone. As we sat there, watching the lurid sunset and the darkening waters, we had dreams of an excursion to be made in the days to come. When Bell's long exile in the West was over, we were to meet somewhere about this point. We were suddenly to disappear from human ken into the wilds of the Adirondacks. We should live on the produce of our own guns and fishing-rods; we should sleep in the log-huts on the cool summer nights; we should become as dexterous as Indians in the use of our canoes. We had heard vague rumors of similar excursions through these virgin wilds: why should not we also plunge into the forest primeval?

Mr. Von Rosen said nothing at all when he heard this proposal; but he laughed, and looked at his wife.

"When I am set free to get back to England," said the ranchwoman, with great gentleness—for she was obviously profiting by her brief companionship with civilized folks—"I don't think—I really do not think—that you will catch me foolin' around here."

In the mean time, however, she was just as eager to see everything as anybody else. Look, for example, at what happened on the very first morning after our arrival at Montreal. We had, on the previous evening, left Lake Champlain at Plattsburg, and got into the train there. We had made our first acquaintance with the Canadians in the persons of four as promising-looking scoundrels as could be found in any part of the world, who conversed in guttural French in whispers, and kept their unwashed faces and collarless throats so near together as to suggest a conspiracy to murder. We had parted from these gentlemen as soon as the train had crossed the St. Lawrence bridge and got into Montreal, and we had reached our hotel about midnight. Now what must this German do but insist on every one getting up at a nameless hour in the morning to start away by train and intercept a boat coming down over the Lachine Rapids. His wife assented, of course; and then the other two women were not to be outdone. A solemn tryst was made. Ridicule was unavailing. And so it happened that there was a hushed hurrying to and fro in the early dawn, and two or three wretched people, who ought to have been in bed, went shivering out into the cold air. As for the Lachine Rapids, the present writer has nothing to say about them. They are said to be very fine, and there is a picture of them in every bookseller's shop in Canada. It is also asserted that when the steamer goes whirling down, the passengers have a pleasing sensation of terror. All he knows is that, as he was sitting comfortably at breakfast, four objects made their appearance, and these turned out to be human beings, with blue faces and helpless hands. When they had got thawed somewhat, and able to open their mouths without breaking bones, they said that the descent of the rapids was a very fine thing indeed.

Nor was it possible for one to learn anything of the character of the Canadian nation because of these insatiable sight-seers. The writer of these pages, finding that he would have two whole days to spend in Montreal, had proposed to himself to make an exhaustive study of the political situation in Canada, and to supplement that by a comparison between the manners, customs, costume, and domestic habits of the Canadians and those of the

Americans. It was also his intention to devote a considerable portion of this time to a careful inquiry as to the number of Canadians who would prefer separation from Great Britain. But these projected studies, which would have been of immense value to the world at large, were rendered impossible by the conduct of this group of frivolous tourists, who were simply bent on profitlessly enjoying themselves. And this they seemed to do with a great good-will, for they were delighted with the cool fresh air and the brilliant atmosphere, which gave to this city a singularly bright and gay appearance. They were charmed with the prettily decorated cabs in the street. When they entered the Cathedral of Notre Dame, it seemed quite appropriate to find colors and gilding there that in England would have suggested a certain institution in Leicester Square. Then we had to climb to the tower to have a view over the beautiful, bright city, with its red-brick houses set amidst green trees; its one or two remaining tin domes glinting back the morning sunlight; its bold sweep of the St. Lawrence reflecting the blue sky. What was that, too, about the vagus nerve, when the striking of the great bell seemed to fill our chests with a choking sound? Our ranch-woman was not ordinarily scientific in her talk, but she was rather proud of the vagus nerve. Indeed, we grew to have a great affection for that useful monitor within, of whose existence we had not heard before; and many a time afterward, when our desire for dinner was becoming peremptory, we only recognized the friendly offices of this hitherto unknown bell-man, who was doubtless, in his own quiet way, sounding the tocsin of the soul.

In fact, these trivial-minded people would have nothing to do with a serious study of the Canadian character. They said that they approved of the political institutions of this country because they got French bread at dinner. They were quite sure that the Canadians were most loyal subjects of the Crown, and that everything was for the best, simply because some very kind friends called on them with a couple of carriages, and whirled them away up to the summit of Mount Royal Park, and showed them the great plain beneath, and the city, and the broad river. They went mad about that river. You would have fancied that Bell had been born a barge-woman, and had spent her life in shooting rapids. We knew that the old-fashioned song of our youth kept continually coming back to her idle fancy, for we heard faint snatches of it hummed from time to time when the rest of us were engaged in talk.

> "Why should we yet our sail unfurl?
> There is not a breath the blue wave to curl;
> But when the wind blows off the shore,
> Oh, sweetly we'll rest our weary oar!
>
> *   *   *   *   *   *
>
> "Utawa's tide! this trembling moon
> Shall see us float over thy surges soon.
> Saint of this green isle, hear our prayers—
> Oh, grant us cool heavens and favoring airs!
> Blow, breezes, blow! the stream runs fast,
> The rapids are near, and the daylight's past!"

And the daylight was indeed past when we left Montreal; for these unconscionable tourists insisted on starting at the unholy hour of ten at night, so that they should accomplish some foolish plan or other. It was an atrocious piece of cruelty. We got into a sleeping-car, and found the brightest and cleanest of bunks awaiting us. We were pretty tired, too, with rushing up and down belfry stairs, and what not. It was no wonder, therefore, that we speedily forgot all about our having to get up in the middle of the night at some wretched place called Prescott.

We were summoned back from the calm of dream-land by a hideous noise. We staggered out of the carriage, and found ourselves in a small and empty railway station at two in the morning. But the more we rubbed our eyes, the more we were bewildered. Everything was wrapped in a cold thick fog, so that the train was but the phantom of a train, and we seemed to each other as ghosts. The only light was from a solitary lamp that sent its dazzling glare into the fog, and seemed to gather about it a golden smoke. Then these fierce cries in the distance:

"Dan'l's? Who's for Dan'l's? All aboard for Dan'l's?"

The poor shivering wretches stared helplessly at each other, like ghosts waiting for Charon to take them somewhither.

"Dan'l's?" again resounded that unearthly cry, which had a peculiar rising inflection on the second syllable. "Who's for Dan'l's? All aboard for Dan'l's?"

Then it crossed the mind of the bewildered travellers that perhaps this Dan'l's was some hostelry in the neighborhood—some haven of refuge from this sea of fog—and so they stumbled along until they made out the glare of another lamp, and here was an omnibus with its door flung wide open.

"Dan'l's?" sung out the plaintive voice again. "Who's for Dan'l's Hotel. All aboard for Dan'l's?"

We clambered into the small vehicle and sat down, bound for the unknown. Then the voice outside grew sharp. "ALL ABOARD!" it cried. The door was banged to, and away we went through the fog, plunging and reeling, as if we were climbing the bed of a stream.

Then we got into the hostelry, and there was an air of drowsiness about it that was ominous. The lights were low. There was no coffee-room open.

"I think," said the lieutenant, rubbing his hands cheerfully—"I think we could not do better than have some brandy or whiskey and hot water before going to bed."

The clerk, who had just handed him his key, politely intimated that he could have nothing of that sort—nothing of any sort, in fact. The lieutenant turned on him.

"Do you mean to tell me that this is a temperance house?" he said, with a stare.

"No, it ain't," said the clerk. "Not generally. But it is on Sunday; and this is Sunday."

It certainly was three o'clock on Sunday morning.

"Gracious heavens, man!" exclaimed the lieutenant, "is this a civilized country? Don't you know that you will play the very mischief with our vagus nerves?"

The clerk clearly thought he had nothing to do with our vagus nerves, for he simply turned and lowered another lamp. So the lieutenant lit his candle and departed, muttering to himself.

"Dan'l's?" we heard him growl, as he went up the wooden stair. "All aboard for Dan'l's? Confound me if I ever come within a dozen miles of Dan'l's again!"

CHAPTER XXXV.

A THOUSAND ISLANDS.

THE next day was a Sunday, still, calm, and blue; and we sat or patiently walked along the wooden pier, waiting for the steamer that was to come up the broad waters of the St. Lawrence. The river lay before us like a lake. The sun was warm on the long planks. There was not a flake of cloud in the sky.

Hour after hour passed, and the steamer, that had been detained in the fog of the preceding night, did not appear. We got into a drowsy and dreamy state. We watched the people come and go by the other boats, without interest or curiosity. Who were these, for example, this motley group of Indians, with their pale olive complexion, and their oval eyes like the eyes of the Chinese? They spoke a guttural French, and they were clad in rags and tatters of all colors. Hop-pickers? The squalid descendants of the old Iroquois? And when these had gone, the only man who did remain was a big sailor-looking person, who walked up and down, and eagerly whittled a bit of wood. Him we did regard with some languid interest; for hitherto we had not seen any one engaged in this occupation, and we wished to know the object of it. Surely this was no idle amusement, this fierce and energetic cutting down of the stick? Was he not bent on making a peg? Or on sharpening his knife? Suddenly he threw the bit of wood into the river, and shut up his knife with an air of much satisfaction: the mystery remains a mystery until this day.

Perhaps it is to beguile this tedium of waiting—and be it remembered that the Lake of a Thousand Islands lay right ahead of us, and Niagara too: while at Niagara we expected to get letters from England—that one of us begins to tell a story. It is a pathetic story. It is all about a bank clerk who lived a long time ago in Camdentown, and who used to walk in every day to the City. One day, as he was passing a small shop, he saw in a corner of the window about half a dozen water-color drawings in a somewhat dirty and dilapidated state; and it occurred to him

that, if he could get these cheap, he might have them fresh
mounted and framed, and then they would help to decorate a certain tiny house that he had his eye on for a particular reason.
He bought the pictures for a few shillings, and he very proudly
carried them forthwith to a carver and gilder whose shop lay in
his line of route to the City.   He was to call for them on the following Monday.   He called in at the appointed time, and the
carver and gilder seemed suddenly to recollect that he had forgotten the drawings; they would be ready on the next Monday.
The bank clerk was in no great hurry—for the fact is, he and his
sweetheart had quarrelled—and he somewhat listlessly called in on
the next Monday.   The drawings, however, were not yet ready.
And so it came to pass that every Monday evening, as he went
home to his lodgings, the bank clerk — with a sad indifference
growing more and more apparent in his face—called in for the
water-colors, and found that they were not in the frames yet, and
promised, without any anger in his voice, to call again.   Years
passed, and quite mechanically, on each Monday evening, the bank
clerk called in for the pictures, and just as mechanically he walked
home without them to his lodgings.   But these years had been
dealing hardly with the bank clerk.   His sweetheart had proved
faithless, and he no longer cared for anything that happened to
him.   He grew negligent about his dress; he became prematurely-
ly gray; he could not trust his memory in the fulfilment of his
duties.   And so in time they had to ask him to resign his situation in the bank; and he became a sort of messenger or hall por-
ter somewhere, with his clothes getting dingier and his hair whiter
summer by summer and autumn by autumn.   And at last he fell
sick, and his wages were stopped, and he thought there was nothing for him to do now but to turn his face to the wall and die.
But—said the narrator of this true story—would you believe it?
one night the pictures came home!   There was a noise on the
little wooden stair—not the heavy tramp of the undertaker, but
the uncertain footsteps of the carver and gilder, who had himself
grown a tottering, white-headed old man.   And when he came
into the room he burst into tears at sight of the poor bank clerk;
but all the same he cried out, "Now, see what I have done for
you!   I have kept your pictures until they have become OLD MAS-
TERS!   I have been offered £300 apiece for them; you can have
the money to-morrow."   And the poor bank clerk wept too; and

he got up, and shook his friend by the hand; he could scarcely
express his gratitude. But what does he do now? Why, on the
strength of the sum of money he got for his pictures he started
a Bath-chair; and you may see him any day you like being
wheeled along the broad walks in Regent's Park; and whenever
he sees a young man with a beard, a velveteen coat, and unwashed
hands, he imagines him to be an artist, and he stops and says to
him, "I beg your pardon, sir; but don't be hard on the poor
carver and gilder. He is only increasing the value of your pictures. It will all come right in time." This was the story of
the poor bank clerk.

The steamer! What business have we to be thinking about
Regent's Park, here on the banks of the broad St. Lawrence?
We enter the great vessel, and have a passing look at its vast saloons and rows of cabins and rows of life-belts. We start away
into the wide stream, and go swiftly cutting through the clear
green water; while the wooded and rocky banks and the occasional clusters of white houses glide noiselessly back into the sunny haze of the east. Then the vagus nerve has to be appeased;
for it is a long time since we left the coffee-room at Dan'l's.
When we go out on the high deck again, the afternoon is wearing on, and we are nearing that great widening of the river which
is known as the Lake of a Thousand Islands.

But surely this is neither a river nor a lake that begins to disclose itself—stretching all across the western horizon, with innumerable islands and gray rocks and dark clusters of firs and bold
sweeps of silver where a current passes through the dark green
reflections of the trees. It is more like a submerged continent
just reappearing above the surface of the sea; for as far as the
eye can range there is nothing visible but this glassy plain of water, with islands of every form and magnitude, wooded down to
the edge of the current. It is impossible to say which is our
channel, and which the shore of the main-land; we are in a wilderness of water and rock and tree, in unceasing combinations, in
perpetual, calm, dream-like beauty. And as we open up vista after vista of this strange world—seeing no sign of life from horizon to horizon but a few wild-duck that go whirring by—the
rich colors in the west deepen; the sun sinks red behind some
flashing clouds of gold; there is a wild glare of rose and yellow
that just misses the water, but lights up the islands as if with

fire; one belt of pine in the west has become of a deep violet, while all around the eastern sky there is a low-lying flush of pink. And then, after the sun has gone, behold! there is a pale, clear, beautiful green all across the west; and that is barred with russet, purple, and orange; and the shadows along the islands have grown dusky and solemn. It is a magical night. The pale, lambent twilight still fills the world, and is too strong for the stars—unless we are to regard as golden planets the distant lights of the light-houses that steadily burn above the rocks. There is a gray, metallic lustre on the surface of the lake, now ruffled by the cool winds of the night. And still we go gliding by these dark and silent islands, having the sharp yellow ray of a light-house now on this side and now on that; and still there seems to be no end to this world of shadowy foliage and rock and gleaming water. Good-night—good-night—before the darkness comes down! The Lake of a Thousand Islands has burned itself into our memory in flashes of rose-color and gold.

What is this strange thing that awakens us in the early morning—a roaring and rushing noise outside, a swaying of the cabin that reminds us of "the rolling Forties" in mid-Atlantic, and sudden dashes of green water across the dripping glass of the porthole? We stagger up on deck, and lo! there is nothing around us but driving skies and showers and hurrying masses of green water, that seem to have no boundary of main-land or island. We congregate in the forward part of the saloon, and survey this cheerless prospect; our only object of interest being the rapid flight of some wild-fowl that scud by before the wind. Have we drifted away, then, from the big, hot continent they call America, and floundered somehow into the Atlantic or Pacific? We are withdrawn from this outward spectacle by the pathetic complaints of a tall and lank Canadian, who has made friends with everybody, and is loudly discoursing—in a high, shrill, plaintive key—of his troubles, not the least of which is that he declares he will shortly be sea-sick if this plunging of the steamer continues. It appears that he came on board at some port or other about six in the morning, with his wife, who, an invalid, still remains in her cabin.

"Yes, sir. The landlord shet up at 'leven o'clock, and we didn't know when the boat was comin' 'long; and me and the old woman we had to go bamboozlin' round moren hef the night; and that makes a man kiner clanjammery, you bet!"

He looked through the dripping winds with an uncomfortable air.

"There's a pretty riley bit o' sea on," he remarked.

He became more and more serious, and a little pale.

"If this goes on," said he, suddenly, "by Gosh, I'll heave!"

So we considered it prudent to withdraw from the society of this frank and friendly person; and while the vessel went plunging on through the wild chaos of green and gray mists and vapors, we busied ourselves in purchasing knick-knacks manufactured by the Canadian Indians, little dreaming that ere long we should be the guest of the red man in his wigwam in the Far West, and be enabled to negotiate for the purchase of articles deposited by the innocent children of the forest at a sort of extemporized pawnshop at the agency. It was then that one of our number —her name shall not be mentioned, even though thousands of pounds be offered—made a joke. It was not an elaborate joke. But when she said something, in a very modest and sly way, about a Pawnee, we forgave her wickedness for the sake of the beautiful color that for a second suffused her blushing face.

Even Lake Ontario, shoreless as it seemed when we went on deck in the morning, must end some time; and so it was that at length we came in sight of its north-western boundaries, and of Toronto. By this time the weather had cleared up a bit; and we landed with the best disposition in the world toward this great collection of business buildings and private dwellings, all put down at right angles on the sandy plain adjoining the lake.

"*Now* will you study the history, literature, and political situation of Canada?" asked the only serious member of this party, when we had reached the spacious and comfortable hotel, which was an agreeable relief after being on board that fog-surrounded ship.

"I will not," is the plain answer.

"What did you come to America for?"

If she had been honest, she would have confessed that one of her plans in coming to America was the familiar one of delivering a series of lectures—all at the head of one innocent young wife. But she says, boldly,

"To amuse myself."

"And you have no care for the ties which bind the mother country to these immense colonies—you have no interest in their demands—"

"Not the slightest."

"You would see them go without concern?"

"Yes. Are we not always giving them a civil hint to that effect?"

"It is nothing to you that the enterprise of your fellow-subjects has built this great town, in a surprisingly short time, on this arid plain—"

"It is a great deal to me," she says. "I must buy a dust-coat, if I can get one. And what about the arid plain? I see as many trees here as I have seen in any city on this side of the Atlantic."

And so it was always; the most earnest of students would have broken down in his efforts to impress on this tourist party the necessity of learning anything. If you spoke to them about theatres, or carriages, or dry champagne, perhaps they might condescend to listen; but they treated with absolute indifference the most vital questions regarding the welfare of the nation whose guests they were. The kindly folks who drove them about Toronto, through the busy streets of the commercial district, through the sandy thoroughfares where the smart villas stood amidst the gardens, and through that broad and pleasant public park, tried to awaken their concern about the doings of this person and that person whose name was in all the newspapers; and they paid no more heed than they might have done had the Legislature at Ottawa been composed of the three tailors of Tooley Street. But there was one point about Toronto which they did most honestly and warmly admire, and that was the Norman-Gothic University. To tell the truth, we had not seen much that was striking in the way of architecture since crossing the Atlantic; but the simple grace and beauty of this gray stone building wholly charmed these careless travellers; and again and again they spoke of it in after-days, when our eyes could find nothing to rest upon but tawdry brick and discolored wood. There is a high tower at this Toronto College, and we thought we might as well go up to the top of it. The lieutenant, who was never at a loss for want of an introduction, speedily procured us a key, and we began to explore many curious and puzzling labyrinths and secret passages. At last we stood on the flat top of the square tower, and all around us lay a fresh and smiling country, with the broad waters of Ontario coming close up to the busy town. We went walking quite carelessly about this small inclosed place; we were chatting with each other, and occasionally leaning on the parapet of gray stone.

Who was it who first called out? Far away over there, in the haze of the sunlight, over the pale ridges of high-lying woods, a faint white column rose into the still sky, and spread itself abroad like a cloud. Motionless, colorless, it hung there in the golden air; and for a time we could not make out what this strange thing might be. And then we bethought ourselves—that spectral column of white smoke, rising into the summer sky, told where Niagara lay hidden in the distant woods.

CHAPTER XXXVI.

A GLANCE BACK.

MEANWHILE, what of the widower whom we had left behind in England? It was fairly to be expected that Balfour, once he had seen his wife handed over to that wise and tender counsellor who was to cure her of all her sentimental sufferings, would go straightway back to England and rejoice in the new freedom that allowed him to give up the whole of his time and attention to public affairs. At all events that was what Lady Sylvia expected. Now he would have no domestic cares to trouble him. As far as his exertions were necessary to the safety of the State, England was secure. For Lady Sylvia always spoke of her husband as having far more serious duties to perform than any home secretary or lord chancellor of them all.

Balfour, having taken a last look — from the deck of his friend's yacht—at the great dark ship going out into the western horizon — got back to Queenstown again, and to London. No doubt he was free enough; and there was plenty at this time to engage the attention of members of Parliament. But he did not at all seem to rejoice in his freedom; and Englebury had about as little reason as Ballinascroon to applaud the zeal of its representative. He went down to the House, it is true; and he generally dined there; but his chief cronies discovered in him an absolute listlessness, whenever, in the intervals between their small jokes, they mentioned some bill or other; while, on the other hand, he was greatly interested in finding out which of these gentlemen had made long sea-voyages, and was as anxious to get information about steamers, storms, fogs, and the American climate as if he were about to arrange for the transference of the whole population of England to the plains of Colorado. The topics of the hour seemed to have no concern whatever for this silent and brooding man, who refused all invitations, and dined either at the House or by himself at a small table at the Reform. The Public Worship Regulation Bill awoke in him neither enthusiasm nor aversion. The duty on third-class passengers—they might have made it a guinea a head if they liked. In other days he had been an eager demonstrator of the necessity of our having a public prosecutor; now he had scarcely a word to say. There were only two subjects in which, at this moment, he seemed keenly interested; the one was the report which Mr. Plimsoll's commission had just published, and the other was, singularly enough, the act just passed in America about the paper currency. What earthly reason could he have for bothering about the financial arrangements of America? He did not own a red cent of the American debt.

One forenoon he was walking through St. James's Park when he was overtaken by a certain noble lord — an ingenuous youth whom he had known at Oxford.

"Balfour," said this young man, walking on with him, "you are a Scotchman—you can tell me what I have to expect. Fact is, I have done rather a bold thing—I have taken a shooting of 13,000 acres, for this autumn only, in the Island of Mull; and I have never been there. But I sent my own man up; and he believes the reports they gave were all right."

"What you are to expect?" said Balfour, good-humoredly. "Plenty of shooting, probably; and plenty of rain, certainly."

"So they say," continued the young man. "And my *avant-courier* says there may be some difficulty about provisions—he hints something about hiring a small steam-yacht that we might send across to Oban at a pinch—"

"Yes, that would be advisable, if you are not near Tobermory."

"Eighteen miles off."

Then the young man was fired with a sudden generosity.

"Your wife has gone to America, hasn't she?"

"Yes," was the simple answer.

"Are you booked for the 12th?"

"No."

"Come down with me. I sha'n't leave till the 10th, if that will suit you. The House is sure to be up—in fact, you fellows have nothing to do—you are only gammoning your constituencies."

"It's lucky for some people that they can sit in Parliament without having any constituency to gammon," said Balfour.

"You mean we mightn't find it quite so easy to get in," said the young man, with a modest laugh; for indeed his service in Parliament was of the slightest sort—was limited, in fact, to procuring admission for one or two lady friends on the night of a great debate. "But what do you say to Mull? If we don't get much of a dinner, we are to have a piper to play to us while we eat. And of course there will be good whiskey. What do you say?"

"I say that it is very good of you; and I should like it extremely; but I think I shall stay in town this autumn."

"In town!"

"Yes."

"All the autumn?" exclaimed the young man, with an air as though he half expected this maniac to turn and bite him on the arm.

"Yes," said Balfour; and then he stammered a sort of apology. "The fact is that a married man feels himself taken at an unfair advantage if he goes anywhere without his wife. I hate nothing so much as dining as a single man with a lot of married people. They pity you and patronize you—"

"But, my dear fellow, there won't be any married people up at this place—I can't pronounce the name. There will be only two men besides ourselves—a regular bachelor party. You surely can't mean to stop in town the whole of the autumn, and be chased about your club by the cleaning people. You will cut your throat before the end of August."

"And what then? The newspapers are hard pushed at that time. If I committed suicide in the hall of the Reform Club, I should deserve the gratitude of the whole country. But seriously, I am sorry I can't go down with you to Scotland—much obliged all the same."

"When does Lady Sylvia return?" asked his companion, care-lessly.

"About the end of October, I should think," Balfour said; and then he added, "Very likely we shall go to Italy for the winter."

He spoke quite calmly. He seemed to take it as a mere mat-ter of ordinary arrangement that Lady Sylvia and himself should decide where they should spend the winter. For of course this ingenuous youth walking with him was not to know that Lady Sylvia had separated herself from her husband of her own free-will and choice.

"Good-bye, Balfour," said the young Lord L——, as he turned off and went down toward Queen Anne's Gate. "I would have sent you some game if Lady Sylvia had been at home: it would be no use to a club man."

Balfour walked on, and in a second or two found himself be-fore the clock tower of the Houses of Parliament, rising in all its gilded pride into the blue summer sky. Once upon a time—and that not so long ago—all the interests of his life were centred in the great building beneath that tower; when he first entered it— even in the humble capacity of member for Ballinascroon—a new world of activity and ambition seemed opening up before him. But at this very moment, strangely enough, the mere sight of the Houses of Parliament appeared to awaken in him a curious sort of aversion. He had been going down to a morning sitting, rather because he had nothing else to do than that he was inter-ested in the business going forward. But this first glimpse of the Parliament buildings caused him suddenly to change his mind; he turned off into Parliament Street, and called in at the offices of Mr. Billy Bolitho.

Mr. Bolitho was as cheerful and bland as usual. Moreover, he regarded this young man with sympathy, for he noticed his re-served and almost troubled air, and he at once divined the cause. Did not everybody know that some of these large firms were be-ing hardly hit just then? The fine old trade in Manchester goods had broken down before markets glutted with gray shirtings and jeans. The homeward consignments of teas and silks were no longer eagerly competed for by the brokers. The speculations in cotton to which some of the larger houses had resorted were wilder than the wildest gambling on the Stock Exchange. It was a great thing, Mr. Bolitho knew, to have belonged to such a firm as Balfour, Skinner, Green, & Co., in the palmy days of commerce, but these fine times could not last forever.

"Come, Balfour," said Mr. Bolitho, brightly, "have a glass of sherry and a cigar. You don't look quite up to the mark this morning."

"Thank you, I will. I believe idleness is ruining my health and spirits—there is nothing doing at the House."

"Why don't you start a coach, and spend your forenoons that way?" said Bolitho, gayly.

"I'll tell you what I will do with you, if you like," said Balfour, "I will drive you down to The Lilacs. Come. It is a fine day, and they will give you some sort of dinner in the evening. You can be here by ten to-morrow morning."

Mr. Bolitho was seated on a table, his legs dangling in the air, and he was carefully cutting the end off a cigar.

"Done with you," said he, getting on his feet again, "if you first lunch with me at the Devonshire."

This, too, was agreed upon, and Balfour, as the two walked up to St. James's Street, did his very best to entertain this kind friend who had taken compassion on his loneliness. And as they set out in the shining afternoon, to drive away down into the quiet of Surrey, Balfour strove to let his companion know that he was greatly obliged to him, and talked far more than was his wont, although his talk was mostly about such roads as Lady Sylvia knew, and about such houses as Lady Sylvia had admired.

"Have you heard the last about Englebury?" he asked.

"No."

"Old Chorley has been struck with remorse of conscience, and has handed over that piece of filched common to the town, to make a public green."

"That public green was nearly keeping you out of this Parliament," observed Mr. Bolitho, with a demure smile.

"And there is to be a public gymnasium put up on the ground; and I have promised to go down and throw the thing open. What do you say, Bolitho? will you take a run down there, and drink a glass of wine with old Chorley, and show the boys how to twist round a trapeze?"

"I am very glad you have made friends with Chorley," said Mr. Bolitho. "He might have done you a deal of mischief. But

I do think you are becoming a little more prudent; no doubt you have found that all constituencies are not Ballinascroons."

"I may have become more prudent," said Balfour, with the indifference of a man who is mentally sick and out of sorts, "but it is not from any desire to remain in Parliament. I am tired of it—I am disgusted with it—I should like to quit it altogether."

Bolitho was not surprised. He had known a good many of these spoiled children of fortune. And he knew that, when by chance they were robbed of some of their golden toys—say, that an income of £30,000 a year was suddenly cut down to £5000 —they became impatient and vexed, and spoke as if life were no longer worth having.

"Try being out of Parliament for a year or two, and see if you don't change your mind," said Mr. Bolitho, shrewdly. "There is something in the old proverb that says you never know the value of anything until you have lost it."

"That is true enough," said Balfour, with decision; but he was not thinking of Ballinascroon, nor yet of Englebury, nor of any seat in any Parliament.

It was the cool of the evening when they got down to The Lilacs, and very quiet, and still, and beautiful looked the cottage amidst its rose-bushes and honeysuckle. No doubt there was a deserted air about the rooms. The furniture was covered with chintz; everything that could be locked and shut up was locked and shut up. But all the same Mr. Bolitho was glad to be taken round the place, and to be told how Lady Sylvia had done this and had done that, and how that the whole designing and decoration of the place was her own. Mr. Bolitho did not quite enter into this worship at the shrine of a departed saint, because he knew very well that if Lady Sylvia had been at The Lilacs that evening, he would not have been there; but of course he professed a profound admiration for the manner in which the limited space had been made the most of, and declared that, for his part, he never went into the country and saw the delights of a country house without wishing that Providence had seen fit to make him a farmer or squire.

And Mr. Bolitho got a fairly good dinner, too, considering that there were in the place only the house-keeper and a single servant, besides the gardener. They would not remain indoors after dinner on such a beautiful evening. They went out to smoke a cigar in the garden, and the skies were clear over them, and the cool winds of the night were sweetened with the scent of flowers.

"They have no such refreshing coolness as this after the hot days in America," said Balfour; "at least, so they tell me. It must be a dreadful business, after the glare of the day, to find no relief—to find the night as hot as the day. But I suppose they have got over the hottest of the weather there."

"Where is Lady Sylvia now?" asked Mr. Bolitho, seeing that the thoughts of the young man—troubled as they must be by these commercial cares—were nevertheless often turned to the distant lands in which his wife was wandering.

"Up toward Canada, I should think," he said. "Soon she will be out in the West, and there it is cool, even in the heat of summer."

"I don't wonder you remained in England," said Mr. Bolitho, frankly.

"Why?" said Balfour, who could not understand Mr. Bolitho's having an opinion about the matter in any direction.

"Things have not been going well in the City," said Mr. Bolitho, cautiously.

"I suppose not," said Balfour, carelessly. "But that does not concern me much. I never interfere in the business arrangements of our firm; the men whom my father trusted I can afford to trust. But I suppose you are right. There has been over-speculation. Fortunately, my partners are sufficiently cautious men. They have already made money; they don't need to gamble."

Bolitho was troubled in his mind. Was the young man acting a part; or was he really ignorant of the rumor that his partners, finding the profits on their business gradually diminishing, and having sustained severe losses in one or two directions, had put a considerable portion of their capital into one or two investments which were at that very time being proved to be gigantic frauds? After all, Bolitho was a generously disposed man.

"Balfour," said he, "you won't mind my speaking frankly to you?"

"Certainly not."

"Well, I don't know how far you examine into the details of the business transactions of your firm; but, you know, commercial things have been in a bad way of late; and you ought—I mean any man situated as you are—ought to be a little particular."

"Oh, I am quite satisfied," Balfour said. "I don't know much about business; but I can understand the Profit and Loss and Capital Accounts in the ledger, and these I periodically examine. Why, the firm gave £1000 to the last Mansion House Fund!"

Bolitho had heard before of firms hopelessly bankrupt making such dramatic displays of wealth, in order to stave off the evil day; but of course he did not mention such a thing in connection with such a house as Balfour, Skinner, Green, & Co. He only said that he was glad to find that Balfour did examine the books

---

CHAPTER XXXVII.

FARTHER LOOKINGS BACK.

WHAT was it, then, this feeling of inexplicable unrest and anxiety that possessed us as we drew near Niagara? Was it the fear of being disappointed? Was it the fear of being overawed? Or was it that mysterious vagus nerve catching something of the vibration that the vast cataracts sent shuddering through the land?

It was a blazing hot day; and the two scraggy horses were painfully hauling the rumbling old omnibus up a steep and dusty hill to the Clifton House hotel. Through the small window we could look down into the deep gorge; and there were no foaming rapids, but a deep, narrow, apparently motionless river of a singularly rich green color. It was an opaque, solid green—not unlike sealing-wax—and the smooth shining surface had here and there a bold swirl of white. Then the sides of the gorge showed masses of ruddy rocks and green trees; and there was the brilliant blue overhead: altogether, a German lithograph.

But why this curious unrest, while as yet the Falls were far away and out of sight? Well, there were two of us in that little omnibus who once upon a time saw a strange thing, never to be forgotten. We had climbed up from Chamounix to the small hostlery of Montanvert. We were going down the rugged little mountain-path to cross the Mer de Glace. But where the great glacier lay in the high valley, and all over that, and all beyond that, nothing was visible but a vague gray mist that seemed to be enclasping the world. We stumbled on through the cold, damp atmosphere, until we found before us the great masses of ice in their spectral greens and whites. I think it was just about this time, when we had reached the edge of the glacier, that we were suddenly arrested by a wonderful sight. Right overhead, as it were, and far above the floating seas of mist, gleamed a wild break of dazzling blue; and far into this—so far away that the very distance seemed awful—rose a series of majestic peaks, their riven sides sparkling with sunlit snows. It was a terrible thing to see. All around us the solemn world of ice and shadows: above us the other, and silent, and bewildering world of light, with those glittering peaks cleaving the blue as if they would pierce to the very throne of Heaven. The phantasmal fog-clouds went this way and that, taking strange shapes as they floated over the glacier and showed us visionary glimpses of the lower mountains; but there was neither cloud, nor fog, nor mist in that distant dome, and the giant peaks stood unapproachable there in their lonely and awful splendor. To have seen this sight once is a thing to be remembered during a man's lifetime; it is an experience that perhaps few of us would care to repeat. Was this strange unrest, then, a sensation of fear? Did we shrink from the first shock of a sight that might be too terrible in its majesty?

If that were so, we were speedily reassured. Through this port-hole of a window we caught a glimpse of something white and gray; and, as we recognized from many pictures the American Falls, it was with a certain sense of comfort that we knew this thing to be graspable. And as we got farther along, the beautiful, fair, calm picture came better into view; and it seemed to be fitting that over this silent sheet of white water, and over the mass of dark rocks and trees beyond, there should be a placid pale-blue summer sky. Farther on we go, and now we come in sight of something vaster—but still placid, and beautiful, and silent. We know from the deep indentation and the projection in the middle that these are the Horseshoe Falls; and they seem to be a stupendous semicircular wall, of solid and motionless stalactites, with a touch of green at the summit of the mighty pillars of snow. We see no motion, we hear no sound; they are as frozen falls, with the sunlight touching them here and there, and leaving their shadows a pale gray. But we knew that this vast white thing was not motionless; for in the centre of that semicircle rose a great white column of vapor, softly spreading itself abroad as it ascended into the pale-blue sky, and shutting out altogether the dark table-land beyond the high line of the Falls. And as we got out of the vehicle, and walked down toward the edge of the precipice, the air around us was filled with a low and murmuring sound—soft, continuous, muffled, and remote; and now we could catch the downward motion of these falling volumes of water, the friction of the air fraying the surface of the heavy masses into a soft and feathery white. There was nothing here that was awful and bewildering; but a beautiful, graceful spectacle—the white surface of the descending water looking almost lace-like in its texture—that accorded well with the still pale blue of the sky overhead. It was something to gaze on with a placid and sensuous satisfaction: perhaps because the continuous, monotonous murmur of sound was soothing, slumberous, dream-like.

But Bell's quick eye was not directed solely to this calm and beautiful picture. She saw that Lady Sylvia was disturbed and anxious.

"Had we not better go into the hotel at once?" said she. "There is no use trying to see Niagara in a minute. It has to be done systematically. And, besides, there may be letters waiting for us."

"Oh yes, certainly," said Lady Sylvia; and then she added, seriously, as if her whole thoughts had been centred on the Falls, "It is a very hopeful thing that we have not been disappointed at the first sight. They say nearly every one is. I dare say it will be some days before we get to understand the grandeur of Niagara."

"My dear Lady Sylvia," said one of us, as we were all walking up to the hotel, "you might spend thirty years here in such weather as this without knowing anything of the grandeur of Niagara. There is no mysticism possible with a pale-blue sky. I will endeavor to expound this matter to you after luncheon—"

"Gott bewahre!" exclaims the German, flippantly.

"—and I will show you that the size of any natural object has nothing to do with the effect it produces on the mind. I will show you how, with a proper atmospheric effect, an artist could make a more impressive picture of an insignificant island off the coast of Mull than he could if he painted Mont Blanc, under blue skies, on a canvas fifty feet square. The poetry of nature is all a question of atmosphere; failing that, you may as well fall back on a drawing-master's notion of the picturesque—a broken mill-wheel and a withered tree. My dear friends—"

"Perhaps you will explain to us, then," said Bell, not caring how she interrupted this valuable lecture, "how, if we can put grandeur into anything by waiting till a little mist and gloom gets round it—if there is nothing in size at all—how we were so foolish as to come to Niagara at all? What did we come for?"

"I really don't know."

"He is only talking nonsense, Bell!" says a sharper voice; and we reach the hotel.

But there are no letters.

"I thought not," says Queen T——, cheerfully; as if news from England was a matter of profound indifference to every one of us. "But there is no hurry. There is no chance of our missing them, as we shall be here some days."

"I suppose they will have some English newspapers here?" suggested Lady Sylvia, just as if she had been in Brussels or Cologne.

"I should think not. If there are any, they will be old enough. What do you want with English newspapers, Lady Sylvia?"

"I want to see what has been going on in Parliament," she answers, without the least flinching.

"What a desperate patriot you are, Lady Sylvia!" says Bell, laughing, as we go up the stairs to our rooms. "I don't think I ever read a debate in my life—except about Mr. Plimsoll."

"But your husband is not in Parliament," returns Lady Sylvia, with blushing courage.

"And where your treasure is there will your heart be," says Queen T—— in a gay and careless fashion; but she has a gentle hand within her friend's arm; and then she takes the key to open the door of her room for her, treating her altogether like a spoiled child.

The after-luncheon lecture on the sublime in nature never came off; for these careless gadabouts, heedless of instruction and the proper tuition of the mind, must needs hire a carriage to drive forthwith to the rapids above the Falls.   And Queen T—— had begged Lady Sylvia to take her water-proof with her; and the lieutenant, perched up beside the driver, was furnished with a couple of umbrellas.   So we set out.

And very soon we began to see something of the mighty volume of water falling over the Horseshoe Fall; for right away in there at the middle of the bend there was no white foam at all, but a projecting, unceasing bound of clear crystal of a curiously brilliant green, into which the sun struck deep.   And what about the want of vapor and atmospheric effect?   Presently we found ourselves in a sort of water-witch's paradise.   Far below us boiled that hell-caldron of white smoke—roaring and thundering so that the ground around us trembled—and then this mighty pillar, rising and spreading over the landscape, enveloped us in clouds of shifting shapes and colors through which the gleaming green islands by the side of the road appeared to be mere fantasies of the eye.   The earth and the sky seemed to be inextricably mixed up in this confusion of water and sunlight.   We were in a bewilderment of rainbows—the pale colors coming right up to the wheels of the carriage, and shining between us and the flowing streams and water-weeds a few yards off.   And then again we drove on and right through this Undine world; and, behold! we were in hot sunshine again, and rolling along a road that sent volumes of dust over us.   It was only a trick of the great mother Nature.   She had been treating her poor children to a bath; and now took this effectual method of drying them.   And the dust about Niagara is the most dry and choking dust in the world.

We drove away round so as to get beyond the Falls, and then descended to the side of the noble river.   Here we found the inevitable museum of photographs and pebbles; and a still stranger exhibition.   We were professed sight-seers; and we agreed to see the burning spring of the Indians, no matter what the wild excitement might cost.   So we were conducted into a little dark room, in the floor of which was a hole, covered over.   The performer—who was not attired in the garb of the wild man of the woods, as he ought to have been—removed the lid, and began to play a great many pranks with the gas which rose from the well. It was really wonderful.   Some of us were carried away in imagination to the beautiful days in which a penny paid on entrance to a canvas tent unlocked more marvels than were known to all the wise men of the East. But this performance was monotonous. In vain we waited for our friend to open another door and show us the Fat Woman of Scandinavia. It was merely trifling with our feelings to offer each of us a glass of the fire-water to drink. We resented this insult; and sought the outer air again, having paid—what was it?—for that revelation of the wonders of nature.

There was a grander sight outside—the great rapids whirling by at our very feet toward the sudden and sheer descent. The wild plain of waters seemed broader than any river; the horizon line was as the horizon of the sea, but it was a line broken by the wild tossing of the waves as they came hurrying on to their doom. High over the green masses of the water the white crests were flung this way and that, in the maddening race and whirl these wild uprearings resembled—who made this suggestion?—the eager outstretched hands of the dense crowd of worshippers who strive for the holy fire passing over their heads. And here, too, the noise of the rushing of the waters still sounded muffled and remote; as if the great river were falling, not into the chasm below, but into the very bowels of the earth, too far away from us to be seen or heard.

A fiery red sunset was burning over the green woods, and the level landscape, and the dusty roads, as we drove away back again, and down to the whirlpool below the Falls. Indeed, by the time we reached the point from which we were to descend into the gorge, the sun had gone down, the west had paled, and there was a cold twilight over the deep chasm through which the dark green river rolls. There was something very impressive in these sombre waters—their rapidity and force only marked by the whirling by of successive pine-trees—and in the sheer precipices on each side, scarred with ruddy rocks and sunless woods. Down here, too, there were no photographs, or Indians selling sham trinkets, or museums; only the solemnity of the gathering dusk, and the awful whirling by of the sullen water, and the distant and unceasing roar. The outlines of the landscape were lost, and we began to think of the sea.

And very pleasant it was that evening to sit up in the high balcony, as the night came on and the moon rose over the dark trees, and watch the growing light touch the edge of the far-reaching Falls just where the water plunged. The great pillar of foam was dark now, and the American Falls, opposite us, were no longer white, but of a mystic gray; but out there at the bend of the Horseshoe Falls the moonlight caught the water sharply—gleaming between the black rocks and trees of Goat Island and the black rocks and trees of the main-land.

It was a beautiful sight, calm and peaceful, and we could almost have imagined that we were once more on the deck of the great vessel, with the placid night around us, and the sound of the waves in our ears, and Bell singing to us, " Row, brothers, row, the daylight's past." You see, no human being is ever satisfied with what is before his eyes. If he is on land, he is thinking of the sea; if he is on the sea, he is dreaming of the land. What madness possessed us in England that we should crave to see the plains of the Far West, knowing that our first thought there would be directed back to England? For Bell and her husband all this business was a duty; for us, a dream. And now that we had come to these Niagara Falls, which are famous all over the world, and now that we could sit and look at them with all the mystery and magic of a summer night around us, of what were we thinking?

" It will be beautiful up on Mickleham Downs to-night," says Bell, suddenly.

It is the belief of the present writer that every one of these senseless people was thinking of his or her home at this moment, for they set off at once to talk about Surrey as if there was nothing in the world but that familiar English county, and you would have imagined that a stroll on Mickleham Downs, on a moonlight night, was the extreme point to which the happiness of a human being could attain.

" Lady Sylvia," says Queen T——, in a gentle undertone, and she puts a kindly hand on the hand of her friend, " shall we put on our bonnets and walk over to The Lilacs now? There might be a light in the windows."

CHAPTER XXXVIII.

SAMBO.

On a blazing, hot, dry day in August, two strange creatures might have been seen carefully picking their steps down a narrow path cut in the steep precipice that overlooks the whirling and hurrying waters of Niagara. They were apparently Esquimaux; and they were attended by a third person, also apparently an Es-quimau. All three wore heavy and amorphous garments of a blue woollen stuff; but these were mostly concealed by capacious oil-skins. They had yellow oil-skin caps tightly strapped on their head; yellow oil-skin jackets, with flapping sleeves; yellow oil-skin trousers of great width but no particular shape; and shoes of felt. One of the two travellers wore—alas!—spectacles.

These heavy garments became less hot as the Esquimaux be-gan to receive shooting spurts of spray from the rocks overhead; and when, following their guide, they had to stand in a shower-bath for a few seconds while he unlocked a small and mysterious portal, the cool splashing was not at all uncomfortable. But when, having passed through this gate, they had to descend some exceedingly steep and exceedingly slippery wooden steps, they discovered that even a shower-bath on a hot day may become too much of a good thing. For now they began to receive blows on the head, and blows on the shoulders, as though an avalanche of pebbles was upon them; while strange gusts of wind, blowing up from some wild caldron below, dashed across their faces and mouths, blinding and choking them. And in the booming and thundering sound all around them, had not the taller of the two travellers to stop, and seize his companion's arm, and yell with all his might before he could be heard,

"Donnerwetter! what a fellow that was in the guide-book! I will swear he never came through that gate! He said you must take off your collar and gloves, or you will get them wet! Ho, ho! Your collar and gloves! Ho, ho!"

But the laughter sounds wild and unearthly in the thunder of

the falling waters and the pistol-shots hammering on one's head.
Still farther down the slippery steps go these three figures; and
the roar increases; and the wild gusts rage with fiercer violence,
as if they would whirl these three yellow phantoms into mid-air.
The vagus nerve declares that in all its life it never was treated in
this way before; for what with the booming in the ears, and the
rattling on the head, and the choking of the mouth, it has got altogether bewildered. The last of the wooden steps is reached;
the travellers are on slippery rocks; and now before them is a
vast and gloomy cave, and there is a wild whirlpool of lashing
water in it, and outside it, between the travellers and the outside
world is a blinding wall of water, torn by the winds into sheets
of gray and white, and plunging down as if it would reach the
very centre of the earth. The roar is indescribable. And how is
it that the rushing currents of wind invariably sweep upward, as
if to fight the falling masses of white water, and go whirling a
smoke of foam all about the higher reaches of this awful cavern?

Here ensues a piteous and painful spectacle. No doubt these
two travellers had gone down to this Cave of the Winds to be
suitably impressed. No doubt they had read with deep attention the description of getting behind the Falls written by gentlemen who had adventured some little way behind the Horseshoe
Falls—on the other side—and who had gone home, with damp
gloves, to write an account of the business, and to invoke the
name of their Maker in order to give strength to their intransitive
verbs. But could anything in the world be more ludicrous than
the spectacle of a man, with Niagara tumbling on his head, trying
to keep his spectacles dry? It was in vain that the guide had
warned him to leave these behind him. It was in vain that his
companion had besought him. And there he stood, in the midst
of this booming and infernal cavern, trying to get furtive snatches
through his miserable spectacles by rapidly passing over them a
wet handkerchief. Then a fiercer gust than usual whirled the
handkerchief out of his hand and sent it flying upward until it
disappeared in the smoke of the spray. After that, mute despair.

For now, as dumb signs declared, it was necessary to pass
round the back of this wild cavern by a narrow path between the
lashing waters and the rocks; one hand on the rocks, the other
gripped by the guide, the eyes keeping a sharp lookout, as far as
was possible in the gloom, for one's footing. But how could this

miserable creature with the swimming spectacles accomplish this feat? Blind Bartimeus would have been safer; for he, at least, would have had both hands free. It was with a piteous look that he held out the spectacles and shook his head. The face of the attendant Esquimau plainly said, "I told you so"—speech was impossible amidst this thunder.

And now this helpless person, being left alone at the entrance to the cave, and alternating the efforts of spray-blinded eyes with quick glances through spectacles dried by a dripping oil-skin sleeve, saw some strange things. For at first it appeared to him that there was nothing visible in the outer world but this unceasing plunge of masses of water, that crashed upon the rocks, and sprung out into mid-air, whirling about in mad fashion with the twisting hurricanes of wind. But by-and-by—and apparently immeasurable leagues away—he caught fitful glances of a faint roseate color—a glow that seemed to have no form or substance. And then again, with the rapidity of a dream, a glimmer appeared as of sunlight on brown rocks; and for an instant he thought he saw some long wooden poles of a bright red, supported in mid-air. Was that, then, the bridge outside the Falls by which the other two phantoms were to return? But the whole thing was fleeting and unsubstantial; and again the wild gray mists closed over it; while the vagus nerve protested horribly against this perpetual hammering on the head. For a moment the frantic thought occurred to him that he would sacrifice these accursed spectacles—that he would dash them into the foaming caldron—that he would, at all risks, clamber round the black walls with both hands unencumbered. But the vagus nerve—which seems to form a sort of physical conscience—intervened. "*Think of your loving wife and tender babes,*" it said. "*Think of your duty as one of the magistrates of Surrey. Above all, consider what the wise Frenchman said: 'When one is dead, it is for a very long time;' and cheerfully, and without a pang, sacrifice the dollars you have paid.*"

Another vision through this Walpurgis dance of waters. Far away—as if another world altogether was revealing itself—two figures appeared in mid-air, and they seemed to be clambering along by the rose-red poles. But there was no substance in them. They were as aërial as the vapor through which they faintly gleamed. They passed on, apparently descending toward certain

phantasmal shadows that may have been rocks; and were seen
no more.

It was about ten minutes thereafter that the wooden portal
above was reopened; and the three Esquimaux, dripping inside
and out, stood in the dry air. And now it seemed as if the great
landscape around was dyed in the intensest colors; and the eyes,
long harassed by these bewildering grays and whites, roved in a
delighted manner over the ruddy rocks, and the green woods,
and the blue of the skies. And the hot air was no longer too
hot after this mighty shower-bath; while the lieutenant, his face
glowing after the wet, and his beard in twisted and flaky tangles,
was declaring that the passage along these slippery boards was
about as bad as the Mauvais Pas. Was it to flatter him — as
every captain is ready to flatter his passengers on getting them
into port by telling them he has not experienced such a storm
for five-and-twenty years—that the attendant Esquimau observed
that it was an unusually bad day for the Cave, owing to the direction of the wind. In any case, the lieutenant answered, it was
a good thing he had not asked any of his lady friends to accompany him.

But of course these gentle creatures insisted on going down to
the old and familiar passage behind the Horseshoe Falls which
has been the theme of much eloquent writing; and accordingly,
in the afternoon, we all went along to a big building that reminded us at once of Chamounix, so crammed was it with photographs,
trinkets, guides, and tourists. Here, for a trifling charge, we were
accommodated with a few loose water-proofs to throw over our
ordinary costumes; and, thus attired, we crossed the road and
struck down the narrow and sloppy path leading to the Falls.
We would have no guide. If there was a guide at all, it was a
courageous person who had boldly left his spectacles in the building above, and had sworn—in his purblind state—to accomplish
this desperate enterprise, or perish in the attempt. Undaunted,
he and his companions passed by several ladies who were busy
making water-color drawings—having cunningly chosen positions
where they could get a good lump of red rock and some bushes
for their foreground. Undaunted, they met the preliminary
challenges, as it were, of the Horseshoe Falls in the shape of
little spouts of water; in fact, these were only the playful and
capricious attentions that Undine's knight received when her

uncle was in a good humor and attended him through the gloomy forest. These spouts and jets increased to a shower; and the path grew narrower, so that we had to exercise some caution in allowing returning explorers to pass us — more especially as we were shod, not in gripping felt, but in galoches of enormous size. But what of that? We should have pressed forward, if each foot had been in a canoe.

And it was shameful to see at this time how the lieutenant paid almost no heed at all to his wife—to the mother of his children—to the friendless and forlorn creature who had been banished from her native land; but almost exclusively devoted himself to Lady Sylvia, whom he led in the van of the party. Not only did he give her his hand at all the narrow places; but even, in order to do so, was bold enough to venture outside on the broken and brittle slate, in a fashion which no father of a family should permit himself. But as for Bell, she was not born in Westmoreland for nothing. She walked along this ledge as freely and carelessly as if she had been walking in Oxford Street. When she looked down the sheer precipice, it was only to admire the beautiful colors of the green water, here swirling in great circles of foam. We firmly believed that she was singing aloud the mermaid's song in "Oberon;" but of course we could not hear her.

For now the booming of the Falls was close at hand; and we found in front of us a ledge or plateau running away in between the high wall of rock and the mighty masses of water shooting downward in a confusion of mist and spray. One by one we entered into this twilit hall of the water-gods; and, after trying to overmaster or get accustomed to the thundering roar, placed our backs to the rocks and confronted the spectacle before us. What was it, then? Only perpetual downward streaks of gray; a slight upward motion, as if the wind was fraying the surface of these masses; a confused whirling overhead of gray vapor; and at our feet a narrow ledge of black and crumbling rock that trembled with the reverberation of the crash below. The strange twilight of this hall of waters was certainly impressive; and there was something in our enforced silence, and in the shaking of the ground on which we stood, to add to the impression. Here, too, there were none of the fierce hurricane-gusts of the Cave of the Winds to buffet the eyes and choke the mouth and nostrils.

Nor had the vagus nerve to contend with the hammering of tongs on the head. No doubt, a cultivator of the emotions might come down here with a fair presumption that beautiful feelings would arise within him. He might even bring a chair with him, and sit down and wait for them. And when he clambered up into the dry air again, he would find himself none the worse, except, perhaps, that his gloves might be damp.

But onward—onward. The goal has to be reached: let those whose vagus nerve remonstrates remain behind. And now the darkness increases somewhat; and the narrow ledge, rising and falling, and twisting round the edge of the rocks, is like a black snake at one's feet; and the wind and water around one's face seem more inextricably mixed than ever. But has the world come to an end? Have the rocks, too, been mixed up with the vapor? Have we got to the verge of the visible universe, to find ourselves confronted by nothing but misty phantoms? Suddenly one feels a hand on one's shoulder. With caution, and a tight grip, one turns. And what is this wild thing gleaming through the gray vapor—a great, black face, shining and smiling and dripping, brilliant rows of teeth, and coal-black eyes? And what is this thing that he yells high and clear—so that it is heard even through the roar and thunder around—"You kent go no forder den dawt!" 'Tis well, friend—Sambo, or Potiphar, or whatever you may be. You are very like the devil, down here in this wild place; but there has been a mistake about the element. 'Tis well, nevertheless; and a half-dollar shall be thine, when we get back to dry air and daylight.

Our women-folk were greatly pleased with this excursion, and began to assume superior airs. At dinner there was a wild and excited talk of the fearful things they had seen and done—a jumble of maddened horses, runaway coaches, sinking boats, and breaking ice—so that you would have thought that such an assemblage of daring spirits had never met before under one roof.

"These are pleasant things to hear of," it is remarked, "especially for the father of a family. When one listens to such pranks and escapes on the part of respectable married people, one begins to wonder what is likely to be happening to two harum-scarum boys. I have no doubt that at this moment they are hewing off their thumbs with jack-knives; and trying to

hang the pony up to a tree; and loading the gardener's gun
with four pounds of powder and three marbles. What do you
say, Bell?"

"I have no doubt they are all asleep," answered that practical
young matron, who has never been able to decide whether American time is before English time, or the reverse.

Well, we got our letters at Niagara; and were then free to set
out for the Far West. There was nothing in these letters but
the usual domestic tidings. Lord Willowby expressed surprise
to his daughter that Balfour should intend, as he understood, to
remain in London during the autumn; that was all the mention of her husband that Lady Sylvia received. Whether she
brooded over it, can only be conjectured; but to all eyes it was
clear that she was not at this time solely occupied in thinking
about Niagara.

Our favorite points of view had by this time come to be certain chosen spots on the American side, close by those immense
bodies of green water that came gliding on so swiftly and smoothly, that fell away into soft traceries of white as the wind caught
their surface, and that left behind them, as they plunged into the
unknown gulf below, showers of diamonds that gleamed in the
sun as they remained suspended in the upward currents of air.
But perhaps our last view was the finest of all, and that as we
were leaving, from the Canadian side. The clear blue day was
suddenly clouded over by a thunder-storm. Up out of the south-
west came rolling masses of cloud, and these threw an awful
gloom over the plain of waters above the Falls, while the narrow
neck of land adjacent was as black as night. Then from a break
in these sombre clouds one gleam of light fell flashing on the
very centre of the Horseshoe Falls, the wonderful green shining out more brilliantly than ever; while nearer at hand one or
two random shafts of light struck down on the white foam that
was whirling onward into the dark gorge. That was our final
glimpse of Niagara; but perhaps not the one that will remain
longest in the memory. Surely we had no intention of weaving
anything comic or fantastic into our notion of Niagara when we
went down that dripping path on the hot August afternoon. But
now we often talk of Sambo—if such was his name—of the tall
and dusky demon who burst upon us through floating clouds of
vapor. Does he still haunt that watery den—a gloomy shape—

yet not awful, but rather kind-hearted and smiling, in the midst of these unsubstantial visions? Or have the swift waters seized him, long ago, and whirled him away beyond the reach of human eyes and ears?

CHAPTER XXXIX.

THE COLLAPSE.

LORD WILLOWBY had heard of the arrival of his son-in-law at The Lilacs; and on the following morning he drove over to see if he were still there. He found Balfour alone, Mr. Bolitho having gone up to town by an early train.

"What a lucky chance!" said Lord Willowby, with one of his sudden and galvanic smiles. "If you have nothing better to do, why not go on with me to The Hollow; you know this is the first day of the sale there."

"Well, yes, I will go over with you for an hour or so; I need not be up in town before the afternoon," answered Balfour. "And I should like to see how that fellow lived."

He certainly did not propose to himself to buy any second-hand chairs, books, or candlesticks at this sale; nor did he imagine that his father-in-law had much superfluous cash to dispose of in that way. But he had some curiosity to see what sort of house this was that had had lately for its occupant a person who had given rise to a good deal of gossip in that neighborhood. He was a man who had suddenly inherited a large fortune, and who had set to work to spend it lavishly. His reputation and habits being a trifle "off color," as the phrase is, he had fallen back for companionship on a number of parasitical persons, who doubtless earned a liberal commission on the foolish purchases they induced him to make. Then this Surrey Sardanapalus, having surrounded himself with all the sham gorgeousness he could think of, proceeded to put an end to himself by means of brandy-and-soda. He effected his purpose in a short time; and that is all that need here be said of him.

It was a pitiable sight enough—this great, castellated, beplastered, ostentatious house, that had a certain gloom and isolation about it, handed over to the occupancy of a cheerfully inquisitive crowd, who showed no hesitation at all in fingering over the dead man's trinkets, and opening his desks and cabinets. His very clothes were hanging up there, in a ghastly row, each article numbered off as a lot. In the room in which he had but recently died, a fine, tall, fresh-colored farmer—dressed for the occasion in broadcloth—was discussing with his wife what price the bedstead would probably fetch. And there was a bar, with sherry and sandwiches. And on the lawn outside the auctioneer had put up his tent; and the flag erected over the tent was of the gayest colors.

Lord Willowby and Balfour strolled through these rooms, both forbearing to say what they thought of all this tawdry magnificence—panellings of blue silk and silver, with a carpet of pink roses on a green ground; candelabra, costing £1800, the auctioneer's reserve price on which was £300; improvised ancestors, at a guinea a head, looking out of gorgeous frames; and so forth, and so forth. They glanced at the catalogue occasionally. It was an imposing volume; and the descriptions of the contents of the house were almost poetical.

"Look at the wines," said Lord Willowby, with a compassionate smile. "The claret is nearly all Lafitte. I suppose those toadies of his have supplied him with a *vin ordinaire* at 120 shillings a dozen."

"I should not be surprised if a lot of these spurious things sold for more than he gave for them," Balfour said. "You will find people imagining everything to be fine because a rich man bought it. That claret would fetch a high price, depend on it, if it was all labelled 'Château Wandsworth.'"

Then there was the ringing of a bell; and the people began to stream out of the house into the marquee; and the auctioneer had an improvised rostrum put up for himself at the end of the long table; and then the bare-armed men began to carry out the various articles to be bid for. It was soon very evident that prices were running high. No doubt the farmers about would be proud to show to their friends a despatch-box, a bird-cage, a hall table—anything that had belonged to the owner of The Hollow. And so the ostentatious trash, that even Tottenham Court Road would have been ashamed of, was carried piecemeal out into the light of the day; and in some instances these simple folk considered it to be so beautiful that a murmur of admiration ran round the tent when the things were brought in. It was altogether a melancholy sight.

Balfour had accompanied Lord Willowby solely from the fact of his having an idle forenoon to dispose of; but he could not quite make out what his father-in-law's purpose was in coming here. For one thing, he appeared to be quite indifferent about the sale itself. He had listened to one or two of the biddings; and then—saying that the prices were ridiculously high—had proposed a farther stroll through the rooms. So they entered the house again, and had another look at the old masters (dating from the latter half of the nineteenth century) and at the trumpery gilt and satin.

"Ah, well, Balfour," said Lord Willowby, with a pensive air, "one can almost pity that poor fellow, having his house overhauled by strangers in this way. Fortunately he knows nothing about it. It must be much worse when you are alive and know what is going on; and I fancy — well, perhaps there is no use speaking of it—but I suppose I must go through it. What distresses me most is the thought of these merry people who are here to-day going through my daughter's room, and pulling about her few little treasures that she did not take with her when she married—"

Lord Willowby stopped; doubtless overcome by emotion. But Balfour—with a face that had flushed at this sudden mention of Lady Sylvia—turned to him with a stare of surprise.

"What do you mean, Lord Willowby?"

"Well," said his lordship, with a resigned air, "I suppose I must come to this, too. I don't see how I can hold on at the Hall any longer—I am wearing my life out with anxiety—"

"You don't mean to say you mean to sell Willowby Hall?"

"How can I help it? And even then I don't know whether I shall clear the mortgages—"

"Come," said Balfour, for there were several of the auctioneer's men about, "let us go out into the garden and have a talk about this business."

They went out. It did not occur to Balfour why Lord Willowby had been so anxious for him to come to this sale; nor did he consider how skilfully that brief allusion to Lady Sylvia's room in her old home had been brought in. He was really alarmed by this proposal. He knew the grief it would occasion to his wife;

he knew, too, that in the opinion of the world this public humiliation would in a measure reflect on himself. He remonstrated severely with Lord Willowby. What good could be gained by this step? If he could not afford to live at the Hall, why not let it for a term of years, and go up to London to live, or—if the shooting of rabbits was a necessity—to some smaller place in the country? And what sum would relieve his present needs, and also put him in a fair way of pulling his finances together again? He hoped Lord Willowby would speak frankly, as no good ever came of concealing parts of the truth.

That Lord Willowby did disclose the whole truth it would be rash to assert; but at all events, his dramatic little scheme worked so well that, before that talk and walk in the grounds of The Hollow were over, Balfour had promised to make him an immediate advance of £10,000, not secured by any mortgage whatever, but merely to be acknowledged by note of hand. Lord Willowby was profoundly grateful. He explained, with some dignity, that he was a man of few words, and did not care to express all his feelings, but that he would not soon forget this urgently needed help. And as to the urgency of the help he made one or two references.

"I think I might be able to see my partners this afternoon," Balfour said, in reply. "Then we should only have to step across to our solicitors. There need be no delay — if you are really pressed for the money."

"My dear fellow," said Lord Willowby, "you don't know what a load you have taken from my breast. I would have sold the Hall long ago, but for Sylvia's sake—I know it would break her heart. I will write out at once to her to say how kind you have been—"

"I hope you will not do that," Balfour said, suddenly. "The fact is — well — these business matters are better kept among men. She would be disturbed and anxious. Pray don't say anything about it."

"As you please," Lord Willowby said. "But I know when she comes back she won't be sorry to find the old Hall awaiting her. It will be her own in the natural course of things—perhaps sooner than any one expects."

It was strange that a man who had just been presented with £10,000 should begin to indulge in these melancholy reflections;

but then Lord Willowby had obviously been impressed by this
sad sight of the sale; and it was with almost a dejected air that
he consented—seeing that his son-in-law would now have no time
to get luncheon anywhere before leaving by the mid-day train—
to go to the refreshment-bar and partake of such humble cheer
as was there provided. It was not the dead man's sherry they
drank, but that of the refreshment contractor. They stood for a
few moments there, listening to the eager comments of one or
two people who had been bidding for a box of games (it cost £10,
and went for £23) and a cockatoo; and then Lord Willowby had
the horses put to, and himself drove Balfour all the way to the
station. He shooks hands with him warmly. He begged of him
not to hurry or bother about this matter; but still—at the same
time—if there was no obstacle in the way—it was always com-
forting to have such things settled quickly—and so forth.

Balfour got up to London, and went straight to the offices of
his firm in the City. Perhaps he was not sorry to make the visit
just at this juncture; for although it would be exaggeration to
say that the hints dropped by Bolitho had disquieted him, they
had nevertheless remained in his mind. Before this, too, it had
sometimes occurred to him that he ought to take a greater interest in that vast commercial system which it had been the pride of
his father's life to build up. It seemed almost ungrateful that he
should limit his interference to a mere glance at the Profit and
Loss and Capital accounts. But then, on the other hand, it was
his own father who had taught him to place implicit confidence
in these carefully chosen partners.

Balfour was shown up-stairs to Mr. Skinner's room. That gentleman was sitting alone, at his desk, with some letters before
him. He was a small, prim, elderly, and precisely dressed person,
with gray whiskers and a somewhat careworn face. When Balfour entered, he smiled cheerfully, and nodded toward a chair.

"Ah, how do you do, Balfour? What's new with you? Anything going on at the House? I wish Parliament would do something for us business men."

"You have plenty of representatives there, anyhow, Mr. Skinner," said Balfour—the "Mr." was a tradition from his boyish
visits to the office, when the young gentleman used to regard his
father's partners with considerable awe—"but at present my
call is a personal and private one. The fact is, I want to oblige

a particular friend of mine—I want you to let me have £10,000 at once."

"£10,000? Oh yes, I think we can manage that," said Mr. Skinner, with a pleasant smile.

The thing was quite easily and cheerfully settled; and Balfour proceeded to chat about one or two other matters to this old friend of his, whom he had not seen for some time. But he soon perceived that Mr. Skinner was not hearing one word he said. Moreover, a curious gray look had come over his face.

"You don't look very well," said this blunt-spoken young man.

"Oh yes, thank you," said Mr. Skinner, quite brightly. "I was only thinking—since you were here, anyway—we might have a short talk about business matters, if Mr. Green agrees. I will see whether he is in his room."

He rose, opened the door, and went out. Balfour thought to himself that poor old Skinner was aging fast; he seemed quite frail on his legs.

Mr. Skinner was gone for fully ten minutes, and Balfour was beginning to wonder what could have occurred, when the two partners entered together. He shook hands with Mr. Green—a taller and stouter man, with a sallow face and spectacles. They all sat down; and, despite himself, Balfour began to entertain suspicions that something was wrong. Why all this nervousness and solemnity?

"Balfour," said Mr. Skinner, "Green and I are agreed. We must tell you now how we stand; and you have to prepare yourself for a shock. We have kept you in ignorance all this time— we have kept our own clerks in ignorance—hoping against hope —fearful of any human being letting the secret go out and ruin us; and now—now it is useless any longer—"

It was no ordinary thing that had so disturbed this prim old man. His lips were so dry that he could scarcely speak. He poured out a glass of water, and drank a little. Meanwhile, Balfour, who merely expected to hear of heavy business losses, was sitting calm and unimpressed.

"But first of all, Mr. Green, you know," said he, "don't think that I am pressing you for this £10,000. Of course, I would rather have it; but if it is necessary to you—"

"£10,000!" exclaimed the wretched old man, with the frankness and energy of despair, "if we go into the *Gazette*, it will be for a half a million !"

The *Gazette!* The word was a blow ; and he sat stunned and bewildered, while both partners were eagerly explaining the desperate means that had been taken to avoid this fatal issue, and the preliminary causes, stretching back for several years. He could not understand. It was as if in a dream that he heard of the Investments Account, of the China Capital Account, of the fall in property in Shanghai, of speculations in cotton, of bill transactions on the part of the younger partners, of this frantic effort and that. It was the one word *Gazette* that kept dinning itself into his ears. And then he seemed to make a wild effort to throw off this nightmare.

"But how can it be ?" he cried. "How can these things have been going on ? Every six months I have looked over the Profit and Loss Account—"

The old man came over, and took his hand in both of his. There were tears in his eyes.

"Balfour," said he, " your father and I were old friends while you were only a child; if he were alive, he would tell you that we acted justly. We dared not let you know. We dared not let our own clerks know. We had to keep accounts open under fictitious names; if we had written off these fearful losses to Profit and Loss we should have been smashed a year ago. And now—I don't think any further concealment is possible—"

He let the hand fall.

"Then I understand you that we are hopelessly bankrupt," said Balfour.

He did not answer ; his silence was enough.

"You mean that I have not a farthing," repeated the younger man.

"You have the money that was settled on your wife," said Mr. Skinner, eagerly. "I was very glad when you applied for that—"

"It will be returned to you ; I cannot defraud my father's creditors," said Balfour, coldly.

And then he rose ; no one could have told what he had undergone during that half-hour.

"Good-bye, Mr. Skinner ; good-bye, Mr. Green," said he. "I can scarcely forgive you for keeping me in ignorance of all this, though doubtless you did it for the best. And when is the crash to be announced ?"

"Now that we have seen you, I think we might as well call in our solicitors at once," said Mr. Skinner.

"I think so too," said the other partner; and then Balfour left.

He plunged into the busy, eager world outside; the office-boy was whistling merrily as he passed, the cabmen bandying jokes, smart young clerks hurrying over the latter part of their duties to get home to their amusements in the suburbs. He walked all the way down to the House, and quite mechanically took his seat. He dined by himself—with singular abstemiousness, but then no one was surprised at that. And then he walked up to his house in Piccadilly.

And this was the end—the end of all those fine ambitions that had floated before his mind as he left college, equipped for the struggle of public life with abundant health, and strength, and money, and courage. Had his courage, then, fled with his wealth, that now he seemed altogether stunned by this sudden blow? Or was it rather that, in other circumstances, he might have encountered this calamity with tolerable firmness; but that now, and at the same time, he found himself ruined, forsaken, and alone.

———

CHAPTER XL.

A FLASH OF NEWS.

WE dragged a lengthening chain. As soon as we had left Niagara and its hotels and holiday-making, and plunged into that interminable forest-land that lies between Lakes Huron and Erie, one could have noticed that the gravity of our women-folk was visibly increased. Did they half expect, then—while they were idling about these show-places—some sudden summons, which they could readily answer? Bell, at least, could have no such hope; but all the same, as this big and ornate car was quietly gliding away westward, in the direction of her future home, she was as sad as any of them.

What was the matter? It was a beautiful afternoon. The

country through which we were passing was sufficiently cheerful; for this forest was not dark, gloomy, and monotonous like the Schwarzwald, but, on the contrary, bright, varied in hue, and broken up by innumerable clearances. Every few minutes the window next us became the frame of a pleasant little picture—the sudden open space among the trees; a wooden house set amidst orchards in which the ruddy apples showed in the evening light; a drove of cattle homeward going along the rough road; tall silver-gray stems of trees that had been left when the wood was burned down; and everywhere—in every available corner—maize, maize, maize.

"What is the matter?" says the German ex-lieutenant to his wife, who is gazing somewhat absently out of the window.

"I know," says Queen T——, with a gentle smile. "She is thinking how she could ever make her way back through this perpetual forest if she were all by herself and with no road to guide her. Fancy Bell wandering on day and night—always toward the East—toward her children. She might take some food from the country-people; but she would not enter their houses; she would go on day after day, night after night, until she got to the sea. And you want to know what she is thinking of now? I believe she is consumed with hatred of everything lying westward of the river Mole; and that she considers the Pullman car a detestable invention. That is the pretty result of Colonel Sloane's ingenuity!"

It certainly was not fair to talk in this slighting fashion of poor old Five-Ace Jack, who was but recently dead, and who had done what he considered his best with such worldly possessions as Providence had allowed him to thieve and amass. But at this moment the lieutenant struck in.

"Oh, that is quite foolish!" he cried. "There is no longer any such thing as distance—it is only time. It is foolish to think of the distance between the Rocky Mountains and Surrey; it is only how many days; and you may as well be living in a pleasant car, and having good food, and very capital beds, as in a hotel, while all the time you are travelling. And indeed," continued this young man, seriously addressing his wife, "there is very little difference of time either now. You want to speak to your children? You speak to them through the telegraph. It is an hour or two—it is nothing. In the morning you send them a message—you say, ' How do you do ?'—in the evening, as you sit down to dinner, you have the answer. What is that separation ? It is nothing."

" I think," says Bell, with savage ferocity, but with tears springing to her eyes, " I will spend the whole of the first year's income of this wretched property in telegrams to the children. One might just as well be dead as living without them."

And if she was to derive any comfort from this reflection, that the telegraph was a constant link of communication between herself and those young folks left behind in Surrey, she was not likely to be allowed to forget the fact for any length of time. Even out in this forest wilderness, the most prominent feature of the smallest hamlet we passed was its telegraph posts and wires. Very plain, unpretending, unpicturesque hamlets these were, even in the ruddy glow now shining over the land. They consisted of a number of wooden shanties, all set down in rectangular rows— the thoroughfares being exceedingly broad and bare—the whole place having an oddly improvised and temporary look, as if the houses and shops could in a few minutes be put on wheels and carried along to the next clearance in the forest. But what could even the smallest of these here-to-day-and-gone-to-mor-row-looking places want with such a multiplicity of telegraph-wires ?

That night the three women, having been bundled into the prettily decorated state-room that had been secured for them, and being now doubtless fast asleep, saw nothing of a strange thing that occurred to us. Had Von Rosen gone mad, or had the phrase " state-room " confused his fancies, that, looking out of the car-window, he suddenly declared we were at sea ? Rubbing his eyes—perhaps he had been dozing a bit—he insisted on it. Then he must needs hurry out to the little iron gangway at the end of the car, to see if his senses were forsaking him.

Here, certainly, a strange sight was visible. We were, no doubt, standing on a railroad-car; but all around us there was nothing but black and lapping water through which we were rapidly moving, propelled by some unknown power. And the blackness of this mysterious lake or sea was intensified by the flashing down on the waves of one or two distant lights that seemed to be high above any possible land. Then, as our eyes became accustomed to the darkness, lo! another phenomenon—a great black mass, like a portion of a city, moving after us through the night. We began to make it out at last. The bewildering lights ahead were two lofty beacons. We were crossing a lake, or a bit of a lake. The long train had been severed into lengths, and each portion of the huge serpent placed on a gigantic steam ferry-boat, which was taking us across the black waters. And when this night-passage ceased, we scarcely knew whether we were on sea or on shore, whether on a boat or a line of rail. But people began to talk about Detroit; and here, undoubtedly, was a railway-station, to say nothing of a refreshment-bar.

"I believe we have got into the States again," observed the lieutenant, thereby showing a knowledge of geography which was not surprising in a German.

Next morning our little party had most obviously improved in spirits. Perhaps there was some secret hope among the women-folk that they would have further news from England when they arrived at Chicago, though what good could come of that it was hard to say. Or perhaps they were delighted to find that they had suffered no discomfort at all in passing a night on board a railway-train. They praised everything—the cleanness and com-fort of the beds, the handiness of the lavatories, the civility of the attendants. There was no fatigue at all visible in their fresh and bright faces. And when they sat down to breakfast, it was quite clear that they meant to make it a comic breakfast, whereas breakfast in an American railway-car is a serious business, to be conducted with circumspection and with due regard for contin-gencies. For one thing, the hospitable board is not spacious, and with even the most smoothly going of cars there are occasional swayings which threaten peril to coffee-cups. But the chief oc-casion for fear arises from the fact that your travelling American is a curious person, and insists on experimenting upon every pos-sible form of food that the districts through which he is passing produce. Moreover, he has a sumptuous eye, and likes to have all these things spread out before him at once. No matter how sim-ple the central dish may be—a bit of a prairie-chicken, for exam-ple, or a slice of pork—he must have it, perhaps merely for the delight of color, graced by a semicircle of dishes containing va-ried and variously prepared vegetables. Now, we never could get the most intelligent of negroes to understand that we were only plain country folk, unaccustomed to such gorgeous displays and

varieties of things, and not at all desirous of eating at one and
the same time boiled beans, beet-root in vinegar, green corn,
squash, and sweet-potatoes. Sambo would insist on our having
all these things, and more, and could not be got to believe that we
could get through breakfast without an assortment of boiled
trout, pork, and apple-sauce, and prairie-chicken. The consequence was that this overloaded small table not unfrequently
reminded one or two of us of certain experiences in Northern
climes, when the most frugal banquet—down in that twilit saloon
—was attended by the most awful anxiety.

"She pitches a good deal," said Bell, raising her cup so as to
steady it the better; "the sea must be getting rougher."

"Madame Columbus," asked the lieutenant, "when shall we
come in sight of land? The provisions will be running short
soon. I have never seen people eat as these people eat. It is
the fine air, is it not?"

"Mr. Von Rosen," said Lady Sylvia, "do you know that you
can have Milwaukee lager-beer on board this ship?"

"Do I know?" said the young man, modestly. "Oh yes, I
know. I had some this morning at seven o'clock." And then
he turned to his shocked wife, "I was very thirsty; and I do not
like that water of melted ice."

He would have explained further; but that his wife intimates
that such excuses are unnecessary. She has got used to this kind
of thing. Happily her children are now beyond the sphere of
his evil example.

"Ah," said he, "this is all very poor and wretched as yet—
this crossing of the American continent. I am a prophet. I can
see the things that will come. Why have we not here the saloon
that we have across the Atlantic—with a piano? I would sing
you a song, Lady Sylvia."

"Indeed," said that lady, very sweetly, "you are very kind."

"But it is a long time ago since we used to have songs in our
travelling. I can remember when we had to try a new piano every day—some of them very queer; but always in any case we
had the guitar, and 'Woodstock Town' and 'The Flowers of the
Forest'—"

"And '*Prinz Eugen, der edle Ritter,*'" says Bell, in a suddenly deep and tragical voice, "'*wollt' dem Kaiser wiedrum
krrrrrrrriegen Stadt und Festung Belga-rrrrrr-ad!*'"

"Ah, Bell," says Queen T——, " do you remember that morning at Bourton-on-the-Hill ?"

Did she remember that morning at Bourton-on-the-Hill! Did she remember that bunch of fiddle-sticks! No doubt they were very pleased to get away from the small inn where they had had ham, and eggs, and whiskey for supper, and ham, and eggs, and tea for breakfast; but here, in this bountiful and beneficent land, flowing over with broiled blue-fish, Carolina widgeon, marrow squash, and Lima beans, what was the use of thinking about Bourton-on-the-Hill and its belongings? I do not believe we were charged more than a shilling per head for our lodging in that Worcestershire hostlery; here we were in a country where we could pay if we chose a couple of shillings extra for having a bottle of wine iced. And, if it came to that, what fresher morning could we have had anywhere than this that now shone all around us? We dragged these nostalgic persons out on to the pleasant little iron balcony at the end of the car. There had been a good deal of rain for some time before; so there was little dust. And what could be brighter and pleasanter than these fair blue skies, and the green woods, and the sweet, cool winds that blew about and tempered the heat of the sun? We seemed to be rolling onward through a perpetual forest, along a pathway of flowers. Slowly as the train went, we could not quite make out these tall blossoms by the side of the track; except to guess that the yellow blooms were some sort of marigold or sunflower, and the purple ones probably a valerian, while the rich tones of brownish red that occurred among the green were doubtless those of some kind of rumex. And all through this forest country were visible the symptoms of a busy and shifty industry. Clearing followed clearing, with its enclosures of split rails to keep the cattle from wandering; with its stock of felled timber close to the house; and with, everywhere, the golden-yellow pumpkins gleaming in the sunlight between the rows of the gray-green maize.

"What a lonely life these people must lead!" said Lady Sylvia, as we stood there.

"Yes, indeed," responded her monitress. "They are pretty nearly as far removed from telegraphs and newspapers and neighbors as we are in Surrey; but no doubt they are content —as we might be, if we had any sense. But if the newspaper

is ten minutes late, or the fire not quite bright in the breakfast-
room—"

"Or the temper of the mistress of the house," says another
voice, "of such a demoniacal complexion that the very mice are
afraid of her—"

"—Then, no doubt, we think we are the most injured beings
on earth. Oh, by-the-way, Lady Sylvia, how did your dado of
Indian matting look?"

This was a sudden change; and, strangely enough, Lady Sylvia seemed rather embarrassed as she answered.

"I think it turned out very well," said she, meekly.

"I suppose some of your guests were rather surprised," is the
next remark.

"Perhaps so," answers the young wife, evasively. "You know
we never have given many dinner-parties in Piccadilly. . I—I
think it is so much better for my husband to get into the country whenever he can get away from the House."

"Oh yes, no doubt," says Queen T——, with much simplicity. "No doubt. But you know you are very singular in your
tastes, Lady Sylvia. I don't know many women who would spend
the season in Surrey if they had the chance of spending it in Piccadilly. And what did you say those flowers were?"

Our attention was soon to be called away from the flowers.
The forest became scantier and scantier—finally, it disappeared
altogether. In its place we found a succession of low and
smooth sand-hills—of a brilliant yellowish-brown in this warm
sunlight, and dotted here and there with a few scrubby bushes.
This was rather an odd thing to find in the midst of a forest;
and we were regarding these low-lying mounds with some interest when, suddenly, they dipped. And lo! in the dip a dark-
blue line—and that the line of the horizon. The sea!—we cried.
Who can imagine the surprise and delight of finding this vast
plain of water before the eyes, after the perpetual succession of
tree-stems that had confronted us since the previous morning?
And surely this blue plain was indeed the sea; for far away we
could pick out large schooners apparently hovering in the white
light, and nearer at hand were smart little yachts, with the sunlight on their sails.

"Madame Columbus," cried the lieutenant, "have we crossed
the continent already? Is it the Pacific out there?"

"Why, you know," says the great geographer, with a curtness unworthy of her historic name and fame. "It is Lake Michigan. It is a mere pond. It is only about as long as from London to Carlisle; and about as broad as—let me see—as Scotland, from the Clyde to the Forth."

It was a beautiful sight, however insignificant the size of the lake may have been. Nothing could have been more intensely blue than the far horizon line, just over those smooth and sunlit sand-hills. No doubt, had we been on a greater height we should have caught the peculiar green color of the water. Any one who has unexpectedly come in view of the sea in driving over a high-lying country — say in crossing the high moors between Launceston and Boscastle — must have been startled by the height of the suddenly revealed horizon line. It seems to jump up to meet him like the pavement in the story of the bemuddled person. But down here on this low level we had necessarily a low horizon line; and what we lost in intrinsic color we gained in that deep reflected blue that was all the stronger by reason of the yellow glow of the sand-hills.

We got into Michigan City. We were offered newspapers. We refused these—for should we not have plenty of time in Chicago to read not only the newspapers, from which we expected nothing, but also our letters from England, from which we expected everything? As it turned out, there was nothing at all of importance in our letters; whereas, if we had taken these newspapers, we could not fail to have noticed the brief telegraphic announcement—which had been sent all over the commercial world—of the suspension of the well-known firm of Balfour, Skinner, Green, & Co., liabilities £500,000. In happy ignorance we travelled on.

It was about mid-day, after skirting the southern shores of Lake Michigan through a curiously swampy country, that we entered Chicago, and drove to the very biggest of its big hotels.

CHAPTER XLI.

CHICAGO.

WE knew nothing of this dire announcement, though it was in every one of the newspapers published in Chicago that day. We were full of curiosity about this wonderful city that had sprung up like Jonah's gourd; and as we drove through its busy thoroughfares — the huge blocks of buildings looking like the best parts of Glasgow indefinitely extended; and as we saw the smoky sky over our head streaked in every direction with a black, rectangular spider's web of telegraphic wires; and as we caught glimpses at the end of the long thoroughfares of the tall masts of ships — we knew that we had indeed reached the great commercial capital of the Far West. And, indeed, we very speedily found that the genius of this big, eager, ostentatious place was too strong for us. We began to revel in the sumptuousness of the vast and garishly furnished hotels; we wanted more gilding, more marble, more gaudy coloring of acanthus leaves. A wild desire possessed us to purchase on speculation all the empty lots available; we would cover every frontage foot with gold, and laugh at all the assessments that were ever levied. Look at this spacious park on the south side of the town; shall we not have a mansion here more gorgeous than the mind of man can conceive, with horses to shoot along these wide drives like a flash of lightning? We began to entertain a sort of contempt for the people living on the north side of the town. It was hinted to us that they gave themselves airs. They read books, and talked criticism. They held aloof from ordinary society — looked on a prominent civic official as a mere shyster — and would have nothing to do with a system of local government controlled by thirty thousand bummers, loafers, and dead-beats. Now, we condemned this false pride. We gloried in our commercial enterprise. We wanted to astound the world. Culture? This was what we thought about culture: " It is with a still more sincere regret that the friends of a manly, vigorous, self-supporting, and self-dependent people, fitted for the exercise of political liberty, see that the branches of culture called blacksmithing, corn-growing, carpenter-ing, millinery, bread-making, etc., are not included in the course of studies prescribed for the Chicago public schools. Society is vastly more concerned in the induction of its youthful members into these branches of culture than it is in teaching them to bawl harmoniously and beat the hewgag melodiously." Yes, indeed. Confound their hewgags, and all other relics of an effete civiliza-tion! And, again: "This city, and every other American city, is crowded with young persons of both sexes that have been 'cult-ured' by a vicious and false public-school system in music, draw-ing, and other fanciful and fashionable but practically useless arts, but that are actually incapable, by reason of their gross ignorance, of earning an honest living. They have acquired, under some well-paid 'professor' (who has bamboozled himself into the erro-neous belief that he and his profession are necessary to the ex-istence of society), some smattering of 'musical culture,' pencil sketching, etc., but of the practical arts and sciences of living and getting a living they are more profoundly ignorant than South African Hottentots." What would our friends on the north side say to that?

"Bell," said the lieutenant, as we were driving through this spacious southern park, in the clear light of the afternoon, "I suppose that we shall be allowed to come up here occasionally from the ranch—what do you say?—for a frolic, and for to spend a little money? I would like to have one of these little traps— it is like the ghost of a trap—*hé!* look at that fellow now!"

We looked at him as well as we could; but he had flashed by before we could quite make out what he was sitting on. In fact, there was nothing visible of the vehicle but two large and phan-tom wheels and a shaft like a prolonged spider's leg; while the driver, with his hands stretched forward, and his feet shot out before him, and therefore almost bent double, was, according to all appearance, clinging on as if for dear life to the horse's tail.

"It would be very fine to go whizzing through the air like that —and very good exercise for the arms, too—"

"But where should I be?" asked his wife, with some indigna-tion. Certainly a vehicle that seemed to have no inside at all— that appeared to be the mere simulacrum of a vehicle—could not very well contain two.

"Where would you be?" said the lieutenant, innocently. "It is Chicago. You would be divorced."

It was this recalling of the divorce business that led us to see the announcement of the failure of Messrs. Balfour & Co. To tell the truth, we were not much interested in American politics; and while there were plenty of new things to be seen everywhere around us, we did not spend much time over the papers. But on this evening Queen T—— had got hold of one of the daily journals to look at the advertisements about divorce. She read one or two aloud to us.

"There, you see," she remarked, addressing Bell more particularly, "you can run up here from the ranch any time you like and become a free woman. 'Residence not material.' 'Affidavits sufficient proof.' 'No charge unless successful.' And the only ground that needs to be stated is the safe one of incompatibility. So that whenever husband and wife have a quarrel, here is the remedy. It is far more swift than trying to make up the quarrel again."

"And a good deal more pleasant, too," remarks a humble voice.

Whither this idle talk might have led us need not now be guessed. The little woman's face suddenly grew ghastly pale. Her eye had been carelessly wandering away from that advertising column, and had lit on the telegram announcing the suspension of Balfour's firm. But she uttered no word, and made no sign.

Indeed, there is a great courage and firmness in this gentle creature when the occasion demands. In the coolest possible manner she folded up the newspaper. Then she rose, with a look of weariness.

"Oh, dear me!" said she, "I suppose I must go and get all these things out. I wish you would come and open my big box for me," she adds, addressing her humble slave and attendant.

But all that affectation of calmness had gone by the time she had reached her own room.

"See!" she said, opening the paper with her trembling, small, white fingers. "See! Balfour is ruined—he has lost all his money—half a million of debts—oh, what shall I do—what shall I do? Must I tell her? Shall I tell her at once?"

Certainly the news was startling, but there was no need to cry over it.

"Oh, I know," she said, with the tears starting to her eyes, "if I were to tell her now, she will start for England to-morrow morning. And I will go back with her," she adds, wildly, "I will go back with her. You can go on to Colorado by yourself. Oh the poor child! she will fly to him at once—" And still she stares through her wet eyes at this brief announcement as if it were some talisman to change the whole course of our lives.

"Come, come, come," is the patient remonstrance. "You have got to consider this thing quietly, or you may blunder into an awkward position and drag her with you."

"How, then?" she says. "It must be true, surely."

"You are taking heaps of things for granted. If you consider that absence and distance and a good deal of covert lecturing have told on the girl's mind—if you think that she would now really be glad to go back to him, with the knowledge that people have got to put up with a good deal in married life, and with the intention of making the best of it—that is all very well—that is first-rate. You have effected a better cure than I expected—"

"Don't you see it yourself?" she says, eagerly. "Don't you see how proudly she talks of 'my husband' now? Don't you see that every moment she is thinking of England? *I know.*"

"Very well. Very good. But, then, something depends on Balfour. You can't tell what his wishes or intentions may be. If he had wanted her to know, he would have telegraphed to her, or caused her father to telegraph to her. On the other hand, if you take this piece of news to her, she will appeal to you. If she should wish to go back to England at once, you will have to consent. Then you cannot let her go back alone—"

"And I will not!" says this brave little woman, in a fury of unselfishness.

"Well, the fact is—as it appears to an unemotional person— there might be, you see, some little awkwardness, supposing Balfour was not quite prepared—"

"A man in trouble, and not prepared to receive the sympathy of his wife!" she exclaims.

"Oh, but you must not suppose that Balfour is living in a garret on dry crusts—the second act of an Adelphi drama, and that kind of thing. People who fail for half a million are generally pretty well off afterward—"

"I believe Mr. Balfour will give up every penny he possesses to his creditors!" she says, vehemently; for her belief in the virtue of the men of whom she makes friends is of the most uncompromising sort.

"No doubt it is a serious blow to an ambitious man like him; and then he has no profession to which he can turn to retrieve himself. But all that is beside the question. What you have got to consider is your guardianship of Lady Sylvia. Now, if you were to sit down and write a fully explanatory letter to Mr. Balfour, telling him you had seen this announcement; giving your reasons for believing that Lady Sylvia would at once go to him if she knew, and asking him to telegraph a 'yes' or 'no:' by that time, don't you see, we should be getting toward the end of our journey and could ourselves take Lady Sylvia back. A week or two is not of much consequence. On the other hand, if you precipitate matters, and allow the girl to go rushing back at once, you may prevent the very reconciliation you desire. That is only a suggestion. It is none of my business. Do as you think best; but you should remember that the chances are a hundred to one that Lady Sylvia sees or hears something of this telegram within the next day or two."

A curious, happy light had stolen over this woman's face; and the soft dark eyes were as proud as if she were thinking of a fortune suddenly inherited instead of one irretrievably lost.

"I think," said she, slowly, "I think I could write a letter that would make Mr. Balfour a happy man, supposing he has lost every penny he has in the world."

Any one could see that the small head was full of busy ideas as she mechanically got out her writing materials and placed them on the table. Then she sat down. It was a long letter; and the contents of it were never known to any human being except the writer of it and the person to whom it was sent. When she had finished it, she rose with a sigh of satisfaction.

"Perhaps," said she, with a reflective air, "perhaps I should have expressed some regret over this misfortune."

"No doubt you spoke of it as a very lucky thing!"

"I can't say," she admitted frankly, "that I am profoundly sorry."

Indeed, she was not at all sorry; and from that moment she began to take quite a new view of Chicago. There could be no doubt that this person of High-Church proclivities, who liked to surrender her mind to all manner of mysteriously exalted moods, had from the very first regarded this huge dollar-getting hive with a certain gentle and unexpressed scorn.   What was that she had been hinting about a person being able to carry about with him a sort of moral atmosphere to keep him free from outside influence; and that the mere recollection of the verse of a song would sometimes suffice?   Lady Sylvia and she had been talking of some of Gounod's music.   Were we to conclude, then, that as she wandered through this mighty city, with its tramways, and harbors, and telegraphs, and elevators, that she exorcised the demon of money-getting by humming to herself, "Ring on, sweet angelus!"   As she passed through the Babel of price-quoters in the central hall of the hotel, it was no echo of their talk that got into her brain, but quite a different echo :

> "Hark! 'tis the angelus, sweetly ringing
>   O'er hill and vale;
> Hark how the melody maidens are singing
>   Floats on the gale!
> *   *   *   *   *   *
> "Ring on, sweet angelus, though thou art shaking
>   My soul to tears!
> Voices long silent now with thee are waking
>   From out the years,
>   From out the years!

That may have been so; but, anyhow, on the morning after she had despatched her letter to Balfour, she entered into the business of sight-seeing with quite a new spirit. She declared that Chicago, for a great city, must be a delightful place to live in. Away from the neighborhood of the manufactories the air was singularly pure and clear. Then there were continual cool winds coming in from the lake to temper the summer heat. Had anybody ever seen grass more green than that in the vast projected park on the southern side which would in time become one of the most noble parks in the world? She considered that the park on the northern side was beautifully laid out; and that the glimpses of Lake Michigan which one got through the trees were delightful. She greatly admired the combination of red sandstone and slightly yellowed marble which formed the fronts of the charming villas in those pretty gardens; and as for drives— well, she thought the chief part of the population of Chicago must live on wheels. It was so rare to find this august lady in so generous and enthusiastic a mood that we all began to admire Chicago, and quite envied our relative, the ranch-woman, in that she would be able to forsake her savage wilderness from time to time for this centre of the arts and civilization.

We revelled in all the luxuries of a great city while as yet these were possible to us. We went to theatres, concerts, picture exhibitions. We drove out to the park in the afternoon to hear the band play. We purchased knick-knacks for friends at home—just as if we had been a party of tourists.

"Come," said our German ex-lieutenant, on the final day of our stay there, "this is our last great town, is it not, before we go away to the swamps, and the prairies, and to the bowie-knives? Shall we not dress for dinner? And I propose that the dinner is at eight. And we will drink a glass of wine to the prosperity of this fine town."

The women would not hear of this proposal in its entirety; for as we had to start by train about eleven at night, they did not relish the notion of pulling out all their finery and putting it back again in a hurry. But we dined at eight all the same; and we did not fail to drink a glass of wine to the prosperity of that fine town. Long before midnight we were all fast asleep in snug berths, the train whirling us on through the darkness toward the country of the Mississippi.

CHAPTER XLII.

LIFE ON WHEELS.

WE rub our eyes. Have we wandered into a Brazilian swamp, then, during the long dark night? The yellow light of the early morning is shining down on those dusky pools of sluggish water, on the dense forest, on the matted underwood, and the rank green grass. How the railway-track does not sink into this vast mere passes our comprehension; there seems scarcely sufficient mud on these scattered islands to support the partly submerged trees. But, as we are looking out, a new object suddenly confronts the eyes. Instead of that succession of still creeks, we

come on a broad expanse of coffee-colored water that broadens
out as it rolls southward; and we cry "The Mississippi!" And
over there, on the other side, we see a big and straggling town
picturesquely built along the bluffs, and all shining in the early
sunlight. But the Mississippi detains us not, nor Burlington
either. Our mission is westward, and forever westward—through
the perpetual forest, with its recurrent clearances and farms and
fields of maize. Surely it is a pleasant enough manner of passing this idle, beautiful day. The recent rains have laid the dust;
we sit outside the car and lazily watch the rich colors of the underwood as we pass. Could anything be deeper in hue than the
lake-red of those sumach bushes? Look at that maple—its own
foliage is a mass of pale, transparent gold; but up the stem and
out the branches runs a creeper, and the creeper is of a pure ver-
milion that burns in the sun. Westward—and forever westward.
We lose consciousness of time. We resign ourselves to the slow
passing-by of the trees, and the farms, and the maize. It is like
a continuous dream.

And was this, we asked ourselves — was this, after all, America? In the by-gone days, before we ever thought of putting
foot on this vast continent, we had our imaginary pictures of it;
and surely these were bigger and nobler things than this trivial
recurrence of maize—maize—maize—an occasional house—endless trees and bushes, and bushes and trees? Who does not remember those famous words that thrilled two nations when they
were spoken?—"*I have another and a far brighter vision before
my gaze. It may be but a vision, but I will cherish it. I see
one vast confederation stretching from the frozen North in unbroken line to the glowing South, and from the wild billows of
the Atlantic to the calmer waters of the Pacific main—and I see
one people, and one language, and one law, and one faith, and, over
all that wide continent, the home of freedom, and a refuge for the
oppressed of every race and of every clime.*" But where were the
condor's wings to give us this vision, now that we were about
midway between the Atlantic and the Rocky Mountains? We
only saw maize. And then we tried to imagine an American's
mental picture of England—something composed of Stratford-on-
Avon, and Westminster Abbey, and Rydal Mount, and Milton,
and Shakspeare, and Cromwell—and his bitter disappointment
on sailing up the Mersey and coming into view of the squalor

of Liverpool.   This was the nonsense that got into our heads on this sleepy and sunny day.

But by-and-by the horizon widened, for we had been slowly ascending all this time; and you may be sure there was a little excitement throughout our party when we began to get our first glimpses of the prairie-land.   Not the open prairie just yet; but still such suggestions of it as stirred the mind with a strange and mysterious feeling.   And, of course, all our preconceived notions about the prairies were found to be wrong.   They were not at all like the sea.   They were not at all melancholy and oppressive. On the contrary, they were quite cheerful and bright in the sunshine; though there was still that mysterious feeling about them; and though the unaccustomed eye could not get quite reconciled to the absence from the horizon of some line of hill, and would keep searching for some streak of blue.   Surely there was nothing here of the dreary wastes we had imagined?   First of all, and near us, was a rich wilderness of flowers, of the most bountiful verdure and variegated colors—masses of yellow sunflowers, and lilac Michaelmas-daisies, and what not, with the blood-red of the sumach coming in.   Farther off, the plain rose and fell in gentle undulations covered with variously tinted grass; and here and there were the palisades of a few ranches.   Farther away still were wider and barer undulations, marked by one or two clusters of the minutest specks, which we took to be cattle.   Then beyond that again the open prairie-land—long, level swathes, of the very faintest russet, and gray-green, and yellow-gray, going out—out— out until the blue sky of the horizon seemed quite close and near to us compared with that ever and mysteriously receding plain. This vast distance was not awful, like the sea.   It was beautiful in its pale colors; it was full of an eager interest—for the eye appealed to the imagination to aid it in its endless search; and if it was an ocean at all, it was an ocean that broke at our feet in a brilliant foam of flowers.   This similitude was, indeed, so obvious that we unanimously were of opinion that it must have been used by every American poet who has ever written about the prairie- lands.

We had for our nearest travelling companions two commercial gentlemen of a facetious turn, who certainly did their best to amuse our women - folk.   It was the lieutenant, of course, who had made their acquaintance.   One was a Philadelphian, the other a New-Yorker; but both were in the sewing-machine business; and it was their account of their various experiences in travelling that had induced Von Rosen to join their conversation. They were merry gentlemen. They ventured to ask what might be his line of business—white goods, or iron, or Western produce?"

"And if it is white goods, what then?" said the ex-soldier, with great *sang-froid*.

"Why, sir," said the Philadelphian, gravely taking out a number of cards, "because money is money, and biz is biz; and you want to know where to buy cheap. That's Philadelphia, sure— the American metropolis—the largest city in the world—yes, *sir!* —eighteen miles by eight—two rivers—going to have the Centennial—the best shad—"

He was regarding the New-Yorker all this time.

"Yes—shad!" said his companion, with affected contempt; for we could see that they were bent on being amiably funny. "If you want shad, go to Philadelphia—and cat-fish, too—cat-fish suppers at the Falls only seventy-five cents a head. And fresh butter, too—go to Philadelphia for fresh butter, and reed-birds, and country board—best country board outside of Jersey—keep their own cows—fresh milk, and all that. But if you WANT TO TRADE, colonel, come to New York! New York ain't no village; no one-horse place; no pigs around our streets. We've got the finest harbor in the world; the highest steeples; the noblest park; the greatest newspapers; the most magnificent buildings —why, talk about your Coliseums, and Tuileries, and Whitechapel, and them one-horse shows; come and see our Empire City!"

"Yes; and leave your purse in Philadelphia before you go!" sneered his enemy, who quite entered into the spirit of the thing. "And ask your friend here to show you the new court-house, and tell you how much *that* cost! Then let him drive you up the avenues, and have your life insured before you start, and show you the tar-and-sand, the mush-and-molasses pavements—patent pavements! Then ask him to introduce you to his friend the Boss, and mebbe he'll tell you how much the Boss got away with. And then about the malaria! And the fever and ague! And the small-pox! And people dying off so fast they've got to run special trains for the corpses! And the Harlem Flats!"

"Now hire a hall, won't you?" said the Knickerbocker. "Hasn't our cat got a long tail? Why, you could roll up Philadelphia into a bundle and drop it into a hole in the Harlem Flats. But I wouldn't mislead you—no, sir: if you want water-power, go to Philadelphia—and grass—splendid grass—and mosquitoes. Tell him about the mosquitoes now! Friend of mine in the sugar line married and went to Philadelphia for his honey-moon. Liked a quiet country-life—no racket, except the roosters in the morning—liked the cows, and beauties of nature—and took his bride to a first-class hotel. Fine girl—bin chief engineer on a double-stitch sewing-machine. Well, sir, the Philadelphia mosquitoes were alive—you bet. In the morning he took her to a hospital—certain she had small-pox—two weeks before the doctors could find it out. The man's life was ruined—yes, sir: never recovered from the shock; business went to the dickens; and he ran away and jined the Mormons."

"Jined the Mormons!" cried the Philadelphian. "Why don't you tell the general the story straight? Don't fool the man! Jined the Mormons! He threw her into a sugar-vat—sweets to the sweet, sez he—and married her mother—and went to New York, and was elected mayor as the friend of Ireland—eleven hundred thousand Irishmen, all yelling for the Pope, voted for him. No, general, if you want to trade with Americans, with white men, you come to Philadelphia; we live cheap and we sell cheap; and with our new line of steamers, and our foreign trade—"

"Tell him about the canal-boats—why don't you tell him about the three canal-boats?" said the other, scornfully. "It is a fact, general—when three canal-boats loaded with pop-corn and sauerkraut got to Philadelphia, the mayor called out the militia for a parade—yes, *sir!*—the town was illuminated — the newspapers had leaders on the revival of commerce, and the people all had two inches sewed on to their coat-tails. And mind, general, when you go to Philadelphia, you tell the conductor where to stop— tell him the wood-and-water station opposite Camden—the train stops by signal—"

Whither this conflict might have led us can only be conjectured. It was interrupted by our halting at a small station to have a mid-day dinner. And we did not fail to remark that the shy and handsome girls who waited on the crowd of ravenous people in this humble hostlery had bright complexions and clear eyes that spoke well for the air of this high-lying country. The lieutenant was furious because he could get nothing but water or iced tea to drink; his wife remarked that she hoped he would always be as well off—showing that she had had her speculations about her probable life as a ranch-woman. But another member of the party was anxious to get away as soon as possible from the devouring multitude; and when she was outside again, on the platform, she revealed the cause of that pensiveness, that had at times dwelt over her face during the morning.

"Really now, *really*, do you think I was right?" she says, in a low voice. "I have been thinking over it. It seems so cruel. The poor thing is just breaking her heart over the mistake she has made—in ever leaving him; and now, when she would have this excuse, this opportunity of appealing to him — of going to him without any appeal—it seems dreadful to keep her in ignorance."

"Tell her, then."

"But the responsibility is terrible," she pleads again.

"Certainly. And you absolve yourself by waiting to know what Balfour's wishes are. What more?"

"If—if I had a daughter—of her age," she says, with the usual quiver of the under lip; "I do not think I should let her go farther and farther away from her husband just when there was a chance of reconciling them—"

"Will the chance be less next week, or the week after? However, do as you like. If you tell her, you must appeal to her not to do anything rash. Say you have written. Or you might suggest — if she is so very penitent — that she should write to her husband—"

"Oh, may I do that?" exclaims this tender-eyed hypocrite; as if she ever demanded permission to do anything she had set her mind on.

You never saw one woman so pet another as she petted Lady Sylvia during the rest of that day. She had never shown so much solicitous attention for the comfort of her own children, as far as any of us had ever noticed. And it was all because, no doubt, she was looking forward to a sentimental scene when we should arrive at Omaha, in which she should play the part of a beneficent fairy, and wise counsellor, and earnest friend. Happily it did not occur to her to have a scene in the railway-car before a score of people.

This railway-car, as the evening fell, was a sore distress to us. Our wish to have that fleeting glimpse of the Mississippi had led us to come on from Chicago by one of the slow trains; and from Burlington there was no Pullman car. Ordinarily this is about the pleasantest part of the long trans-continental ride from New York to San Francisco; for on it are dining-cars, which have within their narrow compass pretty nearly every luxury which the fancy of man could desire, and which therefore offer a capital way of passing the time. If one must go on travelling day after day without ceasing, it is surely a pleasant thing to occupy the last two or three hours of the evening by entertaining your friends to a banquet—and, if you are alone, the conductor will accept an off-hand invitation—of twelve or fourteen dishes, while the foaming grape of eastern France, if Catawba will not content you, is hard by in an iced cellar. With these wild delights we should have been disposed to dispense, had we obtained the comparative seclusion of a Pullman car; but as the long and dull evening set in we learned something of the happiness of travelling in an ordinary car in America. During the day we had spent most of the time outside; now we had to bear with what composure we could show the stifling odors of this huge and overcrowded compartment, while the society to which we were introduced was not at all fastidious in its language, or in its dress, or in the food which it plentifully ate. The lieutenant said nothing when a drunken woman sat down on his top-coat and refused to allow it to be removed; but he did remonstrate pitifully against the persistent shower of beetles that kept falling on our heads and necks. We could not understand whence these animals came. Their home could not be the roof of the car; for they were clearly incapable of maintaining a footing there. Or were we driving through an Egyptian plague of them; and did they come in through the ventilators? It was a miserable evening. The only escape from the foul odors, and the talk, and the shreds of food was sleep; and the close atmosphere gave its friendly help; but sleep is apt to disarrange one's head-covering; and then, that guard removed, the sudden sensation of having a beetle going down the back of one's neck banishes sweet dreams. About half-past eight or nine we got to Council Bluffs; and right glad were we to get out for a walk up and down the wet platform—for it had been raining—in the pitch-darkness.

Nor shall we forget Council Bluffs soon. We spent three mortal hours there. All that we saw was a series of planks, with puddles of dirty water reflecting the light of one or two gas-lamps. We were now on one bank of the Missouri; and Omaha, our destination, was immediately on the other side; while there intervened an iron bridge. An engine would have taken us across and returned in a very short time. But system must be followed. It was the custom that the passengers by our train should be taken over in company with those arriving by a train due from somewhere else; and as that train had not made its appearance, why should we not continue to pace up and down the muddy platform? It was not the least part of our anxiety that, after an hour or so had passed, ex-lieutenant Oswald Von Rosen seemed disposed to eat six or seven railway porters, which would have involved us in a serious claim for damages.

He demanded whether we could not be allowed to walk across the bridge and on to Omaha. Certainly not. He wanted to have some clear understanding as to how late this other train was likely to be. Nobody knew.

"Du lieber Himmel!" we heard him muttering to himself, somewhere about eleven o'clock, "and in this confounded country the very sky is black with telegraph-lines, and they cannot tell you if we shall be here all the night! *Is it the beetles that have stopped the train?*" he suddenly demanded of a guard who was sitting on a hand-barrow and playfully swinging a lamp.

"I guess not," was the calm answer.

"We might have been over the river and back half a dozen times—eh?"

"That's so," said the guard, swinging the lamp.

It was near midnight when the other train arrived; and then the station resounded with the welcome cry of "All aboard!" But we flatly declined to re-enter one of those hideous compartments full of foul smells and squalor. We crowded together on the little iron balcony between the cars, clinging to the rails; and by-and-by we had a dim impression that we were in mid-air, over the waters of the Missouri, which we could not see. We could only make out the black bars of the iron bridge against the black sky, and that indistinctly. Still, we were glad to be moving; for by this time we were desperately hungry and tired; and the sumptuous hospitality of Omaha was just before us.

Alas! alas! the truth must be told. Omaha received us in the most cruel and hard-hearted fashion. First of all, we imagined we had blindly wandered into a kingdom of the bats. There were some lights in the station, it is true; but as soon as we had got into the hotel-omnibus and left these gloomy rays it appeared as though we had plunged into outer darkness. We did not know then that the municipal authorities of the place, recognizing the fact that business had not been brilliant, and that taxes lay heavily on themselves and their neighbors, had resolved to do without gas in order to save expense. All we knew was that this old omnibus went plunging frantically through absolute blackness; and that in the most alarming manner. For what were these strange noises outside? At one moment we would go jerking down into a hollow; and the "swish" of water sounded as if we had plunged into a stream; while we clung to each other to prevent our being flung from one end to the other of the vehicle. And then, two seconds afterward, it really did appear to us that the horses were trying to climb up the side of a house. There was one small lamp that threw its feeble ray both outward and inward; and we saw through a window a wild vision of a pair of spectral horses apparently in mid-air; while inside the omnibus the lieutenant was down at the door, vainly trying to keep his wife from tumbling on the top of him.

"It is my firm conviction," said Queen T——, panting with her struggles, "that we are not going along a road at all. We are going up the bed of the Missouri."

Then there were one or two more violent wrenches, and the vehicle stopped. We scrambled out. We turned an awe-stricken glance in the direction we had come; nothing was visible. It was with a great thankfulness that the shipwrecked mariners made their way into the hotel.

But was it hospitable, was it fair, was it Christian, of the Grand Central of Omaha to receive us as it did, after our manifold perils by land and water? Had we been saved from drowning only to perish of starvation? In the gloomy and echoing hall loud sounded the remonstrances of the irate lieutenant.

"What do you say?" he demanded of the highly indifferent clerk, who had just handed us our keys. "Nothing to eat? Nothing to drink? Nothing at all? And is this a hotel? *Hé!* It is nonsense what you say: why do you let your servants go away, and have everything shut up? It is the business of a hotel to be open. Where is your kitchen—your larder—what do you call it?"

In reply the clerk merely folded up his book of names, and screwed out one of the few remaining lights. Happily there were ladies present, or a deed of blood would have dyed that dismal hall.

At this moment we heard the click of billiards.

"Ha!" said the lieutenant.

He darted off in that direction. We had seen something of billiard-saloons in America. We knew there were generally bars there. We knew that at the bars there were frequently bread and cheese supplied gratis. Behold! the foraging soldier returns! His face is triumphant. In his hands, under his arms, are bottles of stout; his pockets are filled with biscuits; he has a paper-packet of cheese. Joyfully the procession moves to the floor above. With laughter and gladness the banquet is spread out before us. Let the world wag on as it may, there is still, now and again, some brief moment of happiness. And we forgave the waiting at Council Bluffs, and we forgot the beetles, and we drank to the health of Omaha!

But it was too bad of you, Omaha, to receive us like that, all the same.

CHAPTER XLIII.

IN ENGLAND.

"I AM not frightened, but stunned—completely stunned," said Balfour; his hands on his knees, his head bent down. The ever-faithful Jewsbury had at once gone to him on hearing the news; and now the small man with the blue spectacles stood confronting him, all the joyousness gone out of his resonant voice. "I feel there must be a clean sweep. I will go down to The Lilacs, and send over one or two things belonging to—to my wife—to her father's; then everything must go. At present I feel that I have no right to spend a shilling on a telegram—"

"Oh," said Mr. Jewsbury, "when the heavens rain mountains, you needn't be afraid of stones." What he exactly meant by this speech he himself probably scarcely knew. He was nervous, and very anxious to appear the reverse. "Nobody will expect you to do anything *outré*. You won't bring down the debts of the firm by giving up the postage-stamps in your pocket-book; and of course there will be an arrangement; and—and there are plenty of poor men in the House—"

"I have just sent a message down to Englebury," he said, showing but little concern. "I have resigned."

"But why this frantic haste?" remonstrated his friend, in a firmer voice. "What will you do next? Do you imagine you are the only man who has come tumbling down and has had to get up again—slowly enough, perhaps?"

"Oh no! not at all," said Balfour, frankly. "I am in no despairing mood. I only want to get the decks clear for action. I have got to earn a living somehow—and I should only be hampered by a seat in Parliament—"

"Why, there are a hundred things you could do, and still retain your seat!" his friend cried. "Go to some of your friends in the late government—get a private secretaryship—write political articles for the papers—why, bless you, there are a hundred ways—"

"No, no, no," Balfour said, with a laugh; "I don't propose to become a bugbear to the people I used to know—a man to be avoided when you catch sight of him at the end of the street—a button-holer—a perpetual claimant. I am off from London, and from England, too. I dare say I shall find some old friend of my father's ready to give me a start—in China or Australia—and as I have got to begin life anew, it is lucky the blow fell before my hair was gray. Come, Jewsbury, will you be my partner? We will make our fortune together in a half-dozen years. Let us go for an expedition into the Bush. Or shall we have a try at Peru? I was always certain that the treasures of the Incas could be discovered."

"But, seriously, Balfour, do you mean to leave England?" the clergyman asked.

"Certainly."

"Lady Sylvia—"

The brief glimpse of gayety left his face instantly.

"Of course she will go to her father's when she returns from America," said he, coldly.

"No, she will not," replied his friend, with some little warmth. "I take it, from what you have told me of her, that she is too true a woman for that. It is only now you will discover what a good wife can be to a man. Send for her. Take her advice. And see what she will say if you propose that she should abandon you in your trouble and go back to her father! See what she will say to that!"

Jewsbury spoke with some vehemence; and he did not notice that his companion had become strangely moved. It was not often that Balfour gave way to emotion.

"Why," said he—and then he suddenly rose and took a turn up and down the room, for he could not speak for a moment, "Jewsbury, she left me! She left me!"

"She left you?" the other vaguely repeated; staring at the young man, who stood there with clenched hands.

"Do you think," Balfour continued, rapidly—with just a break here and there in his voice, "that I should be so completely broken down over the loss of that money? I never cared for money much. That would not hurt me, I think. But it is hard, when you are badly hit, to find—"

He made a desperate effort to regain his composure, and succeeded. He was too proud to complain. Nay, if the story had to be told now, he would take all the blame of the separation on himself, and try to show that his wife had fair grounds for declaring their married life unendurable. Mr. Jewsbury was a little bit bewildered, but he listened patiently.

"You have done wrong in telling me all that," said he, at last. "I need never have known, for I see how this will end. But how fortunate you were to have that friend by you in such a crisis, with her happy expedient! No one but a married woman could have thought of it. If you had formally separated—if she had gone back to her father's—that would have been for life."

"How do you know this is not?"

"Because I believe every word of what that lady-friend of hers said to you. And — if I don't mistake," he added, slowly, "I don't think you will find this loss of money a great misfortune. I think if you were at this moment to appeal to her—to suggest a reconciliation — you would see with what gladness she would accept it."

"No," said the other, with some return to his ordinary reserve and pride of manner. "She left me of her own free-will. If she had come back of her own free-will, well and good. But I cannot ask her to come now. I don't choose to make an *ad misericordiam* appeal to any one. And if she found that my Parliamentary duties interfered with her notion of what our married life should be, what would she think of the much harder work I must attack somewhere or other if I am to earn a living? She would not accompany me from Surrey to Piccadilly: do you think she would go to Shanghai or Melbourne?"

"Yes," said his friend.

"I, at least, will not ask her," he said. "Indeed, I should be quite content if I knew that her father could provide her with a quiet and comfortable home; but I fear he won't be able to hold on much longer to the Hall. She was happy there," he added, with his eyes grown thoughtful. "She should never have left it. The interest she tried to take in public affairs—in anything outside her own park—was only a dream—a fancy; she got to hate everything connected with the actual business of the world almost directly after she was married—"

"Why?" cried his friend, who had as much shrewdness as most people. "The cause is clear—simple—obvious. Public life was taking away her husband from her a trifle too much. And if that husband is rather a reserved person—and rather inclined to let people take their own way, instead of humoring them and reasoning with them—"

"Well, now, I think you are right there," said Balfour, with some eagerness. "I should have tried harder to persuade her. I should have had more consideration. I should not have believed in her refusals— But there," he added, rising, "it is all over now. Will you go out for a stroll, Jewsbury? I sha'n't bore you with another such story when you take a run out to see me at Melbourne."

Now it happened that when they got out into Piccadilly, the Kew omnibus was going by; and the same project struck both friends at the one moment—for the wilder part of the Gardens had at one time been a favorite haunt of theirs. A second or two afterward they were both on the top of the omnibus, driving through the still, warm air, greatly contented, and not at all afraid of being seen in that conspicuous position. The brisk motion introduced some cheerfulness into their talk.

"After all, Balfour," said Mr. Jewsbury, with philosophic resignation, "there are compensations in life, and you may probably live more happily outside politics altogether. There was always the chance—I may say so now—of your becoming somebody; and then you would have gone on to commit the one unforgivable sin—the sin that the English people never condone. You might have done signal service to your country. You might have given up your days and nights—you might have ruined your health—you might have sacrificed all your personal interests and feelings—in working for the good of your fellow-countrymen; and then you know what your reward would have been. That is the one thing the English people cannot forgive. You would have been jeered at and ridiculed in the Clubs; abused in the papers; taunted in Parliament; treated everywhere as if you were at once a self-seeking adventurer, a lunatic, and a fiend bent on the destruction of the State. If you had spent all your fortune on yourself; given up all your time to your own pleasures; paid not the slightest attention to anybody around you except in so far as they ministered to your comfort, then you would have been regarded as an exemplary person, a good man, and honest Englishman. But if you had given up your whole life to trying to benefit other people through wise legislation, then your reward would be the pillory, for every coward and sneak to have his fling at you."

"My dear Jewsbury," Balfour said, with a rueful smile, " it is very kind of you to insist that the grapes are sour."

"Another advantage is, that you will have added a new experience to your life," continued the philosopher, who was bent on cheering his friend up a bit, "and will be in so much the completer man. The complete man is he who has gone through all human experiences. Time and the law are against any single person doing it; but you can always be travelling in that direction."

"One ought, for example, to pick a pocket and get sent to prison?"

"Certainly."

"And run away with one's neighbor's wife!"

"Undoubtedly."

"And commit a murder?"

"No," replied this clerical person, "for that might disturb the' experiment—might bring it to an end, in fact. But there can be no doubt that Shakspeare committed several diabolical murders, and was guilty of the basest ingratitude, and was devoured with the most fiendish hatred—in imagination. In turns he was a monster of cupidity, of revenge, of blood-thirstiness, of cowardice. Other men, who have not the power to project themselves in this fashion, can only learn through action. It therefore follows that the sooner you get yourself sent to the tread-mill, the better."

"And indeed I suppose I am nearer it now than I was a week ago," Balfour admitted. "And perhaps I shall soon begin to envy and imitate my esteemed father-in-law in the little tricks by which he earns a few sovereigns now and again. I used to be very severe on the old gentleman, but I may have to take to sham companies myself."

With this and similar discourse the two sages passed the time until they arrived at Kew. It will be observed that as yet it was only a theoretical sort of poverty that had befallen Balfour. It was a sort of poverty that did not prevent the two friends from having a fairly comfortable luncheon at a hotel down there; or from giving up the day to idle sauntering through the wilder and uncultivated portion of the Gardens; or from indulging in useless guesses as to what might have been had Balfour been able to remain in Parliament.

"But in any case you will come back," continued Mr. Jewsbury, who was trying to espy a squirrel he had seen run up the trunk of an elm, "and you will be burdened with wealth, and rich in knowledge. Then, when you get into Parliament, shall I tell you what you must do? Shall I give you a project that will make your name famous in the political history of your country?"

"It won't be of much use to me," was the answer; "but I know one or two gentlemen down at Westminster who would be glad to hear of it."

"Take my proposal with you now. Brood over it. Collect facts wherever you go. Depend on it—"

"But what is it?"

"The total abolition of that most pernicious superstition—trial by jury. Why, man, I could give you the heads of a speech that would ring through the land. The incorruptibility of the

English bench—the vast learning, the patience, the knowledge of the world, the probity of our judges. Then you draw a picture of one of these judges laboriously setting out the facts of a case before the jury, and of his astonishment at their returning a verdict directly in the teeth of the evidence. Think of the store of anecdotes you could amass, to get the House into a good humor. Then a burst of pathetic indignation. Whose reputation, whose fortune is safe, if either depends on the verdict of twelve crass idiots? A bit of flash oratory on the part of a paid pleader may cost a man a couple of thousand pounds in the face of common-sense and justice. Balfour," said Mr. Jewsbury, solemnly, "the day on which the verdict in the Tichborne case was announced was a sad day for me."

"Indeed," said the other. "I have got an uncle-in-law who believes in Tich yet. I will give you a note of introduction to him, and you might mingle your tears."

"I was not thinking of Tich," continued Mr. Jewsbury, carefully plaiting some long grass together, "I was thinking of this great political project which I am willing to put into your hands; it will keep a few years. And I was thinking what a great opportunity was lost when those twelve men brought in a verdict that Arthur Orton was Arthur Orton. I had almost counted on their bringing in a verdict that Arthur Orton was Roger Tichborne; but if that was too much to hope for, then, at least, I took it for granted that they would disagree. That single fact would have been of more use to you than a hundred arguments. Armed with it, you might have gone forward single-handed to hew down this monstrous institution—" and here Mr. Jewsbury aimed a blow at a mighty chestnut-tree with the cord of grass he had plaited. The chestnut-tree did not tremble.

"However, I see you are not interested," the small clergyman continued. "That is another fact you will learn. A man without money pays little heed to the English Constitution, unless he hopes to make something out of it. What is the immediate thing you mean to do?"

"I can do nothing at present," Balfour said, absently. "The lawyers will be let loose, of course. Then I have written to my wife requesting her—at least making the suggestion that she should give up the money paid to her under the marriage-settlement—"

"Stop a bit," said Mr. Jewsbury. "I won't say that you have been Quixotic; but don't you think that, before taking such a step, you ought to have got to know what the—the custom is in such things—what commercial people do—what the creditors themselves would expect you to do ?"

"I cannot take any one's opinion on the point," Balfour said, simply. "But of course, I only made the suggestion in informing her of the facts. She will do what she herself considers right."

"I cannot understand your talking about your wife in that tone," said Jewsbury, looking at the impassive face.

"I think they mean to transfer —— to the Lords," said Balfour, abruptly; and so for a time they talked of Parliamentary matters, just as if nothing had happened since Balfour left Oxford. But Jewsbury could see that his companion was thinking neither of Lords nor of Commons.

And indeed it was he himself, despite all his resolve, who wandered back to the subject; and he told Jewsbury the whole story over again, more amply and sympathetically than before; and he could not give sufficient expression to the gratitude he bore toward that kind and gracious and generous friend down there in Surrey who had lent him such swift counsel and succor in his great distress.

"And what do you think of it all, Jewsbury ?" said he, with all the proud reserve gone from his manner and speech. "What will she do ? It was only a sort of probationary tour, you know —she admitted that—there was no definite separation—"

Mr. Jewsbury gave no direct answer.

"Much depends," he said, slowly, "on the sort of letter you wrote to her. From what you say, I should imagine it was very injudicious, a little bit cruel, and likely to make mischief."

CHAPTER XLIV.

THE DISCLOSURE.

"LADY SYLVIA," said Queen T——, going up to her friend, whom she found seated alone in her room in this Omaha hotel, "I am going to surprise you."

"Indeed," said the other, with a pleasant smile; for she did not notice the slightly trembling hands, and most of Queen T——'s surprises for her friends were merely presents.

"I—hope I shall not frighten you," she continued, with some hesitation; "you must prepare yourself for—for rather bad news—"

She caught sight of the newspaper. She sprung to her feet.

"My husband!" she cried, with a suddenly white face. But her friend caught her hands.

"He is quite well—don't be alarmed—it is only a—a—misfortune."

And therewith she put the paper into her hand, with an indication as to where she should look; while she herself turned aside somewhat. There was silence for a second or two. Then she fancied she heard a low murmur—a moan of infinite tenderness, and pity, and longing—"*My husband! My husband!*" and then there was a slight touch on her arm. When she turned, Lady Sylvia was standing quite calmly there, with her eyes cast down. Her face was a little pale, that was all.

"I think I will go back to England now," said she, gently.

And with that, of course, her friend began to cry a bit; and it was with a great deal of difficulty and of resolute will that she proceeded to speak at all. And then she bravely declared that, if Lady Sylvia insisted on setting out at once, she would accompany her; and it needed equal bravery to admit what she had done—that she had written to Mr. Balfour, begging him to let us know what his plans were, and that she had told him where he might telegraph—

"The telegraph!" cried Lady Sylvia, with a quick light of joy leaping to her eyes. "I can send him a message now! He will have it this very day! I will go at once!"

"Yes, there is the telegraph," stammered her friend, "and there is an office below in the hall of the hotel. But—don't you think—it might be awkward—sending a message that the clerks will read—"

Lady Sylvia seized her friend's hands, and kissed her on both cheeks, and hurried out of the room and down-stairs. The elder woman was rather taken back. Why should she be so warmly thanked for the existence of the telegraph, and for the fact that Mr. Balfour, M.P., was ruined?

Lady Sylvia went down-stairs, and in the hall she found the telegraphic office. She was not afraid of any clerk of woman born. She got a pencil, and the proper form; and clearly and firmly, after she had put in the address, she wrote beneath, "*My darling husband, may I come to you?*" She handed the paper to the clerk, and calmly waited until he had read it through, and told her what to pay. Then she gave him the necessary dollars, and turned and walked through the hall, and came up the stairs, proud and erect — as proud, indeed, as if she had just won the battle of Waterloo.

And she was quite frank and fearless in speaking about this failure, and treated it as if it were an ordinary and trivial matter that could be put right in a few minutes. Her husband—she informed Mr. Von Rosen, who was greatly distressed by the news, and was consoling with her very sincerely—was quite capable of holding his own in the world without any help from his father's business. No doubt it would alter their plans of living, but Mr. Balfour was not at all the sort of man likely to let circumstances overpower him. And would it please us to set out at once on our inspection of Omaha? for she would like to get a glimpse of the Missouri, and there was the possibility that she might have to start off for England that night.

"*Nee!*" cried the lieutenant, in indignant protest. "It is impossible! Now that you have only the few days more to go on —and then your friends to go back—"

Here one of the party intimated her wish—or, rather, her fixed intention—of accompanying Lady Sylvia.

"Oh no!" our guest said, with quite a cheerful smile. "I am not at all afraid of travelling alone — not in the least. I have

seen a great deal of how people have to help themselves, since I
left England. And that is not much hardship. I believe one
can go right through from here to New York; and then I can
go to the Brevoort House, which seemed the quietest of the hotels, and wait for the first steamer leaving for Liverpool. I am
not in the least afraid."

Our Bell looked at her husband. That look was enough; he
knew his fate was sealed. If Lady Sylvia should set out that
evening, he knew he would have to accompany her as far as New
York anyhow.

I think she quite charmed the hearts of the kind friends who
had come to show us about the place. The truth was that the
recent heavy rains had changed Omaha into a Slough of De-
spond, and the huge holes of mud in the unmade streets were
bridged over by planks of wood that were of the most uncertain
character; but she seemed rather to like this way of laying out
streets. Then we climbed up to the heights above the town on
which is built the High School—a handsome building of red-
brick; and she betrayed the greatest interest in the system of
education followed here, and listened to the catechising of the
children by the smartly dressed and self-composed young ladies
who were their teachers, just as if she understood all about co-
sines and angles of reflection. And when we clambered up to
the tower of this building, she was quite delighted with the spacious panorama spread out all around. Far over there was a
mighty valley—a broad plain between two long lines of bluffs—
which was no doubt in former times worn down by the Missouri;
and now this plain, we could see, was scored along by various
channels, one of them, a little darker in hue than the neighboring sand, being the yellow Missouri itself. We were rather disappointed with the mighty Missouri, which we expected to find
rolling down in grandeur to the sea—or, rather, to the Mississippi, if the poet will allow us to make the correction. We considered that even the name they give it out here, the Big Muddy,
was misapplied; for it did not seem broader than the Thames at
Richmond, while the mud-banks and sand-banks on both sides of
it were of the dreariest sort. But she would not hear a word
said against the noble river. No doubt at other times of the
year it had sufficient volume; and even now was there not something mysterious in this almost indistinguishable river rolling

down through that vast, lonely, and apparently uninhabited plain? As for Omaha, it looked as bright as blue skies and sunshine could make it. All around us were the wooden shanties, and the occasional houses of stone, dotted about in a promiscuous fashion out there on the green undulations where the prairie began; on the sides of the bluffs where the trees were; and along the level mud bed of the river, where the railway works and smelting-works were sending up a cloud of smoke into the still clear air. We visited these works. She listened with great interest to the explanations of the courteous officials, and struck up a warm friendship with a civil engineer at the railway works, doubtless because he spoke with a Scotch accent. But, after all, we could see she was becoming anxious and nervous; and rather before mid-day we proposed to return to the hotel for luncheon.

Four hours had elapsed.

"But you must not make sure of finding an answer awaiting you, my dear Lady Sylvia," said her ever-thoughtful friend. "There may be delays. And Mr. Balfour may be out of town."

All the same she did make sure of an answer; and when, on arriving at the hotel, she was informed that no telegram had come for her, she suddenly went away to her own room, and we did not see her for some little time. When she did make her appearance at lunch, we did not look at her eyes.

She would not go out with us for our farther explorations. She had a headache. She would lie down. And so she went away to her own room.

But the curious thing was that Queen T—— would not accompany us either. It was only afterward that we learned that she had kept fluttering about the hall, bothering the patient clerks with inquiries as to the time that a telegram took to reach London. At last it came, and it was given to her. We may suppose that she carried it up-stairs quickly enough, and with a beating heart. What happened in the room she only revealed subsequently, bit by bit, for her voice was never quite steady about it.

She went into the room gently. Lady Sylvia was seated at a table, her hands on the table, her head resting on them, and she was sobbing bitterly. She was deserted, insulted, forsaken. He would not even acknowledge the appeal she had made to him. But she started up when she heard some one behind her, and would have pretended to conceal her tears, but that she saw the telegram. With trembling fingers she opened it, threw a hasty glance at it, and then, with a strange, proud look, gave it back to her friend, who was so anxious and excited that she could scarcely read the words—"*No. I am coming to you.*" And at the same moment all Lady Sylvia's fortitude broke down, and she gave way to a passion of hysterical joy—throwing her arms round her friend's neck, and crying over her, and murmuring close to her, "Oh, my angel—my angel—my angel—you have saved to me all that was worth living for!" So much can imaginative people make out of a brief telegram.

The two women seemed quite mad when we returned.

"He is coming out! Mr. Balfour is coming to join us!" says Queen T——, with a wild fire of exultation in her face, as if the millennium were at hand; and Lady Sylvia was sitting there, proud enough, too, but rosy-red in the face, and with averted eyes.

And here occurred a thing which has always been a memorable puzzle to us.

"Ha!" cried the lieutenant, in the midst of an excitement which the women in vain endeavored to conceal, "that rifle! Does he remember that wonderful small rifle of his? It will be of such use to him in the Rocky Mountains. I think—yes, I think—it is worth a telegram."

And he went down-stairs to squander his money in that fashion. But, we asked ourselves afterward, did he know? Had he and his wife suspected? Had they discussed the affairs of Lady Sylvia and her husband in those quiet conjugal talks of which the outsider can never guess the purport? And had this young man, with all his bluntness and good-natured common-sense, and happy matter-of-fact-ness, suddenly seize the dramatic situation, and called aloud about this twopenny-half-penny business of a pea-shooter all to convince Lady Sylvia of the general ignorance and put her at her ease? He came up a few moments afterward, whistling.

"There is antelope," said he, seriously, "and the mountain-sheep, and the black-tailed deer, and the bear. Oh, he will have much amusement with us when he comes to Idaho."

"You forget," says Lady Sylvia, smiling, though her eyes were quite wet, "that he will be thinking of other things. He has got to find out how he has got to live first."

"How he has got to live?" said the lieutenant, with a shrug of his shoulders. "That is simple. That is easy. Any man can settle that. He has got to live—happy, and let things take their chance. What harm in a holiday, if he comes with me to shoot one or two bears?"

"Indeed, you will do nothing of the kind," said his wife, severely. She had too much regard for her babes to let the father of them go off endangering his life in that fashion.

That was a pleasant evening. Our friends came to dine with us, and we settled all our plans for our expedition to the Indian reservations lying far up the Missouri valley. And who was first down in the morning—and who was most delighted with the clear coolness of the air and the blue skies—and who was most cheerful and philosophical when we discovered, at the station, and when it was too late, that the carpet-bag we had stuffed with wine, beer, and brandy for our stay in these temperate climes had been left behind at the hotel?

The small branch line of railway took us only about forty miles on our way. We went up the immensely broad valley of the river, which was at this time only a rivulet. The valley was a plain of rich vegetation—long water-color washes of yellow, and russet, and olive-green. The farther side of it was bounded by a distant line of bluffs, bright blue in color. Close by us were the corresponding bluffs, broken with ravines which were filled with cotton-trees, and which opened out into a thick underwood of sunflowers ten feet high and of deep-hued sumach. Overhead a pale-blue sky and some white clouds. Then, as we are looking up into the light, we see an immense flock of wild-geese making up the stream, divided into two lines representing the letter V placed horizontally, but more resembling a handful of dust flung high into the air.

About mid-day we reached the terminus of the line, Tekamah, a collection of wooden shanties and houses, with a few cotton-trees about. We had luncheon in a curious little inn which had originally been a block-house against the Indians—that is to say, it had been composed of sawn trees driven into the earth, with no windows on the ground-floor. By the time we had finished luncheon, our two carriages were ready—high-springed vehicles with an awning, and each with a moderately good pair of horses. We set out for our halting-place, Decatur, sixteen miles off.

That drive up the bed of the Missouri we shall not soon forget. There was no made road at all, but only a worn track through the dense vegetation of this swampy plain, while ever and anon this track was barred across by ravines of rich, deep, black, succulent mud. It was no unusual thing for us to see first one horse and then its companion almost disappear into a hole, we looking down on them; then there would be a fierce struggle; a plunge on our part, and then we were looking up at the horses pawing the bank above us. How the springs held out we could not understand. But occasionally, to avoid these ruts, we made long détours through the adjacent prairie-land lying over the bluffs; and certainly this was much pleasanter. We went through a wilderness of flowers, and the scent of the trampled may-weed filled all the air around us. How English horses would have behaved in this wilderness was a problem. The sunflowers were higher than our animals' heads; they could not possibly see where they were going; but, all the same, they slowly ploughed their way through the forest of crackling stems. But before we reached Decatur we had to return to the mud swamp, which was here worse than ever; for now it appeared as if there were a series of rivers running at right angles to the broad black track, and our two vehicles kept plunging through the water and mud as if we were momentarily to be sucked down into a morass. The air was thick with insect life, and vast clouds of reed-birds rose, as we passed, from the sunflowers. There was a red fire all over the west as we finally drove into the valley of the Decatur.

It was a strange-looking place. The first objects that met our eyes were some Indian boys riding away home to the reservations on their ponies, and looking picturesque enough with their ragged and scarlet pantaloons, their open-breasted shirt, their swarthy face and shining black hair, and their arms swinging with the galloping of the ponies, though they stuck to the saddle like a leech. And these were strange-looking gentlemen, too, whom we met in the inn of Decatur—tall, swanking fellows, with big riding-boots and loose jacket, broad-shouldered, spare-built, unwashed, unshaven, but civil enough, though they set their broad-brimmed hats with a devil-may-care air on the side of their head. We had dinner with these gentlemen in the parlor of the inn. There were two dishes—from which each helped himself with his fingers—of some sort of dried flesh which the lieutenant declared to be peli-

can of the wilderness; and there were prunes and tea. We feared
our friends were shy, for they did not speak at all before our
women-folk. In a few minutes they disposed of their meal, and
went out to a bench in front of the house to smoke. Then the
lieutenant — so as not to shock these temperate people — produced one of several bottles of Catawba which he had procured
at some way-side station before we left the railway. In appearance, when poured out, it was rather like tea, though not at all so
clear; and, in fact, the taste was so unlike anything we had ever
met before, that we unanimously pronounced in favor of the tea.
But the lieutenant would try another bottle; and that being a
trifle more palatable, we had much pleasure in drinking a toast.
And the toast we drank was the safety of the gallant ship that
was soon to carry Lady Sylvia's husband across the Atlantic.

CHAPTER XLV.

FIRE CHIEF.

NEXT morning, as we drove away from Decatur, a cold white
fog lay all along the broad valley of the Missouri; but by-and-
by the sun drank it up, and the warm light seemed to wake into
activity all the abounding animal life of that broken and wooded
country that skirts the prairie. There were clouds of reed-birds
rising from the swamps as we approached; now and again a
mourning-dove quietly flew across; large hawks hovered high in
air; and so abundant were the young quail that it seemed as
if our horses were continually about to trample down a brood
coolly crossing the road. We saw the gopher running into his
hole, and the merry little chipmunk eying us as we passed; and
at one point we gave a badger a bit of a chase, the animal quietly trotting down the road in front of us. The air was cool and
pleasant. Dragon-flies flashed, and butterflies fluttered across in
the sunlight: it was a beautiful morning.

And at last we were told that we were on the reservation
lands, though nothing was visible but the broken bluffs and the
open prairie beyond, and on our right the immense valley of the
Missouri. But in time we came to a farm, and drove up to a

very well-built house, and here we made the acquaintance of H—— F——, who most courteously offered to act as our guide for the day. He took a seat in our vehicle; and though he was rather shy and silent at first, this constraint soon wore off. And Lady Sylvia regarded our new acquaintance with a great friendliness and interest; for had she not heard the heroic story of his brother, the last chief of the Omahas, "Logan of the Fires?"—how, when his tribe was being pursued by the savage Sioux, and when there seemed to be no escape from extermination, he himself, as night fell, went off and kindled fire after fire so as to lead the enemy after him, and how he had the proud satisfaction of knowing, when he was taken and killed, that he had saved the life of every man, woman, and child of his followers. We did not wonder that the brother of the hero was regarded with much respect by the Omahas—in fact, there was a talk, at the time of our visit, of the smaller chiefs, or heads of families, electing him chief of the tribe. Indeed, the story reflected some romantic lustre on the peaceful Omahas themselves, and we began to cherish a proper contempt for their neighbors, the Winnebagoes—the broken remnant of the tribe which committed the horrible massacres in Minnesota some years ago, and which, after having been terribly punished and disarmed, was transferred by the Government to the prairie-land adjoining the Missouri.

But for the time being we kept driving on and on, without seeing Winnebago, or Omaha, or any sign of human life or occupation. Nothing but the vast and endless billows of the prairie—a beautiful yellow green in the sun—receding into the faint blue white of the horizon; while all around us was a mass of flowers—the Michaelmas-daisy being especially abundant; while the air was everywhere scented with the aromatic fragrance of the may-weed. We had now quite lost sight of the Missouri valley, and were pursuing a path over this open prairie which seemed to lead to no place in particular. But while this endless plain seemed quite unbroken, bare, and destitute of trees, it was not really so. It was intersected by deep and sharp gullies, the beds of small tributaries of the Missouri, and the sides of these gullies were lined with dense brushwood and trees. It was certainly a country likely to charm the heart of a tribe of Indians, if only they were allowed to have weapons and to return to their former habits; for it offered every facility for concealment and ambuscade. But all that is a thing of the past, so far as the Missouri Indians are concerned; their young men have not even the chance — taken by the young men of apparently peaceable tribes living on other reservations—of stealing quietly away to the Sioux; for the Sioux and the Omahas have ever been deadly enemies.

The danger we encountered in descending into these gullies was not that of being surprised and having our hair removed, but of the vehicle to which we clung toppling over and going headlong to the bottom. These breakneck approaches to the rude wooden bridges—where there were bridges at all—were the occasion of much excitement; and our friendly guide, who seemed to treat the fact of the vehicle hovering in air, as if uncertain which way to fall, with much indifference, must have arrived at the opinion that Englishwomen were much given to screaming when their heads were bumped together. In fact, at one point they refused to descend in the carriage. They got out and scrambled down on foot; and the driver, with that rare smile one sees on the face of a man who has been hardened into gravity by the life of an early settler, admitted that, if the vehicle had been full, it would most assuredly have pitched over.

At length we descried, on the green slope of one of the far undulations, three teepees — tall, narrow, conical tents, with the tips of the poles on which the canvas is stretched appearing at the top, and forming a funnel for the smoke—and near them a herd of ponies. But there were no human beings visible, and our path did not approach these distant tents. The first of the Indians we encountered gave us rather a favorable impression of the physique of the Omahas. He was a stalwart young fellow; his long black hair plaited; a blue blanket thrown round his square shoulders. He stood aside to let the vehicle pass, and eyed us somewhat askance; the few words that F—— addressed to him, and which he answered, were of course unintelligible to us. Then we overtook three or four more, men and women, in various attire; but, altogether, they were better in appearance and more independent in manner than the gypsy-looking Indians we had seen skulking around the confines of the towns, in more or less " civilized " dress, and not without a side-glance for unconsidered trifles. These, we were told, were mostly Pawnees; though the Winnebagoes have in some measure taken to the neighborhood of the towns on the chance of getting a stray dollar by digging.   After we passed these few stragglers, we were apparently once more on the tenantless prairies; but doubtless the Indians who prefer to live in their teepees out on the plain rather than accept the semicivilization of the Agency, had taken to the hollows; so that the country around us was not quite the desert that it seemed to be.

But a great honor was in store for us.   When it was proposed that we should turn aside from our path and visit the wigwam of Fire Chief, one of the heads of the small communities into which the tribe is divided, some scruples were expressed; for we held that no human being, whether he was a poet-laureate or a poor Indian, liked to have his privacy invaded from motives of mere curiosity.   Then we had no presents to offer him as an excuse.

"No tobacco?" said our good-natured guide, with a smile. "An Indian never refuses tobacco."

The news of our approach to the wigwam was doubtless conveyed ahead; for we saw some dusky children scurry away and disappear like rabbits.   The building was a large one; the base of it being a circular and substantial wall of mud and turf apparently about ten feet high, the conical roof sloping up from the wall being chiefly composed of the trunks of trees, leaving a hole at the summit for the escape of smoke.   We descended from our vehicles, and, crouching down, pushed aside the buffalo-skin that served for door, and entered the single and spacious apartment which contained Fire Chief, his wives, children, and relatives. For a second or two we could scarcely see anything, so blinding was the smoke; but presently we made out that all round the circular wigwam, which was probably between thirty and forty feet in diameter, were a series of beds, toward which the squaws and children had retreated, while in the middle of the place, seated on a buffalo-skin in front of the fire, was the chief himself.   He took no notice of our entrance.   He stared into the fire as we seated ourselves on a bench; but one or two of the younger women, from out the dusky recesses, gazed with obvious wonder on these strange people from a distant land.   Fire Chief is a large and powerful-looking man, with a sad and worn face; obviously a person of importance, for he wore an armlet of silver and earrings of the same material, and his moccasons of buffalo-hide were very elaborately embroidered with beads and porcupine quills, while the dignity of his demeanor was quite appalling.

"Will you take a cigar, sir?" said the lieutenant, who had vainly endeavored to get one of the children to come near him.

Fire Chief did not answer. He only stared into the smouldering wood before him. But when the cigar was presented to him, he took it, and lit it with a bit of burning stick, resuming his air of absolute indifference.

"Does he not speak English?" said Lady Sylvia, in an undertone, to our guide, who had been conversing with him in his own tongue.

"They don't know much English," said F——, with a smile, "and what they do know they don't care to speak. But he asks me to tell you that one of the young men is sick; that he is in the bed over there. And he says he has not been very well himself lately."

"Will you tell him," said Lady Sylvia, gently, "that we have come about five thousand miles from our homes, and that we are greatly pleased to see him, and that we hope he and the young man will very soon be well again?"

When this message was conveyed to the chief, we rose and took our departure, and he took no more notice of our leaving than our coming. Shall we say that we felt, on getting outside, rather "mean"—that the fact of our being a pack of inquisitive tourists was rather painful to us — that we mentally swore we should not "interview" another human being, Indian or poet-laureate, during the whole course of our miserable lives? Our self-consciousness in this respect was not at all shared by our good friend from Omaha who was driving one of the two vehicles, and who seemed to regard the Indian as a very peculiar sort of animal, decidedly less than human, but with his good points all the same. Was it not he who told us that story about his wife having been one day alone in her house—many years ago, when the early settlers found the Indians more dangerous neighbors than they are now—and engaged in baking, when two or three Indians came to the door and asked for bread? She offered them an old loaf; they would not have it; thay insisted on having some of the newly baked bread, and they entered the house to seize it; whereupon this courageous house-mistress took up her rolling-pin and laid about her, driving her enemy forthwith out of the door. But the sequel of the story has to be told. Those very Indians, whenever they came that way, never passed the house without bringing her a present—a bit of venison, some quail, or what not —and the message they presented with the game was always this : "Brave squaw! brave squaw!" which shows that there is virtue in a rolling-pin, and that heroism, and the recognition of it, did not die out with the abandonment of chain-armor.

We also heard a story which suggests that the Indian, if an inferior sort of animal, is distinctly a reasoning one. Some years ago a missionary arrived in these parts, and was greatly shocked to find, on the first Sunday of his stay, that these Indians, who had taken to agriculture, were busily planting maize. He went out and conjured them to cease; assuring them that the God whom he worshipped had commanded people to do no work on the Sabbath, and that nothing would come of their toil if they committed this sin. The Indians listened gravely, and, having staked off the piece of ground they had already planted, desisted from work. After that they never worked on Sunday except within this enclosure; but then this enclosure got the extra day's hoeing and tending. When harvest came, behold! the space that had been planted and tended on Sundays produced a far finer crop than any adjacent part, and no doubt the Indians came to their own conclusions about the predictions of the missionary. Anyhow, whether the legend be true or not, the Omahas retain their original faith.

At length we reached the Agency—a small collection of houses scattered about among trees—and here there were some greater signs of life. Small groups of Indians, picturesque enough with their colored blankets and their leggings of buffalo-hide, stood lounging about, pretending not to see the strangers, but taking furtive glances all the same; while now and again a still more picturesque figure in scarlet pants and with swinging arms would ride by on his pony, no doubt bound for his teepee out on the plain. Alas! the only welcome we received from any of the Indians was accorded us by a tall and bony idiot, who greeted us with a friendly "How?" and a grin. We had our horses taken out, we were hospitably entertained by the agent, a sober and sedate Quaker, and then we went out for a stroll round the place, which included an inspection of the store, the blacksmith's shop, and other means for assisting the Indians to settle down to a peaceful agricultural life.

Our party unanimously came to the opinion—having conversed to the extent of "How?" with one Indian, and that Indian an idiot—that the preference of the Indians for remaining paupers on the hands of the Government, rather than take to tilling the ground, is natural. The Indian, by tradition and instinct, is a gentleman. Of all the races of the world, he is the nearest approach one can get to the good old English squire. He loves horses; he gives up his life to hunting and shooting and fishing; he hasn't a notion in his head about "boetry and bainting;" and he considers himself the most important person on the face of the earth. But the Indian is the more astute of the two. Long ago he evolved the ingenious theory that, as his success in the chase depended on his nerves being in perfect order, it would never do for him to attack the ordinary rough work of existence; and hence he turned over to his wife or wives the tending of the horses, the building of the teepees, the procuring of fuel—in fact, all the work that needed any exertion. This is one point on which the English country gentleman is at a disadvantage, although we have heard of one sensible man who invariably let his wife fill and screw up his cartridges for him.

And you expect this native gentleman to throw aside the sport that has been the occupation and passion of his life, and take to digging with a shovel for a dollar a day? How would your Yorkshire squire like that? He would not do it at all. He would expect the Government that deprived him of his land to give him a pension, however inadequate, and the wherewithal to keep body and soul together. He would go lounging about in an apathetic fashion, trying to get as much for his money as possible at the Government stores, smoking a good deal, and being the reverse of communicative with the impertinent persons who came a few thousand miles to stare at him. And if the Government stopped his drink, and would not let him have even a glass of beer— But this is carrying the parallel to an impossibility: no existing Government could so far reduce Yorkshire; there would have been such an outburst of revolution as the world has never yet seen.

We set out on our return journey, taking another route over the high-lying prairie land. And at about the highest point we came to the burial-mound, or rather burial-house, of White Cow. When the old chief was dying, he said, "Bury me on a high place, where I can see the boats of the white men pass up and down the river." Was his friendly ghost sitting there, then, in the warm light of the afternoon, amidst the fragrant scent of the may-weed? Anyhow, if White Cow could see any boats on the Missouri, his spectral eyes must have been keener than ours; for we could could not see a sign of any craft whatsoever on that distant line of silver.

Strangely enough, we had just driven away from this spot, when an object suddenly presented itself to our startled gaze which might have been White Cow himself "out for a dauner." A more ghastly spectacle was never seen than this old and withered Indian — a tall man, almost naked, and so shrunken and shrivelled that every bone in his body was visible; while the skin of the mummy-like face had been pulled back from his mouth, so that he grinned like a spectre. He was standing apart from the road, quite motionless, and he carried nothing in his hand; but all the same, both our horses at the same moment plunged aside so as nearly to leave the path, and were not quieted for some minutes afterward. We forgot to ask F—— if he knew this spectre, or whether it was really White Cow. Certainly, horses don't often shy because of the ghastly appearance of a human being.

That night we reached Decatur again, and had some more pelican of the wilderness and prunes. Then the women went upstairs, doubtless to have a talk about the promised addition to our party, and we went outside to listen to the conversation of the tall, uncouth, unkempt fellows who were seated on a bench smoking. We heard a good deal about the Indian, and about the attempts to "civilize" him. From some other things we had heard out there, we had begun to wonder whether civilization was to be defined as the art of acquiring greenbacks without being too particular about the means. However, it appears that on one point the Indians have outstripped civilization. The Indian women, who had in by-gone years sometimes to go on long marches with their tribe in time of war, are said to have discovered a secret which the fashionable women of Paris would give their ears to know. But they keep it a profound secret; so perhaps it is only a superstition.

CHAPTER XLVI.

SCHEMES.

SHALL we ever forget that sunrise over the vast plain through which the Missouri runs—the silence and loneliness and majesty of it? Far away—immeasurable leagues away, it seemed—a bar of purple cloud appeared to rest on the earth, all along the flat horizon; while above that the broad expanse of sky began to glow with a pale lemon-yellow, the grassy plain below being of a deep, intense olive-green. No object in the distance was to be descried, except one narrow strip of forest; and the trees, just getting above the belt of purple, showed a serrated line of jet-black on the pale-yellow sky. Then a flush of rose-pink began to fill the east, and quite suddenly the wooden spire of the small church beside us—the first object to catch the new light of the dawn—shone, a pale red, above the cold green of the cotton-trees. There was no one abroad at this hour in the wide streets of Decatur, though we had seen two Indians pass some little time before, with shovels over their shoulders. Our object in getting up so early was to try to get over the swampiest part of our journey before the heat of the day called up a plague of flies from the mud.

One thing or another, however, delayed our departure, and when at last we got into the swamps, we were simply enveloped in clouds of mosquitoes. If we could only have regarded these from behind a glass mask, we should have said that they formed a very beautiful sight, and so have discovered the spirit of good that lurks in that most evil thing. For we were in shadow— our vehicles having a top supported by slender iron poles arising from the sides—and, looking out from this shadow, the still air seemed filled with millions upon millions of luminous and transparent golden particles. Occasionally we got up on a higher bit of ground, and could send the horses forward, the current thus produced relieving us from these clouds. But ordinarily our slow plunging through the mire left us an easy prey to these insatiable myriads. Indeed, there were more mosquitoes within our vehicle—if that were possible—than in the same space without; for these creatures prefer to get into the shade when the blaze of the sun is fierce, though they do not show themselves grateful to those who afford it. The roof of our palanquin-phaeton was of blue cloth when we started. Before we had been gone an hour it was gray; there was not anywhere the size of a pea visible of the blue cloth. But this temporary retirement of a few millions in no wise seemed to diminish the numbers of those who were around us in the air. At last even the patience of the lieutenant broke down.

"Lady Sylvia," said he, "I have now discovered why there is so much bad language in America. If ever we go up the Missouri again, you ladies must go in one carriage by yourselves, and we in another carriage; for the frightful thing is that we cannot say what we think." And here he slapped his cheek again, and slew another half-dozen of his enemies.

"But why not speak?" his wife said.

> "'It was an ancient privilege, my lords,
> To fling whate'er we felt, not fearing, into words.'"

Lady Sylvia was supposed to say something; but as she had tied a handkerchief tightly round her face, we could not quite make out what it was.

He continued to complain. We had delayed our return to Decatur on the previous day, so that we should avoid driving on to Tekamah in the evening, when the plague is worse: he declared it could not be worse. He even complained that we had not suffered in this fashion a couple of days before, in driving over the same ground; forgetting that then we had a fresh and pleasant breeze. And we were soon to discover what a breeze could do. Our friendly guide and driver suddenly plunged his horses off the path into a thicket of tall reeds. We thought we should have been eaten up alive at this point. But presently we got through this wilderness, and began to ascend a slope leading up to the bluffs. Was there not a scent of cooler air? We clambered higher and higher; we got among our old friends, the sunflowers and Michaelmas-daisies; and at last, when we emerged on to the sunlit and golden plain, the cool breeze, fragrant with may-weed, came sweeping along and through our vehicle, and, be-

hold! we were delivered from our enemies. We waxed valiant.
We attacked their last stronghold on the roof; we flicked off
these gray millions; and they, too, flew away and disappeared.
We sent a victorious halloo to the vehicle behind us, which was
joyfully answered. We fell in love with the "rolling" prairies,
and their beautiful flowers and fresh breezes.

But the cup of human happiness is always dashed with some
bitterness or another. We began to think about that vast and
grassy swamp from which we had emerged. Was not that, in
effect, part of the very Mississippi valley about which such
splendid prophecies have been made? Our good friends out here,
though they made light of their river by calling it the Big Muddy, nevertheless declared that it was the parent of the Mississippi,
and that the Mississippi should be called the Missouri from St.
Louis right down to New Orleans. Had we, then, just struggled
upward from one branch of the great basin which is to contain
the future civilization of the world? We had been assured by
an eminent (American) authority that nothing could "prevent
the Mississippi valley from becoming, in less than three generations, the centre of human power." It was with pain and anguish
that we now recalled these prophetic words. Our hearts grew
heavy when we thought of our children's children. O ye future
denizens of Alligator City, do not think that your forefathers
have not also suffered in getting through these mud-flats on an
August day!

At length we got back to Tekamah and its conspicuous tree,
which latter, it is said, has done the State some good service in
former days. We were much too early for the train; and so we
had luncheon in the block-house inn (the lieutenant in vain offering a dollar for a single bottle of beer), and then went out to
sit on a bench and watch the winged beetles that hovered in the
sunshine and then darted about in a spasmodic fashion. That
was all the amusement we could find in Tekamah. But they say
that a newspaper exists there; and, if only the Government would
open up a road to the Black Hills by way of the Elkhorn valley,
Tekamah might suddenly arise and flourish. In the end, we left
the darting beetles, and drove to the station. Here we saw two
or three gangs of "civilized" Indians digging for the railway
company. Whether Pawnees, Omahas, or Winnebagoes, they were,
in their tattered shirt and trousers, not an attractive-looking lot of

people; whereas the gentlemen-paupers of the reservations have at least the advantage of being picturesque in appearance. There were a few teepees on the slopes above, with some women and children. The whole very closely resembled a gypsy encampment.

And then, in due course of time, we made our way back to Omaha, the capital of the Plains, the future Chicago of the West; and we were once more jolted over the unmade roads and streets, which had now got dry and hard. And what was this?—another telegram?

Lady Sylvia took it calmly, and opened it with an air of pride.

"I thought so," she said, with assumed indifference; and there was a certain superiority in her manner, almost bordering on triumph, as she handed the telegram to her friend. She seemed to say, "Of course, it is quite an ordinary occurrence for my husband to send me a telegram. There, you may all see on what terms we are. I am not a bit rejoiced that he has actually sailed, and on his way to join us."

The word was passed round. Balfour's telegram was from Queenstown, giving the name of the vessel by which he had sailed. There was nothing for her to be proud of in that; she did well to assume indifference.

But when, that evening, we were talking about our further plans, she suddenly begged to be left out of the discussion.

"I mean to remain here until my husband arrives," said she.

"In Omaha!" we all cried; but there was really no disparagement implied in this ejaculation; for it must be acknowledged that Omaha, after its first reception of us, had treated us with the greatest kindness.

"He cannot be here for a fortnight at least," it is pointed out to her. "We could in that time go on to Idaho and be back here to meet him, if he does not wish, like the rest of us, to have a look at the Rocky Mountains."

"I cannot tell what his wishes may be," said the young wife, thoughtfully, "and there is no means of explaining to him where to find us if we move from here."

"There is every means," it is again pointed out. "All you have to do is to address a letter to the New York office of the line, and it will be given to him even before he lands."

This notion of sending a letter seemed to give her great delight. She spent the whole of the rest of the evening in her own room; no human being but him to whom they were addressed ever knew what were the outpourings of her soul on that occasion. Later on, she came in to bid us good-night. She looked very happy, but her eyes were red.

Then two members of our small party went out into the cool night air to smoke a cigar. The broad streets of Omaha were dark and deserted; there were no roisterers going home; no lights showing that the gambling-houses were still open. The place was as quiet as a Surrey village on a Sunday morning when everybody is at church.

"I have been thinking," says one of them; and this is a startling statement, for he is not much given that way. "And what these ladies talk about Balfour doing when he comes out here—oh, that is all stuff—that is all folly and nonsense. It is romantic—oh yes, it is very fine to think of; and for an ordinary poor. man it is a great thing to have one hundred and sixty acres of freehold land—and very good land—from the Government; and if he knows anything about farming, and if he and his family will work—that is very well. But it is only romantic folly to talk about that and Balfour together. His wife—it is very well for her to be brave—and say this thing and that thing; but it is folly; they cannot do that. That is the nonsense a great many people in England think—that, when they have failed at everything, they can farm. Oh yes; I would like to see Lady Sylvia help to build a house, or to milk a cow even. But the other thing, that is a little more sensible. They say the railway has beautiful grazing land—beautiful grazing land—that you can buy for a pound or thirty shillings an acre; and a man might have a large freehold estate for little. But the little is something; and there is the cost of the stock, and the taxes; and if Balfour had enough money for all that, how do you know that he will be able to make his fortune by stock-raising?"

"I don't know anything about it."

"No," said the lieutenant, with decision, "these things are only romantic folly. It is good for a laboring man who has a little money to have a homestead from the Government, and work away; and it is good for a farmer who knows about cattle to buy acres from the railway, and invest his money in cattle, and look after them. As for Balfour and his wife—"

A semicircular streak of fire in the darkness—a wave of the

15

hand indicated by the glowing end of the cigar—showed how the lieutenant disposed of that suggestion.

"Do you think," said he, after a time—"you have known him longer than I have—do you think he is a proud man?"

"As regards his taking to some occupation or other?"

"Yes."

"He will have to put his pride in his pocket. He is a reasonable man."

"There was one thing that my wife and I talked of last night," said the lieutenant, with a little hesitation; "but I am afraid to speak it, for it might be—impertinent. Still, to you I will speak it; you will say no more if you do not approve. You know, at the end of one year, my wife and I we find ourselves with all this large property on our hands. Then we have to decide what to do with it."

"Sell every stick and stone of it, and take the proceeds back with you to England. You cannot manage such a property five thousand miles away. Bell's uncle, mind you, trusted to nobody; he was his own overseer and manager, and a precious strict one, if all accounts be true. You carry that money back to England, buy a castle in the Highlands, and an immense shooting, and ask me, each August, to look in on you about the 12th. That is what a sensible man would do."

"But wait a bit, my friend. This is what my wife says—yes, it is her notion—but she is very fearful not to offend. She says if this property is going on paying so well, and increasing every year, would it not be better for us to give some one a good salary to remain there and manage it for us? Do you see now? Do you see?"

"And that was your wife's notion? Well, it is a confoundedly clever one; but it was her abounding good-nature that led her to it. Unfortunately, there is a serious drawback. You propose to offer this post to Balfour."

"Gott bewahre!" exclaimed the lieutenant, almost angrily, for he was indeed "fearful not to offend;" "I only say to you what is a notion—what my wife and I were speaking about—I would not have it mentioned for worlds—until, at least, I knew something about—about—"

"About the light in which Balfour would regard the offer. Unless he is an ass, which I don't believe, he would jump at it.

But there is the one objection, as I say : Balfour probably knows as much about the raising of cattle as he knows about mining—which is nothing at all. And you propose to put all these things into his hands ?"

"My good friend," said the lieutenant, "he is a man; he has eyes; he is a good horseman; he can learn. When he comes out here, let him stay with us. He has a year to learn. And do you suppose that Bell's uncle he himself looked after the cattle, and drove this way and that, and sold them ? No, no ; no more than he went down into the mines and watched them at the work. If Balfour will do this—and it is only a notion yet—he will have to keep the accounts, and he will judge by the results what is going on right. And so we too. If it does not answer, we can sell. I think he is a patient, steady man, who has resolution. And if he is too proud — if he is offended — we could make it an interest rather than salary—a percentage on the year's profits—"

"Well, if you ask me what I think of it, I consider that he is very lucky to have such a chance offered. He will live in the healthiest and most delightful climate in the world ; he and his wife, who are both excessively fond of riding, will pass their lives on horseback ; he may make some money ; and then he will be able to come up here and go in for a little speculation in real estate, just by way of amusement. But, my dear young friend, allow me to point out that when you talk of the women's schemes as romantic, and of your wife's and yours as a matter of business, you try to throw dust into the eyes of innocent folks. You are contemplating at present what is simply a magnificent act of charity."

"Then," said he, with real vexation, "it is all over. No, we will make him no such offer unless it is a matter of business ; he will only resent it if it is a kindness."

"And are there many people, then, who are in such a wild rage to resent kindness ? Where should we all be but for forbearance, and forgiveness, and charity ? Is he a god that he is superior to such things ?"

"You know him better than I do," is the gloomy response.

But the lieutenant, as we walked back to the hotel, was rather displeased that his proposal was not looked upon as a bit of smart commercial calculation.

CHAPTER XLVII.

AND here also, as at Chicago, the demon of speculation was nearly getting the better of our small and not by any means wealthy party. It was a terrible temptation to hear of all those beautiful grazing-lands close by in the Platte valley, the freehold of which was to be purchased for a song. The fact is, things were rather bad at Omaha while we were there; and although everybody tried to hang on to his real estate in hopes of better times, still the assessments pressed hard, and one could have very eligible "lots" at very small prices. No doubt there were ominous rumors about. We heard something, as we went farther west, about county commissioners, elected by the homesteaders and pre-emptors who are free from taxation, going rather wild in the way of building roads, schools, and bridges at the cost of the mere speculators. It was said that these very non-resident speculators, whose ranks we had been tempted to join, were the curse of the country; and that all laws passed to tax them, and to relieve the real residents, were just. Very well; but what was that other statement about the arrears of taxes owing by these unhappy wretches? Was it fair of the Government of any State or any country in the world to sell such debts by auction, and give the buyer the right of extorting forty per cent. per annum until the taxes were paid? We regarded our friends. We hinted that this statement was a capital credulometer. The faith that can accept it is capable of anything.

These profound researches into the condition of public affairs in Omaha, during the further day or two we lingered there, were partly owing to vague dreams of the pleasure of proprietorship, but no doubt they were partly due to the notion that had got into the heads of one or two of our party that the idyllic life of a shepherd in the Platte valley must be a very fine thing. The lieutenant combated this notion fiercely, and begged Lady Sylvia to wait until she had seen the harshness of life even amidst the comparative luxury of a well-appointed ranch. Lady Sylvia retorted gently that we had no further knowledge of life at a ranch than herself; that she had attentively listened to all that had been said about the subject by our friends in Omaha; that harshness of living was a relative thing; and that she had no doubt Bell and her husband would soon get used to it, and would not complain.

"Oh no, she will not complain," said he, lightly. "She is very reasonable—she is very sensible. She will never be reconciled to the place while her children are away, and she will have a great deal of crying by herself; but she will not complain."

"Nor would any woman," said Lady Sylvia, boldly. "She is acting rightly; she is doing her duty. I think that women are far more capable of giving up luxuries they have been accustomed to than men are."

This set the lieutenant thinking. On the morning on which we left Omaha, he came aside, and said,

"I, too, have written a letter to Mr. Balfour: shall I post it?"

"What is in it?"

"The proposal I told you of the other night, but very—very—what do you call it?—roundabout. I have said perhaps he is only coming out to take his wife home sooner than you go—that is well. I have said perhaps he is waiting until the firm starts again; if that is any use, when they must have been losing for years. Again, that is well. But I have said perhaps he is coming to look how to start a business—an occupation; if that is so, will he stay with us a year?—see if he understands—then he will take the management, and have a yearly percentage. I have said it is only a passing thought; but we will ask Lady Sylvia to stay with us at Idaho until we hear from him. He can telegraph from New York. He will tell her to remain until he comes, or to meet him somewhere; I will get some one to accompany her. What do you say?"

"Post the letter."

"It will be very pleasant for us," said he, in a second or so, as he rubbed his hands in an excited fashion, "to have them out for our neighbors for a year at the least—it will be pleasant for Bell —how can she get any one in Denver or Idaho to know all about her children and Surrey? My dear friend, if you have any sense, you will stay with us too. I will show you bears."

He spoke as if he were already owner of the Rocky Mountains.

"And we will go down to Kansas—a great party, with covered wagons, and picnics, and much amusement—for a buffalo hunt. And then we will go up to the Parks in the middle of the mountains—what it is, is this, I tell you : if our stay here is compulsive, we will make it as amusing as possible, you will see, if only you will stay the year too."

A sigh was the answer.

And now, as we again set out on our journey westward, the beautiful prairie-country seemed more beautiful than ever ; and we caught glimpses of the fertile valley of the Platte, in which our imaginary freehold estates lay awaiting us. On and on we went, with the never-ending undulations of grass and flowers glowing all around us in the sunlight; the world below a plain of gold, the world above a vault of the palest blue. The space and light and color were altogether most cheerful; and as the train went at a very gentle trot along the single line, we sat outside, for the most part, in the cool breeze. Occasionally we passed a small hamlet, and that had invariably an oddly extemporized look. The wooden houses were stuck down anyhow on the grassy plain; without any trace of the old-fashioned orchards, and walled gardens and hedges that bind, as it were, an English village together. Here there was but the satisfaction of the most immediate needs. One wooden building labelled "Drug Store," another wooden building labelled "Grocery Store," and a blacksmith's shop were ordinarily the chief features of the community. All day we passed in this quiet gliding onward; and when the sun began to sink toward the horizon, we found ourselves in the midst of a grassy plain, apparently quite uninhabited and of boundless extent. As the western sky deepened in its gold and green, and as the sun actually touched the horizon, the level light hit across this vast plain in long shafts of dull fire, just catching the tops of the taller rushes near us, and touching some distant sandy slopes into a pale crimson. Lower and lower the sun sunk, until it seemed to eat a bit out of the horizon, so blinding was the light; while far above, in a sea of luminous green, lay one long narrow cloud, an island of blood-red.

In a second, when the sun sunk, the world seemed to grow quite dark. All around us the prairie-land had become of a cold, heavy, opaque green, and the only objects which our bewildered eyes could distinguish were some pale-white flowers—like the tufts of canna on a Scotch moor. But presently, and to our intense surprise, the world seemed to leap up again into light and color. This after-glow was most extraordinary. The immeasurable plains of grass became suffused with a rich olive-green; the western sky was all a radiance of lemon-yellow and silvery gray; while along the eastern horizon—the most inexplicable thing of all—there stretched a great band of smoke-like purple and pink. We soon became familiar with this phenomenon out in the West—this appearance of a vast range of roseate Alps along the eastern horizon, where there was neither mountain nor cloud. It was merely the shadow of the earth, projected by the sunken sun into the earth's atmosphere. But it was an unforgettable thing, this mystic belt of color, far away in the east, over the dark earth, and under the pale and neutral hues of the sky.

The interior of a Pullman sleeping-car, after the stalwart colored gentleman has lowered the shelves and made the beds and drawn the curtains, presents a strange sight. The great folds of the dusky curtains, in the dim light of a lamp, move in a mysterious manner, showing the contortions of the human beings within who are trying to dispossess themselves of their garments; while occasionally a foot is shot into the outer air so that the owner can rid himself of his boot. But within these gloomy recesses there is sufficient comfort; and he who is wakeful can lie and look out on the gathering stars as they begin to come out over the dark prairie-land. All through the night this huge snake, with its eyes of yellow fire, creeps across the endless plain. If you wake up before the dawn and look out, behold! the old familiar conditions of the world are gone, and the Plough is standing on its head. But still more wonderful is the later awakening; when the yellow sunlight of the morning is shining over the prairies, and when within this long caravan there is a confused shuffling and dressing, everybody wanting to get outside to get a breath of the fresh air. And what is this we find around us now? The vast plain of grass is beautiful in the early light, no doubt; but our attention is quickened by the sight of a drove of antelope which trot lightly and carelessly away toward some low and sandy bluffs in the distance. That solitary object out there seems at first to be a huge vulture; but by-and-by it turns out to be a prairie-wolf—a coyote—sitting on its hind legs and chewing at a bone. The chicken-hawk lifts its heavy wings as we go by, and flies across the plain. And here are the merry and familiar little prairie dogs — half rabbit and half squirrel — that look at us each from his little hillock of sand, and then pop into their hole only to reappear again when we have passed. Now the long swathes of green and yellow - brown are broken by a few ridges of gray rock; and these, in some places, have patches of orange-red lichen that tell against the pale-blue sky. It is a clear, beautiful morning. Even those who have not slept well through the slow rumbling of the night soon get freshened up on these high, cool plains.

At Sydney we suddenly came upon an oasis of brisk and busy life in this immeasurable desert of grass; and of course it was with an eager curiosity that we looked at these first indications of the probable life of our friend the ranch-woman. For here were immense herds of cattle brought in from the plains, and large pens and enclosures, and the picturesque herders, with their big boots and broad-rimmed hats, spurring about on their small and wiry horses.

"Shall you dress in buckskin?" asked Lady Sylvia of our lieutenant; "and will you flourish about one of those long whips?"

"Oh no," said he; "I understand my business will be a very tame one—all at a desk."

"Until we can get some trustworthy person to take the whole management," said Bell, gently, and looking down.

"What handsome fellows they are!" the lieutenant cried. "It is a healthy life. Look at the keen brown faces, the flat back, the square shoulders; and not a bit of fat on them. I should like to command a regiment of those fellows. Fancy what cavalry they would make—light, wiry, splendid riders—you could do something with a regiment of those fellows, I think! Lady Sylvia, did I ever tell you what two of my company—the dare-devils!—did at —— ?"

Lady Sylvia had never heard that legend of 1870; but she listened to it now with a proud and eager interest; for she had never forsaken, even at the solicitation of her husband, her championship of the Germans.

"I will write a ballad about it some day," said the lieutenant, with a laugh. "'Es ritt' zwei Uhlanen wohl über den Rhein—'"

"Yes!" said Lady Sylvia, with a flash of color leaping to her face, "it *was* well over the Rhine — it was indeed well over the Rhine that they and their companions got before they thought of going home again!"

"Ah, yes," said he, humbly, "but it is only the old seesaw. To-day it is Paris; to-morrow it is Berlin that is taken. The only thing is that this time I think we have secured a longer interval than usual; the great fortresses we have taken will keep us secure for many a day to come; our garrisons are armies; they cannot be surprised by treachery; and so long as we have the fortresses, we need not fear any invasion—"

"But you took them by force: why should not the French take them back by force?" his wife said.

"I think we should not be likely to have that chance again," said he; "the French will take care not to fall into that condition again. But we are now safe, and for a long time, because we have their great fortresses, and then our own line of the Rhine fortresses as well. It is the double gate to our house; and we have locked all the locks, and bolted all the bars. And yet we are not going to sleep."

We were again out on the wide and tenantless plains, and Bell was looking with great curiosity at the sort of land in which she was to find her home; for over there on the left the long undulations disappeared away into Colorado. And though these yellow and gray-green plains were cheerful enough in the sunshine, still they were very lonely. No trace of any living thing was visible — not even an antelope, or the familiar little prairie-dog. Far as the eye could reach on this high-lying plateau, there was nothing but the tufts of withered-looking buffalo-grass, with here and there a bleached skull, or the ribs of a skeleton breaking the monotony of the expanse. The lieutenant, who was watching the rueful expression of his wife's face, burst out laughing.

"You will have elbow-room out here, eh?" said he. "You will not crowd your neighbors off the pavement."

"I suppose we shall have no neighbors at all," said she.

"But at Idaho you will have plenty," said he; "it is a great place of fashion, I am told. It is even more fashionable than Denver. Ah, Lady Sylvia, we will show you something now. You have lived too much out of the world, in that quiet place in Surrey. Now we will show you fashion, life, gayety!"

15*

"Is it bowie-knives or pistols that the gentlemen mostly use in Denver?" asked Lady Sylvia, who did not like to hear her native Surrey despised.

"Bowie - knives! Pistols!" exclaimed the lieutenant, with some indignation. "When they fight a duel now, it is with tubes of rose-water. When they use dice, it is to say which of them will go away as missionaries to Africa—oh, it is quite true —I have heard many things of the reformation of Denver. The singing-saloons, they are all chapels now. All the people meet once in the forenoon and once in the afternoon to hear an exposition of one of Shakspeare's plays, and the rich people, they have sent all their money away to be spent on blue china. All the boys are studying to become bishops—"

He suddenly ceased his nonsense, and grasped his wife's arm. Some object outside had caught his attention. She instantly turned to the window, as we all did; and there, at the distant horizon, we perceived a pale transparent line of blue. You may be sure we were not long inside the carriage after that. The delight of finding something to break the monotony of the plains was boundless. We clung to the iron barrier outside, and craned our necks this way and that, so that we could see from farthest north to farthest south the shadowy, serrated range of the Rocky Mountains. The blue of them appeared to be about as translucent as the silvery light in which they stood; we could but vaguely make out the snow-peaks in that long serrated line; they were as a bar of cloud along the horizon. And yet we could not help resting our eyes on them with a great relief and interest, as we pressed on to Cheyenne, at which point we were to break our journey and turn to the south. It was about mid-day when we reached that city, which was a famous place during the construction of the Union Pacific Railway, and which has even now some claim to distinction. It is with a pardonable pride that its inhabitants repeat the name it then acquired, and all right to which it has by no means abandoned. The style and title in question is "Hell on Wheels."

CHAPTER XLVIII.

"HELL ON WHEELS."

WE step out from the excellent little railway-hotel, in which we have taken up our quarters, on to the broad platform, and into the warm light of the afternoon.

"Bell," says our gentle Queen T——, looking rather wistfully along the pale rampart of the Rocky Mountains, "these are the walls of your future home. Will you go up to the top of an evening and wave a handkerchief to us?—And we will try to answer you from Mickleham Downs."

"On Christmas-night we will send you many a message," said Bell, looking down.

"And my husband and myself," said Lady Sylvia, quite simply, "you will let us join in that too."

"But do you expect to be out here till Christmas?" said Bell, with well-affected surprise.

"I don't think my husband would come to America," said Lady Sylvia, in the most matter-of-fact way, "after what has happened, unless he meant to stay."

"Oh, if you could only be near us!" cried Bell; but she dared not say more.

"That would be very pleasant," Lady Sylvia answered, with a smile; "but of course I don't know what my husband's plans are. We shall know our way more clearly when he comes to Idaho. It will seem so strange to sit down and shape one's life anew; but I suppose a good many people have got to do that."

By this time the lieutenant had secured a carriage which was standing at the end of the platform, along with a pony for himself.

"Now, Mrs. Von Rosen," said he, "air you ready? Guess you've come up from the ranch to have a frolic? Got your dollars ready for the gambling-saloons?"

"And if I have," said she, boldly, "they are licensed by the Government. Why should I not amuse myself in these places?"

"Madame," replied her husband, sternly, "the Puritan nation into which you have married permits of no such vices. Cheyenne must follow Homburg, Wiesbaden, Baden-Baden—"

"No doubt," said the sharper-tongued of our women-folk, who invariably comes to the assistance of her friend—"no doubt that will follow when your pious emperor has annexed the State."

"I beg your pardon, madame," says the lieutenant, politely, "but Wyoming is not a State; it is only a Territory."

"I don't suppose it would matter," she retorts, carelessly, "if the Hohenzollerns could get their hands on it anyhow. But never mind. Come along, Bell, and let us see what sort of neighbors you are likely to have."

They were no doubt rather rough-looking fellows, those gentlemen who lounged about the doors of the drinking-saloons; but there were more picturesque figures visible in the open thoroughfares riding along on stalwart little ponies, the horsemen bronzed of face, clad mostly in buckskin, and with a good deal of ornament about their saddle and stirrups. As for Cheyenne itself, there was certainly nothing about its outward appearance to entitle any one to call it "Hell on Wheels." Its flat rectangular streets were rather dismal in appearance; there seemed to be little doing even in the drinking-saloons. But brisker times, we were assured, were at hand. The rumors about the gold to be had in the Black Hills would draw to this point the adventurers of many lands, as free with their money as with their language. Here they would fit themselves out with the wagons and weapons necessary for the journey up to the Black Hills; here they would return—the Sioux permitting—to revel in the delights of keno, and poker, and Bourbon whiskey. Cheyenne would return to its pristine glory, when life—so long as you could cling on to it—was a brisk and exciting business. Certainly the Cheyenne we saw was far from being an exciting place. It was in vain that we implored our Bell to step down and bowie-knife somebody, or do something to let us understand what Cheyenne was in happier times. There was not a single corpse lying at any of the saloon-doors, nor any duel being fought in any street. The glory had departed.

But when we got away from these few chief thoroughfares, and got to the outskirts of Cheyenne, we were once more forcibly reminded of our native land; for a better representation of

Epsom Downs on the morning after the Derby-day could not be found anywhere, always with the difference that here the land is flat and arid. The odd fashion in which these wooden shanties and sheds, with some private houses here and there, are dotted down anyhow on the plain—their temporary look, the big advertisements, the desolate and homeless appearance of the whole place—all served to recall that dismal scene that is spread around the grandstand when the revellers have all returned to town. By-and-by, however, the last of these habitations disappeared, and we found ourselves out on a flat and sandy plain, that was taking a warm tinge from the gathering color in the west. The Rocky Mountains were growing a bit darker in hue now; and that gave them a certain grandeur of aspect, distant as they were. But what was this strange thing ahead of us, far out on the plain? A cloud of dust rises into the golden air; we can hear the faint foot-falls of distant horses. The cloud comes nearer; the noise deepens. Now it is the thunder of a troop of men on horseback galloping-down upon us as if to sweep us from the road.

"Forward, scout!" cried Bell, who had been getting up her Indian lore, to her husband on the pony; "hold up your right hand and motion them back; if they are friendly they will retire. Tell them the Great Father of the white men is well disposed toward his red children—"

"—And wouldn't cheat them out of a dollar even if he could get a third term of office by it."

But by this time the enemy had borne down upon us with such swiftness that he had gone right by before we could quite make out who he was. Indeed, amidst such dust the smartest cavalry-uniforms in the United States army must soon resemble a digger's suit.

We pushed on across the plain, and soon reached the point which these impetuous riders had just left—Fort Russell. The lieutenant was rather anxious to see what style of fortification the United States Government adopted to guard against any possible raid on the part of the Indians exasperated by the encroachments of the miners among the Black Hills; and so we all got down and entered Fort Russell, and had a pleasant walk round in the cool evening air. We greatly admired the pretty little houses built for the quarters of the married officers, and we appreciated the efforts made to get a few cotton-wood trees to grow on this arid soil; but as for fortifications, there was not so much as a bit of red-tape surrounding the enclosure. Our good friend who had conducted us hither only laughed when the lieutenant expressed his surprise.

"The Indians would as soon think of invading Washington as coming down here," said he.

"But they have come before," observed the lieutenant, "and that not very long ago. How many massacres did they make when the railway was being built—"

"Then there were fewer people—Cheyenne was only a few shanties—"

"Cheyenne!" cried the lieutenant, "Cheyenne a defence?—a handful of Indians, they would drive every shopkeeper out of the place in an hour—"

"I don't know about that," responded our companion for the time being. "The most of the men about here, sir, I can assure you, have had their tussles with the Indians, and could make as good a stand as any soldiers could. But the Sioux won't come down here; they will keep to the hills, where we can't get at them."

"My good friend, this is what I cannot understand, and you will tell me," said the lieutenant, who was arguing only to obtain information. "You are driving the Indians to desperation. You make treaties; you allow the miners to break them; you send out your soldiers to massacre the Indians because they have killed the white men, who had no right to come on their land. Very well: in time you will no doubt get them all killed. But suppose that the chiefs begin to see what is the end of it. And if they say that they must perish, but that they will perish in a great act of revenge, and if they sweep down here to cut your railway line to pieces—which has brought all these people out— and to ravage Cheyenne, then what is the use of such forts as this Fort Russell and its handful of soldiers? What did I see in a book the other day? that the fighting-men of these Indians alone were not less than 8000 or 10,000, because the young men of the Red Cloud and Spotted Tail people could easily be got to join the Sioux; and if they are to die, why should they not do some splendid thing?"

"Well, sir," said our friend, patting the neck of one of his horses, as the ladies were getting into the carriage, "that would be fine—that would be striking in a book or a play. But you don't know the Indians. The Indians are cowards, sir, take my word for it; and they don't fight except for plunder. They are revengeful—oh yes—and malicious as snakes; but they wouldn't kill a man unless they could get his rifle, or his oxen, or something. The young men are different sometimes; they want scalps to make themselves big in the eyes of the gals; but you wouldn't find a whole tribe of Indians flinging their lives away just to make a fuss in the New York papers."

At this point we started off again across the plains; and the discussion was adjourned, as the Irish magistrate said, *sine die* until the evening. Only Bell was anxious to be assured that if Sitting Bull and his merry men should meditate one grand and final act of revenge, they would not make their way down to the plains of Colorado and take up their abode there; and she was greatly comforted when she heard that the chief trouble of the Government was that it could not get the Indians to forsake their native hills in the north and go down to the Indian Territory in the south.

"I think, Mrs. Von Rosen," said Lady Sylvia, "that you will have some romantic stories to tell your children when you return to England. You would feel very proud if you compelled the Indians to address you as 'Brave squaw! brave squaw!'"

"I can assure you I am not at all anxious to become a heroine," our Bell said, seriously; no doubt remembering that romantic incidents have sometimes a knack of leaving children motherless.

And now "the Rockies" had grown quite dramatic in their intensity of plum-color, and there were flashing shoots of crimson fire high over the dusky peaks. But as we were driving eastward, we saw even more beautiful colors on the other horizon; for there were huge soft masses of color that had their high ridges of snow touched with a pale saffron as the light went down. And then, when the sun had really sunk, we found that strange phenomenon again appear along the eastern horizon—a band of dull dead blue lying close to the land, where no clouds were, and fading into a warm crimson above. Had this belt of colored shadow been a belt of mountains, we should have estimated them to be about 5000 feet above the level of these plains, which are themselves 5000 or 6000 feet above the level of the sea; and a strange thing was that this dusky blue and the crimson above remained well into the twilight, when all the world around us was growing dark. It was in this wan twilight that we drove out to a lake which will, no doubt, form an ornamental feature in a big park when the Black Hills miners, gorged with wealth, come back to make Cheyenne a great city. The chief attraction of the lake, as we saw it, was the presence of a considerable number of wild-duck on the surface; but we did not stay long to look at them, for the reason that there were several boats out after them; and the tiny jets of pink fire that were from time to time visible in the silvery twilight showed that the occupants of the boats were firing pretty much at random. As we did not wish to have a charge of No. 5 shot for supper, we drove off, and eventually were landed at the railway inn at Cheyenne.

We were quite conscious of having done an injustice to "Hell on Wheels" in taking only this cursory glance at so famous a place; but then we knew that all our letters—and perhaps telegrams—were now at Idaho, and we wished to get on as soon as possible. But as the present writer was unanimously requested by the party to pay a tribute of gratitude to the clean and comfortable little inn at the station, he must now do so; only he must also confess that he was bribed, for the good-natured landlord was pleased, as we sat at supper, to send in to us, with his compliments, a bottle of real French champagne. Good actions should never go unrewarded; and so the gentle reader is most earnestly entreated, the first time he goes to Cheyenne—in fact, he is entreated to go to Cheyenne anyhow—to stay at this inn and give large orders. Moreover, the present writer, not wishing to have his conduct in this particular regarded as being too mercenary, would wish to explain that the bottle of champagne in question was, as we subsequently discovered, charged for in the bill, and honestly paid for too; but he cannot allow the landlord to be deprived of all credit for his hospitable intentions merely on account of an error on the part of the clerk. We drank to his health then, and we will do so now. Here is to your health, Mr. ——, and to yours, you kind friend, who showed us the non-fortified Fort Russell; and to yours, you young Canadian gentleman, who told us those sad stories about Denver; and we hereby invoke a malison on the Grand Central Hotel of that city, on account of its cockroaches, and its vinous decoctions, and its incivility; but all this is highly improper, and premature, and a breach of confidence.

We did indeed spend a pleasant evening that night at Cheyenne; for we had ordered for our banquet all the strangest dishes on the bill of fare, just to give our friends a notion of the sort of food they would have to encounter during their stay in the West. And then these steaks of antelope, and mountain sheep, and black-tailed deer derived a certain romance from the presence, on the walls of the room, of splendid heads and antlers, until it appeared to us that we must be mighty hunters just sitting down to supper with the trophies won by our own sword and spear hung up around us. And then our Prussian strategist —who had acquired such a vast and intimate acquaintance with the Indians from his conversation with the Omaha idiot—proceeded to explain to us his plan of an Indian campaign; which showed that he was quite fitted to take the command of all the red men in Dakota. We were treated to a dose of history, too; to show that, in desperation, the Indians have often risen to commit a general massacre, apparently with no ulterior motive whatever. And of course, when Sitting Bull had swept down on Cheyenne and drunk its taverns dry; and when he had swept down on Denver, and filled his pockets—if any—with sham French jewellery, surely he would come up to Idaho to pay a certain young lady a friendly call?

"Bell," said her husband, "you shall have a laurel wreath ready, and you will have all the neighbors trained and ready; and, when the great chief approaches, you will all burst out with 'Heil dir im Siegerkranz!'"

"In the mean time," said Bell, sedately, "if we are to catch the train for Denver at five in the morning, we had better get to bed."

CHAPTER XLIX.

IN SOCIETY.

FIVE in the morning—pitch-darkness all around the station—a clear starlit sky—the flashing belt and sword of Orion almost right overhead. We had our breakfast of bread and apples in the great empty saloon; then we went out on to the platform, wondering when the Cyclops eye of the train would come flaring through the dark. For now we were within a few hours' journey of the point to which those messages were to be directed which would finally set at rest one or two grave problems; and there was a good deal of nervousness visible among our women-folk when we touched on these probabilities. But Lady Sylvia showed no nervousness at all. She was eager, buoyant, confident. She was clearly not afraid of any telegram or letter that might be awaiting her at Denver. Nay, when her friends, shivering in the cold and darkness of the early morning, were complaining of the railway arrangements that compelled us to get up at such an hour, she made light of the matter, and showed how, as we went south, we should have the beautiful spectacle of the sunrise breaking on the Rocky Mountains.

At length the train came along, and we got into the warm carriage, in which the conductor was engaged in cramming a blazing stove with still further blocks of wood. Very soon we were away from the scattered shanties of Cheyenne, out on the lone prairie-land that was to be our Bell's future home. And as we sat and silently looked out of the windows, watching a pale glow arise in the east, and trying to make out something on the dark plains below, suddenly we caught sight of some flashing lights of red and yellow. These were the breakfast fires of some travellers camping out—probably miners or traders making for the Black Hills with a train of wagons and oxen. The light in the east increased; and then we saw all along the western horizon the great wall of the Rocky Mountains become visible in a stream of color—the peaks the faintest rose, the shadowy bulk below a light, transparent, beautiful blue. The morning came on apace; the silvery grays of the east yielding to a glowing saffron. There seemed to be no mists lying on these high plains, for, as the sun rose, we could see an immense distance over the yellow prairie-land. And the first objects we perceived in this lonely desert of grass were a number of antelope quietly grazing within rifle-range of the railway line, taking no heed whatever, though occasionally one of the more timid would trot off on its spider-like legs to a safer distance. Bell began to laugh. She saw the misery of her husband's face.

"Ah, well," said he, with a sigh, "I suppose if the train were to stop, and you went down with a gun, they would be away like lightning. *But a time will come;* and your husband, Lady Sylvia, will be with me to help me, I hope."

There was certainly no misery on Lady Sylvia's face, now that the brilliant light of the new day filled the carriage. Was this the pale sad soul who had come away from England with us, out of sorts with the world, and almost aweary of her life? There was a color in her cheeks that nearly rivalled Bell's apple-blossom tints. There was an unusual gladness in her eyes this morning that we could not at first account for; but she let the secret out: she had been making elaborate calculations. The telegram she received at Omaha from Queenstown had been waiting for her two days before she got it. Then, taking into account the number of days we stayed at Omaha and the leisurely fashion in which we had come across the plains, there was at least a chance —so she proved to herself—that her husband might at that very moment be landing at one of the New York wharves. It all depended on the steamer. Who knew anything about that steamer? Notoriously it belonged to the fastest of all the lines. Was it possible, then, that as we were chatting and laughing in this railway-carriage on the Colorado prairies, Balfour might be on the same continent with us? You could almost have imagined that his stepping ashore had communicated some strange magnetic thrill to his wife's heart.

"We are getting near to Greeley now," said Queen T—— to her friend Bell, looking rather eagerly out of the window.

"Yes," said the practical lieutenant, "and we shall have twenty minutes there for a real breakfast. An apple and a bit of bread is not enough, if you are travelling in Colorado air."

But I do not think it was altogether the breakfast—though that, as it turned out, was excellent—that led us to look out with unusual interest for this little township set far among the Western plains; there were other reasons, which need not be mentioned here. And, indeed, we have the most pleasant memories of Greeley, as it shone there in the early sunlight. We walked up the broad main thoroughfare, with its twin rows of cotton-wood trees; and no doubt the empty street gained something from the fact that the end of it seemed closed in by the pale-blue line of the Rocky Mountains, the peaks here and there glittering with snow. A bright, clean, thriving-looking place, with its handsome red-brick school-house and its capacious white church; while many of the shanties about had pleasant little gardens attached, watered by small irrigation canals from the Cache-la-poudre River. As we were passing one of those tiny streams, a great heron rose slowly into the air, his heavy wings flapping, his legs hanging down; but a large hawk, crossing a field beyond, took no notice of him; and we were disappointed of a bit of extempore falconry. We had only a look at the public park, which is as yet mostly a wilderness of underwood, and a glimpse at the pretty villas beyond; in fact, our explorations nearly lost us our train. As we think of Greeley now—here, in England, in the depth of winter —it shines for us still in the light of the summer morning, and the trees and fields are green around it, and the mountains are blue under the blue of the sky. May it shine and flourish forever!

It is most unfair of the Americans to speak slightingly of Denver. It is a highly respectable city. We were quite astounded, on our first entrance, by the number of people who appeared in black coats and tall hats; and the longer we stayed in the place, the more we were impressed by the fashion in which the Denverites had removed the old stains from their reputation by building churches. They have advanced much further in the paths of civilization than the slow-moving cities of the East. In New York or Boston hotels, the servants merely claim a free-and-easy equality with the guests; in Denver they have got far beyond that. The wines are such triumphs of skilful invention as no city in the world can produce. And then, when one goes into the streets (to escape from the beetles in one's bedroom), the eye is charmed by the variety of nationalities everywhere visible. A smart Mexican rides by, with gayly decorated saddle, on his long-tailed pony. Chinese women hobble on their small shoes into an ironmongery-shop. The adjoining saloon is called "Zur goldenen Trauben;" and at the door of it a red-haired Irish-woman is stormily quarrelling with an angry but silent and sulky negress. Over this seething admixture of population dwell the twelve patrician families of Denver, shining apart like stars in a silent heaven of their own. We were not permitted to gaze upon any one of these—unless—unless? Those two people who stood on the steps of the hotel after dinner? They were distinguished-looking persons, and much bediamonded. The lady wore beauti-ful colors, and the red-faced gentleman had a splendid gold chain round his neck; and thus—so far as we could make out—they spake:

"Jim," said the lady, "don't you remember that hop of Steve Bellerjean's that he giv after he run away wi' Dan Niggles's gal, to make up all around, when he found pay-gravel, and married the gal?"

"No," said the other, reflectively, "I disremember."

"Well, that woman in yaller fixins that stared at me all din-ner, I could swear was Steve's woman."

"But Steve run away from her," said the gentleman, who seemed to remember some things, if not the hop. "She didn't pan out well. Tried to put a head on him with a revolver—jeal-ousy and rum. Steve went to Sonora; tried to bust the Gov-ernment; and the Greasers ketched him with a lariat, and his chips were passed in."

The gentleman in the gold chain had suddenly grown melan-choly.

"Yes; Steve's chips were called," chimed in his spouse.

"That's what's the matter with all of us," continued her com-panion, in a sad tone. "That's what no Fifteenth Amendment can stop; the chips must be paid. That's what I told the boys down at Gridiron Bend, when I giv my experiences and jined the church, and Euchre-deck Billy heaved that rock into the chris-tenin'-place; sez I, Boys, sez I, life gen'rally begins with a square deal, leastways outside the idiot asylum. 'Cordin' as you play your hand, will the promises be kep'. Sure enough, some has aces, and some not, and that's luck; and four aces any day is as good a hand as the Ten Commandments. With four aces, I'd buck agin the devil. But we don't have four aces in the first deal, unless mebbe the Czar of Russia, or the Prince of Wales, or some of them chaps; and so life and religion is pretty much as we play the hand we've got."

The lady seemed to put another aspect on these moral truths.

"Hosea Kemp," said she, practically, "that pig-skinned Mormon fraud, diskivered that when you raised him ten thousand, and raked in his pile; and he had a full, and you were only king high."

"That was before I knowed better, and I hadn't seen the vanities," said the repentant sinner. "But when I played, I played my hand for all that it was worth; and that's what's the matter with me. You kent fool away your hand and keep the chips; and that's what you find in the Commandments. That's the idee." What the idea was we were rather at a loss to discover; but we were not exactly in search of conundrums at this moment.

Indeed, our arrival at Denver had put an end for the time being to our idling and day-dreaming. First of all, there were the letters (there were no telegrams for any one, so we imagined that Balfour had not yet reached New York); and in the general selfishness of each seizing his or her own packet, no one noticed the expression with which Lady Sylvia broke open the only envelope addressed to her. There was a turmoil of news from home, mostly of a domestic and trivial nature, but none the less of tremendous importance to the two mothers. And when they turned to Lady Sylvia, she was sitting there quite calm and undisturbed, without any trace of disappointment on her face.

"So Mr. Balfour has not reached New York yet," said Queen T——, in her gentle way.

"I suppose not," was the answer. "I was calculating on the very shortest time possible. This letter was written some time before he left England. It is only about business affairs."

It was not until that evening that Lady Sylvia communicated the contents of this letter to her friend, and she did so without complaint as to the cold and formal manner in which her husband had written. Doubtless, she said, he was perfectly right. She had left him of her own accord; she deserved to be treated as a stranger. But the prompt answer to her message to him convinced her—this she said with a happy confidence in her eyes —of the spirit in which he was now coming out to her; and if, when he came out here, she had only five minutes given to her to tell him— But the present writer refuses to reveal further the secrets that passed between these two women.

In fact, he would probably never have known, but that at this juncture he was privately appealed to for advice. And if, in the course of this faithful narrative, he has endeavored as far as possible to keep himself in the background, and to be the mere mouth-piece and reporter of the party, that rôle must be abandoned for a moment. He must explain that he now found himself in a position of some difficulty. Balfour had written out to Lady Sylvia, informing her of the collapse of his father's firm. It was hopeless, he said, to think of the firm resuming business; the trade that had made his father's fortune was played out. In these circumstances, he considered himself bound to give up everything he possessed to his creditors, and he wished to know whether she, Lady Sylvia, would feel disposed to surrender in like manner the £50,000 settled on her before her marriage. He pointed out to her that she was not legally bound to do so, and that it was a very doubtful question whether she was morally bound; it was a matter for her private feeling. If she felt inclined to give up the money, he would endeavor to gain her father's consent. But he thought that would be difficult, unless she also would join in persuading him; and she might point out that, if he refused, she could in any case pay over the annual interest of the sum. He hoped she was well; and there an end.

Now, if Lady Sylvia had had a bank-note for £50,000 in her pocket, she would have handed it over with a glad heart. She never doubted for a moment that she ought to pay over the money, especially as she now knew that it was her husband's wish; but this reference to her father rather bewildered her, and so she indirectly appealed for counsel.

Now, how was it possible to explain to this gentle creature that the principle on which an antenuptial settlement is based is that the wife is literally purchased for a sum of money, and that it is the bounden duty of the trustees to see that this purchase-money shall not be inveigled away from her in any manner whatever? How was it possible to point out to her that she might have children, and that her husband and father were alike bound by their duties as trustees not to let her defraud these helpless things of the future? Nay, more: it would be necessary to tell her that these hypothetical young people might marry; and that, however they might love their mamma, papa, and grandpapa, some cantankerous son-in-law could suddenly come down on the papa and grandpapa and compel them to make good that money which they had allowed, in defiance of their trust, to be dissipated in an act of quixotic sacrifice.

"I always thought the law was idiotic," says Queen T——.

"The law in this case is especially devoted to the protection of women, who are not supposed to be able to take care of themselves."

"Do you mean to say that if Lady Sylvia, to whom the money belongs, wishes to give it up, she cannot give it up ?"

"It does not belong to her; it belongs to Balfour and Lord Willowby, in trust for her; and they dare not give it up, except at their own risk. What Balfour meant by making himself a trustee can only be imagined; but he is a shrewd fellow."

"And so she cannot give up the money! Surely that is a strange thing—that one is not allowed to defraud one's self !"

"You can defraud yourself as much as you like. If she chooses, she can pay over the £2000 a year, or whatever it is, to Balfour's creditors; but if she surrendered the original sum, she would be defrauding her children: do you see that? Or does your frantic anxiety to let a woman fling away a fortune that is legally hers blind you to everything ?"

"I don't see that her children, if she has any," says this tiny but heroic champion of strict morality, "would benefit much by inheriting money that ought never to have belonged to them. That money, you know very well, belongs to Mr. Balfour's creditors."

"This I know very well: that you would be exceedingly glad to see these two absolute beggars, so that they should be thrown on each other's helpfulness. I have a suspicion that that is the foundation for this pretty anxiety in the cause of morality and justice. Now there is no use in being angry. Without doubt, you have a sensitive conscience, and you are anxious that Lady Sylvia's conscience should be consulted too; but all the same—"

By this time the proud blood has mounted to her face.

"I came to you for advice, not for a discourse on the conscience," she says, with a splendid look of injured dignity. "I know I am right; and I know that she is right, children or no children. You say that Lord Willowby will probably refuse—"

"Balfour says so, according to your account."

"Very well; and you explain that he might be called on to make good the money. Could not he be induced to consent by some guarantee—some indemnity—"

"Certainly, if you can get a big enough fool to become responsible for £50,000 to the end of time. Such people are not common. But there, sit down and put aside all these fantastic speculations. The immediate thing you want is Lord Willowby's consent to this act of legal vandalism. If he refuses, his refusal will be based on the personal interests of his daughter. He will not consider children or grandchildren. Long before her eldest born can be twenty-one, Lord Willowby will be gathered to his fathers; and as for the risk he runs, he has not a brass farthing that any one can seize. Very well: you must explain to Lady Sylvia, in as delicate a way as you can, that there might be youthful Balfours in the days to come, and that she must consider whether she is acting rightly in throwing away this provision—"

"But, gracious goodness! her husband wants her to do so, and she wants to do so—"

"Then let that be settled. Of course, all husbands' wishes are law. Then you must explain to her what it is she is asking her father to do, and point out that it will take a good deal of appealing before he consents. He has a strictly legal right to refuse; further, he can plead his natural concern for his daughter's interests—"

"He ought to have more regard for his daughter's honor!" says she, warmly.

"Nonsense! You are talking as if Balfour had gone into a conspiracy to get up a fraudulent settlement. It is no business of hers that the firm failed—"

"I say it is a matter of strict honor and integrity that she should give up this money; and she *shall* give it up!" says Queen T——, with an indignant look.

"Very well, then; if you are all quite content, there only remains that you should appeal to Lord Willowby."

"Why do you laugh?"

"Lord Willowby thought he would get some money through Balfour marrying his daughter. Now you are asking him to throw away his last chance of ever getting a penny. And you think he will consent."

"His daughter shall make him," said she, confident in the sublime and invincible powers of virtue. Her confidence, in this instance, at least, was not misplaced—so much must be admitted.

CHAPTER L.

A NEW COMPANION.

THE arrival of the new sovereign to take possession of the ceded dominions had been made known to the people at Eagle Creek Ranch; and soon our poor Bell was being made the victim of continual interviews, during which agents, overseers, and lawyers vainly endeavored to get some definite information into her bewildered head. For what was the use of reporting about the last branding of calves, or about the last month's yield of the Belle of St. Joe, or about the probable cost of the new crushing-machines, when the perpetual refrain of her thinking was, "Oh, good people, wouldn't you take the half of it, and let me have my children?"

Fortunately her husband was in no wise bewildered, and it was with not a little curiosity that he went off to inspect the horses and two carriages that had been sent on to Denver for us from the ranch. My lord was pleased to express his approval of these; albeit that one of the vehicles was rather a rude-looking affair. The other, however—doubtless Colonel Sloane's state carriage—was exceedingly smart, and had obviously been polished up for the occasion; while, as regards the horses, these were able to elicit even something more than approval from this accomplished critic. He went back to the hotel highly pleased. He believed he had got some inkling that life at the ranch was not wholly savage. The beautiful polished shafts and the carefully brushed dark-blue cushions had had an effect on his imagination.

And then, right in the midst of all this turmoil, Lady Sylvia got a telegram from New York. We had just sat down to dinner in the big saloon, at a separate table; and we were a sufficiently staid and decorous party, for Mr. and Mrs. Von Rosen were dressed in black, and the rest of us had donned whatever dark attire we had with us, out of respect to the memory of the lamented Jack Sloane. (One of the executors was to call in on us after dinner; but no matter.) This telegram produced quite a flutter of excitement, and for the moment we forgot all about Texan herds and placer mines. Lady Sylvia became a trifle pale as the telegram was handed to her, and she seemed to read it at one glance; then, despite herself, a smile of pleasure came to her lips, and the color returned to her face.

"But what is this, Mr. Von Rosen?" she said, and she endeavored to talk in a matter-of-fact way, as if nothing at all had happened. "My husband speaks of some proposal you have made to him."

"Yes," said the lieutenant, blushing like a guilty school-boy.

He looked at his wife, and both were a trifle embarrassed; but at this moment Lady Sylvia handed the telegram across the table.

"You may read it," she said, indifferently; as if it had conveyed but little news to her. And yet it was a long telegram— to be sent by a man who was not worth sixpence.

"*Hugh Balfour, New York, to Lady Sylvia Balfour, Central Hotel, Denver : Have got your letter; all is right. Shall reach you Saturday. Please tell Von Rosen that, subject to your wishes, I accept proposal with gratitude.*"

"Lady Sylvia," said the lieutenant, with his bronzed face as full of triumph as if he himself had brought about the whole business, "Will you let me cry 'hurrah?' Bell, shall I cry 'hurrah?' Madame, do you object?"

And he held up the bit of paper for a signal, as if we were about to shock the calm proprieties of Denver.

"May I see the telegram, Lady Sylvia?" said Mrs. Von Rosen, taking no notice of her mad husband.

"Certainly. But please tell me, Mr. Von Rosen, what the proposal is. Why do you wish to cry 'hurrah?'"

"Ah, yes, you may well ask," said the young man, moderating his fervor, "for I was too soon with my gladness. I will have to persuade you before we can cry any hurrahs. What I was thinking of was this—that you and Mr. Balfour would be a whole year with us, and we should have great amusement; and the shooting that I have heard of since yesterday—oh! I cannot tell you of it. But he says it is all subject to your wishes; now I must begin to persuade you to stay away from England for a whole year, and to give us the pleasure of your society. It is a great favor that my wife and myself we both ask of you; for we shall be lonely out here until we get used to the place and know our neighbors; but if you were our neighbors, that would be very pleasant. And I have been very busy to find out about Eagle Creek—oh no, it is not so bad as you would think; you can have everything from Denver—I do not know about ladies' saddles, but I will ask—and it is the most beautiful and healthy air in the world, Lady Sylvia—"

"My dear Mr. Von Rosen," said Lady Sylvia, interrupting him with a charming smile, "don't seek to persuade me; I was persuaded when I got the message from my husband; for of course I will do whatever he wishes. But if you will let me say so, I don't think this proposal of yours is very wise. It was scarcely fair of you to write to New York and inveigle my husband into it, without letting me know. It is very charming, no doubt; and you are very kind; and I have not the least doubt we shall enjoy ourselves very much; but you must remember that my husband and myself have something else to think of now. We cannot afford to think only of shooting and riding, and pleasant society. Indeed, I took it for granted that my husband had come out to America to find some profession or occupation; and I am rather surprised that he has accepted your proposal. It was too tempting, I suppose; and I know we shall enjoy ourselves very much—"

Husband and wife had been glancing at each other, as if to inquire which should speak first. It was the lieutenant who took the burden on his shoulders, and certainly he was extremely embarrassed when he began. Fortunately in these Western hotels you are expected to order your dinner all at once, and it is put on the table at once; and then the waiter retires, unless he happens to be interested in your conversation, when he remains, and looks down on your shoulders. In this case, our colored brother had moved off a bit.

"Lady Sylvia," said he, "I wish Mr. Balfour had explained to you what the proposal is in a letter; but how could that be? He will be here as soon as any letter. And I am afraid you will think me very impertinent when I tell you."

He looked at her for a second; and then the courage of this

man, who had been through the whole of the 1866 and 1870–'71 campaigns, and done good service in both, fell away altogether.

"Ah," said he, lightly—but the Germans are not good actors, "it is a little matter. I will leave it to your husband to tell you. Only this I will tell you, that you must not think that your husband will spend the whole year in idleness—"

"It is a mystery, then?" she said, with a smile. "I am not to be allowed to peep into the secret chamber? Or is it a conspiracy of which I am to be the victim? Mrs. Von Rosen, you will not allow them to murder me at the ranch?"

Mrs. Von Rosen was a trifle embarrassed also, but she showed greater courage than her husband.

"I will tell you what the secret is, Lady Sylvia," she said, "if my husband won't. He is afraid of offending you; but you won't be offended with me. We were thinking, my husband and myself, that Mr. Balfour was coming out to America to engage in some business; and you know that is not always easy to find; and then we were thinking about our own affairs at the same time. You know, dear Lady Sylvia"—and here she put her hand gently on her friend's hand, as if to stay that awful person's wrath and resentment—"we run a great risk in leaving all these things, both up at Idaho and out on the plains, to be managed by persons who are strangers to us—I mean, when we go back to England. And it occurred to my husband and myself that if we could get some one whom we could thoroughly trust to stay here and look into the accounts and reports on the spot— well, the truth is, we thought it would be worth while to give such a person an interest in the yearly result rather than any fixed salary. Don't you think so?" she said, rather timidly.

"Oh yes, certainly," Lady Sylvia replied. She half guessed what was coming.

"And then," said our Bell, cheerfully, as if it were all a joke, "my husband thought he would write to Mr. Balfour telling him that if he liked to try this for a time—just until he could look round and get something better—it would be a great obligation to us; and it would be so pleasant for us to have you out here. That was the proposal, Lady Sylvia. It was only a suggestion. Perhaps you would not care to remain out here, so far away from your home; but in any case I thought you would not be offended."

She was, on the contrary, most deeply and grievously offended, as was natural. Her indignant wrath knew no bounds. Only the sole token of it was two big tears that quietly rolled down her face—despite her endeavors to conceal the fact; and for a second or two she did not speak at all, but kept her head cast down.

"I don't know," said she, at length, in a very low and rather uncertain voice, "what we have done to deserve so much kindness—from all of you."

"Oh no, Lady Sylvia," our Bell said, with the utmost eagerness, "you must not look on it as kindness at all—it is only a business proposal; for, of course, we are very anxious to have everything well looked after in our absence—it is of great importance for the sake of the children. And then, you see, Mr. Balfour and yourself would be able to give it a year's trial before deciding whether you would care to remain here; and you would be able to find out whether the climate suited you, and whether there was enough amusement—"

"Dear Mrs. Von Rosen," said Lady Sylvia, gently, "you need not try to explain away your kindness. You would never have thought of this but for our sakes—"

"No," she cried, boldly; "but why? Because we should have sold off everything at the end of the year, rather than have so much anxiety in England. But if we can get this great business properly managed, why should we throw it away?"

"You forget that my husband knows nothing about it—"

"He will have a year to learn; and his mere presence here will make all the difference."

"Then is it understood, Lady Sylvia?" the lieutenant said, with all the embarrassment gone away from his face. "You will remain with us for one year, anyway?"

"If my husband wishes it, I am very willing," she said, "and very grateful to you."

"Ha!" said the lieutenant, "I can see wonderful things now—wagons, camp-fires, supper-parties; and a glass of wine to drink to the health of our friends away in England. Lady Sylvia, your husband and I will write a book about it—'A Year's Hunting in Colorado and the Rocky Mountains.'"

"I hope my husband will have something else to do," Lady Sylvia said, "unless you mean to shame us altogether."

"But no one can be working always. Ah, my good friends," he said, addressing the remaining two of the party, "you will be sorry when you start to go home to England. You will make a great mistake then. You wish to see the Alleghany Mountains in the Indian summer? Oh yes, very good; but you could see that next year; and in the mean time think what splendid fun we shall have—"

"Ask Bell," said Queen T——, with a quiet smile, "whether she would rather return with us now, or wait out here to hear of your shooting black-tailed deer and mountain-sheep?"

At this point a message was brought in to us; and it was unanimously resolved to ask Bell's business friend to come in and sit down and have a glass of wine with us. Surely there were no secrets about the doings of Five-Ace Jack unfit for us all to hear? We found Mr. T. W. G—— a most worthy and excellent person, whose temper had not at all been soured by his failure to find the philosopher's stone. It is true, there was a certain sadness over the brown and wrinkled face when he described to us how the many processes for separating the gold from the crushed quartz could just about reach paying expenses, and without doing much more; and how some little improvement in one of these processes, that might be stumbled on by accident, would suddenly make the discoverer a millionnaire, the gold-bearing quartz being simply inexhaustible. It was quite clear that Mr. G—— had lost some money in this direction. He was anxious we should go up to Georgetown, when we were at Idaho, to see some mines he had; in fact, he produced sundry little parcels from his pocket, unrolled them, and placed the bits of stone before us with a certain reverent air. Our imagination was not fired.

He had known Colonel Sloane very well, and he spoke most discreetly of him; for was not his niece here in mourning? Nevertheless, there was a slight touch of humor in his tone when he told us of one of Bell's mines—the Virgin Agnes—which led one or two of us to suspect that Five-Ace Jack had not quite abandoned his tricks, even when his increasing riches rendered them unnecessary. The Virgin Agnes was a gulch mine, somewhere in the bed of the stream that comes rolling down the Clear Creek cañon, and it was originally owned by a company. It used to pay very well. But by-and-by the yield gradually diminished, until it scarcely paid the wages of the men; and, in fact, the mine was not considered worth working further. At this point it was bought by Colonel Sloane; and the strange thing was that almost immediately it began to yield in a surprising manner, and had continued to do so ever since. Mr. G—— congratulated our Bell on being the owner of this mine, and said he would have much pleasure in showing it to her when she went up to Idaho; but he gravely ended his story without dropping any hint as to the reason why the Virgin Agnes had slowly drooped and suddenly revived. Nor did he tell us whether the men employed in that mine were generously allowed by Colonel Sloane to share in his good fortune.

He asked Bell whether she proposed to start for Idaho next day. She looked at her husband.

"Oh no," said the lieutenant, promptly. "We have a friend arriving here on Saturday. We mean to wait for him."

"Pray don't delay on his account," Lady Sylvia said, anxiously. "I can very well remain here for him, and come up to you afterward."

"Oh, we shall have plenty to do in these three or four days—plenty," the lieutenant said; "I must see about the ladies' saddles to-morrow, and I want to buy an extra rifle or two, and a revolver, and a hunting-knife. And then this list of things for the house at Idaho—"

No doubt there was a good deal to be done; only one would have thought that three or four days were pretty fair time in which to prepare for a short trip up the Clear Creek cañon. It was not, however. On the Saturday morning every one was most extraordinarily busy, especially as the time approached for the arrival of the train from Cheyenne. Next day all the shops would be shut; and on Monday morning early we started.

"Lady Sylvia," said the lieutenant, with ingenuous earnestness, "I must really go after those saddles again. Tell Mr. Balfour I shall be back to lunch, will you, if you please?"

Indeed, one went away on one mission, and the other on another, until there was no one of the party left in the hotel with Lady Sylvia but Queen T——. The latter was in her own room. She rung, and sent a servant to ask her friend to come and see her. She took Lady Sylvia's hand when she entered.

"I am going to ask you to excuse me," said she, with great innocence. "I feel a little tired; I think I will lie down for an hour, until luncheon-time. But you know, dear Lady Sylvia, if there are none of them down-stairs, all you have to do is to get into the omnibus when it calls at the door, and they will drive you to the station; and you will not have long to wait."

The white hand she held was trembling violently. Lady Sylvia said nothing at all; but her eyes were moist, and she silently kissed her friend, and went away.

About an hour thereafter, four of us were seated at a certain small table, all as mute as mice. The women pretended to be very busy with the things before them. No one looked toward the door. Nay, no one would look up as two figures came into the big saloon, and came walking down toward us.

"Mrs. Von Rosen," said the voice of Lady Sylvia, in the gayest of tones, "let me present to you your new agent—"

But her gayety suddenly broke down. She left him to shake hands with us, and sat down on a chair in the dusky corner, and hid away her face from us, sobbing to herself.

"Ha!" cried the lieutenant, in his stormiest way, for he would have none of this sentiment, "do you know what we have got for you after your long journey? My good friend, there is a beefsteak coming for you; and that—do you know what that is?—that is a bottle of English alc!"

CHAPTER LI.

OUR LAST NIGHT TOGETHER.

On that Monday morning when we left Denver to seek Bell's distant home in these pale-blue mountains, there was no great rejoicing among us. It was the last day of our long journeying together, and we had been pleasantly associated; moreover, one of us was going to leave her dearest friend in these remote wilds, and she was rather down-hearted about it. Happily the secret exultation of Lady Sylvia, which could not altogether be concealed, kept up our spirits somewhat: we wondered whether she was not going to carry her husband's portmanteau for him, so anxious was she about his comfort.

The branch line of rail that pierces for some distance the Clear

Creek cañon takes a circuitous course on leaving Denver through some grassy plains which are intersected by narrow and muddy rivulets, and are sufficiently uninteresting; so that there was plenty of opportunity for these sojourners to sketch out something of their plans of living for the information of the new-comer. But Balfour—who, by-the-way, had got thoroughly bronzed by his travelling—would not hear of all the fine pleasure-excursions that the lieutenant was for planning out.

"We are under enough obligation to you," said he, "even if I find I can do this thing; but if I discover that I am of no use at all, then your charity would be too great. Let us get to work first; then, if the way is clear, we can have our play afterward. Indeed, you will be able to command my attendance, once I have qualified myself to be your servant."

"Yes, that is reasonable," said the lieutenant.

"I am quite sure," said Lady Sylvia, "that my husband would be a poor companion for you, so long as our affairs are unsettled—"

"And, besides," said Balfour, with a laugh, "you don't know what splendid· alternative schemes I have to fall back on. On the voyage over, I used to lie awake at night and try to imagine all the ways in which a man may earn a living who is suddenly made penniless. And I got up some good schemes, I think: good for a man who could get some backing, I mean."

"Will you please to tell us some of them?" said Queen T——, with no apparent sarcasm. "We are so often appealed to for charity; and it would be delightful to be able to tell poor people how to make a fortune."

"The poor people would have to have some influence. But would you like to hear my schemes? They are numberless; and they are all based on the supposition that in London there are a very large number of people who would pay high prices for the simplest necessaries of life, provided you could supply these of the soundest quality. Do you see? I take the case of milk, for example. Think of the number of mothers in London who would pay a double price for milk for their children, if you could guarantee them that it was quite unwatered, and got from cows living wholesomely in the country instead of in London stalls? That is only one of a dozen things. Take bread, for example. I believe there are thousands of people in London who would pay extra for French bread if they only knew how tb get it supplied to them. Very well: I step in with my association—for the wants of a great place like London can only be supplied by big machinery—and I get a duke or two, and a handful of M.P.'s with me, to give it a philanthropic look; and, of course, they make me manager. I do a good public work, and I benefit myself."

"Do you think you would succeed as the manager of a dairy?" said Queen T——, gently.

"As well, probably," said he, laughing, "as the manager of Mrs. Von Rosen's mines and farms! But having got up the company, you would not ask me to look after the cows."

"Oh, Hugh," said Lady Sylvia, anxiously, "I hope you will never have anything to do with any company. It is that which has got poor papa into such trouble. I wish he could leave all these things for a time, and come out here for a holiday; it would do him a great deal of good."

This filial wish did not seem to awaken any eager response, though Mrs. Von Rosen murmured something about the pleasure it would give her to see Lord Willowby. We had not much hope of his lordship consenting to live at a ranch.

And now we drew near the Rockies. First of all, rising from the plains, we encountered some ridges of brown, seared, earthy-looking hills, for the most part bare, though here and there the crest was crowned by a ridge of pine. At the mouth of one of the valleys we came upon Golden City, a scattered hamlet of small houses, with some trees, and some thin lines of a running stream about it. Then, getting farther into the mountains, we entered the narrow and deep gorge of the Clear Creek cañon, a naturally formed highway that runs and winds sinuously for about thirty miles between the huge walls of rock on either side. It was not a beautiful valley, this deep cleft among the mountains; but a gloomy and desolate place, with lightning-blasted pines among the grays and reds of the fused fire-rocks; an opaque gray-green river rushing down the chasm; the trees overhead, apparently at the summit of the twin precipices, black against the glimmer of the blue sky. Here and there, however, were vivid gleams of color: a blaze of the yellow leaves of the cotton-wood, or a mass of crimson creeper growing over a gray rock. We began to wonder, too, whether this small river could really have cut this deep and narrow chasm in the giant mountains; but there, sure enough, far above us on the steep slopes, were the deep holes in the intertwisted quartz out of which the water in by-gone ages must have slowly worked the bowlders of some alien material. There were other holes, too, visible on the sides of this gloomy gorge, with some brown earth in front of them, as if some animal had been trying to scrape for itself a den there: these were the "prospect holes" that miners had bored to spy into the secrets of the everlasting hills. Down below us, again, was the muddy stream, rushing between its beds of gravel; and certainly this railway-carriage, on its narrow gauge, seemed to tilt dangerously over toward the sheer descent and the plunging waters. The train, indeed, as it wound round the rocks, seemed to be some huge python, hunted into its gloomy lair in the mountains.

We were glad to get out of it, and into the clear sunshine, at the terminus—Floyd Hill; and here we found a couple of stage-coaches, each with four horses, awaiting to carry us still farther up into the Rockies. They were strange-looking vehicles, apparently mostly built of leather, and balanced on leather springs of enormous thickness. But they soon disappeared from sight. We were lost in such clouds of dust as were never yet beheld by mortal man. Those who had gone inside to escape found that the half-dozen windows would not keep shut; and that, as they were flung hither and thither by the plunging of the coach up the steep mountain-paths, they lost sight of each other in the dense yellow clouds. And then sometimes a gust of wind would cleave an opening in the clouds; and, behold! a flashing picture of pine-clad mountains, with a dark-blue sky above. That jolting journey seemed to last for ever and ever, and the end of it found us changed into new creatures. But the coat of dust that covered us from head to heel had not sufficed to blind us; and now before our eyes we found the end and aim of our journey—the far hamlet of Idaho.

Bell looked round bewildered; she had dreaded this approach to her future home. And Queen T——, anxious above all things that her friends' first impressions should be favorable, cried out,

"Oh, Bell, how beautiful, and clean, and bright it is!"

And certainly our first glance at Idaho, after the heat and dust we had come through, was cheering enough. We thought for an instant of Chamounix as we saw the small white houses by the side of the green, rushing stream, and the great mountains rising sheer beyond. There was a cool and pleasant wind rustling through the leaves of the young cotton-wood trees planted in front of the inn. And when we turned to the mountains on the other side of the narrow valley, we found even the lofty pine-woods glowing with color; for the mid-day sun was pouring down on the undergrowth—now of a golden yellow—so that one could almost believe that these far slopes were covered with butter-cups. The coaches had stopped at the inn—the Beebee House, as it is called—and Colonel Sloane's heiress was received with much distinction. They showed her Colonel Sloane's house. It stood on a knoll some distance off; but we could see that it was a cheerful-looking place, with a green-painted veranda round the white walls, and a few pines and cotton-woods about. In the mean time we had taken rooms at the inn; and speedily set to work to get some of the dust removed. It was a useful occupation; for no doubt the worry of it tended to allay that nervous excitement among our women-folk, from which Bell, more especially, was obviously suffering. When we all assembled thereafter at our mid-day meal, she was still somewhat pale. The lieutenant declared that, after so much travelling, she must now take a long rest. He would not allow her to go on to Georgetown for a week at least.

And was there ever in all the world a place more conducive to rest than this distant, silent, sleepy Idaho up here in the lonely mountains? When the coaches had whirled away in the dust toward Georgetown, there was nothing to break the absolute calm but the soft rustling of the small trees; there was not a shred of cloud in the blue sky to bar the glare of the white road with a bit of grateful shadow. After having had a look at Bell's house, we crossed to the other side of the valley, and entered a sort of tributary gorge between the hills which is known as the Soda Creek cañon. Here all vestiges of civilization seemed to end, but for the road that led we knew not whither; and in the strange silence we wandered onward into this new world whose plants, and insects, and animals were all unfamiliar to us, or familiar only as they suggested some similarity to their English relatives. And yet Queen T—— strove to assure Bell that there was nothing wonderful about the place except its extreme silence and a certain sad desolation of beauty. Was not this our identical Michaelmas-daisy, she asked? She was overjoyed when she discovered a real and veritable harebell—a trifle darker in color than our harebell, but a harebell all the same. She made a dart at a cluster of yellow flowers growing up among the rocks, thinking they were the mountain-saxifrage; but they turned out to be a composite plant—probably some sort of hawkweed. Her efforts to reach these flowers had startled a large bird out of the bushes above; and as it darted off, we could see that it was of a dark and luminous blue: she had to confess that he was a stranger. But surely we could not have the heart to regard the merry little chipmonk as a stranger—which of all living creatures is the friendliest, the blithest, the most comical. In this Soda Creek cañon he reigns supreme; every rock and stone and bush seems instinct with life as this Proteus of the animal world scuds away like a mouse, or shoots up the hill-side like a lizard, only, when he has got a short distance, to perch himself up on his hind-legs, and curl up his bushy tail, and eye us demurely as he affects to play with a bit of may-weed. Then we see what the small squirrel-like animal really is—a beautiful little creature with longitudinal bars of golden brown and black along his back; the same bars on his head, by the side of his bright, watchful eyes; the red of a robin's breast on his shoulders; his furry tail, jauntily cocked up behind, of a pale brown. We were never tired of watching the tricks and attitudes of this friendly little chap. We knew quite well that his sudden dart from the lee of some stone was only the pretence of fright; before he had gone a yard he would sit up on his haunches and look at you, and stroke his nose with one of his fore-paws. Sometimes he would not even run away a yard, but sit quietly and watchfully to see us pass. We guessed that there were few stone-throwing boys about the Rocky Mountains.

Behold! the valley at last shows one brief symptom of human life; a wagon drawn by a team of oxen comes down the steep road, and the driver thereof is worth looking at, albeit his straw sombrero shades his handsome and sun-tanned face. He is an ornamental person, this bull-whacker; with the cord tassels of his buckskin jacket just appearing from below the great Spanish cloak of blue cloth that is carelessly thrown round his shoulders. Look at his whip, too—the heavy thongs of it intertwisted like serpents: he has no need of bowie-knife or pistol in these wilds while he carries about with him 'that formidable weapon. The oxen pass on down the valley, the dust subsides; again we are left with the silence, and the warm sunlight, and the aromatic odors of the may-weed, and the cunning antics of our ubiquitous friend the chipmonk.

"There," said the lieutenant, looking up to the vast hill-slopes above, where the scattered pines stood black among the blaze of yellow undergrowth, "that is the beginning of our hunting-country. All the secrets are behind that fringe of wood. You must not imagine, Lady Sylvia, that our life at Idaho is to be only this dulness of walking—"

"I can assure you I do not feel it dull at all," she said; "but I am sorry that our party is to be broken up—just when it has been completed. Oh, I wish you could stay with us!" she adds, addressing another member of the party, whose hands are full of wild-flowers.

"My dear Lady Sylvia," says this person, with her sweetest smile, "what would you all do if you had not us to take back your messages to England? We are to teach Bell's little girl to say Idaho. And when Christmas comes, we shall think of you at a particular hour—oh, by-the-way, we have never yet fixed the exact difference of time between Surrey and Idaho—"

"We will do that before you leave, madame," says the lieutenant, "but I am sure we will think of you a good many times before Christmas comes. And when Mr. Balfour and I have our bears, and buffaloes, and elephants, and all these things, we will see whether we cannot get something sent you in ice for your Christmas party. And you will drink our good health, madame, will you not? And perhaps, if you are very kind, you might send us one bottle of very good Rhine wine, and we will drink your health, too. Nee! I meant two bottles, for the four of us—"

"I think we shall be able to manage that," says she; and visions of real Schloss Johannisberg, each bottle swathed in printed and signed guarantees of genuineness, no doubt began to dance before her nimble brain.

But at this moment a cold breeze came rushing down the narrow gorge; and almost at the same instant we saw the edge of a heavy cloud come lowering over the very highest peak of the mountains. Some little familiarity with the pranks of the weather in the Western Highlands suggested that, having no water-proofs, and no shelter being near, we had better make down the valley again in the direction of Idaho; and this we set about doing. The hot afternoon had grown suddenly chill. A cold wind whistled through the trembling leaves of the cotton-woods. The mountains were overshadowed, and by the time we reached Idaho again it seemed as if the night had already come down. The women, in their thin dresses, were glad to get in-doors.

"But it is this very thing," the lieutenant cried—for he was anxious that his wife should regard her new home favorably— "that makes these places in the Rocky Mountains so wholesome; so healthful, I mean. I have heard of it from many people, who say here is the best sleeping-place in the world. It is no matter how warm it is in the day, it is always cold at night; you always must have a blanket here. The heat—that is nothing, if you have the refreshing cold of the night; people who cannot sleep anywhere else, they can sleep here very well. Every one says that."

"Yes, and I will tell you this," he added, turning to Balfour; "you ought to have stayed some days more in Denver, as all people do, to get accustomed to the thin air, before coming up here. All the doctors say that."

"Thank you," said Balfour, laughing, "my lungs are pretty tough. I don't suffer any inconvenience."

"That is very well, then; for they say the air of these places will kill a consumptive person—"

"Oh, Oswald!" his wife cried. "Don't frighten us all."

"Frighten you?" said he. "Will you show me the one who is likely to be consumptive? There is not any one of us does look like it. But if we all turn to be consumptive, cannot we go down to the plains? and we will give up the mountain-sheep for the antelope—"

"I do believe," said his wife, with some vexation, "that you had not a thought in coming out here except about shooting!"

"And I do believe," he said, "that you had no thought except about your children. Oh, you ungrateful woman! You wear mourning—yes; but when do you really mourn for your poor uncle? When do you speak of him? You have not been to his grave yet."

"You know very well it was yourself who insisted on our coming here first," said she, with a blushing face; but it was not a deadly quarrel.

The chillness of the night did not prevent our going out for a walk later on, when all the world seemed asleep. And now the clouds had passed away from the heavens, and the clear stars were shining down over the mystic darkness of the mountains. In the silence around us we only heard the plashing of the stream. It was to be our last night together.

CHAPTER LII.

AUF WIEDERSEHN!

IN the early morning—the morning of farewell—we stood at the small window—we two who were leaving—and tried to fix in our memories some picture of the surroundings of Bell's home; for we knew that many a time in the after-days we should think of her and endeavor to form some notion of what she was engaged in at the moment, and of the scene around her. And can we remember it now? The sunlight seems to fall vertically from that blazing sky, and there is a pale mist of heat far up in the mountains, so that the dark pine-woods appear to have a faint blue fog hanging around them. On the barer slopes, where the rocks project in shoulders, there is a more brilliant light; for there the undergrowth of cotton-wood bushes, in its autumn gold, burns clear and sharp, even at this distance. And then the eye comes down to the still valley, and the scattered white houses, and the small and rustling trees. We seem to hear the running of the stream.

And what was that little bit of paper thrust furtively, almost at the last moment, into our Bell's trembling hand? We did not know that we had been entertaining a poetess unawares among us; or had she copied the verses out of a book, just as one takes a flower from a garden and gives it as a token of remembrance—something tangible to recall distant faces and by-gone friends?

"O Idaho! far Idaho!   . –
A last farewell before we go—"

That was all that the companion of this unhonored Sappho managed to make out as the paper was snatched from her hand. No doubt it invoked blessings on .the friends to whom we were bidding good-bye. No doubt it spoke of the mother's thinking of her children far away. And there certainly was no doubt that the verses, whether they were good verses or bad verses, served their turn, and are treasured up at this moment as though their like had never been seen.

On that warm, clear, beautiful morning, when the heavy coach came rolling up to the door of the inn, Balfour and Lady Sylvia did not at all seem broken down by emotion; on the contrary, they both appeared to be in high spirits. But our poor Bell was a wretched spectacle, about which nothing more shall be said here. Her last words were about her children; but they were almost inaudible, through the violence of her sobbing. And we knew well, as we caught the last glimpse of that waved handkerchief, that this token of farewell was not meant for us: it was but a message we were to carry back with us across the seas to a certain home in Surrey.

Hier hat die Mär' ein Ende; and yet the present writer, if he is not overtaxing the patience of the reader, would like to say a word about the fashion in which two people, living pretty much by themselves down in the solitudes of Surrey, used to try to establish some link of interest and association with their friends far away in Colorado, and how, at these times, pictures of by-gone scenes would rise before their minds, soft, and clear, and beautiful; for the troubles and trials of travelling were now all forgotten, and the pleasant passages of our journeying could be separated and strung like lambent beads on the thread of memory.

Or shall we not rather take, as a last breach of confidence, this night of all the nights in the year—this Christmas-eve—which we more particularly devote to our dear and absent friends? It is now drawing away from us. We have been over to Bell's almost deserted house; and there, as the children were being put to bed, we heard something about Ilaho. It was as near as the little girl could get to it; it will suffice for a message.

And now, late as it is, and our own house being wrapped in silence after all the festivities of the evening—well, to tell the truth, there *was* a wild turkey, and there *were* some canvas-back

duck; and we were not bound to tell two eagerly inquisitive boys
that these could not well come from Colorado, though they did
come from America—a madness seems to come over our gentle
Queen Titania, and she will go out into the darkness, though the
night is cold and there is snow on the ground. We go forth
into the silent world. The thin snow is crisp and dry underfoot.
The stars are shining over our heads. There is no wind to stir
the black shadows of the trees.

And now, as the time draws near when we are to send that un-
spoken message to the listening ones across the seas, surely they
are waiting like ourselves? And the dark night, even up here
on Mickleham Downs, where we go by the dusky yew-trees like
ghosts, becomes afire with light, and color, and moving shapes;
for we are thinking once more of the many scenes that connect
us by an invisible chain with our friends of the past. How long
ago was it that we sat in the long saloon, and the fog-horn was
booming outside, and we heard Lady Sylvia's tender voice singing with the others, "Abide with me; fast falls the eventide," as
the good ship plunged onward and through the waste of waters?
But the ship goes too slow for us. We can outstrip its speed.
We are already half-way over to Bell's retreat, and here we shall
rest; for are we not high over the Hudson, in the neighborhood
of the haunted mountains?—and we have but to give another call
to reach the far plains of Colorado!

*   *   *   *   *   *   *

"Ho, Vanderdecken — Heinrich Hudson — can you take our
message from us and pass it on? This is a night, of all the nights
in the long year, that you are sure to be abroad, you and your
sad-faced crew, up there in the lonely valleys, under the light of
the stars. Can you go still higher and send a view-halloo across
to the Rocky Mountains? Can you say to our friends that we
are listening? Can you tell them that something has just been
said—they will know by whom—about a certain dear mother at
Ilaho? Give a call, then, across the waste Atlantic that we may
hear! Or is it the clamor of the katydids that drowns the ghostly
voice? We cannot hear at all. Perhaps the old men are cowering
in their cave, because of the sacred time; and there is no mirth
in the hills to-night; and no huge cask of schnapps to be tapped,
that the heavy beards may wag. Vanderdecken—Hendrick Hud-

son—you are of no use to us: we pass on: we leave the dark mountains behind us, under the silent stars.

* * * * * * *

> "'Saint of this green isle, hear our prayer,
> Grant us cool heavens and favoring air !
> Blow, breezes, blow, the stream runs fast ;
> The rapids are near and the daylight's past !'

"Look at the clear gold ray of the light-houses, and the pale green of the sunset skies, and the dark islands and trees catching the last red flush. And is not this Bell's voice singing to us, with such a sweetness as the Lake of a Thousand Islands never heard before—

> "'Soon as the woods on shore look dim,
> We'll sing at St. Ann's our parting hymn.'

The red flame in the west burns into our eyes; we can see no more.

* * * * * * *

"We are startled by this wild roaring in our ears, as if the world were falling, and we are in a mystical cavern; and the whirling gray cataracts threaten to tear us from the narrow foothold. Our eyes are blinded, our throats are choked, our fingers still clutch at the dripping rocks; and then all at once we see your shining and smiling face — you giant black demon — you magnificent Sambo—you huge child of the nether world of waters! We KENT GO NO FORDER DEN DAWT? Is that what you say? We shout to you through this infernal din that we can—we can—we can! We elude your dusky fingers. We send you a mocking farewell. Let the waters come crashing down; for we have dived—and drifted—and come up into the white sunlight again !

* * * * * * *

"And now there is no sound at all. We cannot even hear Bell's voice; for she is standing silent in front of the Chief's grave; and she is wondering whether his ghost is still lingering here, looking for the ships of the white man going up and down the great river. For our part, we can see none at all. The broad valley is deserted; the Missouri shows no sign of life; on the wide plains around us we find only the reed-bird and the grasshopper. Farewell, White Cow; if your last wish is not gratified, at least the silence of the prairie is reserved to you, and no alien plough crosses the solitude of your grave. You are an amiable ghost, we think; we would shake hands with you, and give you a friendly 'How?' but the sunlight is in our eyes, and we cannot see you, just as you cannot make o″t the ships on that long line of river. May you have everlasting tobacco in the world of dreams!

*   *   *   *   *   *   *

"You infamous Hendrick Hudson, will not you carry our message now—for our voices cannot reach across the desert plains? Awaken, you cowled heads, and come forth into the starlight; for the Christmas bells have not rung yet; and there is time for a solemn passing of the glass! High up in your awful solitudes, you can surely hear us; and we will tell you what you must call across the plains, for they are all silent now, as silent as the white skulls lying in the sand. Vanderdecken, for the sake of Heaven —if that has power to conjure you—call to our listening friends; and we will pledge you in a glass to-night, and you and your ghastly crew will nod your heads in ominous laughter—"

*   *   *   *   *   *   *

But what is this that we hear, suddenly shaking the pulses of the night with its tender sound? O friends far away! do you know that our English bells are beginning to ring in the Christmas-time? If you cannot hear our faint voice across the wild Atlantic and the silent plains, surely you can hear the sounds you knew so well in the by-gone days! Over the crisp snow, and by the side of the black trees and hedges, we hurry homeward. We sit in a solitary room, and still we hear outside the faint tolling of the bells. The hour nears; and it is no dire spirit that we expect, but the gentle soul of a mother coming with a message to her sleeping children, and stopping for a moment in passing to look on her friends of old.

And she will take our message back, we know, and tell that other young wife out there that we are glad to hear that her heart is at peace at last. But what will the invisible messenger take back for herself? A look at her children: who knows?

A second to twelve. Shall we give a wild scream, then, as the ghost enters; for the silence is awful? Ah no! Whether you are here or not, our good Bell, our hearts go forth toward you, and we welcome you; and we are glad that, even in this silent fashion, we can bring in the Christmas-time together. But is the gentle spirit here—or has it passed? A stone's-throw from our house is another house; and in it there is a room dimly lit; and in the room are two sleeping children. If the beautiful mother has been here with us amidst the faint tolling of these Christmas bells, you may be sure she only smiled upon us in passing, and that she is now in that silent room.

THE END.

VALUABLE AND INTERESTING WORKS

FOR

PUBLIC AND PRIVATE LIBRARIES

PUBLISHED BY HARPER & BROTHERS, NEW YORK.

☞ *For a full List of Books suitable for Libraries, see* HARPER & BROTHERS' *Trade-List and* CATALOGUE, *which may be had gratuitously on application to the Publishers personally, or by letter enclosing Nine Cents in Postage Stamps.*

☞ HARPER & BROTHERS *will send their publications by mail, postage prepaid [excepting certain books whose weight would exclude them from the mail], on receipt of the price.* HARPER & BROTHERS' *School and College Text-Books are marked in this list with an asterisk* (*).

FIRST CENTURY OF THE REPUBLIC. A Review of American Progress. 8vo, Cloth, $5 00; Sheep, $5 50; Half Morocco, $7 25.

Contents.

Introduction: I. Colonial Progress. By EUGENE LAWRENCE.—II. Mechanical Progress. By EDWARD H. KNIGHT.—III. Progress in Manufacture. By the Hon. DAVID A. WELLS.—IV. Agricultural Progress. By Professor WILLIAM H. BREWER.—V. The Development of our Mineral Resources. By Professor T. STERRY HUNT.—VI. Commercial Development. By EDWARD ATKINSON. —VII. Growth and Distribution of Population. By the Hon. FRANCIS A. WALKER.—VIII. Monetary Development. By Professor WILLIAM G. SUMNER.—IX. The Experiment of the Union, with its Preparations. By T. D. WOOLSEY, D.D., LL.D.—X. Educational Progress. By EUGENE LAWRENCE. —XI. Scientific Progress: 1. The Exact Sciences. By F. A. P. BARNARD, D.D., LL.D. 2. Natural Science. By Professor THEODORE GILL.—XII. A Century of American Literature. By EDWIN P. WHIPPLE.—XIII. Progress of the Fine Arts. By S. S. CONANT.—XIV. Medical and Sanitary Progress. By AUSTIN FLINT, M.D. — XV. American Jurisprudence. By BENJAMIN VAUGHAN ABBOTT.—XVI. Humanitarian Progress. By CHARLES L. BRACE. —XVII. Religious Development. By the Rev. JOHN F. HURST, D.D.

MOTLEY'S DUTCH REPUBLIC. The Rise of the Dutch Republic. A History. By JOHN LOTHROP MOTLEY, LL.D., D.C.L. With a Portrait of William of Orange. 3 vols., 8vo, Cloth, $10 50; Sheep, $12 00; Half Calf, $17 25.

MOTLEY'S UNITED NETHERLANDS. History of the United Netherlands: from the Death of William the Silent to the Twelve Years' Truce—1609. With a full View of the English-Dutch Struggle against Spain, and of the Origin and Destruction of the Spanish Armada. By JOHN LOTHROP MOTLEY, LL.D., D.C.L. Portraits. 4 vols., 8vo, Cloth, $14 00; Sheep, $16 00; Half Calf, $23 00.

MOTLEY'S LIFE AND DEATH OF JOHN OF BARNEVELD. The Life and Death of John of Barneveld, Advocate of Holland: with a View of the Primary Causes and Movements of "The Thirty-years' War." By JOHN LOTHROP MOTLEY, LL.D., D.C.L. Illustrated. In 2 vols., 8vo, Cloth, $7 00; Sheep, $8 00; Half Calf, $11 50.

*HAYDN'S DICTIONARY OF DATES, relating to all Ages and Nations. For Universal Reference. Edited by BENJAMIN VINCENT, Assistant Secretary and Keeper of the Library of the Royal Institution of Great Britain; and Revised for the Use of American Readers. 8vo, Cloth, $3 50; Sheep, $3 94.

HILDRETH'S UNITED STATES. History of the United States. FIRST SERIES: From the Discovery of the Continent to the Organization of the Government under the Federal Constitution. SECOND SERIES: From the Adoption of the Federal Constitution to the End of the Sixteenth Congress. By RICHARD HILDRETH. 6 vols., 8vo, Cloth, $18 00; Sheep, $21 00; Half Calf, $31 50.

HUME'S HISTORY OF ENGLAND. The History of England, from the Invasion of Julius Cæsar to the Abdication of James II., 1688. By DAVID HUME. 6 vols., 12mo, Cloth, $4 80; Sheep, $7 20; Half Calf, $15 30.

HUDSON'S HISTORY OF JOURNALISM. Journalism in the United States, from 1690 to 1872. By FREDERIC HUDSON. 8vo, Cloth, $5 00; Half Calf, $7 25.

JEFFERSON'S DOMESTIC LIFE. The Domestic Life of Thomas Jefferson: compiled from Family Letters and Reminiscences, by his Great-granddaughter, SARAH N. RANDOLPH. Illustrated. Crown 8vo, Cloth, $2 50.

JOHNSON'S COMPLETE WORKS. The Works of Samuel Johnson, LL.D. With an Essay on his Life and Genius, by ARTHUR MURPHY, Esq. 2 vols., 8vo, Cloth, $4 00; Sheep, $5 00; Half Calf, $8 50.

KINGLAKE'S CRIMEAN WAR. The Invasion of the Crimea: its Origin, and an Account of its Progress down to the Death of Lord Raglan. By ALEXANDER WILLIAM KINGLAKE. With Maps and Plans. Three Volumes now ready. 12mo, Cloth, $2 00 per vol.; Half Calf, $3 75 per vol.

LAMB'S COMPLETE WORKS. The Works of Charles Lamb. Comprising his Letters, Poems, Essays of Elia, Essays upon Shakspeare, Hogarth, &c., and a Sketch of his Life, with the Final Memorials, by T. NOON TALFOURD. With Portrait. 2 vols., 12mo, Cloth, $3 00; Half Calf, $6 50.

LAWRENCE'S HISTORICAL STUDIES. Historical Studies. By EUGENE LAWRENCE. Containing the following Essays: The Bishops of Rome.—Leo and Luther.—Loyola and the Jesuits.—Ecumenical Councils.—The Vaudois.—The Huguenots.—The Church of Jerusalem. —Dominic and the Inquisition.—The Conquest of Ireland.—The Greek Church. 8vo, Cloth, uncut edges and gilt tops, $3 00.

MYERS'S REMAINS OF LOST EMPIRES. Remains of Lost Empires: Sketches of the Ruins of Palmyra, Nineveh, Babylon, and Persepolis, with some Notes on India and the Cashmerian Himalayas. By P. V. N. MYERS. Illustrated. 8vo, Cloth, $3 50.